THE HEART OF MAGIC

Book One: Merlin in Moab

CARYL SAY

Contact the author via e-mail at carylsay.author@gmail.com

Edited and designed by:
Relham LLC
P.O. Box 1055
Silver City, NM 88062
www.relham.com
575.534.4841

Front cover design and image of "Merlin" copyright 2014 © by Keegan Stewart. Delicate Arch image in public domain. Back cover image of Hidden Valley copyright 2014 © by Caryl Say. Author photo copyright 2014 © by Barb Webb.

ISBN 10: 151207375X
ISBN 13: 978-1-512073751

DEDICATION

For author Mary Stewart.

Without your wonderful books—*The Crystal Cave*, *The Hollow Hills*, and *The Last Enchantment*—my story might never have been written.

ACKNOWLEDGEMENTS

Several people deserve a special and heartfelt "thank you" for their time and expertise, not to mention friendship, love, and moral support: Lisa Albert, Jean Carson, Arlene Heintz, Keegan Stewart, and Richard Mahler. I could not have done it without you.

And to all my friends and coworkers at The Synergy Company, I thank you for your patience and understanding.

Part 1:

Awakening

CHAPTER 1
April 20 Morning

MANY CENTURIES HAD GONE BY after Arthur's death before I heard the voice calling me. I had been sleeping in the Crystal Cave again, dreaming of the past, when I heard the voice say, "It is time to awake, Emrys, and follow your Heart. The world is in dire straits and needs Arthur to return, and it is, as it has always been, your destiny to bring back the Once and Future King. You must follow the Power to a new beginning for all mankind."

I opened my eyes slowly, trying to remember where I was, *when* I was. I was lying on my back in bed, amid a pile of blankets, within a cavern. I had on my favorite robe, but even its warmth had not protected me from the chill and I shivered, pulling the blankets up around my shoulders as I sat up. I looked at the thousands of crystals surrounding me, glowing softly with the brilliance of an inner light, and I recognized the familiar surroundings of my unusual home. I sighed and stretched, wondering what was happening in the world outside now, and pondering the meaning of the voice's message in my dream.

"'...follow the Power to a new beginning...'" I muttered. "By the gods, what is that supposed to mean?" And of course, since I was quite alone, the words hung, unanswered, in the cold, damp air.

I stood up slowly and walked across the room to the large flat crystal next to my writing table that worked best for scrying, and gazed curiously into its depths. I needed to know what had happened in the world during my most recent period of unconsciousness. I would soon have to absorb new language patterns, and more, to fully understand why I had awakened at this particular time, but for now I would just take a quick look. As I witnessed the years of history flowing past, the scenes revealed in the crystal included unfamiliar faces, strange clothing and hairstyles, and even stranger modes of transportation. I could never have imagined changes such as these. I saw strange metal shapes that appeared to convey people from one place to another using an unknown energy source. Thriving cities amid unusual landscapes and rock formations indicated that people had traveled to lands unknown in my time and established new settlements. Despite the fact that I had slept long periods before, and had witnessed interesting developments in civilization, this current time seemed even more unusual than I could have foreseen.

After a time, I closed my eyes, allowing the images to fade from the crystal. However, they stayed sharp and clear in my memory. It was apparent to me that before I could emerge from my self-styled cocoon and proceed with plans to reunite with Arthur, I would need to conduct a more detailed study of the current era. I needed to figure out the best way to interact with the people of this time period without calling too much attention to myself. During past forays to the outside world, I had discovered that the stories about King Arthur and the Knights of the Round Table, and about my own role in the building of a united Britain, had grown to mythic proportions. I could only imagine the uproar should my true identity be discovered.

I sat at my desk and leaned back in my chair, reflecting upon the decision I had made so long ago to stay in the cave.

When living in Camelot had begun to seem pointless with Arthur gone, and with Guinevere having settled into her reign most competently, I had decided to move into the Crystal Cave to pursue my studies of herbs, medicine and sorcery. I had arranged with a local family loyal to the realm to keep me supplied with food and wine, and to assist me in caring for my horse and household. And when I realized what I had to do, when I knew that I would spend many centuries in a state of unconsciousness awaiting the time of Arthur's return, I arranged for the caretaker's family to pass along that responsibility to their descendants, so as to be prepared for the times when I would awaken and require their services.

Many times in the centuries after Arthur's death, I had ventured out into the world, hoping his return was imminent, only to retreat again and again to the refuge of this enchanted cave when the disappointment, loneliness and isolation became too much to bear. I would sleep and dream of past events, until something, such as the voice in my dream, should awaken me.

The voice that had spoken to me this morning seemed familiar somehow, but I could not recall where or when I had heard it before. I had not thought of myself as Emrys since that long ago time at the edge of the lake at Avalon, when I begged the gods to save Arthur. Pain lanced through me as if it was only minutes ago when I watched the boat carrying Arthur's body disappear into the mist. In reality, it had been more than 1500 years since I rode back to Camelot, alone, with the weight of my failure sitting heavily on my shoulders.

I sighed, wishing as I did every time I awoke that I could somehow have changed the outcome of that last battle; but as hard as it was to accept, it had been destined to occur, and who was I to question the wisdom of the gods?

I stopped chastising my past self as it was too late to change what was, and turned my attention to my immediate needs. From what I had seen of my reflection in the crystals, hair down my back to my waist, and beard cascading over my chest, it was obvious that I needed to bathe, shave, and trim my hair. Food was also in order, as my stomach was complaining loudly about the lack of nourishment over the last three hundred years. *Imagine that,* I thought in amusement.

As I seemed to have misplaced my bronze razor, I used a simple spell to remove the hair from my face. I shortened the long hair on my head the same way. Apparently the fashionable length of men's hair now varied from very short to quite long, so

I chose the middle path and made my hair shoulder length. It turned out a bit shaggy, but it would do.

I then drew water out of the spring at the back of the cave, drank my fill, cleaned my teeth and proceeded to wash the years off my skin. Although I preferred my heavy warm robe, I decided my soft pants, tunic and vest would be less conspicuous and possibly more appropriate to the weather outside. I dressed hurriedly in the cold air and studied my reflection mirrored in the faceted face of another large crystal.

I looked just as I remembered myself, which was a good thing I suppose; tall and slender, with straight, black hair and green eyes that would change color depending on the light, or upon my mood or my magic. There were a few lines around my eyes and mouth, but I still looked no older than I had those many years ago in Camelot. A pleasant face one might think, although perhaps a bit narrow, with a straight nose, and high cheekbones. I grinned humorlessly at myself and noted that my teeth still looked white and mostly straight, obviously not the normal oc-currence for the time period in which I had lived. Being born of magic had its benefits in more ways than one, I thought, and yet this virtual immortality had its drawbacks when all the people you have ever cared for had died and turned to dust, lost to hu-man memory. But not lost to mine; although perhaps I was not entirely human anymore, if I ever was...

Forcing myself to focus on the present, I decided I need-ed more time to study the images in the crystal. I felt a sense of urgency to discover as much as possible before venturing out of the cave. I used a focusing spell to speed up the viewing and learning process, especially in regards to language, and deter-minedly ignored the rumbling in my empty belly.

Some time later, feeling over-full with the quantity of in-formation I had absorbed, but decidedly empty in the gut, I pulled on my boots and donned my jacket. Then I strapped on a belt and grabbed my dagger, my staff and my crossbow, and strode towards the opening of the cave, anxious to begin. The staff, inscribed with runes and other markings of magic, and topped by a multi-faceted crystal, was one of the primary instruments of my craft, and I always carried it with me when I left the cave. This time I felt the need to have the weapon with me also, although I truly hoped I would not have to use it. I was not an accomplished bowman.

Just to be cautious, I took a moment to close my eyes, still my thoughts, and to extend my awareness outside, ensuring that I would be alone when I emerged from my hiding place. To my relief, the protective wards that I had set long ago to discourage people and animals from getting too close to my concealed entrance were still in place, and active, and there was no one outside to witness me exiting the cave. Since the way seemed clear, I gathered my will and said firmly *"Aperi."* The short tunnel opened to the world outside, and I stepped into the sunlight for the first time in over three hundred years.

CHAPTER 2
April 20 Noon

I RE-SET THE WARDS OUTSIDE the cave and murmured the spell "*Cludo et invisibil,*" causing the entrance to close and become unseen once more. I tested the effectiveness of the spell, and it held to my satisfaction. *Good work, Merlin, considering that you are out of practice,* I thought to myself. I closed my eyes, and taking a deep breath of the freshest air that had entered my lungs in centuries, I actually felt content, an emotion I had not experienced since I lived in Camelot. Perhaps it was time to let go of the guilt...

As I started down the slope I wondered if anything remained of the shed that had sheltered my horse three centuries ago. Even a pile of rubble would be sufficient to hide my crossbow—now that I was outside my fears seemed groundless and it was a heavy weapon to bear unnecessarily. I walked along an overgrown path that headed more or less in the right direction, the bright sunlight dimming somewhat under a thick stand of oak trees that was not there the last time I was outside. I heard the rustle of new leaves overhead and the brief call of a bird, felt the cool air under the trees, and noted the thickness of the holly and blackberry hedges; things I had not experienced in years. And it felt good to be alive, to move, to stretch muscles that had been inactive for much too long.

To my surprise, not only was there a small stable built in the same location as my old shed, but it was occupied by a nice bay mare with a black mane and tail. A saddle and bridle for her were hung up neatly above the manger, and it was obvious from her glossy hide that she was well cared-for. I was grateful that my caretakers were following the instructions I had given long ago.

I had intended to walk the distance to the caretaker's

farm, but decided to ride instead. It was a beautiful spring day, complete with a bright blue sky and a few white clouds. With a light breeze ruffling my hair, I whistled while I saddled and bridled the horse, patting her neck in apology for my clumsiness. I left the crossbow in the stable, affixed my staff through a loop on the saddle, then mounted stiffly and turned her towards the caretaker's place, several miles away.

I stopped for a moment to gaze at the countryside. Although the terrain had changed somewhat in the past three hundred years, the difference between the present time and the fifth century was staggering. There were now gentle slopes and open meadows full of grazing sheep where in the past dense forests had stood, and where rushing streams had been, now only slow-moving creeks meandered. I also noticed that the air seemed a bit hazy with smoke, and there was a hum of noise in the distance that I didn't recognize. I would have to ask the current caretaker's family about these things as soon as I arrived. I wondered if the old stone manor house still stood or if new construction had replaced the ancient dwelling.

I had ridden only a short distance when my good mood was abruptly shattered by a sense of impending doom. The horse snorted and tossed her head as I pulled back sharply on the reins. The hairs stood up on the back of my neck, and I could sense dark magic being summoned up ahead in the direction of the caretaker's farm.

This does not bode well, I thought anxiously. As I urged the horse into a gallop and raced towards the farm, I thought I heard screaming.

"No, not again...I will not lose anyone else!" I growled, remembering other battles and other deaths.

As I neared the top of the ridge above the farm, I reined in the horse, threw myself from her back before she even came to a halt, and grabbed my staff. I had left my weapon behind, and it may not have been appropriate in this situation anyway. I did not want to reveal my magic, but I may not have a choice in the matter.

I flattened myself to the ground, crawled over to the edge, and gazed down upon the open space where the house and outbuildings sprawled in the valley. The tableau spread out below me was one of chaos and unreality. The sight of a creature I never expected to see again startled me. What appeared to be a wyvern was attacking a group of people trying to shield themselves behind a machine of some kind. A creature of nightmare, the wyvern had the body of a dragon and the tail of a serpent. One lone man was trying to divert the beast's attention, but he was in immediate danger of being either immolated by the wyvern's fiery breath, or crushed by its heavy tail. His arms were outstretched in a show of power and I could feel the magic he was using against the beast, but clearly he was outmatched. The situation was obviously critical, and I decided that I had no choice but to use my magic in defense of these people. I hastily gathered energy, drawing it up through the earth, from the air, and from the core of my being until I felt an immense pressure in my chest and a tingling throughout my body. There was no time for an intricate spell that might have yielded a more narrow focus. I stood up and pointed my staff at the creature below, sending a wild bolt of energy arcing down to find its target in a burst of white light and an earsplitting sound like thunder on a stormy night. I heard an unearthly shriek from the creature and I prayed that I had stopped it. I immediately turned and raced down the steep path towards the farm, hoping that I had acted in time to save the man who had bravely tried to hold the wyvern at bay.

At the bottom of the hill, I burst from the cover of trees in time to see the beast collapse, and the man slowly crumple to the ground near it.

The group of people, presumably my caretaker and his family, had run from behind their makeshift barricade and towards the house as soon as the wyvern had been hit by the energy bolt. They seemed unhurt, so I quickly approached the fallen wizard; for such he must be to have even attempted to magically control the animal.

As I crouched next to the downed man, I noticed that he was bronze-skinned, with long, straight blue-black hair braided down his back and bound with a narrow strip of leather. His clothing was unusual, with beads worked into the fabric, and his boots were of soft leather laced up the front. It was obvious to me that he was not from Britain.

I suspected that he was already dead, but I felt compelled to put my hands on him, searching for any trace of his life's energy. Suddenly, a vision of this man as he had appeared in life swam before my eyes, and he spoke to me.

"Merlin, listen to me closely, I do not have much time. I came a long way to warn you of the upheaval in the Other World. Many practitioners of magic have sensed unrest and instability in the borders between this world and the next, and it may be connected to the reawakening of the Once and Future King. Be aware that your destiny and your heart's desire can no longer be attained through the traditional entrance at Avalon—that portal has been sealed forever. Heed my words, for I came to tell you of a new portal that will lead to your goal. You will find this portal in a land far to the west. Many attempts will be made to stop you before you reach it. Only in America will you realize the truth. These visions that I now show you will help you find the portal. Your heart and soul will tell you how to proceed. Follow the Power…"

A blast of information in a swirl of colors and forms entered my consciousness, and just as abruptly ended, as my connection to the stranger was severed. I staggered and gasped; his shade was gone. I slowly lifted my hands from the body, thinking about everything the man's spirit had communicated to me. I noticed how similar his words were to the ones that had awakened me this morning. There was something powerful happening and I seemed to be at the center of it. I would reflect upon all that had happened once I returned to the privacy of my cave to make my final plans. But first I needed to confer with my current caretakers.

I closed my eyes for a moment, offering a short prayer to the gods to welcome this heroic stranger's soul to the spirit world. He had died protecting my caretakers and I was most grateful for his sacrifice. I stood up and turned towards what remained of the dead creature. I could sense that the evil and dark magic had already dissipated, and the body of the wyvern had subsided into a mass of jelly-like material, which would soon evaporate and disappear completely from this realm. There was no doubt in my mind that this had been a magical construct rather than a real flesh and blood creature. But that thought led to another—who or what had created this monster, and how strong must that practitioner of magic be?

And the fact that someone had known that I had just awakened disturbed me greatly. The dead wizard at my feet must have begun his journey long before I awoke to have arrived here already. How had he known, unless the gods had guided him? And who had planned and executed such a reception for me?

I assumed that the death blow was meant for me, and yet I had experienced no difficulty in slaying the wyvern. Could the wizard have been the target all along? Had he been killed to prevent him from communicating with me? Or were my caretakers the real target? Either way, the attackers had failed.

I would have to spend some time pondering this sequence of events, but first I needed to see to my caretaker and his family, who were standing in shock near the house. I strode towards them and said, "The beast will not harm you now. Are any of you hurt?"

The family turned towards me as one, and the older man spoke, "We're safe, thank you. We're grateful to you for killing it. May we ask who you are, sir?"

"I am Merlin. I am happy to have been of service in your time of need."

As I was speaking to the caretaker, I overheard the two younger men arguing heatedly. "What the bloody hell just happened here, Rob? Who's that guy talking to Dad? What was that thing anyway, and how did he kill it? And how are we going to explain a dead body to the constable? The villagers already think we're odd, keeping to ourselves out here. And for what, some myth handed down for hundreds of years about some old man in the cave up in the hills?" His tirade was cut short by the other man, Rob, obviously his brother.

"Shut up, Ben! Christ, let's deal with one issue at a time. We're lucky to be alive," Rob replied, as he ran his hand nervously through his short brown hair. The young man seemed to be a bit older than Ben, and to have more sense.

It was apparent that this family, while accomplishing most of the tasks I had long ago assigned to my original caretakers, did not know what their true purpose was, or for whom they were caring. These young people literally had no idea who I was, although the older man standing in front of me now had a shocked look of recognition on his face.

He exclaimed as he bowed low before me, "I'm so sorry for not knowing you, my lord, and please pardon the rudeness of my sons."

The man, Tom, as I soon learned was his name, straightened and turned to the young men. "Hold your tongues and have some respect! This is Lord Merlin himself, the one our family has served for so many years."

Taken aback, Ben blurted out in denial, "No, that's impossible. That old tale about the magician in the cave is just a myth—it's not real!"

"Actually, I am a sorcerer," I said, "and I can assure you, I am quite real."

I was more than ready to bring this encounter to an end.

We needed to respectfully bury the dead, and then sit down and have a conversation and a meal, not necessarily in that order. Despite the gruesome events of the past hour, I was almost faint with hunger. The needs of the living, after all is said and done, must take precedence over the dead.

I glanced over at the women, who were looking at me with both fear and awe, and I addressed the older of the two, obviously the matriarch of the group. "My lady, I apologize for coming to your home unannounced, but I wonder if it would be possible to have a meal as soon as we have finished our sad task here." I gestured towards the body. I assumed that this woman must be the mother of the three young people, and the wife of the man called Tom.

She ducked her head respectfully. "Please call me Sandy, Lord Merlin. I'm truly honored to meet you; I never thought to see you in my lifetime. I'm Tom's wife, and mother to these three." She indicated the two younger men and the girl next to her. "You're certainly welcome here, sir, and I apologize for the surly greeting from my youngest son." She turned and glared at Ben. "We would appreciate any help that you can give us right now. We feel terrible that we weren't able to help that poor man. He had just arrived in our yard and we were trying to find out what he wanted, when that creature appeared out of nowhere. He distracted it until we could get out of harm's way. There was absolutely nothing we could do, and seeing him die right in front of us was *horrible*. We're grateful that you came to our aid, and whatever we can do for you would be our pleasure." Sandy was sincere, friendly and talkative, and I felt comfortable with her immediately. I hoped that the rest of the family would prove to be as cooperative.

"Thank you, Sandy." I turned towards Tom as the older woman and young girl went in the house. "Perhaps you would bring some tools and we will find a good place to bury this man."

The three men glanced worriedly at each other, and Tom said, "You know, in this day and age, we do things differently than in your time, Lord Merlin. If someone is murdered, we are obligated by the law to report it to the local constable."

I looked into his eyes and said sharply, "Although I understand your concern for obeying the current laws, it is not likely that the local constable will be able to bring to justice those responsible for this death, as 'twas by means of dark magic. The man had no family in Britain, and his friends and family across the sea were aware of the risks he faced coming here, so there should be no consequences for failing to report the crime. Tis my responsibility to handle this."

"But how do you know about his family or where he was from? We'd barely met him when the beast showed up, and you never talked to him before he died. We would've seen you," said Rob with a frown.

"His shade spoke to me shortly after his passing, and his last thoughts and wishes were made known to me in a vision," I said. Their eyes widened and they stared without comment.

I stared back at the three men, and said impatiently, "Now please, do as I bid you, and help me bury this man. I know you are all shocked and saddened by what has occurred here today, but we must take action before someone sees him." I noted that it was already mid-afternoon. "And I need to be on my way back to the cave while the light holds. To that end perhaps one of your sons could bring my horse down from the ridge and give her some water."

As I turned back towards the body, I heard Tom giving instructions to his sons, promising that they would talk later. Ben went running up the hill after the mare and Rob headed to one of the outbuildings, apparently to find the tools we needed.

The caretaker and I carried the body to a secluded area away from the buildings and respectfully laid him out on the ground. Rob came running with several shovels and the three of us started digging.

An hour later, we trudged wearily back to the house, which indeed turned out to be the old stone manor house I had known when I was here last, albeit with several rooms added on. We washed the soil and sweat from our hands and faces and sat down to a simple meal, thankful that we were alive to eat it. Tom asked his God to bless the food, and although I did not participate in the blessing, I could not help but be thankful as well.

Soon after the meal was over and the dishes cleared, I began asking questions of the members of this family, and assigned them several tasks: Using whatever means necessary, start making plans for me to travel to the land from which the wizard had come, the harsh land of red rock and heat. Also, I charged them with determining how I could survive in this modern world; what documents I would need, and currency.

For it seemed that I was bound by my destiny to follow the stranger's advice. I would have to leave this land for other shores, and soon.

CHAPTER 3
April 20 Late Afternoon

A FEW HOURS LATER I WAS back at the cave, having learned a great many details from the Reese family about the current state of the world. I learned, among other things, that the smoke and the noise I had noticed this morning were due in part to the number of "cars" now being used to travel from one point to another. Apparently horses had fallen out of favor as the preferred mode of transportation.

My caretakers had been most helpful after they recovered from the initial shock of my presence, on top of the trauma of the attack. I confirmed that the previous generations hadn't been especially diligent in providing accurate information about me. I had expected some loss of understanding over the course of time, but not to this extent. Truthfully, I'd never expected to be out of contact for so long. I'd assumed, wrongly as it turned out, that Arthur would reappear within a few centuries after his death.

I promised to supply the family with additional funds, as they were dangerously close to destitution. The cost of goods and services had so increased that I'd not provided enough gold, silver, or gemstones to their ancestors during my previous time outside the cave. I knew also that I would need funds for my excursion into foreign lands.

As the day waned, Ben had accompanied me on his own horse back to the stable near the cave, so that he could care for and feed my mare. He was apparently responsible for this chore, and I praised him for his efforts; she was a fine, healthy animal. He had calmed down and become quite sociable once my story was told. He was a little in awe of me and I said nothing to dissuade him. Sometimes it was advantageous to seem apart from the rest of humanity. Of course, that was the reason I always ended up alone, so perhaps I needed to rethink that choice.

As I turned to traverse the path to the cave, Ben said, "Wait, Merlin, don't forget these," and handed me a bag containing enough food and wine to last for several days, and also a thick packet of documents. Tom and Sandy had lost their oldest son Michael in an accident a few years earlier and were willing to give me his driving license, birth certificate, and passport. This was most fortuitous, and I was grateful, as I had no documents of my own and would never be able to legitimately attain any—certainly not in my real name. So I would be Michael Reese for the duration of my quest.

I looked at Ben and said, gently, "I do not know how to adequately thank you and your family for your help. I would have no chance to appear normal in your society without these"—I held up the documents in front of me—"to prove that I exist. We needed nothing like this in my time, but that time is long gone and will never come again."

He looked steadily at me and said, "My brother's dead, but you'll be able to carry on in his name. You're rather like him in build and coloring, enough to fool anyone who doesn't look too closely, anyway. And you are a good man, like he was."

"Thank you once again for helping me, Ben. I will do my best to honor the memory of your brother."

Ben paused and said, with a sheepish look on his face, "Sir, I'm sorry for the way I spoke to you earlier. For one thing, I was upset about what happened at the farm today, and also, I couldn't accept that the old stories about you were true. When you looked so young, it just didn't seem possible that you could really be *the* Merlin of Camelot. For centuries, you've been just a fantasy, and I couldn't reconcile the myth with our duties here at the farm. I pictured an old man with a long gray beard and hair, wearing a robe and a pointy hat with stars on it, not a man only a few years older than my brother."

I smiled kindly at him. "It is all right, Ben. Please ask your father to be ready to take me to town within the week; I must journey west across the ocean as soon as possible. Mention that I will need to learn to operate your strange machine, uh, car. It is unlikely that I will be riding horses where I'm going. Be kind to your mother and your siblings, Ben, for they depend on you. I suggest that you start back, as it will be full dark soon enough."

He nodded in agreement, but seemed reluctant to leave me. I decided to give him a parting gift. I uttered a simple spell, "*Mutabo meam apparentia*," which changed my appearance to reflect his vision of me, pointy hat and all. And then, as I whispered, "*Invisibilis*," I simply vanished. I could hear his sudden intake of breath and smiled, then turned and walked away.

CHAPTER 4
April 20 Night

A FEW HOURS LATER, I stood in the middle of my cave, and wondered if I could go through with this wild plan to leave Britain, traveling a long distance to a place that I had never even imagined. I looked around at the crystals, and at my things, and started remembering past times when I had awakened.

In 1191, I had heard rumors that the monks at Glastonbury Abbey had found the graves of King Arthur and Guinevere, and out of curiosity I had ridden there, only to discover that they had already enshrined the remains in the Great Church. I had disguised myself as a monk, using magic, and had made my way to the shrine. I had extended my senses and discovered that these people had not been Arthur and Guinevere, although the individuals had been important in their own right.

I walked over to my writing table and sat down, recalling another time, in 1700, when I had traveled back to Avalon, so sure that Arthur's return was nigh. Twas a shock to discover that the lake was...gone. I had climbed the Tor and found a stone tower crouching upon the crest; the remnants of a Christian chapel that had been built there hundreds of years prior. I had stood for a long while, gazing in all directions, and had seen great changes in the landscape. The vast forests that I had known more than 1000 years before had been replaced by open farmland. And, of course, the castle and keep of King Melwas were no longer there. But as I stood on the Tor, I began to sense the power emanating from the portal to the Elven Kingdom on the eastern slope, through which Arthur should emerge. I had felt hopeful, anticipating an end to the long wait, but alas, it had proved yet again to be a dream unfulfilled, and I remembered the feelings of despair and defeat that had welled up in my being.

As my thoughts returned to the current time, to this

twenty-first century, I felt a lightening of spirit and a sudden sense of adventure. Perhaps now was the time for the reawakening of the Once and Future King.

Part 2:

Arrival

CHAPTER 5
April 21-25

THE DAY AFTER THE WYVERN attack and subsequent death of the Native American shaman, Carlos Sun Chaser (for this, I learned later, was the dead man's identity), I returned to the Reese family's abode. I'd realized the previous night how much help I would require to accomplish my quest. Things were no longer simple. The world in which I now walked was much more complicated than any previous time I had experienced. I'd gazed into my crystals again and found several places in the western world that could be the shaman's homeland. But I needed to be more precise, as the land across the sea was vast and I could not hope to traverse it by myself in a reasonable amount of time.

Sandy had already started searching for information as I had requested, using her "computer," a truly miraculous device and an amazing repository of information, to identify and locate the unique red rock structures I had seen in my vision. She found that they were located in a place called Moab, Utah, in the Southwest area of the United States of America. Therefore, Moab would be my destination.

I had heard of this new land, America, when I awakened around the year 1700, when the settlements there were still in rough colonies on the eastern coast of the continent. I should say, rough in comparison to the ancient civilizations of the Old World. I felt curious about the people now inhabiting that country, for many of them could be the descendants, many times removed, of people I had known in Britain so long ago.

During the next few days, Sandy proceeded to make all the arrangements for me, using the documents that had been her son's, that were now in my possession. I would be traveling aboard some sort of ark that flew through the air. These new technologies seemed to be a form of magic themselves, especially to someone such as I, from a less complicated time in history; a time often steeped in conflict and barbarity.

Tom Reese conceded to my wishes that I learn how to "drive," and helped me to attain the rudimentary skills for operating one of the strange machines. I used a learning spell to enhance my understanding, and with his able tutelage, I was soon able to operate a "car" in a limited fashion.

I also arranged with the Reeses to ship my sorcerer's staff, my dagger, my sword, the crossbow and an assortment of crystals to me as soon as I was settled in my new home. I had to give up my intention to carry my crossbow with me on the ark, since it was apparent that carrying weapons on board the "jet" was not acceptable.

Tom contacted people he normally used to exchange or sell the precious metals and gemstones for currency, and we managed to sell enough that Tom and Sandy's family would be able to continue watching over my cave for years to come—and I now had the means to live comfortably in America.

I did not know how long I might have to be away from Britain, but it could be many decades before I fulfilled my quest. Although time did not mean much to me, what it would mean to others was obvious. Ben would take over as caretaker (for I had decided that he would be Tom and Sandy's successor), and I would have to leave Moab, or create a new identity for myself, to disguise the fact that I had not changed over the years. I hoped someday to create an aging spell that would slowly change my appearance over time, so that I would not have to keep leaving the places and people I had become accustomed to, and fond of.

As I thought about my appearance changing over time, I wondered how I would appear to others in this twenty-first century. I hoped to seem a normal, modern man, not only outwardly, but also in attitude and presentation. I knew that I did not sound the same as the current inhabitants of this time and therefore needed to be conscious of my speech. After many sojourns in other centuries, my accent had changed since the fifth century, but it was still very old-fashioned. I had to continue utilizing learning spells to help me change the habits of a lifetime. Sandy provided me with Michael's clothing, so at least in that way I would be acceptable.

The family had wholeheartedly adopted me, and no longer bowed, or called me Lord Merlin, or sir. I enjoyed feeling normal, if such a thing was possible for someone who was anything *but* normal. Fourteen-year-old Jen hugged me as if I was actually her brother Michael, and although I appreciated her affection I felt false in accepting it. The Reeses persuaded me to share tales of my life in Camelot. They experienced a sense of wonder hearing stories from someone who had been there. Personally, I felt mixed emotions sharing this information with them.

Tom and I packed Michael's documents and various articles of clothing, and my own sparse belongings, into the car, and we were ready to depart. I wore stiff pants—called "Levis"—instead of my usual soft, loose pants, a "T-shirt" instead of my long-sleeved tunic, and "tennis" shoes instead of my boots. These new garments felt very strange and a little uncomfortable, but I was grateful that they fit me perfectly. The gods had truly been kind.

After a journey that in my time would have taken many days, we arrived in Londinium, now called London, in mere hours. The trip was relatively uneventful as the attack I had anticipated did not occur. However, one thing happened that was most odd: An animal of some sort ran in front of the vehicle as if to divert us from our course. We were able to avoid a collision but came very close to going off the road and consequently, off an embankment. It had been an animal neither of us had seen before, a hunched creature running on four legs that gave the impression that it could have stood up and continued running on two; not a man, but not quite an animal. A most suspicious occurrence indeed.

London, the city I had known well in the past, had transformed into a lumbering beast I did not recognize. An overwhelming sense of humanity, the energy of thousands upon thousands of souls, including many with a darkness of spirit, pressed against my being. I had never felt anything like this before and it was not a pleasant sensation. I had been feeling a certain amount of trepidation about the flight, including the fear that the destructive force would affect my journey to America. Feeling that I was responsible for all of humanity as well suffocated me.

As I boarded the enormous "air-craft" that would transport me across the ocean, I felt as if I was being swallowed by a giant bird of prey.

CHAPTER 6
April 25-26

F INALLY, ALMOST A WEEK after my awakening, I was on board the jet and trying to prepare myself for the experience of flying. A feeling of doom settled over me. Dark forces were stirring again, and I knew that everyone onboard was in danger. I extended my inner senses and tried to discover from whence the danger would come, but to no avail.

As the jet began to move down the runway, then gained speed and finally became airborne, the tension seemed to ease somewhat, and I hoped that I had been mistaken. As we continued to ascend, the captain of the airship talked to us through a device that enabled him to speak as if he was in the same room.

Suddenly, the jet shuddered and bucked, tossing people about roughly in their seats. I heard cries of fear and knew that another attack was imminent. I turned in my seat and peered out the window beside me, sensing that the invisible wave of dark energy that had already hit the jet was being followed by an unnatural wall of thick blackness, rolling towards us in an otherwise cloudless sky. I worried that my adventure might be over before it had even begun. At once, I thrust that thought from my mind and reached deep inside myself for my magic, for my connection with the air and the light, and I visualized surrounding the outside of the aircraft with an impenetrable shield of positive energy, protecting it against the onslaught of evil. And as I released the full force of my will in a silent, unseen burst of power into that shield, I thought furiously that I would not allow the darkness to destroy all of these innocent lives.

For a moment I thought I had failed. But as soon as the roiling, seething blackness came in contact with my shield, it erupted in brilliant sparks and a roaring as if from a hundred dragons, then it winked out of existence. The sun again shone brightly on the aircraft and the wind died down. The jet righted itself, and flew on as smoothly as before. The pilot explained that we had just passed through a freak storm, and not to worry, that everything was fine.

Since I had been sitting in the cabin amongst several hundred people and using powerful magic at the time of the attack, I was afraid that others had felt the backwash of energy filtering through the cabin, or noticed the brightened aura surrounding me. I looked around cautiously and saw no sign of interest, and when I opened my senses I felt nothing unusual. I glanced surreptitiously at the woman sitting next to me, but she was reading a book and apparently had not noticed my behavior. No one stared at me or seemed to suspect my participation in this strange occurrence, and I marveled at the willingness of the human mind to deny the existence of magic.

I closed my eyes and relaxed back into my seat, sighing deeply, which prompted my seatmate to put her book down, and lean towards me in concern to ask if I was all right.

I said, roughly, without looking at her, "Tis my first time flying."

"I understand," she said compassionately, "And to have a sudden storm hit us so unexpectedly doesn't help any. It'll be better next time, I promise."

I opened my eyes and turned my head to look at her, pushing my hair back from my face, and said, "How can you know that?"

The lovely young woman just winked and smiled. "I just do, trust me." Then she leaned back against her seat and resumed reading her book.

I leaned back and smiled also, enjoying the exchange. When I thought about this woman sitting so close to me, rather scantily clad compared to the fashions of my day, I felt my body stir in a way that I had almost forgotten about.

Later on, after we had both slept briefly, my seatmate

and I introduced ourselves. Of course I told her that my name was Michael Reese, originally from Wales, and she said her name was Emily Crandall from the state of Utah, USA. She was returning home after several weeks in England, where she had been researching her ancestry. She had been attempting to trace one branch of her family that she had not been able to locate through her research, and she had followed the trail to Glastonbury, Somerset. This interested me greatly, but of course I could not tell her why.

During the remainder of the flight, which included a "layover" in Houston, Emily and I continued to converse about various topics including Celtic symbols, the Druids, and what is now called Stonehenge. I noticed that the initial attraction I felt for her had not diminished, in fact it had increased. I sensed that she might be interested in me also. Neither of us mentioned the "storm" again, and I had no desire to remind her about an occurrence for which I could not provide a satisfactory explanation.

Many uneventful hours later, during which parts my anatomy became numb from sitting and the stiff pants I was wearing had chafed other parts, we landed in Salt Lake City, Utah. I realized that I was that much closer to attaining my goal.

As soon as the aircraft came to a halt and the doors were opened, Emily lifted her bags and hurried up the aisle, turning back towards me for a moment and giving me a brief smile and a wave. Perhaps she was meeting someone. I nodded my head in acknowledgement, feeling a brief jolt of regret that I would probably never see her again.

I stood up carefully, too tall in the confined space, so that I had to stoop. I gathered my few belongings, got off the aircraft, and walked along the ramp to the boarding area, noticing all the families who waited for their loved ones. I stopped for a moment to contemplate what the outcome of the attack would have been had I not been able to repel the menacing cloud; it did not bear thinking about. I had to find some way to end this.

I finally found my way to the exit door of the terminal, and pushing it open, I walked outside. I stood looking around, and for just a moment, I had no idea what to do next.

Just then, Emily appeared. Her long, golden-brown hair was like a beacon to a floundering vessel. She walked right up to me and said in her direct way, "Are you lost?"

I smiled slightly, and said, "I know it sounds most strange, but I feel disoriented and I am not sure how to proceed."

She looked at me quizzically. "What do you want to do, Michael?"

I looked into her expressive hazel eyes and realized in a distracted moment that she was quite tall for a woman, only a hand's breadth shorter than I even in the flat shoes that she wore. I could not help noticing that she was slim, yet had womanly curves that filled out her garments nicely. Her nose was finely sculpted, slightly turned up, and her lips were full. She had a heart-shaped face with a clear, glowing complexion, and quite simply, she was beautiful.

"I wish to travel to the place called Moab. Do you know where that is?" I sounded like the village idiot, but I was overwhelmed with all the changes that had happened in my life recently. I was a powerful sorcerer, but at this moment I was only a man, having an experience that I was surprisingly unprepared for. My crystal-gazing had not been able to prepare me for the emotional impact I felt now. I was an anachronism in this highly technical future society.

Emily responded smugly to my question, "As a matter of fact, I do. I'm driving to Moab myself just as soon as I can get my car out of long-term parking." She seemed amused at the look of confusion on my face as I thought, *And what, by the gods, is long-term parking?*

She finally took pity on me in my bewilderment. "Hey, I have a great idea. The person that was supposed to catch a ride with me is already gone, so why don't you ride with me, Michael, and you can help pay for gas, okay? There's no point in you taking the bus—I'm going there anyway. Here, help me carry my bags since you don't seem to have many of your own." And she unceremoniously thrust her luggage into my hands and started walking away. I just stood there for a moment staring after her. She might have been speaking a foreign tongue for all the sense I could make of her words. She looked back and smiled mischievously. "Come on, Mikey, let's go. It's already after five o'clock and time's a-wastin'."

I think that was the moment when I first felt a connection between us, and I followed her, relieved that for once in my long life someone else was leading the way.

Once we had retrieved her vehicle and left the airport behind us, we headed south on the smooth, black strips of the highway. I sat quietly in the seat next to her, wanting to talk but feeling suddenly uncertain. She and I had conversed during the flight, but this was different: now we were a man and a woman alone in a small space.

I was not particularly experienced when it came to interacting socially with the fairer sex. I had had only brief encounters with women, when my urges had been too strong to ignore. Spending most of my adult life in service to the Pendragons—first to Uther, then to Arthur, and finally to Guinevere—made it impossible to lead a normal life. And even years later, after Arthur's death, I was too bound by sadness and guilt to think about having a woman in my life.

As I considered discussing with Emily the merits of using herbs for healing, she turned to me abruptly and said, "Michael, what are you planning to do in Moab? I mean, do you have any friends or relatives there? Any place to stay?"

Emily seemed nervous now for some reason, perhaps because I was silently staring at her. Perhaps she thought I was behaving strangely. She certainly did not realize *how* strange and different I was from the men she knew.

I finally said, "If I am making you nervous, Emily, I apologize. Please believe that I mean you no harm." I was well aware that women considered me attractive, as evidenced by the coy looks and whispers I had encountered every time I appeared in public, no matter the year. But I was not entirely sure how Emily felt about me. I continued to look at her as she drove, wondering if she sensed anything unusual about me. Though she probably would have noticed my use of magic on the aircraft if she been able to perceive it.

Finally, she glanced over at me and said with a wry smile, "Michael, are you that naïve? You're incredibly hot and I'm attracted to you, so yes, I'm feeling a little nervous with you staring at me that way."

I did not know why she would remark about my body temperature, but I was surprised at her boldness, and it took me a moment before I could speak. "I truly do not know what to say. I find you most comely, my lady…I mean, I am attracted to you as well, Emily. You are a beautiful woman." I felt flustered and my heart was beating faster than normal. My command of the current idiom was disappearing rapidly, and at the same time my accent returned tenfold. I hardly knew this woman, but I wanted her with an intensity that startled me.

Emily looked into my eyes as long as she could, and then returned her gaze to the road ahead of us.

I felt as if I could not breathe.

"Why don't we find a room for the night? We're both too tired from the flight to drive the rest of the way to Moab, don't you think?" She looked over at me almost shyly.

"Yes, indeed" I said with feeling, sensing that she wanted to do something other than sleep, and I was in complete agreement. I wanted her, and soon.

We stopped at an inn called Best Western, and I carried the bags while she arranged for a room. The clerk gave me a knowing look as I walked by, but I ignored him, my eyes on

Emily's shapely backside as she walked ahead of me. I could not believe I was about to share my body with this woman whom I hardly knew, but it felt right and good, and I was not going to deny myself this rare pleasure.

She opened the door with a curious little white card, and we entered our room. She pulled the drapes closed and the room was full of shadows. As I put the bags down on one of the beds, I turned to her and said quietly, "Are you certain this is what you want? You really do not know me." I stood tall next to her, knowing that my dark hair and brooding look would be a stark contrast to her brightness. I hoped that she would say yes.

She smiled widely and said, "Absolutely," as she stepped close to me and held my face in her soft hands, kissing me deeply. I put my arms around her and kissed her back with an urgency I could not deny. My body tightened and swelled with desire, and as I pressed myself against her I felt the magical energy inside me stir as well. This intrigued me, as I had not expected that lust would affect my magic quite this strongly. I did not remember this happening in the past. I drew back for a moment and she said, "What's wrong?"

"Nothing," I said breathlessly, ignoring the pressure in my chest, and guiding her over to the empty bed. We fell onto the mattress together, laughing. We undressed quickly, caressing each other as the removal of each article of clothing revealed sensitive bare skin. Finally, with no more barriers between us, we lay next to each other, kissing and exploring each other's bodies. I cupped each of her breasts in turn and gently sucked on each nipple. Emily inhaled sharply, her breath coming in rapid gasps. I circled my tongue lightly over each breast, watching her reaction from under the thick hair that had fallen into my face. Then I slowly placed soft kisses across her collarbone, along her throat and back up to her mouth.

"Lovely," I murmured, kissing her lips once again. I then gently traced the rim of each delicate ear with the tip of my finger. She shivered and nuzzled my neck. "God, you smell amazing," she sighed. She ran her hands through my hair, then gently stroked across my shoulders and down my chest to the silky dark hair that grew around my nipples and down to my navel. My breath came faster and I groaned aloud.

I stroked with my large palms down the sides of her breasts to her waist, to her slightly rounded belly and flared hips until I reached the apex of her thighs. She quivered and sighed, opening herself to me as she moved my right hand to cover her heated center. I cupped her and noticed that she was ready for me. She reached down between us and caressed the hard length of my erection, then gently squeezed my testicles, causing me to gasp for breath at the intense sensation of a promised ecstasy. I could wait no longer. I raised up slightly, positioned myself, and slowly entered her tight wetness, causing us both to moan with pleasure. We began to move together in the age-old dance between a man and a woman, slowly at first, then faster, until I knew I had to stop for a moment. As I felt myself losing control I gasped, "It has been so long, I am not sure that I can wait."

She tightened up around me and whispered urgently, "Michael, I'm about to come, please don't stop!" And she used her inner muscles to squeeze me until I thought I would burst. I thrust into her deeply again and again, and she started climaxing, which triggered my own intense explosion. At the same time, the magical energy that had been building up inside of me burst out into the room, shattering the light bulbs, knocking over lamp and chair and scattering our belongings. I completely covered her body with mine to protect her from the flying glass. Finally, I pulled away from her, wondering how I was going to explain what had just happened.

Emily sat up and looked around, then said breathlessly, "Wow, that was pretty powerful stuff. Want to do it again?" She grinned wickedly. And we did.

Later, when I thought she was asleep, I arose, and with a

quick spell for light and a wave of my hand, I cleaned up the broken glass, righted the furniture and straightened everything up, then walked into the bathroom to urinate. After a glance at the room to make sure I had not missed anything, I extinguished the little orb. When I returned to bed she stirred and put her arms around me, asking sleepily, "Michael, what were you doing?"

I replied quietly, stroking her hair, "I had to get up for a moment. Go back to sleep, Emily." As I lay in her arms, I realized that we had not eaten an evening meal, but I smiled as I thought about what we had done instead. This experience had been unexpected, and I was surprised at my willingness to risk everything for a mortal woman. And on that thought, I succumbed to sleep.

As I dressed the next morning I chose my own comfortable clothing and boots, hoping that she would not notice the archaic design and fabric, but determined to protect my sensitive areas from further irritation. As we were about to leave the room, we turned and embraced each other tightly, kissing and grinning as if we were the first ones to discover the wonders of sex.

Emily reached up and brushed the hair back from my face, as she said, "Just because I didn't ask you about what happened last night doesn't mean that I've forgotten about it."

I just looked into her wide hazel eyes, traced her jawline with my finger, and said simply, "I know."

"And," she teased, "I couldn't help but notice that your English is really old-fashioned and your accent is unusual. What's up with that? What century are you really from, anyway?" She was smiling playfully, so I presumed that she was not serious.

"Fifth," I said solemnly.

"I would have said the fifteenth," she said with a laugh.

So I responded in kind, "I am familiar with that time as well, my lady." I smiled warmly at her, enjoying the game, though it could prove to be a dangerous one.

Emily smiled back. "You're smart and funny; I like that in a man. You're special, Michael; I've never met anyone like you."

I gazed back at her and said softly, "You have no idea…"

CHAPTER 7
April 26 Morning

WE CHECKED OUT of the inn and stopped for something to eat at a place called the Cracker Barrel, which I thought most odd, as there were no barrels in sight. After breaking our fast we left the valley and drove up into the mountains on Highway 6, talking and enjoying each other's company; so much so that when the attack came I was not prepared. I would soon regret this.

The sudden blast of darkness and icy wind seemed alive as it writhed like a serpent, and wailed like a banshee, battering the small car. This manifestation was eerily similar to the attack on the aircraft, but felt much more personal, and much more intense, directed entirely at me.

Terrified, Emily screamed, "What's happening, Michael?" She was struggling to control the vehicle and I was afraid she would drive off the road.

I yelled, trying to make myself heard over the din, "Pull over to the side of the road, quickly, and let me get out. Stay in the car and get down." I prayed that she would not attempt to get out with me and risk her safety. Also, I did not want her to witness my magical assault on the pulsating darkness. I had already—most foolishly—revealed too much information about myself, even in jest, in our recent conversation.

"Michael, no, what are you doing? Just stay in the car, where it's safe, until it stops!" She raised her voice frantically and grabbed my arm, her eyes wild with fear.

I pulled away from her, threw open the door and leaped out into the dark, menacing cloud, now erupting with bolts of lightening and stinging ice pellets. I could almost see distorted faces in the darkness and hear the wail of lost souls. I knew that this could get much worse and I had to act immediately, no matter the consequences—our lives were at stake.

I assumed a stance with my feet apart, and quickly threw my arms wide into the air, and drawing upon strength and power from deep within myself and from within the earth, I flung a wide band of magical energy at the manifestation, and screamed, *"Recesserimus creaturam malum!...* Be gone evil creature."

With a shriek of fury, the creature of darkness and evil was catapulted through a jagged rift in the sky, as if it was being banished into another realm. Silently, the rift closed behind it.

As the darkness vanished, I lowered my arms and took a deep breath. Behind me I heard the car door slam and Emily say, her voice shaking, "Michael, how did you do that? What *are* you?" She had obviously not done as I bid her. She had watched me use magic.

I knew that I would turn and see a look on her face that I had seen many times before; a look of shock, of fear, perhaps of awe or of worship. I sighed, and prepared myself to do what must be done to protect my identity and to keep her safe, possibly at the cost of our budding romance.

I turned around and walked up to her, a serious look on my face. "Emily, I have magic, and I used my powers just now to defeat this manifestation of evil that was sent to destroy me. I truly regret exposing you to this danger." I put my hands gently on her arms, hoping to calm her.

But Emily surprised me. Though shaken and scared by what had occurred, she definitely was not afraid of *me*; in fact, it seemed that she had expected my confession.

She stared at me and exclaimed excitedly, "I *knew* it! I knew you were different. I don't know how it's possible, but you saved us with magic. How cool is that! I have to tell my friend Derek, he'll have a fit that he wasn't here to see this!"

I groaned to myself, and thought, *Oh, gods, this cannot be happening.* So I cradled her face in my hands and kissed her, and said, "I am so sorry, but I cannot allow you remember this or to tell anyone."

Emily stood still and looked at me in confusion. "I don't understand, Michael, what are you going to do? Don't you trust me?"

I did not answer, feeling as if I was betraying her. I called upon a spell to erase her memory.

"*Oblitus*...forget," I said softly, gazing deeply into her eyes. I could sense the spell taking effect as her eyes lost their focus for a moment. The tension seemed to leave her body, and I stepped back from her, letting my hands drop to my sides. It was a mild spell, meant to erase only the most recent memories, and should not cause any ill effects. She should still remember our night together, and forget only the last few minutes. Unfortunately, I had not had the time to formulate a more intricate spell; hopefully this would be enough.

Emily stirred almost immediately, and looked at me blankly, as if she had forgotten I existed. That would truly be hard to bear, and for a moment, my heart seemed to stop beating.

"Michael, I feel so strange...What are we doing here?" Puzzled, she looked around the clearing, becoming increasingly agitated.

"Do you not remember? We stopped because you wanted to show me something." I hated deceiving her, but I was glad she still remembered me.

Suddenly she seemed like a different person. "Well, there's nothing here, *asshole*, so I don't know why I'd do that," she snarled angrily, becoming tense and irritated. "Get back in the fucking car. I want to get to Moab before dark." She got in the car without looking at me, slammed the door hard and turned the key in the ignition, the tension in her building tenfold.

Concerned that in her altered state she would change her mind and leave me here, I hurried around to the passenger side and jumped in, barely closing the door before she roared back onto the pavement and drove erratically, at high speed, down the highway, cutting across traffic heedlessly.

I was extremely concerned about her reaction. This could end very badly.

"Emily, calm yourself!" I exclaimed, afraid she would wreck the vehicle. Although I knew she was reacting to the spell, I could not imagine what had gone wrong.

She speared me with her gaze, scowling furiously, and yelled loudly, desperately, "I don't know what's going *on*. I'm *really pissed* at you; I know you did something to me, you *bastard*. You did something to me! What happened? Why can't I remember?"

She was now weeping hysterically, and I realized that she must have an extremely strong will. I had never seen any human being respond this way to my magic. I *thought* that Emily was entirely human, but what if I was wrong? The spell was meant only for humans, and I had no idea what effect it would have on someone with Fae blood or..... Oh, gods, could she be Fae, or partly so? An Elf perhaps? I had been in *very* close contact with her—would I not have been able to tell? There were many creatures of Faery that resembled humans, but whose physiology was entirely different.

I had no more time to ponder her heritage as she became increasingly erratic.

She screamed, "You fucker, what did you do to me?" She was driving more and more recklessly, frantically, and I decided that I had no choice. I would have to reverse the spell before she killed us both.

"Stop this machine now, Emily," I commanded, cutting through her screams with a Voice I rarely used.

She immediately slowed down and stopped the car at the side of the road, her body shaking violently. I reached over and pulled her around to face me and demanded, "Look at me!"

She reluctantly obeyed. I gazed deeply into her eyes and murmured the spell's reversal, "*Tenere memoria*...remember."

Immediately, she stopped shaking and her eyes cleared, and I knew that the memory I had tried to erase was once again foremost in her mind. She came back to herself and sighed, finally relaxing.

I could not have allowed her to go on another moment in such torment, but I wondered what the repercussions would be. As we looked at each other I waited to hear what she would say.

She let out another heartfelt sigh. "That really *sucked*. I don't *ever* want to experience something like that again. Michael, I remember everything, the attack, your...*magic*..."

Before I could respond, she continued, "And I *also* remember that you didn't trust me to keep a secret. How *could* you invade my mind and erase my memory like that?" Angry tears welled in her eyes and overflowed in rivulets down her cheeks. It was plain that I had hurt her terribly, and I would understand if she never wanted to see me again, but I had not wanted to take the chance that she would inadvertently betray me. In the past, trusting someone had ultimately meant betrayal.

I sighed and took her in my arms as she sobbed out her frustration and anger. "Emily, I did what I thought best to protect both of us, but something went wrong. I had no idea that your mind, your will, would oppose my spell so strongly. I am truly sorry, but if I had to do it all over again with stronger magic, or a different type of enchantment, I would. Please try to understand. Someone has been trying to kill me for several weeks now and everyone around me is in terrible danger. I realize that I have not been taking this situation as seriously as I ought to. I cannot have innocent people dying because of me. Even if it means hurting the feelings of someone I care about."

Emily wiped her face, said resolutely, "I understand that, but I would never tell anyone, Michael, I promise; I can and will keep your secret." Then she said under her breath, "Although I'm half-tempted to post it on Facebook."

At my baffled look, she laughed briefly. "There's my

sick sense of humor cropping up again, sorry. It's a social media site on the Internet, and *that* probably doesn't mean anything to you either, does it?" She was quiet for a moment, looking at me quizzically, and I could tell that she was starting to understand.

"Things are starting to make sense, in a crazy way. You had never flown before, your speech is awkward, your accent is British but sounds different somehow, archaic, and you seem so...unusual. Even your clothes look out of place. You're literally not from around here, are you?" She finally ran out of momentum and just stared at me, her eyes huge.

Gods, I had been afraid of this happening. "No, Emily, I am not." At least she did not suspect my true name, but I wondered how she could possibly *not* guess the truth, unless she was completely unfamiliar with the legends.

I said nothing further and turned to look out the window, hoping that she would change the subject. Actually, I was surprised that she did not hate me for what I had done.

"Okay, big guy," she said softly, "We'll talk about it later. We have to get going anyway." She guided the car back into the correct lane and slowly accelerated until we were traveling at the posted speed.

I took a cleansing breath and let it out slowly, trying to relax. I started thinking about the three attacks and realized that the length of time in between was getting shorter. Something else could happen before we arrived in Moab. As much I hated the idea, I might have to discuss this possibility with Emily so that she would not be taken by surprise again.

She was too quiet. I already knew enough about her to realize that this was not a good thing.

"Emily, what are you thinking about?" I asked carefully, dreading what she might say.

She glanced over at me and said quietly, "You know, I *did* see you last night, cleaning up the mess—that *you* had made! I saw you make hand gestures, then the chair and the lamp stood back up by themselves, and a little whirlwind of glass shards flew into the wastebasket. You thought I was asleep, but I was watching you use magic. I thought I was dreaming." She smiled at me with a saucy gleam in her eye, and said, "*I* think the fantastic sex caused your magic to spontaneously combust."

Although my face reddened I could not help grinning a little, because that is very close to what happened. I cleared my throat, and said, "Indeed." It took me several minutes to regain my composure, especially because she continued to grin widely and glance my way suggestively.

Then, we both became quiet, and many miles passed in a contemplative silence. I began to notice and appreciate the incredible landscape through which we were traveling. Tall, rugged mountains, sculpted by erosion into strange shapes, and above, the bluest sky I had ever seen. Sear, barren land as far as the eye could see, but dotted here and there with short, scraggly trees and bushes, and occasional brilliantly colored flowers. I had never seen a land such as this before, and I was fascinated by it.

And as I gazed out the window, I thought about everything that had happened. I was beginning to believe that I should trust Emily, and that I should tell her about the attacks. She was extremely intelligent, and I had a feeling she knew more about me than she cared to admit. Could it be that all of this was destined to occur? Apparently, I would have to trust the gods, as I always had.

We had long since passed by the towns of Price and Green River, and were nearing the place where we would turn off to go to Moab, when I finally spoke again.

"Emily, I need to talk to you about what happened on the flight, and up in the mountains this morning. Those were not arbitrary events. They were deliberate attacks on me, I suspect to stop me from reaching Moab."

She turned to look at me and said, "Wait a minute, what

do you mean 'what happened on the flight?' I thought that there was some freak storm...*oh!* Do you mean to tell me that you repelled that...thing...while you were sitting next to me? My God, no wonder you had a strained look on your face." She looked at the road in front of us, and then the rest of my comment registered. "You're from Great Britain—why the hell would this... whatever it is ...want to prevent you from getting to Moab, Utah, of all places?"

"I am not certain; that is what I intend to find out. But in the meantime, I need to warn you that there could be another occurrence before we arrive in Moab. I want you to be prepared this time," I said, gravely.

Her expression grew solemn. "While I appreciate the sentiment, it would have been helpful if I had known about this *before* that debacle up near Soldier Summit."

"I know, and I apologize for my error in judgment, Emily, but the pleasure of your company had me utterly distracted," I said sincerely.

"Oh sure, blame me for it!"

As I looked over at her profile, I wondered if I should have refused to give in to my base desires. Wise practitioners of the magical arts had always warned that sex was a powerful form of magic by itself, and one's personal magic never mixed well with it.

But it felt so good to hold another person in an intimate embrace, so pleasurable and satisfying for body, mind and soul. I swore that I would figure out how to have both magical *and* sexual power, instead of having to choose between them. I was so entrenched in my thoughts that it took me a moment to realize Emily was speaking to me.

"Earth to Michael, hey, I think you'd better take a look at the sky; we have incoming," Emily said worriedly, peering out through the windshield at a dozen dark, rapidly moving specks in the sky.

I came out of my reverie in time to witness a rage of dragons winging directly towards us.

"This cannot be," I cried in stunned disbelief, "dragons have been extinct for more than a thousand years!"

"How in the world do you know that, Michael?" Emily exclaimed.

"I do not know that for sure, Emily, but it makes sense— they are creatures of myth, but myths always start with a grain of truth." I tried to cover up my blunder.

Again, she seemed satisfied by one of my hasty explanations.

The dragons were approaching quickly. We had already turned onto Highway 191 to Moab, traveling in a southerly direction, and I knew that we must get away from the other vehicles, the occupants of which would be in danger when the dragons began their attack.

"Turn onto a side road as soon as possible," I said urgently. "We must divert the creatures away from the highway."

She nodded and soon turned left onto a dirt track leading out into the desert. At our current speed, the car was bouncing through holes in the rough and narrow road.

Suddenly, spears of flame began hitting the ground on each side of the car, incinerating the few bushes and low trees on the sides of the dirt road.

"Watch out!" I yelled, as Emily veered back and forth to try and avoid the fire raining down upon us. I could hear the deep roar of the dragons above us, bent on destruction.

Finally, she pulled off the road and under a massive rock overhang, barely missing the roof of her car. She turned to me and said, "I know this isn't the time or the place for this, but I want you to remember what I said: I will keep your secret, Michael, and I will help you in any way that I can, but I hope that someday you will trust me enough to tell me everything."

I nodded. "We *will* talk about this later, but right now I

must get rid of these dragons before they hurt someone." I opened the door and started to climb out, but she grabbed my arm and pulled me back so that she could kiss me. Apparently, I was forgiven. Surprised, I kissed her back enthusiastically for a second then gently pushed her away. "I *have* to go, Em, *now*."

I strode out into the open and saw the dragons circling, searching for me. It occurred to me that these were magical constructs similar to the wyvern that I encountered recently, conjured from the material of the Other World. They could not be actual dragons, for those had gone from this earth long ago.

There was no more time to think; the dragons were now dropping out of the sky practically on top of me. I could feel the heat from their fire all around me, and one of the beasts actually got close enough to rake my shoulder with his claws. I cried out at the sudden, agonizing pain, but injured or not, I only had this one chance to repel the attack. I reached into my memories and prepared to speak to them as a dragonlord.

I faced the huge creatures above me, and flung my right hand towards them, palm spread wide, directing my will in a pulse of magical energy. As I snarled loudly in the old tongue, I once again called upon the power of my Voice, and chanted "*Ic eower frea, bebeodan ge, dracas. Laefan her nu ac na gecierran.*" I had chosen to use Old English, and although my phrasing might not have been perfect, I was counting on the effect of its abrasive, guttural sounds to influence the dragons.

Constructs or not, when commanded by the Voice of a dragonlord, the creatures had no choice but to obey. They flew swiftly up into the sky, roaring their displeasure, until I could see them no more. I was relieved that the attack had been repelled without killing any of them, and no one but myself had been injured. However, many people traveling to Moab would be telling stories about the dragons they had seen. No one would believe them, certainly, and even if they did, they would not be able to link the dragon sighting to an itinerant sorcerer.

I clutched my injured shoulder, trying to staunch the flow of blood, and turned around, noticing that Emily was standing where she could see the entire confrontation. She had again witnessed my use of magic, but apparently did not realize what had happened.

Then her eyes widened in shock as she saw the blood. "Oh my God, Michael, you're hurt," she exclaimed as she ran towards me.

I smiled crookedly as I swayed on my feet—perhaps my injury was more severe than I thought. Emily quickly braced me under my good arm and helped me back to the car. She found a clean towel in the back seat and pressed it against the wound.

"We have to get you to the hospital, Michael!"

I winced. "*Don ne bisgu*, I mean, do not worry, 'twill heal."

"I'm serious, you've lost a lot of blood," she said worriedly, apparently ignoring the fact that I had just lapsed into the Anglo-Saxon language again.

"And what shall we tell them, that 'twas a dragon that clawed my shoulder?" I grimaced in pain. "Just let me rest until we get to town, please, love."

As we returned to the paved road, and turned left towards Moab, she said, wonderingly, "You just called me 'love,' Michael."

"I did," I said quietly. "I am sorry. I presume too much."

"It's okay, Michael, I don't mind. I'm sorry, but I have to ask: where did dragons...*dragons*...come from? I watched you, and I heard how you commanded them. How did you...?"

I managed to answer her, through a haze of pain, unwittingly revealing even more information about myself. "Twas Old English, from the time of the Saxon occupation, when there were still a few dragons left in Britain. I commanded them, as their master, to leave here *now* and never return."

Her eyes narrowed as she looked at me suspiciously.

"How do you happen to know just the right Old English words to command dragons?"

I thought carefully before I answered her and told a partial truth, "The same way I know Latin—I learned both languages for use with my magic. When creating spells, it is best to use a language that you do not speak on a regular basis." I took a deep breath and pushed the pain away temporarily.

"Look, Michael, I'm having a hard time wrapping my head around this. You use magic, and you speak ancient languages to various mythical creatures, and you're apparently from another *time*. And there are *still* things you're not telling me. Swell. Do you realize how much you're asking of me to….never mind, I won't push you." She shook her head in disbelief.

Finally, Emily turned to me with a sigh. "Okay, big guy, I concede that you're the All-Powerful Wrangler of Dragons. Now, let's talk about what we're going to do when we get to Moab. We'll be there in about twenty minutes, and we still need to get you some medical attention."

I looked at her, puzzled, only hearing the first part of the sentence, and said, "Why do you persist in calling me that?"

She replied, watching the road ahead, "Well, I'm not really comfortable calling you 'honey' or 'dear' so early in our relationship, so I figure 'big guy' will work." And she gazed pointedly down at the bulge in my pants, then looked up at me through her long eyelashes and winked.

I choked as I realized what she was referring to. Then I started laughing until the injury to my shoulder turned mirth into a moan of pain.

"Oh, God, I'm so sorry, Michael! Here I've been talking your ear off and you're hurting," she said regretfully.

"I will be fine," I said firmly. "Now, Emily, please allow me to sit quietly with my eyes closed for a few minutes, and then we can discuss what to do when we get to town."

I did not wait for her to answer. I sat back, closed my

eyes, and started breathing slowly and rhythmically, focusing inside myself, reaching down into the center of my being into the white light within. I immersed myself in that pure light and felt the pain start to recede. I pictured my wounded shoulder in my mind and said silently, *Sanare...heal*, directing the light in the form of healing energy to the torn muscles and ragged, bleeding flesh.

I kept focusing until the pain was gone and I knew that the wound was healed. Then I slowly opened my eyes—to find Emily staring in astonishment at the aura that surrounded me.

"Emily," I began, "I can explain." But as I turned towards her, the blood-soaked towel fell off of my shoulder, revealing new pink skin under the torn shirt.

"You just healed yourself! How in hell is that possible?" Emily gasped.

I just looked at her solemnly and flexed my newly healed arm and shoulder. How could I explain to her what I was, without revealing my true name? I could not. I owed this mortal nothing, yet I wanted to give her some kind of explanation.

"Emily, I have told you that I have magical abilities, and that means I can manipulate energy. The world we are a part of is *made* of energy, and I directed that energy to my wound, facilitating the healing process," I explained. It was the truth, up to a point.

"If you say so, but it just adds one more thing to my list," she said quietly, staring straight ahead again.

I sighed, knowing that she was close to discovering the truth, and I realized that I had been revealing clues to my identity all day. Did I want her to know about me?

"How much longer will it be until we reach Moab?" I asked, trying to divert her attention.

"We just passed Arches National Park, so it's about ten minutes more to my house." She paused a moment then said cautiously, "You're welcome to spend the night with me, Michael, if you don't have anywhere else to go."

"I appreciate your kindness, Emily, and I accept your offer. Tomorrow I will find other lodging. I do not want to intrude upon your life any more than I already have," I said. I really could not blame her if she wished to be quit of me. It had been a most harrowing day for her. She had done well for a normal human being, though, considering everything she had experienced today. If she was indeed human, I added to myself.

I glanced out the window and noticed that we were approaching a bridge arching over a river, and that the surrounding cliff faces were a bright orange-red in the late afternoon sunlight. It was absolutely breathtaking and I smiled, soaking in the beauty.

Without warning, my spirit soared as I felt the gods welcome me, and for a moment, I knew that I was truly headed in the right direction. Then I lost the thread of time and consciousness and went into the light.

CHAPTER 8
April 26 Late Afternoon

M ICHAEL, ARE YOU ALRIGHT? *Michael!"* The car was
stopped in a tree-shaded area, and Emily was shaking me
frantically.

As I came back to my body I sat up and gasped, "I am
well." Apparently I had been in the company of the gods for a
few minutes, and my physical body had gone completely limp in
the seat, appearing as if I had fainted.

Emily reached over and cupped her hand against my
face. She said, worried, "You frightened me, big guy…Let's go
in the house, okay?"

We were stopped in front of her home, and I remembered nothing of the drive from the bridge. I carefully opened the
car door and stepped out into warm, dry air. I reached back inside for the bloodied towel. "I would be happy to clean this for
you, Emily, but I am afraid the stains will not come out."

She said calmly, "Throw it away; I have lots of towels.
We have more important things to do right now." She indicated a
tall bin near the back door and I put the towel inside it. In the
back of my mind, a quiet voice whispered that it was a mistake
to do so. But focused on Emily, I promptly forgot the warning.

We carried our bags into her small living space, her
"mobile home" as she called it, and Emily said, "Just put them
down anywhere. I'm going to turn on the cooler, and then I'll get
us both a drink. We need it."

I agreed that a drink would be welcome, and a few
minutes later when we each had our glasses, we drained them
simultaneously. The amber liquid felt like fire going down my
throat and I coughed and my eyes watered.

She laughed. "Somehow I thought you were tougher
than that, Michael."

"No, I am not 'tough' at all, Emily. However, I would say that *you* are. You have experienced things today that most people would not have been able to endure. You are very brave, and I am proud of you," I said softly, putting the glass down and wrapping my arms around her.

Emily hugged me back, then she tilted her head, and looking into my eyes, she brought her lips to mine, gently kissing me. I returned the kiss, deepening it until our tongues clashed in an intimate duel. We clung to each other as the attraction we felt surfaced once again. I pulled back for moment and gasped, "I need to bathe first, Em."

She murmured, "My thoughts exactly. Come with me." She led me into her bathroom and undressed even before turning on the faucets. I quickly removed my ruined clothing and dropped it on the floor, then turned to her and pulled her naked body into my arms. Her beautiful breasts flattened against my torso, and my erection was pressed firmly against her abdomen.

Emily said breathlessly, "Let's get in the shower and wash before we get too carried away...Oh!" I had picked her up and set her down her in the tub before stepping in myself. Apparently I had surprised her with my strength.

I looked for soap but did not see any, until Emily said, "Here's some shower gel—liquid bath soap—that works really well." She picked up a bottle and poured some of the liquid into the palm of her hand, then proceeded to run her soap-filled hands across my back, my chest and my arms before she reached down and stroked my erection. The feel of her hands gripping me, slippery and warm, was almost more than I could bear.

"Wait," I said roughly. I gestured towards the soap bottle and it flew into my hand; it was now my turn to wash *her* body. I ran my hands around her taut nipples, across her shoulders and down her back to the crease of her buttocks, then I reached underneath and caressed her intimately until she tensed and moaned, "Let's rinse off—I can't wait any longer!"

We rinsed quickly and toweled each other dry, kissing and touching all the while, and then she took my hand and pulled me impatiently into her bedroom. We lay down on the bed, wet hair dampening the pillows, and she rolled with me until she was on top, gazing down at me seductively. I brushed the strands of hair out of her face and kissed her, easing my tongue into her mouth to taste her. We both began breathing hard, desire building. And as I pulled her closer to me, she moved so that she was slowly impaled upon my hardness.

"Oh, God," she groaned as we began moving together. Then, with my arms around her, I rolled over, still inside her, so that she was under me. She reached up and gripped my backside with both hands, pulling me deeper, and I stayed there motionless until we were both feeling crazed with the need to move, then I began thrusting into her over and over until we both cried out in release.

We collapsed against each other and I just gazed at her helplessly. I loved her. I hardly knew this woman, it didn't make sense, and yet I loved her. By the gods, how had I allowed this to happen? She was mortal. I was not entirely sure *what* I was.

Emily smiled and touched my face gently. She looked at me closely and said, "Why do you look so serious? That was just amazing!"

I honestly did not know what to say. My mind went through a tally of things I could *not* say to her: We cannot be in love because you will grow old and die and I will never age...I cannot love you because I must find the portal to Avalon so that I can resurrect the Once and Future King...I am much too old for you...So I settled on saying the simple truth.

"I...think I love you, Emily," I said hesitantly, not wanting to breathe until I heard her answer.

"I love you too, Merlin," she said quietly, with a catch in her voice.

CHAPTER 9
April 26 Evening

I T TOOK ME A MOMENT to grasp what she had just said. She loved me! Then my eyes widened and I asked in disbelief, "You know who I am?"

"I'm not stupid, sweetie, and I finally put it all together after you healed yourself. With everything that has happened since we met, all the incredible, impossible things I've seen you do, who else could you be besides Merlin the Magician?"

I could not believe that ridiculous title had persisted for almost 1600 years. I laughed and shook my head in exasperation as I sat up at the edge of the bed, my damp hair falling around my face. "I swear by all the gods, that if Uther was still alive I would take him to task for naming me that. I am a *sorcerer*, not a magician."

Emily gasped. "You mean Uther Pendragon, King Arthur's father? My God, having you say that out loud somehow makes all of this real..."

I turned to look at her, gazing into her beautiful, intelligent eyes, and surrendered to the inevitable. "But it *is* real, Emily. I was born in the year AD 420; I was serious this morning when I said I was from the fifth century. What year were you born, about 1985? That makes me at least 1500 years too old for you." I grinned at her, surprised that I found the situation humorous.

"It's unbelievable—you look like you're in your early thirties," she said.

"I stopped aging around 452, so I would indeed have been in my early thirties. When Arthur was wounded at Camlann I was actually in my fifties, which was considered an advanced age back then." Strange, I mused, I hadn't thought about that in centuries.

Emily sat up, pressing her breasts against my back and put her arms around me.

"Wow, this isn't easy for me, big guy. Realizing that my lover is a really old legend is pretty intimidating." She laughed a little, and said, "You know, I'm hungry, O Sexy One. Let's get something to eat. We'll have to go out since there's no food in the house." She kissed my shoulder and clambered off the bed, reaching for clean clothes in a chest of drawers.

I got up and turned her around to face me. "I am so sorry for the danger you were in today, because of me."

Emily just pulled my head down so that our foreheads touched, and said softly, "It wasn't your fault that those creatures were trying to kill you. You just wanted to protect me. Merlin, this has been the most exciting day I've ever experienced! And how could I be sorry that I've found the love of my life?" She kissed me sweetly and proceeded to get dressed.

I just looked at her, at a loss for words, and sincerely hoped that fate would indeed smile upon us.

As soon as we were both ready, we walked out of her small dwelling into the cooling air of a spring evening in Moab. It felt good to stretch my legs after several days of being cramped first in Tom's car during the trip to London, then in the jet for an interminable length of time, and then in another small car for an additional four-hour journey. It seemed a very long time ago that I had ridden my horse to Tom and Sandy's farm, and I wondered distractedly how the Reese family was faring. I glanced over at the bright-haired woman beside me for whom I had so recently declared my feelings. I reached out and took Emily's hand in mine and she looked up at me with such undisguised love and longing that I pulled her into my arms and kissed her deeply. We both laughed in joyful abandon as we continued down the street.

The sun had just set behind a towering wall of rock that I

could see over the tops of the homes we passed. I glanced over my right shoulder and saw that sunlight still illuminated the red cliffs on the other side of the valley, and I sensed a latent power in the rocks, deep and strong and as old as time.

We headed down a winding walkway and then crossed a small bridge with a creek rushing below. We passed several couples with their arms twined around each other, and we had to step aside while a family went past us, each person mounted on some kind of wheeled conveyance.

"What are they riding?" I asked, fascinated by the sight.

"Those are bicycles, Merlin," Emily said, amused. "Everyone rides them here."

When we reached Main Street we stopped for a moment so that I could look around at the bustling town. I was really here, in Moab, Utah, and it was a little overwhelming. It was much larger than the village where I grew up, and different in every way from Camelot, but it seemed a friendly, interesting place. Vehicles of all types traveled in both directions, and people walked along gazing into shop windows displaying every kind of merchandise imaginable. There were large inns such as the one in which we had stayed the previous night, and several taverns and eating establishments were nearby. A few lights winked on along the street now and the tantalizing aroma of food cooking reminded me that it was past time to eat, and I was famished. We approached a place called City Diner and were about to open the door, when we heard someone shout, "Emily, wait!"

As we turned around, a husky young man ran up to her and said breathlessly, "Hey, I didn't know you were back in town, Em—it's good to see you." He turned to stare at me suspiciously as he asked, "Who's this?" His tone was mild but I sensed a trace of jealousy in his manner. I wondered if he was Emily's former lover.

Not knowing if she would remember to call me Michael, instead of Merlin, I extended my hand to shake his, as seemed to be the current custom, and said, "Hallo, I am Michael Reese, a new friend of Emily's." The man reluctantly shook hands with me, and to my surprise, I felt a brief warm tingle in that firm grip. Normally, this would be a sign that the other person had at least a small amount of magic, so I was surprised when Emily's friend did not acknowledge that he had felt it. Was he totally unaware of his gift? I was intrigued—I wanted to get to know this man, despite his obvious hesitancy towards me.

He responded politely enough, "Nice to meet you Michael, I'm Derek Colburn. Emily and I have been friends for years. I don't know if she told you, but we both work for the Park Service."

Emily just stood quietly smiling as she watched us interact; an old friend and a new lover. Perhaps I was mistaken. Nothing in her demeanor seemed to indicate anything more than a long-standing friendship with Derek.

"No, she had not yet mentioned it, but we have actually not known each other that long," I said, looking into her eyes and thinking about the intimacy we had shared.

Emily gazed back at me, her eyes acknowledging our connection, and then she said, "Now that you guys have done the male-bonding thing, Michael and I need to eat. Derek, can you join us?" Derek nodded and we all went inside. I wondered if it would be difficult for him to see her interacting with me.

The three of us sat down, Derek facing us across the table. As we consulted our menus, I realized that although I could read it, I had no idea what most of the food choices were. I finally decided on a meal and we ordered our food. As we waited for it to be served, Emily glanced at me mischievously and said to Derek, "Michael is interested in the Dark Ages, and it seems he's quite an expert when it comes to the King Arthur and Merlin legend. Isn't that right, *Michael*?"

I had just taken a sip of water, on which I proceeded to choke. What game was she playing?

As I turned to look at her with my eyebrows raised in a silent question, Derek seemed to come alive as he said excitedly, "Really? Are you a historian, or a professor? I'm fascinated with the old legends and stories about King Arthur and the Knights of the Round Table and I'd be very interested in talkin' to you. If you're going to be in town for awhile, maybe you'd like to hang out, watch a little tube or some DVDs? I have a lot of old Merlin movies you may not have seen and I have some free time right now—I'm on furlough."

I sat there nodding my head and smiling in agreement, but I did not understand most of what he said, except for Arthur's name and my own, and the Knights of the Round Table. I was surprised that Derek's attitude had suddenly turned around.

I looked at Emily askance, and she grinned, enjoying my confusion immensely. I grabbed her hand under the table and squeezed it until she said out loud, "Ow, stop it!" I would have my hands full with her, I could see that already.

Fortunately, steaming plates of food were brought out and our conversation was temporarily forgotten. I was very hungry, as much of my personal energy had been depleted during the magical encounters earlier in the day. The steak that I had ordered was flavorful and tender, the texture unlike the wild boar, venison and mutton that I was accustomed to, and the rest of the meal was hearty. I finished it all.

As soon as our plates were cleared, I felt that I should address Derek's previous comment, for I did not want to appear rude to a new friend. "I thank you for offering to spend time with me, Derek, and I accept with pleasure. I cannot claim to be a teacher of history, but I am certainly interested in the myths about Arthur and Merlin, and in the time called the Dark Ages."

Surprised and amused, Derek glanced from me to Emily and said, "Does he always sound so formal?"

"Yep, that's Michael, old-fashioned and formal," she said gleefully, once again amused at my expense.

I turned to look at her, my forehead creasing into a frown, and said, "Emily, do you really think 'tis a good idea to provoke me?"

"Sorry, Michael. No, uh, I have a feeling it would be an *explosive* situation if you were to lose your temper..." She grinned widely and got up to pay the bill, waving away Derek's money. The minx was clearly enjoying herself and I stared after her in confusion.

"Am I missin' something here? What's goin' on with you two?" asked Derek, as confused as I at Emily's behavior.

"I am sorry, Derek, she and I are both tired and I know not what she is referring to. Since it has been a long eventful day for us, I think we are going to say 'good night.' I would like to meet with you on the morrow however, if that is convenient." I was anxious to find out about his magic, as it would be helpful to have an assistant in searching for the portal. And I confess to being curious about the extent to which twenty-first century inhabitants were interested in the tales of Camelot and Arthur and of course, Merlin.

At that moment, Emily walked over to us. "We probably ought to get going. I just had a call asking me to report for work tomorrow, a day earlier than I expected, so I need to get to bed soon. You know my number, Derek, so just give Michael a call in the morning. You two can go for coffee or something—I'm sure you'll have *a lot* to talk about. Oh, and Derek, do me a favor? Take a picture of us together and then send it to me, please?"

As he got his phone out of his pocket I reflected on the first time I had seen Emily use her device, and how amazed I was at this astonishing piece of modern technology. Derek turned it towards us, taking our picture. It had been centuries since I had seen myself other than reflected in the crystals, so I was curious to see the results.

As we left City Diner I said, "Twas a pleasure to meet

you, Derek, and I will see you on the morrow."

Derek said, "You too, man, lookin' forward to it!" and walked away, whistling, acting as if he was truly reconciled to the fact that Emily had chosen me. I was not sure I could have been as understanding had I been in his position.

As Em and I walked back to her house along the darkened streets, I realized that I was unhappy about her behavior at the restaurant. I wanted an explanation. She could not make light of my secret in public—it was just too dangerous.

She must have sensed that I was upset, because she turned to me and said apologetically, "Merlin, I'm sorry for putting you on the spot. I admit that I have a perverse sense of humor, but I would never have revealed to Derek who you really are. Honestly, though, I think that once you get to know him, you might want to consider him an ally."

I said to her firmly, "Emily, I know you did not mean to cause harm, but you must be most cautious not to draw attention to me or to my magic in that way."

I brooded silently for a few more minutes, then suddenly I was struck by a thought that made me pause. My magic...When Emily and I were intimate earlier, my magic was... quiet. What had caused that?

"It just occurred to me that I did not lose control of my magic during our time together earlier. How could I have forgotten that?" I was excited at this revelation and intended to think more on it later.

"Great, let's see if we can duplicate those results!" Emily said happily and took my hand, pulling me the last few feet up to her house and through the front door.

CHAPTER 10
April 27

T HE FOLLOWING MORNING I awoke just before sunrise and dressed quickly, leaving Emily still fast asleep. I needed some time to myself to think and plan. Barefoot, I quietly went outside and sat on her porch, relishing the early morning coolness. I could see the ridge across the valley starting to glow red as the first rays of the sun touched it. I gazed at the light and drank it in. I drew the fresh air deep into my lungs and noticed that it had a quality that was hard to describe, dry and crisp and a bit spicy. I wondered what the day would bring.

I reminded myself not to lose track of my reason for coming to Moab. And I sincerely hoped that Emily would not prove too much of a distraction. Emily...I shook my head slowly in disbelief. I had never considered that I would find someone who could love me, especially in this time and place. I had always been alone, thinking that I was too different, or too dangerous, to have a normal relationship with a woman. And the destiny that had always seemed so very clear to me now seemed to have become a little obscured. However, I had felt the gods very near to me through all the days I had been awake this century, and even more so since I arrived in Moab the previous day. I needed to trust that all was as it should be. While I wondered about the part Emily would play in the story now being written, there was no doubt in my mind that she was integral to it.

I heard her begin to stir, so I put aside my thoughts for the moment and walked back inside. She was just coming out of the bedroom when she saw me, and her face lit up with joy. I crossed the room and drew her into my arms, and breathing in her scent, I felt truly at peace.

"How was your sleep, sweet lady?" I said softly, kissing her cheek.

Emily said with a saucy grin, "What little sleep I had was fine, thank you. As for the rest of the time, your stamina was truly impressive, old man. And you didn't even wreck the place—although I did notice that your magic misbehaved once, causing my underpants to go flying around the room."

"Easily remedied, my dear," I said, casually flicking my hand in the direction of the bedroom.

Looking skeptical, she went into the other room and inspected the state of her underwear drawer. "I'm impressed. I think you should do the laundry from now on."

I raised my eyebrows imperiously and said in a thick accent, "You truly expect Lord Merlin, the Sorcerer of the Realm, to do lowly servant's chores, madam?" I was playing a game with her; I had done any number of chores over the years for the Pendragons that were far more demeaning than washing a few garments.

Emily's eyes widened at the mention of my title, and said with a smile, "Seriously? *Lord* Merlin?"

"The title is quite real, having been bestowed upon me shortly after I arranged Uther's assignation with Ygraine. However, in this setting, it does seem rather pompous," I admitted.

Emily drew my face to hers and gave me a quick kiss. "Well, *Lord* Merlin, while I wish we could continue this conversation, I have to get ready for work. Why don't you call Derek and see if he's up yet? You two can get some breakfast together—City Diner makes great pancakes."

"At the risk yet again of sounding hopelessly old-fashioned, how do I do that?" I grimaced, wishing I had my scrying crystal.

"Oh, sorry, the phone is over on my desk," she said as she walked over and picked it up. "Just push the buttons like this, press 'Send' and hold the phone up to your ear." She showed me how to do that and wrote Derek's phone number down.

I entered the information as she had instructed and heard

a ringing sound followed by a voice that said, "Hello?"

"Hallo, is this Derek?" I said tentatively. I hoped that I had entered the number correctly.

"Yeah, is this Michael?"

"Yes. Emily will be leaving soon and suggested that we break our fast together this morning," I said.

"Uh, okay, that sounds good. We can meet at City Diner or you can have Emily drop you off at my house," Derek said. "I'm not a *great* cook, but I make a pretty mean omelet. See you soon."

A *mean* omelet? I almost asked him what he meant but decided not to reveal my ignorance.

"I will be there in a short while," I said, feeling somewhat out of my depth. *You can do this Merlin*, I said to myself, taking a deep, steadying breath.

Emily, now dressed in a sort of uniform, came out of the bedroom, and saw that I was feeling a bit ill at ease. She put her hands on her hips. "Merlin, are you nervous? You are the most amazing person in the entire world—you have *nothing* to be nervous about. If Derek knew who you were, he would practically be groveling at your feet. He *idolizes* you. He lives and breathes sword and sorcery stuff—anything and everything pertaining to you and Arthur. How do you think I figured out who you were? I've been listening to Derek *rave* about you for years, never imagining that I would actually sleep...uh, meet you. So just go have fun and relax."

She poured herself a glass of juice and drank it down hurriedly. "I'm sorry, I have to run or I'll be late. I wasn't really expecting to go in this morning, but my boss said it's urgent, so...gotta go." She hurriedly strapped on a belt with a stiff pouch on the side holding what appeared to be a weapon. I was surprised. Did all the people who worked for this "Park Service" carry weapons?

She noticed the look on my face and explained, "I'm a

law enforcement ranger, Merlin, I'm sorry I didn't tell you that yesterday. Somehow with all the magical stuff happening it just didn't seem that important." She kissed me again. "See you about five-thirty this afternoon. I'll probably be at the Park Service office on Resource Boulevard today so I shouldn't be late. Just leave the door unlocked, it's safe enough here. Oh, and I know you haven't had the chance yet to exchange your money, so here's twenty bucks. You can pay me back later, okay?"

She handed me some currency, then ran out the door, got in the car, and drove away.

I realized as soon as she was gone that I had not asked her to give me a ride to Derek's house. Then I remembered the phone, so I called Derek and explained what had happened.

"Yep, that sounds like her, always in a hurry; I'll be right there." He arrived soon thereafter, and we decided to forego his 'mean' omelets and eat at City Diner. I ordered the pancakes Emily recommended, enjoying the meal thoroughly. And I discovered an exceptional beverage: Coffee. I had three cups and felt most agreeable.

As it turned out, I felt more comfortable spending time with Derek alone, without Emily; we were just two men having a meal together and getting to know each other. I was hoping that he would give some indication that he knew about his magic, but he did not.

Derek and I found one subject after another to talk about, including herbs, antique weapons and ancient history. One "fact" that he had discovered in his research seemed strange to me. According to the historical documents he'd read, the Romans had taken their crossbows with them when they left Britain early in the fifth century, and crossbows were not used there again until the time of the Norman Invasion in 1066. I frowned a little when he related this information, because I knew for a fact that it was not true. We had used crossbows in Camelot every day, and the Romans had been gone from Britain since before I was born. But of course I could not tell him the documents were incorrect without revealing myself, so I said nothing.

And it seemed that Derek was most knowledgeable about historical events, enthusiastically mentioning the specific information he had researched. I found I had to be careful how I responded, since I had participated in some of those events over the centuries.

During our conversation, I also found out that his ex-wife was the proprietor of the only herb shop in town. This interested me greatly, as I wanted to find a place to obtain various herbs and potions.

After breakfast, we headed towards the herb shop, only a few blocks away.

I wondered at Derek's acceptance of losing his wife and his ability to remain friendly with her. I was hesitant to inquire as it could be rather awkward. Derek anticipated my question.

"You're probably wonderin' about my relationship with Chris, my ex. We were really young when we got married, and after awhile we realized that we'd be better off as best buds than as husband and wife, so we got divorced years ago. We never had kids so we didn't have to fight about custody. We've been great friends for a long time," Derek explained. Although I truly did not understand the situation, I just nodded sagely.

We arrived at Chris Colburn's shop just as she was opening for the day, and I noticed a sign in the window that read, BUILDING W/ BUSINESS FOR SALE. As I saw those words, a sense of rightness, of inevitability, filled me, and I knew that I had found the means by which I could fit into the Moab community, earn a living, and still be able to search for the portal back to Avalon, and to Arthur.

Derek introduced me to Chris, a small yellow-haired woman with a warm smile. She explained that she wanted to move to another state to be closer to her sister, and needed to sell the business to finance the move. She was pleased that I was interested in the shop, and encouraged me to look around.

I noticed that she had an excellent assortment of herbs, all of which I was thoroughly familiar with. I was particularly interested in a book she had that seemed to be a modern translation of an original Herbarium. I was fascinated by the fact that the contents of an obscure fifth century journal had not only survived, but was actually being used in the twenty-first century. And I chuckled as I realized that it was a reprint of my old journal. I had compiled the information and drawn the illustrations in the years following Arthur's death. I very much wanted this volume to be included in the sale.

Continuing my inspection of the premises, I saw that she had a good-sized area for display in front, and a work area in the back. As I turned to exit the back room, I noticed a door leading to a narrow staircase. Climbing the steep stairs and barely having enough headroom, I ended up in a small apartment that was obviously Chris's living space. I turned away, not wanting to intrude on her private area. But it occurred to me that she would be moving out of it when the sale was done. Not only would I have the shop, but a place to live as well.

I wondered what Emily would think of my plan. I would be spending more than a few nights a week with her, I was certain. However, I needed to have my own place to be alone and this would be the perfect setting. I could work on potions and spells and make plans to search out and defeat my enemy, and all the while pursuing my original quest.

Downstairs again, as I walked through the back room looking for Chris so that we might discuss the details of our transaction, I overheard Derek talking to her softly in the front of the shop. I paused, curious to know what was being said when he thought I could not hear him. I concentrated, using my sorcerer's senses to Listen closely to the conversation.

"...And I'm surprised that I kinda like the guy, but I'm

still a little concerned for Emily. I mean, she just met him on the plane the other day, but he's stayin' at her house and it's obvious they're already havin' sex. She's kind of vulnerable, even though she seems so tough. She's wanted a relationship for a long time, and I hope he won't take advantage of her, you know?" Derek said to Chris, concern for his friend obvious in his voice.

Emily was fortunate to have a friend like Derek, I thought. He could not know that I would never take advantage of her, nor deliberately hurt her. I would try to reassure him in some way. Perhaps when he found out that I intended to move into the apartment above the shop, he would feel more comfortable about the situation.

I deliberately made a sound to warn them that I was coming, and stepped into the front room.

"I hope that you will allow me to purchase your shop, Chris—it would suit my needs well. Perhaps we can discuss the details of the transaction, and I can contact my agent to arrange the transfer of funds," I said.

I would be able to have Tom or Sandy wire the funds to me the following day, so Chris and I completed the necessary paperwork immediately, both of us satisfied with the arrangement. She had inherited the building and owned it outright, so the transaction could be completed faster than normal.

Not being entirely familiar with the value of property in this time, I nearly fainted when a "fair" price was agreed upon. In my day, I could have purchased a large estate including a manor house with servants, and an entire stable full of horses and livery for the amount I was paying for her herb business and the building that housed it. Derek reminded me that the exchange rate from the British pound to the U.S. dollar was currently favorable, which relieved my mind somewhat. And soon I would be the new proprietor of The Moab Herbalist. I felt an enormous sense of accomplishment and a heady excitement; the gods were surely responsible for all that had happened recently.

CHAPTER 11
April 27

A S SHE ALREADY HAD PLANS for later on, I arranged with Chris to meet the following day to learn about operating the business and to obtain her advice regarding the items I might offer in the shop. I was anxious to get started, but she assured me that it would not take more than a few hours to become familiar with the details.

I had a long time to wait until Emily returned home, so I accepted Derek's offer to view several "movies" about Merlin and King Arthur. Of course, he had no way to know that the subject of his "movies" would be sitting right beside him. I smiled to myself in anticipation.

When we arrived at Derek's house and stepped through the front door, I noticed that he had a collection of large, colorful, shiny scrolls on his walls depicting scenes of ancient battles, many with a lone figure in a long robe standing tall upon a hilltop, brandishing a sorcerer's staff.

I cleared my throat, gestured towards the robed figure, and said, "Ah, who is this, is it supposed to be Merlin?"

"Right, that's Merlin the Enchanter, using his magic to protect the people of Camelot." Derek replied with enthusiasm.

Merlin the Enchanter, rather than Merlin the Magician—thank the gods, I thought to myself, *perhaps this culture can be saved after all.*

We selected the "DVDs" out of Derek's personal collection: *Merlin*, a movie starring Sam Neil; the first two "discs" in a "TV series" called *Camelot;* and several in another series called *The Adventures of Merlin,* which had been made in Great Britain and France. And there were many others we would not have time to watch this day.

I was truly startled. I had no idea that this modern society was quite so obsessed with me, and although it was flattering, it made me feel very odd. I was basically a modest man. Despite knowing throughout my entire life that I was a unique and powerful being, I did not dwell upon it; it was just something that I accepted. But I did not necessarily enjoy this misplaced adulation. After all, it was my destiny to serve Arthur, and through him, all mankind. I did not need, nor seek, praise and approval for performing this sacred duty.

Derek made coffee for us, and we started watching the most amazing thing I had ever seen: Moving color pictures, of real people, complete with the sound of their voices, on a glass rectangle called a "television", or "TV." I was completely captivated, especially when these pictures were supposed to be portraying *my* life. Of course, they were grossly inaccurate, but entertaining anyway.

The show called *Camelot* I found most interesting, because the man portraying me had a shaved head, and looked a lot older than I had been when Arthur was sixteen years old. And he was quite troubled about using his powers, which I had not been.

When this sinister Merlin caused the lake to ice over and trap the girl named Excalibur (why would they call the girl by the sword's name?), I was so incensed that I looked over at Derek and exclaimed, "I would *never* have…I mean, Merlin would never have done something like that; to have so little control over one's magic is inexcusable!"

Derek looked at me strangely, and I realized that I had almost given myself away.

"I just meant that Merlin was too responsible to cause a girl's death merely to stop her. He could have just used magic to take the sword away from her…" I was making things worse and decided to stop talking. A bead of nervous perspiration trickled down the side of my face as I realized what I had almost done. One person knowing my secret in this time was more than enough.

Fortunately, Derek interpreted my statements as an intense interest in the story of Merlin and Arthur, rather than evidence of actual involvement, and agreed with me.

The hours passed as we watched more about "Merlin," until my fascination with the experience began to wane.

I was entertained by the BBC interpretation, however. It was done very well, and portrayed me as an innocent young man in his late teens, the same age as Arthur, coming to Camelot for the first time to be under the tutelage of one Gaius, Court Physician to Uther. It is interesting that they used the name Gaius, as that really was my mentor's name when I was young, but *I* was Court Physician during Uther's reign, not Gaius. And at that time, Arthur had not yet been conceived. In this show, Uther was opposed to the use of magic, ruthlessly beheading Druids and any other practitioners of magic that crossed his path. This disturbed me greatly. In reality, he had *encouraged* the practice of magic, first naming me Court Magician, an erroneous title that plagued me even now, and later officially appointing me Sorcerer of the Realm, a role I fulfilled for many years, into Arthur's reign and beyond. The other thing that bothered me was the use of the French castle for Camelot; it was too recent by nine hundred years. It was most certainly a beautiful place, but not appropriate to use as Camelot.

"I have been to Chateau de Pierrefonds, Derek. It is a fine piece of architecture and 'tis no wonder it still stands today," I said, not telling him exactly *when* I had been there, which was after it was built in the late 1300s.

"That's awesome, Michael, and I hope that you'll tell me more about it next time we get together. Since you bought Chris's shop, I assume you'll be stayin' in Moab for awhile. I'm lookin' forward to becomin' good friends."

I nodded, and as I looked at him, I knew that we could be very close friends indeed if he had magical abilities and I was able to trust him with my secret. However, to discover if he had magic, I would have to have my hands on him for more than just a brief handshake, to really Look into his being, and that would be most awkward until I knew him better. It would have to wait.

After we had watched all the DVDs he had chosen, eaten our "snacks" and consumed great quantities of coffee, I decided I would go back to Emily's to await her arrival. I thanked Derek for being a good host and assured him we would meet again soon. I left on foot, relatively certain that I could find my way back, as this town was not large enough in which to get lost.

As it turned out, I did not lose my way, but the walk turned perilous by yet another magical confrontation. I had traveled only a few blocks from Derek's house, enjoying being out in the fresh air, when I sensed a *wrongness*, something that did not belong in this world. I quickly looked around using not only my outer senses, but my inner ones as well, and I saw a shape out of the corner of my eye that I did not recognize. It was most definitely not human. I slowly turned and faced the monstrous form. It was about fifty feet away from me, near the corner of a building that Derek called the "movie theater." It was taller than my above-average height by the breadth of several hands, a pulsing outline of a beast that had no place on this earth, but should be consigned to the realm of Hades. On its head there were horns, and the area where the face should have been was a nightmare visage as eyes and mouth formed and shifted, as far from human as could possibly be. As I quickly reached for my magic and focused my will, I became aware of words being sent to me inside my mind—the sense of evil was overwhelming and I could barely stand to focus on it. I heard the words again, more clearly this time and they sent a chill throughout my being.

Merlin, come with me now...it is time fulfill your true destiny. Your father has waited long for you to take your place at his side in the Underworld, and he has sent me to bring you to him...

No, I am no demon, I gasped mentally, and struggled to

force this abomination from my thoughts. *Oh, gods, this cannot be true.* It is something that I had always feared, but had not wanted to confirm. I struggled against the hideous power of this being, feeling myself being drawn closer and closer to it until I could almost feel the yawning depths of the Underworld at my feet, the very ground I was standing on crumbling away.

Then a spark of sanity prevailed, allowing my fear to recede long enough for me to realize a way to rid myself of this horrifying evil. *What was the opposite,* I asked myself, *of darkness and evil? What always would prevail?* I smiled, because the answer had been there all along: light, goodness and love. And that is what I focused on, immersed myself in. As I felt that light rush through me, banishing the sense of evil that had come with the demon who tried to subdue me, I opened my eyes expecting it to have disappeared. But instead, the shape was increasing in size and coming towards me, its fury apparent at having been thwarted. Immediately, I stretched my hands out in front of me, palms open wide, and directed the full force of my magic in a blast of fire so intense that it instantly destroyed the horned manifestation of evil in a roaring conflagration that consumed itself within seconds. My heart pounding, I slowly dropped my arms and took a few deep breaths. That was much too close.

The encounter had taken only a few minutes, although it seemed like hours, and I carefully looked around to see if anyone had witnessed the confrontation. There was one man standing back somewhat from the scene of the demon's destruction, frozen in shock and fear. I immediately cast a spell to prevent him from moving, then walked up to him, looked into his terrified eyes and said *"Oblitus."* I then walked away from him, releasing him from the first spell. I did not look back, knowing that he would not remember me or what had just happened. Unfortunately, there were burn marks on the sidewalk, and some vegetation had been singed, but that could not be helped.

I realized now how much I needed my staff and my scrying crystal. Since Tom would be wiring the money for the shop and other expenses anyway, he could also send along my things.

As I continued on towards Emily's, I remembered to stop at the bank and open an account, making sure to have enough cash in my pocket to repay her for the money she had loaned me.

When I finally arrived back at the house I noticed that she was already there, even though it was not quite five o'clock, and she had changed out of her uniform into a long, loose, filmy garment. She greeted me with a smile and a kiss as I entered the house, and I relaxed as I basked in her attentions.

"I'll bet you'd like something cold to drink," she said. As she started to turn away to get me a beer, I pulled her back against me and kissed her thoroughly. She noticed my arousal immediately and said in a low voice, "I take it you missed me?"

"I did indeed, my lady," I said as I swung her into my arms and carried her into the bedroom. Emily was not a small woman, but I carried her easily. As I put her down, the loose long dress she was wearing caught on my clothing and rode up, uncovering bare skin.

"I forgot to tell you," Emily whispered in my ear, "I'm not wearing any panties."

She started stroking me through my jeans, then, impatiently, she unzipped them and yanked them down around my ankles along with my underwear. I stepped out of the pants hurriedly, drew Emily's dress over her head, then grabbed her around the waist and we tumbled onto the bed. I felt as if I was starved for her, and I groaned as our bodies came together in passion. And I celebrated the warmth and welcome of her body sheathing mine. As it turned out, we had dinner a bit later than she had originally planned.

We sat in her living room that evening quietly listening to music, another enjoyable aspect of this time period, and I told her that I needed to talk to her about something. I had intended to discuss purchasing The Moab Herbalist, and the fact that I would be moving into the apartment, but encountering the demon this afternoon had driven everything from my mind but the importance of the quest and discovering the reason for the attacks.

And I hesitated to tell her yet of my experience with the demon, as it was too terrifying.

"Emily, perhaps this is not the right time to talk about our relationship, but I feel that I at least need to tell you about my quest, the reason I am here in Moab. I could not speak of it before you guessed my secret, but now that you know who I am, it is time to say what must be said."

"What is it Merlin? Are you leaving me already?" Emily said quietly, in a worried voice.

"No! Gods, no, Emily. I am *madly* in love with you, but the fact is, as soon as I accomplish what I came here to do, I will most likely be transported back to Avalon into the realm of the Fae, who have been keeping Arthur's body for all these centuries, preparing for his return. I could possibly be at Arthur's side for all of eternity, in a place far from here in both space and time."

I gently lifted her hand and placed a light kiss in her palm. I looked into her eyes, huge and worried that I could very well leave her at any time.

"Throughout all of my years of existence, you are the only woman who has ever truly loved me, and I find that I do not *want* to leave you, destiny or no." I stopped and closed my eyes for a moment, sighing deeply. "I swear to you that I am going to find a way to come back to you if I *am* pulled away. But the person that I am, the 'immortal Merlin, Sorcerer of Camelot,' is part of a story that was foretold before I was even born. I do not know what will happen to me if I try to challenge my destiny. I may die immediately and turn to dust, I may become mortal, I could lose my magic—I honestly do not know. And I do not know if I am capable of forsaking the Once and Future King."

I glanced at Emily's drawn, unhappy face, then looked away and said somberly, "I am sorry to frighten you like this, but you need to know exactly what it is you risk in loving me. You have already witnessed the danger that comes with my presence in your life." I hesitated to look at her again, for fear of what I might see on her face.

For just a moment nothing happened, and then I felt cool, soft hands smoothing the hair back from my brow.

Emily said softly, "Merlin, for someone who has been around as long as you have, you *so* do not understand people. When I said I loved you, I didn't say it because I'm in love with your magic, although that is truly incredible, I said it because I love *you*, because of the wonderful man that you are. As unlikely as it sounds, I fell in love with you on the plane with the first thing you said to me in your sexy accent: 'Tis my first time flying.' That was it, love at first sentence."

I looked at her sweet, saucy face, and as her love washed over me I experienced an intense sense of relief.

She pulled me into her arms and held tightly as I buried my face in her neck. I said, somewhat muffled, "Then I might as well tell you the rest. There is a good chance that my father was a demon."

Emily retorted, "I wouldn't care if he was freaking Satan himself; I *love* you!"

I just shook my head and held her against me. By whatever name he was called, the god of death would stand no chance against her, of that I was certain.

CHAPTER 12
April 27-28

A S WE WERE GOING TO BED that night, my second in Moab, I thought to ask Emily why she had needed to go in to work that day, yet had come home so early. Despite the shared intimacy we had experienced earlier and the declarations of love and support, I sensed an undercurrent of tension building in her.

"Em, is there something wrong? You seem worried," I said to her after we had showered and were sitting on the bed holding hands.

"Merlin, I didn't want to tell you this, but in a few days, I will have to go out of town for up to a month, working in Mesa Verde National Park, in Colorado. I will be working constantly and might not be able to come home during that time. I only found out about this today at the special staff meeting we had. Apparently one of the Rangers had an accident in the park and won't be able to work for a while. Until he's recuperated, I'll be on loan to Mesa Verde to cover for him," Emily said, resolutely. She looked miserable, but was trying to be brave in the face of what she perceived as extreme adversity.

I smiled and took her into my arms to comfort her, kissing her cheek. "Emily, I have waited for you for centuries. I am sure I can wait a few more weeks."

She leaned against me and sighed. "I know, but we've just found each other! I hate to miss spending time with you— you may be immortal, but I'm not."

I thought back to my failed attempt to enchant her the other day, and wondered again whether she could have Fae blood. If that was the case, it was possible that she *could* be longer-lived than she knew. I would have to find a way that would tell us for sure. I could Look into her being and see the truth, but I was not sure she would agree to that.

For now, I just said, "Have faith, love, everything is in the hands of the gods, including our relationship."

"Then I guess we'll just have to make the most of the time we have left," she said seductively, trailing her lips over my nipples and down past my abdomen. Those same lips ended up making my night quite interesting, before we finally went to sleep around eleven o'clock.

The next morning, I awoke at six o'clock and quietly went out to the living room to call Tom Reese. I knew that there was an eight-hour time difference so I needed to contact him at once. I wanted him to wire me the money that day, as well as to ship my things. Tom assured me that he would be able to accomplish these tasks immediately. He and Sandy had already packed everything and just needed an address, which I gave him. The large package should be delivered within the week. I told him briefly what had transpired since I had arrived, and inquired also about the health and well-being of his family. He told me everyone was fine, and that his daughter could not stop talking about me. I warned him gently that under no circumstances could she tell her friends about her new "brother." He assured me that she understood her duty to me. We finished our conversation and I hung up, satisfied that my caretakers were attending to their duties as I had instructed.

In the time that I had been conversing with Tom, Emily had gotten out of bed and started the coffee brewing. As soon as we each had a steaming cup in our hands, we sat and discussed my magic's most recent malfunction during our intimate time together the previous night. Her bras had somehow become attached to the ceiling fan in her bedroom. It seems that the one time my magic was quiet during our lovemaking was a fluke.

After putting her bras away, we had a second cup of coffee while I finally shared with her everything that had happened the day before: meeting Chris Colburn and arranging to purchase the shop, spending many hours with Derek watching stories about myself, and fighting off yet another magical attack. Emily congratulated me on my decision to buy the herb shop, and then begged me to tell her about the Merlin stories, which I refused to dwell on overlong as it was embarrassing.

I did mention that I planned on moving into the apartment over the shop as soon as Chris had removed her things. I hoped that this would not be a problem for Emily, but I needed to begin preparing my strategy for the battle I knew was coming. I had to discover the identity of my enemy and figure out how to destroy him. He would only gain strength the longer this situation continued, until it would not be possible to reach Arthur at all. Despite my doubts of the night before in regards to my destiny, I could no more walk away from Arthur than I could walk away from myself—our lives and destinies were one, and had always been so.

Emily could tell I was resolute about this decision and seemed to understand. "Merlin, we all have duties of one sort or another, and I understand your need to do this. I'll be leaving soon for my assignment, though, so I hope we can spend the evenings together, at least."

I stood next to her, looking solemnly into her eyes, and said, "Em, we will be together in the future, for more than just evenings, gods willing. Please do not give up on me."

Emily said, "And don't ever give up on me, *Lord* Merlin, no matter what happens!" She kissed me soundly, and then walked into the bathroom to finish getting ready for work.

As I watched her apply various pastes, creams and powders to her face I remarked, "I do not understand why you use all those things—you are beautiful without them, Em."

Absorbed in her task, she kept looking at herself in the mirror as she replied, "Thanks Merlin, it's sweet of you to say that, but in this century most women wear some sort of makeup daily. It is one of our rituals, especially on a workday."

She paused for a moment as she looked up and studied my reflection in the mirror. "I've been wondering about something. Why do I never see you shave? Your facial hair must be as dark as the hair on your head, but I've never seen any sign of your beard."

I just grinned. "Emily, my hair and beard only grow about six inches every hundred years, or about 1/16 inch per year, so I do not bother to shave—it is easier to use magic."

Her eyes widened and she stared at me for a moment. "God, I keep forgetting how different you are, Merlin."

Then she said suddenly, "Oh, I just remembered, I bought you a present yesterday, to keep the hair out of your eyes." And she handed me a colorful beaded headband, which I accepted and donned immediately. Although it was made very differently, it reminded me a little of the circlet I used to wear in Camelot—it spanned the middle of my forehead, keeping my hair from falling in my face.

"Thank you, Emily," I said softly, kissing her cheek as she grinned at me.

"Glad you like it—looks good on you. I have to run, I'm late. See you later, magic man," she said, giving me a quick kiss on the cheek. She then grabbed her purse and left the house.

At nine o'clock, I walked down to the herb shop and Chris began training me to use the electronic tools of the business. She seemed taken aback that I barely knew how to use a phone, let alone a computer, a cash register and a credit card machine, but she was an excellent teacher and I learned quickly. She was also kind enough to show me how to use the internet and how to send electronic mail messages, for which I was most grateful.

I was extremely careful to keep my magic controlled around the electronic devices. It would be unacceptable to damage them before I had even paid her. An hour later, the wire transfer from Tom came through, and Chris and I headed to the bank and the title company to finish the sale.

After that I helped her pack what few things she was taking with her and I carried them out to her car for her. I had purchased all of her furniture, and things such as linens and dishes, as part of the transaction, so she had only personal items and clothing to load in the vehicle. She mentioned to me that she did not know what to do with her truck—Derek would not want it since he had bought a new one recently. I liked the old black Chevy pickup truck so much that I offered to buy it from her, and she sold it to me gratefully.

"To be honest, I figured I'd have to talk Derek into selling it for me, so I'm glad you wanted it, Michael," Chris said with a smile.

Finally, I had a vehicle. As Derek later described it, I now owned "a short-bed, four-wheel drive with a roll bar." Now I would be able to go out into the countryside and start searching for the portal in earnest. The fact that I had no experience driving a car, let alone a truck, did not deter me. With the aid of learning spells and my scrying crystal, I would learn quickly.

Chris said her goodbyes and drove off, planning to stay at a friend's house until she left for Colorado.

It was now past lunchtime and I was starving, so I went back to Emily's and fixed myself something to eat. I was sitting outside on the front porch step eating a sandwich when I sensed that I had company. I looked around quickly and did not see anyone, then noticed a little black cat sitting there staring at me. I stared back, cautiously, not really familiar with felines. It casually walked over and rubbed against my legs. I had never before kept a pet, and Arthur had kept only dogs, mainly for hunting, so I was not sure what I should do. The animal seemed to want me to stroke its back, so I did, and I immediately noticed how much it appreciated the attention—it started to purr. I found myself smiling and continued to stroke its fur. *Interesting and yet sad*, I thought, *how many simple pleasures I have missed in my life.*

The cat finally left, and as soon as I finished my meal I headed back to the shop.

I decided to call Derek to suggest that he and I take a drive; I wanted to start looking for the portal back to Avalon.

I picked up the phone, keyed in his number and pushed send, marveling at such a convenient device.

Derek answered immediately, "Hello?"

"Derek, it is Michael."

"Hey, Michael, I was hopin' you'd call and save me from the drudgery of housework. What's up?" Derek asked.

"Well, the shop is now mine and so is Chris's truck. Would you have time to take a drive with me, show me around the area?" I asked.

"You bought our old truck, huh? Well, that's great, it's a good vehicle. It'll do the job for you. Sure, I'd enjoy spendin' a few hours out and about. I'll grab some bottled water and see you in about twenty minutes."

"That sounds great, Derek, thank you," I said gratefully.

I wondered how to begin locating the portal, and thought back to the visions the shaman had shown me as he died. At the time I had not focused on any of the details, but I decided that I would have to do that now. I sat down in one of the chairs in the back room, closed my eyes, and went back in my memory to that day in front of the stone manor. I saw once again the shaman attempting to subdue the wyvern, and I remembered how I had used my magic to kill the beast. I felt it as I put my hands on the shaman and experienced the visions his shade had shown me. The scenes of Utah started flashing through my mind just as they had then, and I noticed that many crevices and indentations in the rocks seemed to glow and thus took on a special significance. I noted as best I could, without really recognizing the terrain, where these special points were located. I hoped Derek could find them.

Just then, I heard his truck as he pulled up in back of the

shop. I went out the door to talk to him, and Derek pointed out that my "new" truck was in need of servicing, and low on fuel besides. So we decided to take Derek's this time, but I was disappointed and decided to get my truck fixed as soon as possible. I had wanted to practice driving, but that would also have to wait for another day.

I locked the shop doors, realizing as I did so that in the future I'd need to use a spell to protect the building. Physical locks were not going to be enough once my possessions arrived.

We would only be gone two or three hours, which was convenient for me as I had more work to do at the shop, and I wanted to be back at Emily's when she got home.

Since Derek worked at Arches National Park and he knew the landmarks well, we decided to start there. I hoped that I would recognize some of the terrain from my vision.

We drove out of town, over the Colorado River Bridge, and in a few minutes we were entering the park. As we approached the entrance booth, I could not help but experience a sense of awe when I viewed the towering cliffs ahead of us. We paused for a moment, until the fee collector waved us through, having recognized Derek as a park employee. As we slowly drove up the steep, winding road, I was struck by the incredible beauty and enduring majesty of the rock formations. The view gradually unfolded as we rounded each bend until we could see all over the valley below. As we ascended, I carefully scanned each cliff, crevice and cave for a magical glow that could be evidence of a portal. I noticed a range of mountains to the east that were very different than the red rock cliffs we were passing through, and I asked Derek about them.

"Those are the La Sal Mountains, and they are about 65 million years old, much younger than the formations you see here in the park, which were formed during the Jurassic Period, approximately 150 to 175 million years ago," Derek lectured, obviously used to answering questions for the visitors. "The highest point in the La Sals is Mount Peale, with an elevation of nearly 13,000 feet, which I'll wager is higher that any mountain range you have in Great Britain."

"You are correct, Derek, there are no mountains that high in all of Britain, and have not been in recorded history," I said quietly.

As we traveled on through the rugged landscape I utilized every sense I possessed, and yet I discovered no emanations of magical energy. I did see soaring rock spires and sheer walls of a reddish-orange hue that inspired my senses in other ways, but I did not discover an opening to another realm.

Derek drove slowly, conforming to the posted speed limit, which enabled me to examine a fairly large area all at once. I saw a structure up ahead that particularly fascinated me. It appeared to be a huge ball of rock, a massive boulder, being supported by a pillar of stone, the top of which seemed much too small to support it. It looked as if it would collapse at any time, but it had probably been there for thousands of years.

"Derek, what *is* that up ahead, on the right at the top of the hill?"

He laughed, having evidently been asked that question many times. "That's called Balanced Rock. Would you like to stop and take a closer look at it?"

"Yes, yes I would," I said, my senses telling me that, while it was not a portal, there was an energy signature of some sort around it that intrigued me.

We topped the rise and continued on for a short distance, then turned into a parking area filled with vehicles of all types and sizes.

"This is one of the most popular areas in the Park. It's easy to get to and there's also a good view from there."

"I'd like to get closer, by myself, if you do not mind, Derek," I murmured, opening the vehicle door and stepping out, my attention focused on the monumental object.

"Sure, fine, I've seen it up close many times, so I'll just sit here and wait for you. Take your time." He pushed a button on the dashboard and I could hear music begin to play, something loud and raucous, the words to which I could not decipher.

As I approached the huge structure I knew that it was no portal, but I sensed that magical energy of some kind had affected it in the past. Had the gods intervened at some point to prevent the boulder from falling, and if so, why had they done so?

I reached up to touch the pillar supporting the boulder above me and immediately felt an otherworldly power, and strangely enough, it felt familiar. I frowned and drew back in confusion. How could that be? The energy signature was my own, but had been created long ago. Yet I had never been here before...had I?

As I walked back towards the truck I felt shaken to the core of my being. I had been here in the distant past and had placed an enchantment of some kind on Balanced Rock—and I had absolutely no memory of having done so.

"Michael, what's wrong? Are you okay?" Derek asked, noticing that my face was drained of color.

"Yes, I am alright, thank you." I spoke lightly, as if what I had just experienced did not matter.

We drove in silence for a time, and Derek finally said, "Michael, I get the feeling you're lookin' for something in particular. If you tell me what it is, maybe I can help you find it."

"I am just studying the geological features of the park— it is another one of my interests. I do appreciate your offer, though. I am actually looking for caves, or particularly deep crevices. Sometimes there is a special luminescence emanating from them that may occasionally be seen if one is fortunate enough." I hoped that Derek was not a geologist, or he would realize I did not know what I was talking about.

"Well, that's interestin', I wasn't aware of that, Michael. I'm a law enforcement ranger like Emily, so geology isn't my forté. That information I just spouted about the La Sals, well, I had to memorize it," Derek said, apparently seeing nothing wrong with my explanation. "If I see anythin' like you just described, I'll be sure to point it out to you."

"Thank you, Derek," I said, relieved, again scanning the area for the 'luminescence' that I sought.

"Hey, Michael, we're almost out to Devil's Garden and there's an arch I want you to see. Want to take a quick hike?" Derek asked.

I considered it for a moment and realized that I did want to see more of this unique landscape. My only concern was that another attack could happen, and there were too many people around, including Derek, who could be injured, or at the very least could witness my use of magic. Neither was acceptable to me. But I could not tell him that it was a bad idea because we might be attacked by evil manifestations of black magic.

"Alright, as long as we do not tarry. I still have things to do at the shop, and want to be at Emily's when she gets home," I said.

"I'll just call her and find out her schedule, okay?" Derek pulled out his phone and called her. He talked for a few moments then said, "She's out at Canyonlands and won't be home until at least six o'clock, so we have plenty of time to do the hike."

"That would be fine then, Derek, a hike it is," I agreed reluctantly.

We parked at the end of the road, took a bottle of water each, and started out on the trail to Landscape Arch.

CHAPTER 13
April 28

A S WE STARTED ALONG THE TRAIL between towering walls of rock, I noticed what appeared to be runes upon them. Surprised, I paused to take a closer look and Derek, who seemed to read my mind, said, "I thought they were runes when I first saw them. You know, magical symbols, but they're actually just random markings on the stone."

I looked at him and nodded, more anxious than ever to discover more about this man who was becoming a friend.

We had been walking for less than ten minutes when we approached an intersection with another trail, and I started having the sensation of dread that always preceded a magical confrontation. *Bollocks*, I thought. I started gathering my will and reached out for the energy in the surrounding rocks. I was startled at the power that responded to my call, and had to suppress a gasp as the energy surged into my body. I hoped that Derek would not notice my glowing countenance; I could feel the energy dancing on my skin.

I glanced at Derek and was relieved that he was looking in the opposite direction. I wondered from whence the attack would come and did not have long to find out. An unnaturally strong gust of wind began to blow up the trail, picking up sand and swirling directly towards us, causing the group of hikers in front of us to exclaim in dismay and huddle together at the side of the trail, coughing and covering their mouths and noses.

This was obviously not a normal wind—I could sense that it had been manifested from the Other World and it exuded a deadly intent. Sharp pebbles and stinging sand enveloped us and we literally could not see through it.

Derek was alarmed and reached out to grip my arm, intending to keep me on the trail. He reacted violently to the electrical shock he experienced when he touched me.

"Ow, what the *hell*? Michael, are you alright?"

I quickly pulled away from him, and said, "Derek I am fine, let us stand here until the wind subsides." I extended my senses out into the flying sand and debris and found the center of the disturbance. It was a core of darkness so evil that I recoiled. I did not know how many people were in the midst of this nightmare, although I could hear screams and other sounds of distress along the trail, so I prayed to the gods that I would not injure anyone in trying to destroy this thing. I directed my complete attention to that evil core, raised my right hand with palm spread, and mentally focused on the spell, *Recesserimus tenebris, Begone darkness,* simultaneously releasing a focused beam of white-hot energy. With a loud crack the center of the disturbance suddenly exploded, the sand fell and the wind died away. I dropped my hand quickly and Sighted up and down the trail hoping there were no injured innocents. Many people had stumbled off the trail and were standing in bewilderment and lingering fear, trying to get the sand out of their eyes and hair, but I could sense no serious injuries.

"Derek, are you well?" I was concerned that he had had such an intense response to my magical energy. If he had latent magic that could have amplified the effect.

"Yeah, I guess. Damn, that was a crazy sandstorm. I've never seen anything like it. And that was the worst case of static electricity I've *ever* experienced! When I touched your arm it felt like a bolt of lightnin' hit me!"

"Yes, that was indeed strange, I cannot explain it myself," I said, again having no choice but to lie.

The "storm" had lasted no more than a couple of minutes but it had seemed like hours.

What I could not comprehend was what my enemy was trying to accomplish. I had been able to counter every attack so far, and except for being clawed by a dragon the other day, there were no injuries. And since I had been able to heal myself, even the injuries were a minor thing. Yes, I had used powerful magic every time to counter, or even destroy, the core of each manifestation, but what was the purpose of the attacks? Whoever it was had to know that I could draw energy, power, not only from the center of my own being, but from the very elements around me. If this entity truly wanted to kill me, would it not have happened already? I wondered if, each time there had been an attack, there was a portal in that vicinity. I sent my senses out in all directions, and did indeed discover that there were at least three portals nearby, although the energy emanating from them was weak. I could not help but speculate that the entity perpetrating these events was someone from my past, whose intent had always been to disrupt my quest.

Derek checked with several groups of hikers near us to discover if they were alright, and finally came back to stand beside me. "Do you want to go back? We can always hike again another day. I've got sand in my shirt and in my hair, and I'd just as soon clean up."

"I agree, Derek, I am also uncomfortable, so we had best return to town." I was relieved that he did not want to hike any more this day. I reached down to pick up the bottle of water I had dropped, and we started walking back to the vehicle. There was still no sign of the Avalon portal, although I intended to look closer at the rock formations on the way back. The portals I had sensed along the trail would have to be explored another time, but I could not believe that, as weak as the emanations were, any of them could lead to Avalon.

We arrived back in town sometime after four o'clock and Derek dropped me off at the shop. I offered him a cold beer, but he declined; he was eager to wash the sand off and he admitted that his chores were "callin'" to him.

I brushed as much sand off of myself as I could, and worked in the shop another hour and a half, rearranging the stock and making note of things I would like to sell. I realized that there was a nice corner of the shop that would be suitable for a reading area, so I decided to order some books and invest in a few comfortable chairs. Maybe I would also start a reading and storytelling session. I certainly had enough stories to tell, and the people attending wouldn't have to know that the stories were true.

I was ready to go, but I stopped for a moment and decided how to protect my shop. I locked the front door, then went out the back and locked that door from the outside. I checked to make sure that I was alone, then closed my eyes and centered myself. I drew on the power of my magic then uttered the spell, *"Contego,"* as I visualized the protective energy surrounding the entire building. Shield and defend my store, oh gods. I opened my eyes, sensed the completion of the spell, and smiled. *Yes, that will work.*

I left my truck parked behind the shop in the alley, and walked back to Emily's, still pondering the true intent of the magical attacks. When I arrived, I immediately took a shower to rid myself of dirt and sand, then walked naked into the bedroom to get some clean clothes. *I will need to move my things over to the apartment soon.*

Even though it was late in the afternoon it was still

warm, so I decided to wear shorts and a sleeveless…what was it called? Tank something. I realized that the skin on my arms, face and neck was already losing the paleness of the last sleeping cycle. I looked at my legs, which were very pale and would certainly draw Emily's attention. I decided to magically change that pale skin to match the parts of my body that had already been exposed to the sun, and the result was pleasing to look at in the mirror. *Vain and frivolous, Merlin*, my mind immediately accused.

"'Tis not hurting anyone," I said out loud, daring my mind to respond.

"What isn't hurting who?" Emily said from the living room.

I walked out of the bedroom and stood smiling at her. She placed a bag of groceries on the kitchen table and turned around, her face losing its weary expression. I noticed right away that admiration and lust had taken its place.

"Damn, Merlin, I really didn't need to buy groceries, you look good enough to eat!" Emily exclaimed crudely.

I just laughed self-deprecatingly. "While I appreciate your compliment, I am hardly the stuff of which dreams are made."

Emily glided up to me. "Oh, I beg to differ, big guy," she said softly as she pulled my shirt over my head.

"Em, I just put these clothes on and…" I started to say, but was interrupted by sweet lips kissing mine. I reached out and pulled her against me.

She leaned into my embrace, against my naked torso, and started stroking my back.

I groaned as my body responded to her caresses and deepened the kiss. We turned, still wrapped in each other's arms, and headed into the bedroom.

CHAPTER 14
April 29

A FTER A PEACEFUL AND UNEVENTFUL day at The Moab Herbalist, having ordered the furniture for the reading corner, evaluated the inventory of herbs and potions, and made numerous lists, I finally had a chance to sit and talk with Emily.

She had ordered a pizza for dinner, something that at first had appeared to be quite inedible—until I ate a slice. After I had eaten several more I decided this was definitely acceptable for an evening meal, along with a couple of beers. I took the opportunity, in between bites, to tell her what had transpired during my trip to Arches with Derek the previous afternoon.

"And when Derek touched my arm and was jolted by my magical energy, I thought he would surely know me." I shook my head as I considered what might have occurred.

Later, we were sitting in the living room talking quietly, and Emily decided to show me the photographs from her journey to England. I think she wanted to see if I recognized the current places compared to the ones I had known. I grimaced, knowing that *everything* had changed since I had lived in Camelot, and I was not sure I wanted to revisit my feelings of loss. But I did not want to ruin the evening or stifle Emily's excitement at sharing her memories with me, so I just looked at her expectantly.

"I traveled to Cornwall, to Tintagel, mainly because Derek said I should. At the time I didn't have quite the same interest in King Arthur and in Mer…uh, *you*…as I do now," she said, clearing her throat and glancing at me out of the corner of her eye. "Little did I know who I'd be sharing my bed with, right?" She grinned as she showed me her photos.

"Right," I said softly, smiling at her for a moment before looking back at the images. "Ah, Din Tagell. The cliffs are very nearly the same, as are the caves; perhaps a little more worn. Do you see these ruins on the highest point of the island, here and here? These were the homes of the servants and slaves for Gorlois's castle. He was the Duke of Cornwall whom Uther cuckolded when he slept with Ygraine and Arthur was conceived.

"These ruins," I pointed out the larger castle walls in the foreground, "are much newer. I fear that the Duke's castle is gone, or perhaps the original foundations are underneath these stones."

Emily asked "What about the cave down below the cliff that they call Merlin's Cave? Did you ever use that?"

"No, it always flooded during high tide, so it was not logical to use it for any ongoing purpose. I had spent a short time in it once, though, and perhaps people remembered seeing me there. Legends grow from just such occurrences, so perhaps my short visit became a longer tenancy in the minds of men."

"Did you really change Uther's appearance to that of Gorlois, using magic, so that he could have sex with Ygraine?" Emily asked, avidly curious.

"I did, Emily. Of course, I tried to dissuade him from that course of action but he would not listen. I used a variation on this spell: *"Mutabo meam apparentia."* I uttered the words that I had used not too long ago when I had changed my appearance for Ben, and I knew that I now looked old, with a long gray beard and hair, and wizard's robe and pointed cap. Not my best look, but effective.

"Oh, my God, you look so different, just like in the stories! Does it really change your form or just cause the other person to see an illusion?"

"Touch my face," I said with a smile.

She reached out and gently put her hand on my cheek. "I see a beard but I don't feel one—that is amazing!"

"The illusion fooled the guards long enough to get Uther inside the castle and into bed with the Duchess. I could never understand why she did not notice the difference in Uther's body, especially intimately. Gorlois was an older, heavier man, not at all as lean and fit as Uther was at that time," I said.

"Perhaps she knew and didn't care," Emily said.

"Perhaps," I said, skeptically.

"How old were you when this happened, Merlin?"

"I was no more than 18 years old, and had already been in Uther's service for over a year," I said, remembering the details of this important event that had occurred so long ago.

I released the spell to resume my normal appearance, and we continued looking through the photographs until Emily said excitedly, "Look, here are the pictures I took when I climbed Glastonbury Tor. What do you think?"

I took the pictures from her and looked through them. "The lake into which I threw Excaliber is gone, the forests are gone, and the countryside is ...unrecognizable," I murmured sadly. "It is no wonder the portal has disappeared from Avalon. Avalon itself has disappeared and all that remains is just the Tor—a hill and nothing else. When I was there in 1191, and again in 1700, I still felt the magic emanating from it, but it was blocked to me both times. I have not been back since."

"You were there in 1191...and in 1700," Emily said faintly.

I glanced at her questioningly. "Emily, you know that I awakened many times over the centuries as I waited for Arthur, and I traveled several times to Glastonbury hoping to find the Avalon portal."

Emily took a deep breath and let it out slowly. "I know, Merlin, but sometimes I forget, just for a moment, who you really are. Then you say something, or work your magic, and the truth comes crashing down on me again that you could disappear from my life at any time."

I put the photos down and pulled her into my embrace, so that she could feel my heart beating and my body's warmth; so she could feel my breath on her cheek and my lips on hers.

"I am real, Emily, and I am here with you right now," I reassured her quietly.

"I know, and I'm so glad. I love you, Merlin," Emily said as she hugged me tightly.

"I love you, too," I said softly, rubbing her back.

We sat there for several minutes just holding each other, and I hoped that her fighting spirit would prevail if I did have to leave her.

Finally, she pulled away and picked up a small volume that had my name on it.

"I bought this book in Glastonbury, thinking Derek would like to read it, but because you're here, I decided to read it myself. It has some interesting theories about your existence." She handed me a book entitled *Merlin: The Prophet and His History*, by Geoffrey Ashe.

I examined the cover and saw a slightly distorted but reasonable likeness of me, although much older. That Merlin looked sad and resigned to his fate, as Nimue stood over him, intent upon stealing his powers and entombing him alive. I knew the stories very well, and had no doubt that if she *could* have done that to me, she would have. She had been a very powerful sorceress, but the stories were just that—stories.

I gave the book back to Emily, not really wanting to think about Nimue and her fate.

"Why don't you order a few copies of this for your shop? If you're going to have books available, and tell stories of magic and chivalry, maybe this would be a good one to have in stock," she suggested.

"And have people noticing how much I resemble the Merlin on the cover? I think not," I exclaimed indignantly.

"Well, that's up to you, love." Emily shrugged and went out to the kitchen to get a drink of water.

I decided to tease her. I needed to let go of the melancholy state I was experiencing. So I called upon my magic and whispered, "*Invisibilis.*"

When she walked back into the room she looked around and said, "Merlin, where are you?"

I was actually standing fairly close to her and I was surprised she didn't sense my presence. I leaned over and whispered in her ear, "I am here."

Emily shrieked and jumped back, and would have fallen over the low table we had set up to view the photos. I grabbed her and released the invisibility spell at the same time.

"You scared the hell out of me—I couldn't see you at all. That was just mean, kinda cool, but mean," she said with a frown, pushing away from me.

"Oh, I thought it was actually quite amusing," I said, grinning widely.

"Men! It doesn't seem to matter what century you're from, you're all a bunch of little boys," Emily said, exasperated.

I was in trouble, but it was worth it.

CHAPTER 15
April 30

WE HAD JUST FINISHED breakfast the following morning when I decided to ask Emily to assist me in my quest.

"Do you have to work, Em?" I asked, as I cleared the dishes and poured us each another cup of coffee.

"No, I'm off for the next few days, as it happens," she said. "Why do you ask?"

"I have to continue my search for the portal to Avalon and I had already planned on closing the shop for the day to do that. Will you help me? With your knowledge of the area you should be able to steer us in the right direction."

"What exactly would we be looking for?"

"A crevice in the rocks, or a cave, that gives off a special glow, a strong energy; a place to which people may be drawn but do not know why," I explained.

"Well, in this area that could be any number of places, but I know *I'm* especially drawn to Hidden Valley. Want to go for a hike up there?" Emily asked, and then added softly, "You know I'm still a little upset with you for playing that trick on me last night."

"I *am* sorry, Em," I said, knowing that I did not sound particularly apologetic.

"Yeah, okay, whatever..." She had obviously decided to let it go, at least for now. "Let's get some water and the walking sticks, and we can head out. Are those soft boots all you have?"

"Yes, these are the boots that I wore in Camelot," I admitted.

"How in the world is that possible? Shouldn't they have rotted away by now?" Emily marveled.

"They should have, yes, but they have not, and neither have I. Perhaps the Crystal Cave preserves things."

"I can see how it might have preserved your boots and clothing. But you're unique, magic man. You said yourself that you stopped aging long before you decided to sleep in the cave for centuries," Emily challenged. "In any case, you should probably buy some hiking boots to protect your feet."

"But I like these boots, and they've always served me well," I said, obstinately.

"Okay, I guess that's up to you. Hmm, with your lean lanky body and those muscular legs you should be able to climb like a mountain goat," Emily remarked as she examined my physical attributes.

I looked at her quizzically for a moment, hoping that it was a compliment, as I had never been compared to a goat before. "Uh, thank you?"

Emily laughed and said, "Let's go."

As we got into her car, I remembered sitting in this seat a few days ago, and seeing the look on her face when she realized that I had just healed my ravaged shoulder. Gods, had I only been here four days? It felt like much longer. And I experienced a deep sense of relief that I did not have to lie to Emily any more. I smiled widely.

Emily glanced at me as she started backing out of the driveway. "What?"

"I was just remembering the look on your face when you realized that I had healed my injuries," I said.

"Oh, that look," she nodded. "I had already decided that you were not some run-of-the-mill magician, but when the towel slid off of your shoulder and that nasty wound was just...gone...I knew you were someone very special. Then you looked at me with those slanted green eyes, so full of ancient wisdom, and I knew there was only one person you could possibly be: Merlin."

I sat for a moment contemplating what she had said. "Do you realize that you are the *only* person in the last fifteen centu-

ries who has seen me working my magic, and is still able to remember it? And I find that I am most pleased that you know my
secret."

I glanced over at Emily as she turned left onto Main
Street, and I reached out to lightly caress her cheek.

She couldn't look at me, as the heavy traffic near Town
Market was consuming her concentration, but she smiled and put
her hand on my knee, giving it a little squeeze.

"I think we make a great team, big guy," she said seriously, and I silently agreed with her. "Oh, I meant to ask you if
anything weird has happened in the last few days, other than the
attack on you and Derek out at Arches?"

"No, thank the gods," I replied. "But I have been trying
to understand who this mysterious dark practitioner is. Unless
one of my foes from the past has somehow been able to return
from the dead, it is unlikely to be either Morgana or Morgause,
Arthur's sisters, and it certainly could not be Nimue."

Emily glanced over at me curiously but did not respond.

A few minutes later we pulled into a rough parking area
at the base of the mountain.

"Here we are," Emily announced as she parked off to
one side.

As I got out of the car I stared up at the steep rocky
slope. The angle of the late morning light was such that the rocks
cast few shadows, and looked like a solid expanse. Where was
the trail?

I decided to create a spell to aid in my balance and agility during the hike, perhaps even enabling me to climb like the
mountain goat Emily had likened me to. "*Da mihi statera et agil-
itas,*" I muttered. I felt a slight tingle as the spell took effect.

We got the walking sticks and water bottles out of the
back seat, and I thought about my sorcerer's staff that would be
arriving soon. I would much prefer to be carrying that rather then
this mundane "stick" of Emily's. In reality, the use of my magic

did not depend on anything outside of myself, but the accouterments of sorcery were a great help in focusing and fine-tuning the energy I used for enchantments.

As we climbed up the trail, occasionally clambering over boulders that had fallen from above, I did indeed have the agility of a mountain goat, thanks to the spell I had invoked. However, I found that my lungs were laboring somewhat. Having spent my entire existence at a much lower elevation, I was having a hard time adjusting to the lack of oxygen.

Emily scrambled up ahead of me, easily traversing the steep rocky trail. She had to wait for me several times and of course she teased me.

"Come on, old man, you can do it," Emily called to me.

"I am doing the best I can at the moment, *young woman*," I answered, breathing hard. "Need I remind you that I could easily levitate up the mountain, but I cannot chance someone seeing me 'flying'?"

Suddenly I stopped, a tingling in my body indicating a pocket of power in the rocks nearby.

"Merlin, what is it?" Emily asked.

"I am sensing an energy source, and I am trying to locate...ah, over there." I pointed to a shallow cave above us on the side of the cliff.

"Can you get up there without killing yourself?" Emily asked, sounding worried.

"Em, I do not die that easily, believe me," I said impatiently. I used my abilities to See a route to the cave, and began climbing, putting my feet in the exact places that I had Seen. The walking stick, along with the enchantment, helped me to keep my balance during the climb. As I neared the portal, for such it must be, the output of energy increased, but it felt strange, alien. Although I had hoped that it could be the portal that I had searched for, I knew that it was not. My curiosity was telling me to gaze through this portal, but my sorcerer's senses were warning me not to actually go through it.

"Are you going to check it out?" Emily asked excitedly.

"Just with my senses—it does not feel right." I stood next to the shallow opening in the red rock, not large enough or deep enough to be called a cave, and I cautiously sent my senses through the portal. Immediately I stiffened as I sensed an "otherness" waiting to engulf me; white, cold and inhuman. I pulled my senses back from the portal as fast as I could. I stood for a moment, my eyes closed, trying to re-orient myself.

"Are you alright? What happened?" Emily called out.

"Definitely not the right portal," I gasped, "I would not want to be drawn into that one unawares! I am going to block it—it is just too dangerous. I would never try to access the Other World from this portal and would not want someone drawn in unknowingly."

I climbed back down to her and started to focus my will, calling up energy from the surrounding stones. As had happened at Arches National Park, the power I summoned filled me quickly, and I gestured with my hands and chanted, *"Saxa movere ad malum angustos."* Move the rocks to block the evil, oh gods.

And the huge boulders moved to cover the portal with a rumble that reverberated down into the valley below.

"That was amazing, Merlin! You make it look so *easy*," Emily said.

Puzzled, I turned to her and said, "You have seen me use magic before, Em."

"Yes, but it's still awe-inspiring to witness your power," she admitted, her face radiating admiration and excitement.

I smiled at her and said, "I will have to do it again soon, just to see that look on your face, love."

"Hey, are you two okay?" We heard a man's voice calling from below us on the trail.

Emily yelled back, "Yes, thanks, we're alright; some boulders just settled I guess."

"I had better assure that no one else is around before I do something like that again," I said quietly, concerned about my lapse in judgment.

We continued up the trail until we reached the point where it flattened out, and then we sat down to rest in the shade of a tree that Emily called a pinyon pine.

"There are actually two sections that make up this valley, and you can only see the lower part from here; we still have a ways to go," she said.

"Then it will probably take at least two hours to check the entire area, correct?"

She looked at me and nodded. We drank some water and Emily mentioned that we should have brought something to eat, breakfast having been eaten hours ago.

"Let me try something that I have not done in a while," I said mysteriously, and I held out my hand and closed my eyes, concentrating. In a moment I felt a slight weight in my palm, and heard Emily gasp. I opened my eyes and saw that I held a large red apple. I handed it to Emily and concentrated again. This time I held an orange. I smiled and started peeling the fruit. I noticed that Emily was looking at the apple as if it were a strange, unrecognizable artifact. I ate an orange segment, enjoying the sweet juiciness.

"You can eat that, it will not hurt you. It may not be as nourishing as fruit that grew on a tree, but I guarantee it will be edible." I ate another segment of orange.

She carefully bit into the apple and chewed tentatively, then proceeded to finish it hastily as her hunger overcame her reluctance.

"That was really good," she said, gazing at me in wonderment.

"The last time I conjured an apple was for Ygraine, and she was as hesitant as you were to accept that it was edible," I said.

"Well, you made it out of thin air, Merlin," Emily stated, as if that explained everything.

"You must learn to trust my judgment, Emily," I said seriously, "To accept that I will take care of you no matter what the circumstances. Your life may well depend upon it."

Emily was about to reply when several hikers appeared on the trail and we nodded genially to them, but said nothing until they had passed by us.

"You're right, Merlin," Emily said in a low voice, "and I do trust you, but I'm so used to depending on myself that it's hard to change my way of thinking practically overnight."

"I know, Em, but you must try," I said, as I got up off the ground and prepared to continue our hike. "Now, to return to our current objective, I must devise a way to identify the portals up here so that our time may be spent in the most efficient manner. I shall create a spell that will cause a bright light to shine from each portal, one that only I can see. We do not want any curious hikers around while we are investigating. We almost had a major problem when I moved the boulders; the people that just walked by us noticed an unusual occurrence and will remember it."

I realized that I was getting careless or distracted, or both. And as I glanced at Emily's sweet face I knew which it was. I would not give her up, so I would have to find a way to stay focused on my goal.

I stood still for a moment and closed my eyes, and as I reached inside for my magic, I crafted the spell so that only I could perceive the results. I opened my eyes, stretched my arms wide and threw my head back as I chanted: *"Illuminant ad limina magiae tantum exciderunt."* The magical energy flowed from me and out through both sections of the valley.

As we stood there, beacons of light started winking into existence.

"Alright, we have a couple of hours to check all of these

spots, Emily, and ..."

She was too quiet. I turned around and saw her staring at the brilliance emanating from the portal closest to us.

I looked at her incredulously. "Emily, *you* can see that light?"

"I do see it, Merlin, and I don't understand. I thought only you were supposed to be able to see the lights of the portals." She glanced around at me with a puzzled look on her face.

I had phrased the spell so that only someone who could use magic would be able to see the lights of the portals. I knew she was not a sorcerer, not a wizard nor a witch, nor any other kind of practitioner of magic. But if she was part Fae, perhaps she had some sort of connection to magic, enabling her to perceive the light. But I had created the spell to make sure no one else could see it—was my bond with her that strong? I was not sure what to tell her, as I was truly puzzled. "Perhaps my focus strayed somehow when I created the spell. I am not sure. But this may be fortuitous after all. We'll be able to accomplish more than we had planned, since you can see the sites as well."

As I looked around this first section of the valley, I noticed four bright points of light around the perimeter, which looked fairly accessible. The first one, to our left and ahead several hundred feet, was partially hidden behind a large boulder; it was a mere cleft in the side of the mountain, which rose steeply from the valley floor. I walked up to this small portal, extending my senses carefully. I felt no evil, in fact the benign, odd-looking countryside seemed calm and peaceful enough that I decided to explore. I created a retrieval spell to pull me back through if for some reason I could not access the portal from the other side.

Emily seemed agitated by my decision to explore, however briefly.

"Do not worry, with the spell in place I will be pulled back through the portal within two minutes. I am sure it will be fine," I said calmly.

I cast the spell and entered the portal. I knew immediately that it was not Avalon, nor did it have any connection to Arthur. This part of the Other World resembled Africa, at least according to the various types of wildlife I could see in the distance, or it was possible that the portal actually did connect directly to the other side of the planet. Then, out of the corner of my eye I noticed that I had caught the attention of a lion, and it had started towards me. I turned quickly to go back through the portal, but it had disappeared, and the retrieval spell would not activate for over a minute. I immediately extended my will as a magical shield between myself and the predator. The lion had almost reached the shield when the retrieval spell returned me to Hidden Valley. As I reappeared, I heard Emily breathe a sigh of relief. I warded the portal against accidental entry and labeled it with invisible magical symbols that only another sorcerer, or a wizard with advanced skills, could decipher.

"Where were you; what did you see?" Emily asked.

"Africa. I saw a lion, and some antelope in the distance," I said nonchalantly.

"Oh, well that could be handy if we decided to go on a safari after dinner," she replied.

We continued around to the other three sites in this section of the valley and found, variously, links to what appeared to be a nice little meadow in the south of France (I truly think it was the Other World, as I sensed shapes in the grass that didn't belong in *this* realm), a frightening dark nothingness that I immediately blocked and warded, and lastly, a barren, red landscape without oxygen that I also blocked and labeled with the warning "No Air."

"Emily, I have a feeling that this last portal leads to another planet," I said tentatively.

"It was probably Mars. We'd sent a probe there, so we have images of the surface—looks just like you described. How much do you know about other planets?" Emily asked, curiously.

"During one of the times I was awake, I traveled to the University of Padua, in Italy, and attended some classes. I met someone named Copernicus, who had a lot of revolutionary ideas about the movement of celestial bodies. Interesting young man," I said, as I examined the cliffs above us.

"Copernicus? My God, you met Nicolaus Copernicus? Never mind, of course you did," Emily said, shaking her head.

We decided to continue on to the second and largest part of Hidden Valley, as we still had over an hour until my spell ran out of energy. As we walked along I noticed the variety of wildflowers starting to bloom, and I took a deep breath of the clear air. The day was warm but comfortable, and as I glanced over at Emily, I suddenly felt an emotion that I hardly recognized.

I began to smile. "I feel so...content, so happy. I am not sure that I have ever truly known such happiness."

Emily put a hand on my arm and we stopped for a moment. She looked solemnly into my eyes and said, "Merlin, I promise you that as long as we are together, I will help you to hold on to that feeling." She reached up to touch my face and I turned my head to kiss her hand. Then we continued investigating several small portals that we could see at this end of the valley. None were the Avalon portal and thence were of little interest to me. They were like unfinished seams in the fabric of this reality and led nowhere, merely leaking incidental energy left over from the creation of the universe.

CHAPTER 16
April 30 – May 2

THAT EVENING, AS WE SAT next to each other on the couch discussing our adventure in Hidden Valley, Emily grew more and more quiet, and then with a worried look on her face, she finally turned to me and said, "I have to leave for Mesa Verde the day after tomorrow, Merlin, and I have a really bad feeling about it."

"What do you mean, Em?" I asked as I reached out to stroke her hair.

"I feel like something is going to happen that will affect our relationship in a very negative way. Damn it, I wish I didn't have to go." She grabbed my other hand and held it tightly in her lap.

"My lady, we have known each other only a short while, but I truly believe that we are destined to be together," I said gently. "You have expressed your concern several times about this separation we are about to face, and I think you fear that you will never see me again. Be assured that I will be waiting for you when you return. Take heart and have faith in the gods, in *your* God, that all will be well. When I am in your thoughts, I will be with you."

She looked into my eyes and nodded, but she still did not seem convinced.

We spent that night loving each other, talking softly, and laughing. The next day I helped Emily clean the house, do the laundry and generally prepare for her departure. Whenever we found ourselves near each other we would hug and kiss and hold hands—all those special things that lovers do. And we discussed our intentions to communicate with each other every day, whether by phone, or email, or both. I was pleased that Chris had shown me how to compose and send e-mails.

The night before Emily left, we made love for hours, then fell asleep with our arms wrapped tightly around each other.

On that final morning together, we were up early loading her car, making breakfast and trying not to think about the inevitable. Then there were no more chores to do, and all was in readiness. I could tell that she was struggling to remain cheerful, so I smiled and hugged her, kissing her sweet lips and telling her how much I loved her.

She started to get in the car but turned back to me and said with a determined twinkle in her eye, "Now don't go mesmerizing all the ladies in town; I wouldn't want to have to come back and kick some ass to claim what's mine!"

"Do not worry, my lady, there has never been anyone else who has captured my heart as you have. I will be true to you, Emily," I promised her.

And I waved as she backed out and drove away.

CHAPTER 17
May 2 – June 7

A S THE DAYS AND WEEKS went by, I spent endless hours in my shop, creating new potions and spells, and conducting storytelling sessions and workshops. At Derek's suggestion and guidance, I had purchased a flat-screen television for those sessions when the viewing of a movie was planned.

I also began exploring the mountains and the surrounding desert, which was a pleasure as the energy in that ancient landscape pulsed and sang to me.

I missed Emily more than I thought possible. Not once in my life had I experienced the kind of relationship that I had with her, and I prayed to the gods that when she returned it would continue. I had made promises to her that I was not sure I could keep, but I would try.

I had moved my clothing from Emily's house to my apartment over the shop, but still spent time at her place listening to music and talking to Emily on the phone.

I was adjusting to life in the twenty-first century, although there were times when the vast differences in the details of everyday living were overwhelming. For instance, grocery shopping, a strange yet wondrous activity. Finding everything a person could possibly need for cooking, cleaning, camping, entertainment and personal hygiene, all available in the same place, amazed me. But one had to have money to purchase what one needed. This was almost incomprehensible to someone from my time.

Another aspect of this advanced society that I particularly appreciated was laundering one's garments in machines, instead of scrubbing them by hand in a tub or a stream, then wringing out and draping the clothing over poles or bushes to dry. Technology created convenience and enabled people to enjoy leisure time.

Despite the underlying sense of urgency regarding my quest that accompanied me always, I realized the necessity of keeping my body in good shape and started attending the local aquatic center and gym. Derek had a membership and had been encouraging me to exercise and swim with him. In times past, every day provided the opportunity to exercise and keep fit, merely from trying to survive: running, walking and riding were not optional activities.

I knew how to swim, although I did not remember being taught. There was little time for it when I was at court, but I enjoyed being in the water whenever possible.

So I tried to go to the aquatic center and swim at least twice a week. I felt very comfortable in the water, so much so that I wondered if my father might have been a god of the sea instead of a demon.

At first I was distracted by the women's bathing attire, or rather by the nearly naked bodies being inadequately covered by said bathing attire. But I grew used to it. What I had a hard time getting used to was having women stare blatantly at *me*. I wore trunks rather than the small stretchy things that did not hide what was within, but it didn't seem to matter, women still looked at me as if I was a tasty morsel, which was very disconcerting.

In many ways, I felt surprisingly comfortable in this culture that was so different from my own; but then, I had always been quick to adapt to the changes I had experienced over the centuries. I loved the starkness of the desert environment and the red rock. And here I had a friend in Derek, and a few acquaintances who accepted me; although of course, with the exception of Emily, they had no idea who I really was.

My shipment from the Reeses had finally arrived, and I had created a safe storage area within the walls of the shop's back room in which to keep my treasures. I was not sure if the current situation would remain stable, so I used the scrying crystal regularly to keep abreast of any supernatural activities occurring in town. Despite its size, I kept it on a corner of my desk where I could access it readily.

It seemed strange to feel so protective of this place that in so many ways was alien to me, yet I felt very much at home here, even without Emily's daily presence in my life. I realized that I was literally the only champion the town possessed, and the people here would be at the mercy of the dark sorcerer if I didn't remain vigilant. Of course, I didn't want to think about the fact that these people were in danger *because* of my presence.

Many hours of searching for the Avalon portal yielded an interesting variety of avenues through and around the Other World, as well as dead ends, and openings into places yet to be explored. But I had still not found my desired destination.

Derek was my companion for most of the road trips that I took around Moab. He had helped me to get my truck in shape and coached me in learning how to drive it. If he was surprised at my lack of driving skill, he never mentioned it. Several times a week I experienced a dark and dangerous situation in which I had to defend myself or someone else, and yet not reveal myself or my magic. If I happened to travel alone I carried both my sorcerer's staff and my crossbow. There were a few situations that ended more violently than I had intended. I'd had to kill the beasts that were sent against me because there was no alternative, and I'd had to magically dispose of the bodies so that they were not seen by mortals. I really disliked having to kill a creature whose only crime was to be the pawn of my nemesis, but I did what had to be done.

I always had my sorcerer's staff with me on the treks with Derek, as they usually included hiking, and I could claim that it was my "walking stick." I had placed a surface enchantment upon it, so that it appeared to be just a normal staff for hiking. I wanted to avoid having to answer Derek's questions, but there was a strong possibility that he might be able to sense the power of my staff, and I knew that he would be very curious about the runes inscribed upon it.

We had returned to Arches National Park and finished the hike out at Devil's Garden that had been interrupted by the sandstorm, and I had managed to examine the portals we came across without alerting Derek to their presence. None of the portals in that area gave access to Avalon, although several were back ways into the Other World that I made sure to remember for future reference.

I'd had to cast a spell on Derek on more than one occasion when he witnessed things he should not have seen. Considering his magical heritage, it was surprisingly easy to block his memories, and the spell that had such disastrous results with Emily worked perfectly with Derek. He seemed an intelligent man, a good man, but easily manipulated with the simplest of magic. He was truly an innocent riding ahead of a magical storm of mythic proportions.

So far I had been unsuccessful in identifying my nemesis. It was as if the gods themselves were preventing me from doing so, which made no sense as I felt certain that they had guided me to Moab and had protected me from harm. Though I did not understand, I would continue to study the situation and to search for the Avalon portal. I felt my destiny calling deep in my soul, and I would continue the quest as I always had.

CHAPTER 18
June 8

F IVE WEEKS AFTER SHE LEFT for her temporary assignment in
Colorado, Emily Crandall was finally scheduled to return to
Moab. We had been in constant contact for the first four weeks
she had been gone, talking on the phone at least once a day and
emailing several times a week. When we had spoken over a
week ago, she had assured me she would return on this date, and
I had marked it on my calendar, circling the day several times.
But I had not heard from her since then, and I was becoming
concerned. I had been regularly consulting my scrying crystal
but had seen nothing unusual recently that would explain her
silence.

I had been working busily at the shop all day, preparing
herbal remedies and working on spells. As I completed various
healing concoctions using yarrow, stonecrop and burdock, I rem-
inisced about the times I had created similar medicinal potions
throughout the centuries, when there had been no other treatment
options available. If the herbal medicines did not work, there
were no hospitals to rely upon, and the patient could die of the
slightest infection or complication. At least in this time, there
were many doctors and hospitals to treat illness and injury, and
powerful drugs to combat disease.

Once I looked up and thought I saw Emily walking by
on the sidewalk outside, a small fresh cut on her temple. I ran out
the front door and looked up Main Street in the direction she had
been going. There was no one there. Realizing that I had just had
a vision, I grabbed the phone and entered her cell number. The
phone rang a few times then went to voicemail.

"Emily, if you're back in town, *please* call me at the
shop. I miss you, and I'm worried about you," I said, not happy
about leaving yet another unreturned message. I then called

Derek, hoping he would be able to answer—sometimes he was out of range or on patrol. Perhaps he had some news of her.

"Hello, this is Ranger Derek Colburn, how can I help you?"

"Derek, it's Michael, have you heard from Emily, by chance? I thought I saw her in town a few minutes ago, but then she vanished." And I remembered again the bleeding cut on her temple.

"Oh, hey, Michael, how's it goin'? I still haven't heard anythin' new, but I don't think she's back yet. She should have been done with the assignment today though...just a second, a bulletin just came on the radio. Oh, *crap*, there's been another accident at Mesa Verde...*Shit*, it's Emily! She's wrecked her vehicle and hit her head pretty hard. God *damn* it!" I could hear Derek growling in frustration and fear.

"Derek, we must go to her, where is she?" I was frantic with worry.

"They're airliftin' her to the nearest hospital, which is in Cortez. I'm still out at Arches, but I can pick you up at the shop in fifteen minutes, so be ready," Derek said. "She gave me medical power of attorney years ago when she had no one else she trusted to make those kinds of decisions for her, so we should be able to get in to see her without bein' hassled."

"I will see you soon," I said and ended the call. I told the customers that had just come in that there was an emergency and to please come back the following day, then closed the door behind them. I chose a few potions, one containing thorn-apple, stonecrop and burdock for headache and wounds, and one containing lady's mantle and wood betony which was even more specific to head injuries and protection from evil spells, and put them in the leather pouch fastened to my belt.

I saw Derek pull up outside and I ran out the door, locking it behind me. Silently I projected my regular protection spell for the shop and powerful magic immediately surrounded the

114

building.

I opened the vehicle door and leaped in, and Derek immediately took off, driving through town as quickly as he dared. As soon as we left the city limits he accelerated until we were at least fifteen miles per hour over the speed limit. Fortunately, we were not stopped by law enforcement officers. I met any attempts to block our path with a burst of magical energy directed at the driver, who would veer off to leave the way open for us. I do not know how Derek rationalized the uncanny "coincidence" of every car yielding to our passage—perhaps he was too focused on reaching Emily to notice anything untoward.

We arrived in Cortez, Colorado, in just under two hours, and headed directly for the hospital. As soon as we arrived, we parked and ran in to the reception area, whereupon we discovered that she had been taken for X-rays. I was uncertain what this meant, but could not ask as it would reveal the gaps in my knowledge of this time period.

Derek and I were shown into a room for families and friends of patients. We waited there for what seemed like hours. I grew more and more restless and anxious until I could stand it no longer and started pacing the confines of the seating area.

"Michael, calm down, man, we'll be able to see her soon. She's in good hands," Derek said.

I nodded, but I knew that time was of the essence, and I needed to give her the potions as soon as possible. Finally, we were told that she was back in her room, and that we could see her briefly. As we approached the door, I prayed to the gods that her injuries were not too severe, and that my magic, along with the healing potions, would help her. I told Derek I needed a few minutes alone with her first, which he reluctantly agreed to. As I entered the room, I immediately noticed her bruised and pale countenance, the cut on her temple confirming the vision I had experienced a few hours ago. Her hair was dirty and tangled, but as much as I ached to gently brush it back from her dear face, I knew I needed to treat her immediately.

I approached the bed and drew the potions out of the leather bag, tipping the contents of first one bottle then the other into her mouth. I carefully stroked her throat each time to ensure that she swallowed. I then gathered my will, lightly rested my right palm on her forehead and my left on her chest, and said softly, "*Sanare*," releasing a gentle, white light of healing energy into her body. I had barely removed my hands when Derek came into room with a middle-aged man in a white coat who I presumed was Emily's doctor.

"Michael, this is Dr. Bradshaw, and he's been fillin' me in on the situation."

I reached out and shook the doctor's hand. "How do you do, sir? Thank you for helping Emily." I glanced over and noticed that there was still a warm glow around her body from the healing magic, but I was certain that normal humans wouldn't be able to perceive it. I had forgotten that Derek might have a slightly different perception. He walked over next to the bed and looked closely at Emily, frowning slightly as he stroked her hair.

"Michael, did you notice how the light seems to shimmer around her? What the heck is that?" Derek asked, suspicion tingeing his voice.

I started to say that I didn't know, when Dr. Bradshaw began reciting what he knew about Emily's condition. "She was brought in from Mesa Verde about two hours ago, unconscious, having received a blow to the head when her vehicle went out of control, left the road, and rolled. Fortunately, it was a relatively flat area, not a steep cliff, or we might have lost her. She has various contusions and minor cuts from the broken windows, but overall she is a lucky young woman. Of course, she may suffer from amnesia due to head trauma, but it should be temporary."

Just then, I saw Emily stir and open her eyes, responding to the potions and the spell. Remembering her disastrous first experience with one of my spells, I was very relieved to see that it had worked as planned.

I saw the doctor's eyes widen as he realized she was awake, and he moved to her side to check her pupils and her pulse. "Well, this is a pleasant surprise! How are you feeling young lady?" Dr. Bradshaw asked, puzzled by her miraculous recovery.

Emily blinked as if the light hurt her eyes and said weakly, "I have a little headache and my body feels sore, but other than that I think I'm okay."

"That's good news, but we will still need to keep you under observation for a few days, Miss Crandall. And with rest and time, the prognosis is good. Now just relax, and I'm going to have a nurse come in and help you get cleaned up." The doctor nodded to us and left the room.

CHAPTER 19
June 8

EMILY FOCUSED ON DEREK FIRST. She smiled and said weakly, "Hi Der, I guess you heard about my accident on the park radio. How long have you been here?"

Derek leaned over and kissed her cheek. "About forty-five minutes, but it seemed a lot longer. We were worried about you, kid. Michael and I got here as soon as we could."

Emily looked over at me, puzzled, then smiled politely and said, "Oh, hi, Michael, I'm surprised to see you. Were you just keeping Derek company on the trip from Moab? I haven't seen you since we rode back from the airport together in April."

I just stared at her, a chill running down my spine as I realized that she didn't remember our time together. She had forgotten our love; she had forgotten *me*, Merlin. The doctor had warned us that there might be some memory loss, but I just assumed that the treatment I had administered had healed all of her, mind and body.

Derek glanced at me in confusion. I shrugged unhappily and shook my head. I turned back to Emily, and as I took her hand in mine, I looked into her eyes, and said, "I'm here because you and I are in love and have been in a relationship for the past few months, Emily. Although you have been away working a good deal of that time, we have spoken on the phone every day. Do you not remember any of that?"

Emily just looked confused and nervously pulled her hand away, which almost broke my heart. "No, I'm sorry, I really don't."

I was devastated. I turned to walk out of the room before she could see the pain in my eyes. Derek gripped my arm and said softly, "Michael, it'll be alright, just give her a chance to rest and heal."

I jerked my arm out of his grasp and said gruffly, without looking at him: "I will be outside; I need to be alone for a few minutes."

"Okay, Michael, I understand," Derek said as he turned back to Emily.

As I walked out of that room and then continued out the front door of the hospital, there was a part of my mind that was reconciled to losing her. It would be safer and less complicated for both of us just to let the relationship go. In my heart and soul, however, the part of me that loved her and never again wanted to live without love, screamed in agony at the loss.

"Oh, gods, please allow her to regain her memory!" I cried aloud. An old Native American man sitting on a bench outside the hospital looked up, startled at my vehemence. And then he spoke.

"You know Merlin, what pleases the gods may not be what pleases you," the man said in a strong deep voice. "You have always trusted the gods to give you what you need, whether in good times or in bad, so relax and trust them once again."

Startled, I stared at the old man until he looked up at me in confusion and said in a soft, reedy voice, "Can I help you, son?" And I realized that I had just had a direct answer to my plea, although not the one I had hoped for.

"No, thank you, sir, I apologize for disturbing you," I said calmly, though my thoughts were seething. I quickly walked across the street and out past a grove of trees; I just wanted to be alone. I was convinced now that Emily's injury was no accident. I did not believe that the gods had deliberately *caused* the situation. No, I was completely sure that my enemy had engineered that. But if the gods were indeed watching over Emily as I suspected they were, perhaps they felt it was fortuitous that she lose her memory, to protect her at this point in my quest. Whether she regained those lost memories in the future, well, that remained to be seen.

The pain and the anger boiled up inside of me. "Bollocks!" I growled, furious at my enemy, at the gods, and at myself. Rarely did I curse, or allow my temper to flare out of control, but at this moment I did not care. I could feel the hair all over my body standing up as sparks of energy rippled over my skin, manifesting through my heightened emotions. My chest was tightening with the pressure of the magical energy building up, and as I stretched my arms out, releasing the entire force of my rage and anguish, I threw my head back and screamed, "*No.....!*"

As brilliant white bolts of energy streamed out of my hands in all directions, there was a deep booming sound and everything shook as if from an earthquake. The effect reverberated for miles.

I was immediately horrified at what I had done: I had deliberately unleashed powerful magic without thought as to the consequences, simply to assuage my own inner turmoil. I cast my senses out in all directions, searching for possible damage and any injuries I had caused. There were blasted trees and a few power poles down, and the windows in the path of the energy had been shattered, but I could not sense that any humans were hurt. However, there were many dead birds and stunned animals in the wake of the blast. I ached with remorse. If the gods had been testing me, I had failed utterly.

People were now pouring out of the hospital, looking around. I could hear the shouts and the questions and the fear in their voices.

I ran back across the street and into the building, casting my senses wide to make sure there were no casualties inside. When I realized that there was no damage to the facility or injury to the patients, I breathed a sigh of relief that they had miraculously been spared.

"Thank you," I breathed.

I would have a difficult time forgiving myself for this

inexcusable lack of control. At no time in my life had I ever done such a thing. And I remembered telling Derek that Merlin would never lose control of his magic. Oh, gods, what had I done...

In the past, I *had* used my magic to kill and wound and destroy. I had used my anger to enhance the effects of my magic and I had felt justified in doing so, at the time. But it had happened in battle, and in times that called for dark and desperate measures, not to punctuate my own dissatisfaction with life's challenges.

I tried to pull myself together, and unobtrusively made my way back out to the parking lot to stand next to Derek's vehicle. I took stock of my appearance in the side view mirror and saw that my hair was sticking out in all directions. I smoothed it down with my palms as I applied a slight effort of will until my hair was back to normal.

"Michael! Where've you been? Did you see what happened out here?" Derek came running up to me.

"Ah, no, I did not see anything," I lied. "I just heard a loud noise and felt the earth shake. Is everything alright inside the hospital?"

"Yeah, I think so. People were startled, but there didn't seem to be any damage done. I did hear that there were broken windows all over town, though. It must have been an earthquake, although that's rare in this part of the country." Derek noticed the stricken look on my face. "Hey, are you okay? It must have been a shock that Em didn't remember the time you'd spent together. She said to tell you she's sorry, and that she'll talk to you when she's back in Moab. Honestly, Michael, I think that her memory will come back as soon as she's home and had time to recuperate. She'll probably be released in the next few days and plans to drive her own car back, so there's really nothin' more we can do here. The nurses were pretty adamant that visitin' hours were over, so we might as well get goin'. Maybe they'll let you see her for a few more minutes if you want to say goodbye."

I shook my head. "No, it is not necessary. And I am sure you are right, her memory will return eventually. Let's go home."

We drove a bit slower on the way back and arrived in Moab around nine o'clock. The sun had gone down behind the Rim, but there was enough residual light to see how beautiful the red cliffs were. I felt soothed at the sight, and I experienced again the sense of purpose and of destiny that always helped steer me through the ordeals in my life. I took a deep breath and let it out slowly, feeling calm and centered again. I would get through this just as I always had.

"Why don't we stop for dinner? I'm starvin'," Derek complained, "and I could really use a beer about now."

"I hear you, bro," I replied, finally able to insert a little slang into my daily speech. "How about Moab Brews since it's right up ahead?"

Derek agreed and turned left into the parking lot. We went inside and were seated immediately even though it was Saturday night—it was a little late for most people for dinner.

We got our beers first, and then our server, an attractive woman named Maria, came to take our orders. I could see Derek watching her as she asked me what I wanted; as usual, I ordered the steak, medium rare, with a baked potato and salad. Maria turned to Derek with a smile. He looked into her eyes and smiled back at her, ordering the seafood special. As she walked towards the kitchen to submit our orders, I said, "Derek, I noticed that you seem interested in our server. Do you know her?"

"Yeah, I've wanted to ask her out for a while, but I just haven't done it yet," Derek explained, as his eyes followed her around the restaurant.

"I think you should, Derek, she's interested in you also."

"Really? How do you know?"

I had actually sensed her heart beating faster as she looked at Derek but I couldn't tell him that. "Oh, I can tell when a woman likes a man, trust me, my friend."

As we were waiting for our food, I yearned to tell Derek the truth: About my powers, about my quest, everything. But, of course I didn't. I had seen what happened to Emily and did not want anything to happen to Derek. The difference in his case of course, was his magic, although without revealing *myself* to him I certainly could not confirm his own secret.

Derek was sitting quietly, thinking about Emily now rather than Maria, I was sure.

"Why did you and Emily never have a relationship? You care deeply for each other don't you?" I asked hesitantly.

"That's a good question, Michael. After Chris and I got divorced, I wanted to hook up with Emily—we were already friends and it seemed like a great idea. We did go out a couple of times, but she decided she really didn't want that kind of relationship with me. So I've tried to settle for her friendship. And now that I know you, I can see why she wasn't into me—she likes the tall, dark and slender type."

I smiled briefly as he said that, remembering how she would reach up to run her fingers through my hair, trying to get it out of my face. As other memories surfaced, of passion, love and laughter, my heart ached with loss.

As I was thinking about Emily, Maria brought our food. I could tell that Derek wanted to talk to her, but she had to run back to the kitchen to pick up another order and the opportunity was lost.

Derek picked up his fork and ate a bite of fish, then continued, "I really think that she'll remember you in time, Michael, especially when she gets home and sees the photos of the two of you. You haven't been together that long, but it sure seemed to me like love at first sight. I couldn't believe it when she came back from her trip to England with you in hand like a trophy. And let me tell you, she isn't normally the type to hop into the sack with a stranger."

I smiled a little and said ruefully, "She told me she fell in love with me with the first sentence I uttered. My accent was still strong then, and I had commented that it was my first time flying. She smiled and promised me that it would be better next time. Things just progressed from there." I couldn't tell him about all of the things that had happened on the way to Moab, and how those experiences had created a bond between us. "I didn't realize how much I loved her until we were in bed that first night in her house, and we had just..."

"Whoa, TMI, man!" Derek said, looking horrified.

"Sorry, Derek." I felt embarrassed as I realized what I had almost revealed.

"It's okay, but there are some things you just don't share," Derek said with a laugh, shaking his head.

By this time, we had finished eating and had received the bill. As he had done all the driving to Cortez and back I figured I would pay for dinner, so I placed the appropriate amount of money on the tray and said, "Let's go."

As we left the restaurant that familiar sense of dread and doom again enveloped me and I quickly gathered my power and focused my will in preparation. I tried not to look too conspicuous as I glanced around, but Derek couldn't help but notice my unease.

"What's the matter, Michael?" he said uncertainly.

"Something is wrong, I can feel it." I was afraid of what damage could happen if my nemesis decided to wreak havoc.

Suddenly, all of the overhead lights in the parking lot, as well as in the adjacent street, blew out at once. I immediately pulled Derek down, and directed my energy in an invisible arc over our heads as I thought, *Protege Nos*, protect us. The shards of glass came down upon the shield of magic and were directed away from us.

"What in the hell was *that* about, and how did you know what would happen?" Derek demanded, as I helped him up and we brushed ourselves off.

"I do not know, Derek, perhaps it was a power surge. We could have been hurt badly; we were very lucky," I lied yet again, and avoided answering the second part of his question. I was heartily tired of lying and evading the issues, and I could see from the look on his face that Derek was aware of my lies. I was certain that he had been suspicious of me for some time now.

My enemy once again had threatened not only me, but one of my friends. I swore that I would destroy whoever was causing these things to happen. I felt my rage trying to break through again, which I could not allow. I took several deep calming breaths and let go of the anger; it would destroy me faster than my enemy would. I had always had a temper, but I thought I had learned long ago to purge it. Evidently I had only buried it.

Emotions can be a tool when using magic, but they can also be the catalyst in creating a magical holocaust. Control over one's emotions and control over one's magic go hand in hand. It was time to practice that control more diligently.

The increasing frequency and severity of the attacks would at some point be noticed by Derek and by the more aware inhabitants of Moab, many of whom were my acquaintances and customers. These people lived and breathed a fictional world of swords and sorcery, and would be the first ones to recognize that their fantasy world was real. And I might not always be able to control the situation with enchantments.

By the time Derek pulled up in front of The Moab Herbalist, it was at least ten-thirty, and we were both tired, but we were also wound up from the events of the day—and night.

I glanced at Derek. "I know it is late, but how about coming in for a beer?"

"Sure, I'd like that. You want to watch a movie?" Derek asked.

"Let us watch that episode of *Merlin* in which he becomes Dragonlord," I suggested. It was my favorite episode, making me feel nostalgic for my old life, which made no sense since none of the events in the episode had actually happened. But I could relate to the protectiveness that the fictional Merlin felt for the character of King Arthur.

Derek agreed, and I slipped the DVD into the player. As I sat back in my chair and prepared to watch the episode for the tenth time, I thanked the gods once again that my magic did not short out the electrical devices in the room.

As the scenes unfolded, I relished the idea that the young Merlin had found his father, the Dragonlord, and discovered that he was the son of a good man. The show was fictional, but I was not, and I knew that subconsciously, I feared that I really was the spawn of a demon god, especially when my temper flared hot and unchecked, and it seemed so easy to destroy everything around me.

Derek glanced over at me a couple of times with a questioning look on his face, but I pretended not to notice. However, in my heart I knew that one day he would put the clues together and realize who he had been hanging with the last few months.

CHAPTER 20
June 8-9

As soon as Derek left, I climbed the stairs and went to bed, heedless of my need for a shower. I immediately sank into sleep and began to dream.

I was riding beside Arthur, accompanied by Sir Percival and Sir Leon, as well as several other knights that I did not recognize. We were heading back towards Camelot from a day of hunting, several hinds strapped to the backs of our saddles, when all of a sudden, the sky turned black as night. Frightened, the horses began rearing and bucking, and I realized in the confusion that Sir Leon and Sir Percival had disappeared without a sound. The other unidentified knights had also mysteriously departed. Arthur and I looked for the vanished knights, but I knew that they had been swallowed up by the darkness.

I yelled to Arthur, "Hurry, we must cross the ridge and ride for Camelot forthwith, before 'tis too late!"

Arthur nodded, then yelled something at me and gestured, but I could not hear him. We pushed our horses hard to climb the hill, which had inexplicably steepened. Finally I reached the top of the ridge and could see Camelot. I turned to Arthur triumphantly and started to yell that we were almost there, when I realized that he also was gone, and I was alone.

I screamed, "No! Arthur, where are you? Come back..."

As I searched for Arthur, I realized that my horse was gone and I was afoot, and instead of Camelot in the distance, there was a huge city. It was the city of London as I had experienced it in the twenty-first century, sprawling over a vast plain, swallowing up the countryside.

I fell to my knees with a cry, "Nooo!

And a harsh voice, which could have been male or female, from out of the darkness said, "You will not escape me this time, Merlin... "

I woke up with an agonized gasp, tears running unchecked down my grief-stricken face.

I sat up abruptly, feeling disoriented until I recognized my small apartment over the shop. I took a few deep breaths, then got up and went into the bathroom to wash my face. I knew I would sleep no more this night.

I sat looking out the window at the empty street below, and was resigned once again to the truth: Arthur was gone and Camelot a distant memory.

But I thought I recognized the voice in my dream. It sounded strangely like someone I once knew, in another time and place. But it could not be the woman I thought it was, could it?

As the sky lightened, I decided to take a walk, hoping to clear my head, so I dressed hurriedly and left the shop. I barely remembered to set the wards.

Early June mornings in Moab were cool enough to take a relatively strenuous hike, but I decided just to go up behind Derek's place and walk along the powerline road at the base of the Rim. I breathed in the fresh air and tried to regain my perspective as the new day dawned. I walked for about thirty minutes then decided to head back. I was feeling better, and as I came abreast of the trail that led back down into the subdivision I let my mind wander.

For just a moment I thought about talking to Emily about my dream, and then I remembered that she no longer knew me. I felt such a pain in my heart that I stumbled as I came down the hill and fell, twisting my ankle. I sat on the ground with my head in my hands, wondering what in the god's name I was doing here, when I heard a call from one of the houses below.

I looked up and saw Derek starting up the trail; I had not realized how close I was to his place.

"What happened, Michael?" Derek asked, "You okay?"

"To tell you the truth, I am not feeling very well. I have twisted my ankle, so I would appreciate your help," I said, feeling unusually humble. Obviously, I could heal the injury once I was back home out of sight, but for now I needed someone to lean on. "And I need to open the shop; do you know what time it is?"

"Michael, it's Sunday, and you're normally closed, so you can stay off your feet and rest today," Derek said, looking confused.

"Sorry, I did not sleep well last night and forgot that it was my day off," I mumbled as my friend helped me down to his house and into his vehicle.

Derek pulled up behind the shop and I made sure to disable the protective wards before handing him the keys. He unlocked the door then helped me out of the truck and into the back room of The Moab Herbalist, where I collapsed into the straight-backed chair at my desk.

"Do you want me to help you up to your room?"

"No, thank you anyway, I am going to make up a poultice for my ankle, so I need to be down here," I said. I decided to have him gather the ingredients for me before he left, even though I had no intention of actually using the poultice.

"Just tell me what you need, Michael," Derek said, "and I'd be happy to get those things together for you."

"Alright, I would appreciate it." I tried to sound grateful as I wrote out a list and handed it to him. *Bollocks*, I thought, *I wish he would just leave so I can heal myself.* Then I felt guilty; Derek was being his normal, kind self, wanting to help a friend.

"Okay, let's see what we've got here: watercress, crow-foot and henbane to reduce swelling, St John's wort and asphodel for leg pain, and mallow for sore tendons," Derek read as he started gathering the ingredients from the labeled containers and setting them on the clean counter nearest to me. Everything else I needed to complete the poultice was already at hand.

"That is fine, Derek, thank you, I will take it from here," I said firmly.

"Well, if you're sure I can't do anythin' else for you I'll just take off. I've decided to call Maria today and ask her out—life's too short, right? So I'm keepin' my fingers crossed that I get a date tonight. Hope your ankle feels better, man. I'll call you later." As he headed for the door, Derek paused and glanced back at me. "By the way, I called the hospital and Emily is doin' really well. They're gonna run a few more tests, but she might be released tomorrow."

"That's great news. I will call her this afternoon," I lied.

"I'm sure she'd like that, Michael. Take care." He waved and was out the door, carefully closing it behind him.

I breathed a sigh of relief and gestured with my right hand, locking the back door.

Immediately I closed my eyes, and embracing the light and healing energy inside myself, directed it to my injured ankle. *"Sanare,"* I whispered.

Seconds later I knew it was healed and I got to my feet. I decided to mix together the ingredients for the poultice and package it for sale. The herbs were quite effective and I was sure someone could benefit from the mixture.

As I worked, I thought about what had happened, and shook my head at my foolishness. I loved Emily deeply, but I needed to stop pining over her. Whether she remembered me or not, my attention must be directed to my quest. I would continue on as I had before Emily's accident, searching for the portal and preparing for battle, trusting in the gods. Patience was not my strong point, which was ironic considering the length of time I had already waited to restore true justice to this earth. I would just have to work on it...

Part 3:

Revelations

CHAPTER 21
July 4

EVER SINCE I EXPANDED the storytelling hour to a couple of times a week, I had encouraged participants to talk about their favorite fictional characters, read from their favorite novels, and even recite poetry. This activity had become so popular that I occasionally had evening sessions as well, which could include watching movies or just sitting around talking. After so many years alone I enjoyed the company, and it gave me a chance to talk about my own adventures, altered sufficiently to pass as fiction. Most of the people who attended these sessions became customers, if they weren't already, which was indeed a benefit.

One evening session, on July 4th, it was my turn to tell a tale, and I related how Lancelot first came to Camelot and became a knight in King Arthur's court, and how he also became a close friend of Merlin the Sorcerer. It was particularly easy to weave this story as I was talking about my own experiences. The story differed from what people were used to, because over time facts were forgotten, and people exaggerated the truth, until stories of the actual occurrence were so distorted as to be unrecognizable. And, of course, for most people the tales of King Arthur's Knights of the Round Table were no more than wishful thinking, legend, myth.

The longer I spoke, the more animated I became—my accent became more pronounced and my language changed—and I found myself speaking the old British language to a confused but fascinated audience. When I realized what I had done, I explained that I had studied ancient Celtic languages in university, and I had decided to give the story more realism by speaking the language. I went back to translate what I had said, and gradually brought the session to an end. However, something odd happened at that point. I had a feeling that there was someone in the room who was not as he or she appeared to be. I glanced around casually, smiling at people, not wanting to alert the person to the fact that I sensed something out of place. There were several people I did not recognize, and it was logical to assume that it was one of those individuals. There was a rugged looking yellow-haired man in his thirties that I did not know, and several young women that were new also.

I carefully extended my senses outward, only to encounter...nothing out of the ordinary. I frowned slightly, then changed my expression back to one of casual friendliness, as many people came up to me, thanking me for an entertaining session. Several other people that I knew as dedicated sword and sorcery fans also thanked me as they walked out, but I saw them all glance back at me suspiciously. I decided I would have to take greater care around those particular people.

I smiled and waved as the last customer left the shop, and then I locked the door and closed the blinds. My smile disappeared as I sighed and walked into the back room to get a drink of water, thinking about what I had done. That night I had come close to betraying myself. *Again.* I was weary of having to hide the truth, but I suspected that I would always have to prevaricate to some extent.

Although it was already after eight o'clock, I still had work to do before I left to watch the fireworks, so I began stocking the shelves with the new books I had ordered. Novels of magic and adventure were very popular and I had chosen several, among them stories about King Arthur and the knights. I was still amazed at the intense interest in the Merlin and Arthur "legends." Urban fantasy and wizardry ranked very high in sales nationally at that time, as well as at my shop. People read the Harry Potter books for pure fantasy, and Jim Butcher's books for the quality of writing and depth of involvement he offered. As I stood looking at all these titles and thinking about *my* life, my *real* life, and about losing Emily, I found myself overcome by a wave of intense emotion.

In my life I have been called prince, bastard, demon, and god, and the truth was somewhere in between. I had been born of a mortal woman, although I did not remember her well. A Welsh princess—or was she a peasant? Was I sired by a king, a dragon-lord, or by a demon? The tales abounded, and speculation had only increased in variety—and absurdity—over the centuries.

And yet, I was none of those things. I might be unique among men, or gods, a being both mortal and immortal; at least according to every legend written since my life began. But I have never claimed to be anything more than a man, admittedly with some special gifts. Yet I was here, in the twenty-first century, still alive and somehow unchanged almost 1600 years after my birth.

How could I reconcile this state of…grace, for wont of a better word…other than to think that my ultimate purpose in life has yet to unfold?

I had overcome death itself many times over the centuries in my pursuit of restoring the Once and Future King, surely an accomplishment of which to be proud. But at that moment, pride was worth nothing to me, and I felt lost, sad and alone. I had no family, few friends, and the love of my life no longer remembered who I really was.

Suddenly the phone rang. I opened my eyes, and realized that I was standing in my shop with tears running down my cheeks. Hurriedly wiping my face, as if the person calling would be able to see me in a moment of weakness, I reached over and grabbed the phone from the top of the bookshelf. "Hello, I'm sorry but we're closed now," I said thickly.

"Michael, is that you? Your voice sounds a little strange. I'm glad you're still there though, I was just wonderin' if that book I ordered has come in yet?"

"Just a second, Derek, I'll take a look, I was just putting some books away that came in earlier," I said, taking a few deep breaths as I looked through the open box for the novel he'd requested. "No, I don't see it, but it should be here in the next few days."

I had a sudden urge to throw caution to the winds and finally tell Derek about myself. So I took a step that could possibly destroy a lifetime of secrecy and evasion.

I said, tentatively, "Uh, Derek, can we get together tonight, maybe have a few beers and talk? I have something quite interesting to tell you."

I think he was intrigued, as he immediately said he was home and that I should come on over to watch the fireworks with him. I told him I'd be there in a few minutes, then immediately regretted my impetuous decision to reveal myself. Before I could change my mind, I grabbed the bank bag with the day's receipts and slipped out the back door, making sure it was locked behind me, then headed for my vehicle. I paused a moment, knowing I had forgotten something important. I turned back to ward the shop. I stretched out my right palm towards the door and muttered "*Contego.*" I could feel the magic surge out of me and envelope the building.

I got in the truck and put the key in the ignition, then sat there considering what I planned to do. I was going to trust someone that I had known for only a few months with my secret. Emily knew that secret, but no longer remembered it. She had witnessed my use of magic when we had been attacked on the trip back from the airport in April, and had figured out my true identity. But now, due to the head injury and subsequent amnesia she had suffered the previous month, she remembered nothing of our intimate relationship.

It might be risky to reveal my true name to a virtual stranger and it would certainly give Derek power over me if he chose to abuse my gift. However, I didn't think he would do that, as he admired the *fictional* Merlin so much that I was sure he would respect and honor the real man. I felt better as I took a deep, cleansing breath, focused on the light inside me, and tried to let go of my uncharacteristic nervousness.

I shook my head and chuckled to myself, thinking, here I am, someone who has lived longer than anyone else on the planet, with magical powers at my command, and I'm *nervous*? As Derek would say, what's wrong with this picture?

I started the truck and drove south on Main Street, noticing that the Rim was a dark silhouette against the lighter evening sky. Though my thoughts were in turmoil, I remembered to drop my deposit off at the bank's night repository, then continued on through town. Everywhere people were setting off their own fireworks as they waited for the big show to begin around ten o'clock. I had never experienced fireworks before and I was looking forward to watching them tonight. Of course, knowing what would happen once I revealed myself to Derek, I could very well be creating a light show of my own.

I turned into Derek's driveway as the light in the sky was fading, and his porch light was a welcoming beacon in anticipation of my arrival. I walked up the steps and opened the front door, knowing he must have just unlocked it for me. Despite the fact that there was very little crime in this town, Derek kept his door locked even when he was home.

I stuck my head in, and yelled "Hello, anyone there?" Which came out sounding like "Hallo, anyone theh?" The accent was a dead giveaway for my state of mind. Over the past few months I had made an effort to modify my accent and change my speech patterns, trying to fit in. But at times like this, when I was feeling excited or emotional, I reverted to habits long ingrained from an earlier time.

Derek came out of the bedroom pulling a T-shirt over his head and said genially, "No need to shout, buddy, I'm right here—come on in."

I walked over the threshold and into the living room, then stopped short and just looked at Derek as if I had never seen him before. I saw a muscular, stocky young man in his late twenties, at six-feet tall a few inches shorter than myself, with light sandy-brown hair and warm brown eyes—a handsome guy—someone who liked and accepted me for what I was. Except he was about to have his suspicions confirmed that I had been lying to him for months.

I looked directly into his eyes. "Derek, I must tell you something important about myself."

Derek apparently sensed that something was going on, and he came up to me with a concerned look on his face. He gave me a little punch on the arm as he asked, "Michael, what's wrong, man? Why are you so nervous? You know you can tell me anythin'."

I cleared my throat. Oh, gods…. "I have been keeping a secret from you, Derek, ever since we met. First of all, my name is not Michael." I stopped and took a deep breath. "My real name is Merlin."

Derek started chuckling. "You've really reverted to your old speech patterns—listen to that accent! Michael, it's okay, I totally understand. We've both been so involved in all the King Arthur stuff that I don't blame you for callin' yourself Merlin; he was the coolest dude ever. Maybe I'll start callin' myself Lancelot." He stood there and just grinned at me.

I did not return the smile as I was beginning to feel irritated; this was not going at all the way I expected.

"Derek, please be serious and listen to me. This is important. I have been using the name Michael Reese and trying to live a normal life here so that people would not realize who I truly am. I trust you, and I need your help right now…And by the way, you look *nothing* like Lancelot," I growled, hoping I had not made my biggest mistake in centuries. I crossed my arms and stood there scowling at him.

"I don't understand," he said, smile fading as he realized I was absolutely serious.

"Look, Derek, my friend, I know how difficult this must be for you to believe, but I *am* Merlin, also called Emrys, friend and advisor to King Arthur. And I am a sorcerer, just as the legends claim." My name came out sounding like *Muhr-lin*. "I was born in the year AD 420 in a place called Maridunum, in Wales, and...." I paused for a moment, and then said, "I am essentially immortal."

And with that statement I gave up all pretenses at being normal. I stood tall, as the weight of all the centuries of lies and secrets finally fell from my shoulders. I felt free.

Derek was shocked into silence. He paced across the room and back, looking at me as if I had grown an extra head. He finally turned to me and said, incredulously, "No way! What you're tellin' me is impossible, dude! We've only known each other for a few months, but I consider you to be a more than a friend; I feel like we're family. Hell, it's been great havin' someone to share my interest in the Knights of the Round Table, and swords and magic, and the supernatural, all of it. We've confided in each other, and I thought I knew you. It's obvious that you have a special touch with the herbs, and your storytellin' is awesome, but...it seems I really don't know you at all ..." Derek, glanced towards me warily, shaking his head and avoiding eye contact. "This is just crazy, how can this be happenin', man? It can't be real! I love the concept—I wish it *was* real—but people just don't step out of a legend and end up standin' in my livin' room, sayin', in a British accent 'Oh, by the way, I'm *Muhrlin* and I'm immortal,'" he said, sarcastically.

I wasn't sure why Derek was so upset and angry—did he think that I was mocking him? He should know that I would never do that. Perhaps I should not have blurted out the truth so abruptly; but it was too late to take back what had already been said.

I sighed. "I am truly sorry, Derek, I really should have done this differently. I guess I'm a little bit nervous. Why don't we just sit, have a beer and talk, as I had originally suggested? You must have questions that you would like to ask me." I hoped that he would relax, but the tension in the room was so thick I could practically cut it with my dagger. I walked past him into the kitchen, grabbed a couple of cold beers out of his refrigerator, then turned to him and said, "Why don't we go sit outside?"

Derek nodded slightly, then stood up and pushed past me, banging open the back screen door without holding it for me, so it almost hit me in the face. I followed him out without commenting on his unusual rudeness, and reached for a couple of folding chairs that were leaning against the side of the house. Derek took one and set it down across the patio from me. He sat in silence and waited for me to speak.

I stood still for a moment, noting that the chairs and the concrete patio were dirty and unkempt. Being a bachelor who would rather have fun than do housework, Derek's patio suffered from neglect. However, my memories of the Dark Ages included a lot more dirt than this so it didn't bother me overmuch.

I handed him his beer, then sat down and twisted the cap off my own, raising the bottle to my lips and drinking deeply. "Ah, this tastes good...the ale I remember was warm and very strong, not as thirst-quenching as modern beer." I glanced over at Derek, hoping he would open up to me. He sat still for a few more minutes, silently staring up at the stars, which had just started to be visible in the darkened sky, then turned to me with a serious look on his face and challenged me.

"Prove it, Michael. Convince me. If you are who you say you are, use magic to do somethin' so freakin' incredible that I'll have no choice but to believe you."

I had expected this, so I smiled calmly and said, "Sure, I would be happy to give you a demonstration. With all the fireworks tonight, I don't think I have to worry about revealing myself to your neighbors." I stood up and moved to the edge of the patio away from the house, to give myself enough room. Behind

140

me was a dark field that extended to the base of the Rim; a fitting backdrop for my very own fireworks display.

First, to set the stage, I focused my will and whispered my familiar spell, *"Mutabo Meam Apparentia,"* transforming my appearance to that of the traditional practitioner of magic in a long robe, and with long hair and beard. I heard Derek gasp and saw the shock on his face as he realized that I had been telling the truth. Then I closed my eyes and centered myself, feeling the light and power at the core of my being, and began to draw that energy up through my body. As I felt the familiar tingling sensation, I tilted my face and stretched my arms up to the heavens…and with the words *"Caeruleum igne,"* I released that pent-up energy in a stream of blue fire from my hands. The radiance flowed up thick and bright, and arced twenty feet over my head, spreading out until it created a shield around me. Euphoria washed over me as I basked in the feeling of power, and I'm sure my face reflected this inner glow. I could feel my hair blowing back as if in a stiff wind.

Then I muttered, *"Levo,"* and felt myself rising into the air, surrounded by blue flames. Ah, I had missed this, using my magic for the *pleasure* of it. Why had I so often denied myself this experience of my gift? I had always used magic as a tool, as a duty, as a weapon, but rarely for my own enjoyment.

Finally, as I allowed the power to dissipate a bit, and the blue radiance slowly faded away, I lowered my arms, and looked down at Derek to see his reaction. He sat there staring up at me in awe and wonder. "Oh, my God, Michael, it's really true, you really are a fuckin' sorcerer! You…you *are* Merlin!"

I allowed myself to descend back to earth and my normal appearance to return, and then I smiled at him. "Yes, I really am Merlin, and I was born with magic."

When Derek couldn't contain his natural exuberance, he leaped up and shouted, "Oh, my God, how cool is that! Tell me everythin'! Do somethin' else—can you ride a broom like Harry

Potter? Can you fly? I can't believe this!"

I put my hands up and said, "Slowly, Derek, we've plenty of time; I would be happy to tell you what you want to know, and show you other things I can do, but perhaps not everything tonight. And I normally do not ride brooms like Harry Potter, although I suppose I *could*." I considered it for a moment—it was an interesting thought. "Nor can I fly; I am not Superman." He had just introduced me to the Man of Steel, and I was fascinated by the concept of a being coming to Earth from another planet. Although, I suppose it was no stranger than a sorcerer coming to Moab, Utah, after being alive for almost 1600 years.

I laughed out loud and sat down again, picking up my now warm beer. Gods, I felt good; better than I had in eons. I felt exhilarated from the energy that was still coursing through me. Using magic just because it was enjoyable—what an amazing concept!

Derek reluctantly sat down, leaning forward at the edge of his seat. His eyes sparkled as he asked, "Hey, could you light my fire pit, it's gettin' kinda cool out here."

It really wasn't chilly—it had to be at least eighty degrees—but I humored him. He just wanted to watch me perform more magic.

"I'd be happy to. Creating fire is a simple feat for someone who has magic," I said, glancing over at the fire pit. I focused a slight effort of will, lighting the fire as he had requested. Orange flames erupted suddenly and started dancing merrily over the leftover coals, emitting a bit of unnecessary heat.

The longing on Derek's face was obvious as he looked at the fire. "Damn, I wish I could do that." Then he glanced at me. "So, you don't always need to say a spell out loud, then? I heard you whisper somethin' when you changed yourself to look like a wizard, and when you created the, uh, blue flames comin' out of your hands—God, that sounds so weird—and just before you levitated, but I didn't hear you say anythin' to light the fire just now."

I looked intently at Derek and explained, "People who are born with magical powers and abilities don't necessarily have to create a spell for the simple things. But for more complicated uses of magic, we do use special words to focus the energy and to keep it under control. I generally use Latin for my spells. When I was young I spoke several languages, the old Welsh and British languages, the Anglo-Saxon language that is now called Old English, and Latin as well. Generally, practitioners of magic use for their spells whatever language, real or imagined, that resonates with their emotions; usually something special that they do not use in daily life. One's emotions and state of mind can determine the type and extent of the magical energy that is called forth, and can cause that power to manifest for good or for evil. Many conflicting tales have been told about sorcerers being evil and wizards being good, but truthfully, I think the difference is something else entirely.

"You know, Derek, I have done things in my life that I'm not proud of, but I do not consider myself to be an evil person. The times in which I lived were violent and unpredictable and I did what I had to do to survive and to protect Arthur. However, I would be lying if I said there was no darkness in me." I paused for a moment, wondering how Derek would respond.

He sat back in his chair and was silent for a moment, digesting what I had told him. Then he said something unexpected. "Do you realize that your eyes change color when you do your magic? You had your eyes closed for the blue fire thing, but when you opened them afterwards, for a few seconds your eyes were very dark, almost black. Same thing just now when you lit the fire. Then they just revert back to your usual cat's eye green. Does that happen to all people that work magic?"

No one had ever noticed the change in my eye color before, although I always felt it happen. It normally took someone with enhanced perception to notice a magical "side effect" like that; someone with magical abilities of his or her own. I had suspected that Derek had magic when we first met, and I had noticed it at several other times over the past few months; now I was certain of it.

I answered slowly, "I truly do not know if other practitioners of magic have experienced that phenomenon, Derek. I have never really thought about it. But to tell you the truth, I have never encountered another being with powers exactly like mine either. Perhaps I really am the son of a demon, as legend has it. And if that is true, gods help us all."

I paused to take a long last drink of my beer. I had not intended to bring up *that* bit of old lore again, but it was only a few months ago that I had encountered a demon wanting to take me to Hades, and it was, unfortunately, still fresh in my mind.

It was such a relief to finally tell Derek the truth; I could not bear the burden of this knowledge by myself any longer. My sweet Emily knew, but she had no memory of it now. She had returned to Moab within a week of the accident and had resumed her normal activities—without me.

"You know, there have been dozens of legends, myths and stories written about my life over the centuries, but quite frankly, none of them come close to telling the whole truth. I'm not even sure that *I* remember all of it; 1600 years is a very long time." I paused reflectively and noticed Derek staring at me, slack-jawed.

"When I met you, I figured you were a few years older than me, Michael, but...since you really are Merlin, I guess you are a *lot* older."

I walked over and patted him on the shoulder and said gently, "It's alright, Derek, breathe. It will take some getting used to. But *you* of all people, my biggest fan, are familiar with all of the stories; and I did say I was born in 420. I was in my early thirties when my body stopped aging; I will always appear as I do now." I started pacing around the patio. "You guessed that there was something different about me when I first came to town, didn't you?"

Derek followed me with his eyes. "You really don't look much older than I am. And to answer your question, yeah, you gave off an aura, sort of an 'other worldly' vibe, of age and wisdom. At the time, I told myself I was imaginin' it, since no one else seemed to notice, but I guess I was right all along."

I turned and smiled at him. "Yes, you were, my friend."

He leaned forward and said, "Michael, er, I mean Merlin—damn, I can't seem to get used to this, it's just too unbelievable—I'm glad that you chose to tell me your secret, but what about Emily? You two are, or were, pretty close—doesn't she know about you?"

I nodded. "She did, but since the accident, she only remembers Michael, from our first meeting on the flight; she has no memory of the connection we shared. We've talked a few times since she returned, but... perhaps it's just as well that she doesn't remember." I'm sure my face looked stiff and sad. I sat down, feeling tired.

Derek said, "I'm so sorry, Merlin, but maybe she'll remember some day. Or maybe you should just *show* her, like you just did for me. I know how much you still love her, and it must be hard to deal with sometimes."

I nodded, but I did not want to talk about it anymore.

Derek sat quietly for a few minutes, and I waited patiently for him to speak. Finally he said slowly, "I do want to hear everythin', as much as you want to share with me, but somethin' is botherin' me about this whole scenario. Why would you even come to the United States, to Moab? Don't get me wrong; I'm *glad* you came, but you're British and Arthur should appear again in England, right? This doesn't make any sense."

"Derek, something happened the very day I awakened in the spring, and the signs and portents from that occurrence brought me here. A practitioner of magic, a Native American shaman, came to warn me about dark magic being worked that had blocked any future access to Avalon. Someone conjured a creature of myth, a wyvern, to kill me, but instead my caretakers, my employees, were threatened. The plan did not succeed—in fact I was able to destroy the creature—but not before the shaman was killed. When I touched his body, I had a vision in which he told me what was happening, and that I should follow the Power here, to Utah. So I traveled here, met Emily on the flight—and by the way, there's a lot more to *that* story than I have told you—and then I met you, Derek, bought my shop and the truck, and so on. The energy here in this country of red rocks is so strong that it now calls to me every day. Not only that, but the manifestations of evil have been increasing lately. I cannot wait much longer to move against this thing, and I want you to help me with my quest. It seems that there is a portal to the Other World here, somewhere, hidden in a cave or crevasse, which can transport me back to Avalon and to Arthur. I've been searching for it for months, but still haven't found it. I had already involved Emily in the search, but after she lost her memory, it was no longer appropriate to include her."

Derek seemed surprised that I would need his assistance, would actually include him in my quest, and he said, "But Merlin, what in the world can I do to help? I don't have any magical powers!"

I started to tell him about my suspicions regarding his true nature, but at that moment, a huge burst of fireworks erupted across the valley, brilliant against the velvety blackness of the summer night, and we quieted as we turned our chairs to view the show.

We watched the fireworks for a few minutes, and then Derek smiled at me happily and murmured, "Doesn't compare with yours, Merlin."

Throughout the twenty-minute display of increasingly complex patterns of light and color, we each drank another beer, and laughed and chatted about inconsequential things.

As soon as the show was over, Derek turned to me in the darkness and said quietly, "I'm incredibly honored that you told me about yourself. I promise you that I will *never* reveal your secret to anyone. And I'm sorry that I was so rude earlier. I was upset that you had been lyin' to me for months, and I thought you were teasin' me, jokin' with me about my obsession with Merlin…uh, with you. I can't believe that I've been hangin' out with the real Merlin all this time and never guessed the truth; it's kind of embarrassin'."

"There is no need to be embarrassed, Derek. You know, when I met you, and everything started to fall into place, I felt that our friendship was a gift from the gods. It has been difficult to have friends in my life when I never age, and they inevitably grow old and die. It has always seemed easier to avoid being close to people. But it can be so…lonely…" I sat thinking about that for a moment, then leaned back in my chair and looked at the dark sky.

Derek said, "Hey, I just thought of somethin'. Earlier you said I looked nothin' like Lancelot. You actually knew him, knew all of the Knights of the Round Table, didn't you? Did they know about your magic?"

I gave him a wry look. "Yes, of course I knew them, and they all knew that I was a sorcerer—I had been serving the Pendragons in the capacity of both physician and 'Court Magician' for years. I never liked that title, I preferred Sorcerer of the Realm, but it had been bestowed upon me by Uther and it stuck for some time. Lancelot and Gawain were particular friends of mine and Arthur's, and many an evening we would go to the tavern to drink ale and play a few games of dice. And contrary to what you have seen in several episodes of *Merlin*, the TV series, I did *not* use my magic to win unfairly." I was amused that Derek still believed all the tales.

"Remember the first time we watched DVDs together

back in April? I came very close to revealing myself. I was horrified that people thought I had so little control over my magic," I said.

"Yeah, I do remember that. I thought it was odd, as if you knew by experience that it was all wrong," Derek laughed, then became serious and sighed. "I wish I'd lived in your time— it must have been incredibly excitin'."

I shook my head. "It was exciting, Derek, but believe me, you wouldn't have enjoyed it; it was often brutal and primitive. I lived with the constant threat of danger and violence, and was always surrounded by people who were mortally wounded, or dying of diseases that today can be easily cured. I treated many of those people using herbal potions and spells, but very often they were not effective enough, and thus the individuals died anyway. Camelot *was* an amazing place, but it wasn't the clean, perfect castle they used in the BBC show; that place was built in France almost 1000 years after Arthur's reign. Remember I said I had been there? Well I was, but it was during one of my times of awakening; around 1502, I believe, or perhaps it was in 1399. I still have so much to tell you, Derek..."

On that note, I stood up and said, "I really need to get home now, but I would appreciate it if you would come to my place after work tomorrow, so we can continue this discussion. Also, I imagine you would like to see my dagger, my sword and my sorcerer's staff; they have been with me all these years, and they are quite ancient, just as I am."

Derek's eyes widened and he gasped, "You mean you have Excaliber, here in Moab?"

"No, that was Arthur's sword, remember, and I had thrown it into the lake at Avalon to return it to the Fae realm from whence it came. As far as I know it is still in the hands of the Elves." I swallowed, again faced with painful memories. I turned and walked back into the house, as Derek followed with the empty bottles.

"Well, I'll definitely see you tomorrow after work." Derek reached out and gave me a quick hug and a friendly pat on the back. I smiled. It was nice to have a friend that I didn't have to lie to anymore.

"Great, see you then," I said as I walked light-heartedly out the front door, turning to wave one more time. The porch light winked out as I got into the truck and drove away.

CHAPTER 22
July 5

THE FOLLOWING DAY went by quickly as I mixed and bottled basic herbal concoctions, imbuing them with short-term non-specific spells so that they would work for anyone. I labeled the bottles with the old-fashioned lettering that the customers admired, and arranged them on the shelves by their uses. Also, thinking they would be particularly useful for the tourists, I measured and packaged such single herbs as great water dock, for mouth sores and toothache, feverwort for snakebites, and heliotrope for scorpion's sting. I then unpacked the new shipment of the ordinary but useful herbs comfrey, burdock, rosemary and pennyroyal, which I planned to offer in bulk. Of course, I only had the dried herbs, and in reality many of the herbs I used for ointments and poultices had to be fresh to be the most effective. But I did the best I could with what was available, and the herbs were often as popular with my customers as the potions.

Nothing out of the ordinary happened during the day, and business was slow, but I felt very peaceful and happy knowing that I would see my friend after the workday ended.

And I had made an important decision: It was time to talk to Derek about that spark of magic I had felt the first time he and I had shaken hands. Now that he knew my secret, I needed to confirm the truth about Derek also.

At five o'clock I counted the money, completed my meager deposit, and readied the shop for the next business day. There had not been a storytelling session that afternoon so clean-up was fast. As I finished up, I heard a knock, and went to open the door for Derek. After I let him in and carefully locked up behind him, I politely asked if he would like anything to drink. He declined just as politely, but reflected the same excitement I was feeling, even though he was not yet aware of my intentions.

I did not keep him in suspense for long.

"Derek, there is something we need to pursue, something that I've suspected since we first met. When two people who both have magic touch each other, they can feel a deep tingling sensation, almost like a spark of electricity. When we shook hands at the City Diner the night we first met, I felt that tingling, but I realized that you didn't know what it was. I think that you have magic, Derek; to what extent I don't yet know. But to truly confirm this, I'm going to have to touch you, and Look deeply into your being. Will you allow me to do that?" I sincerely hoped that he would agree.

Derek gaped at me for what seemed an interminable length of time, then sputtered, "What? Are you kiddin' me?"

"I'm quite serious," I said solemnly.

"Oh, my God, yes, absolutely! It would be a dream-come-true—all my life I've wondered what it would be like. What do you have to do?" Excitement, disbelief and yearning competed for first place in his voice.

"I just need to touch your bare skin. Perhaps we could clasp each other's forearms, and I'll Look into your eyes for a short time, is that alright?" I asked.

"Yeah, okay," he said, nervously.

"Alright, just stand in front of me, fairly close. Yes, like that. Now, look into my eyes—it's okay, Derek, don't be afraid—and take some long deep breaths to relax. Give yourself permission to let me in. Now, here we go," I said hypnotically.

I reached out and we grasped each other's arms and I Looked deliberately into his eyes, calling upon my magic to connect with him on the deepest level. This was going to be as powerful an experience for him as it would be for me, because the connection worked both ways; we would See each other as we truly were, in the deepest parts of our beings. It was a dangerous thing to do with someone you didn't know very well, and best avoided unless absolutely necessary, but I was confident that I was doing the right thing. As the connection unfolded, I felt the untapped magical energy within Derek; he did indeed have the potential to be a practitioner of magic. Whether that would be as a simple wizard or a great sorcerer, only time, training and experience would reveal. But then something else happened that would change our perception of each other forever. The deeper I went into his being, experiencing his soul, the more his essence seemed as familiar to me as my own. I was shocked, for there could be only one explanation for this phenomenon— we were related. Somewhere in the mists of time, one of my few, brief liaisons had produced a child who was Derek's ancestor.

And as I experienced this revelation, so did Derek. He now knew that I was his many-times-removed great-grandfather.

No wonder we had felt such a close bond; there was a real flesh-and-blood connection between us. Now, more than ever, I knew that my journey to Moab had been destined.

We pulled away at the same time and just gazed at each other in amazement. Then we hugged each other, grinning and laughing.

As we stepped apart, Derek could hardly speak, but finally managed to say in a voice rough with emotion, "That was the most amazin' thing I've ever experienced. Merlin, I...I'm actually related to you. And I have *magic*, oh my God!" he said exuberantly, then, in a hushed, awed tone of voice, he continued, "I saw your soul..."

"And I saw yours, Great-grandson, and it is as pure as I have ever seen; considerably more so than my own. And your magic can one day become strong with the proper training." I grinned proudly.

"So, what happens now?" Derek asked excitedly.

"Well, we need to get started on your training as soon as possible. I am going to need magical assistance finding the portal that leads to Avalon, but you will need to learn and practice some fundamentals first. We will have to coordinate our daily schedules and plan some uninterrupted time for you to practice. And I cannot begin to stress the importance that, however much you want to share this discovery with your friends, you must not let anyone discover the truth, unless I allow it," I said firmly.

"I'll do whatever I have to do, Merlin, you have my word." He frowned. "My parents didn't have magic—I would've noticed. Shouldn't one of them have had magic in order to pass it along to me?"

"Not necessarily; sometimes it can skip many generations. Did you ever hear any family stories about an ancestor who was accused of witchcraft or sorcery?"

Derek thought about it for a moment. "Yeah, as a matter of fact, on my dad's side, there *was* a woman back in the 1600s in Salem, Massachusetts, who was actually burned at the stake for bein' a witch. I guess she really *was* one..."

"So it would be your father, rather than your mother, who is my descendant. Is he still alive?" I asked curiously.

"No, he died in a car accident several years ago."

"I'm so sorry, Derek, I'd like to have met him," I said.

"It's alright, Merlin, I still miss him, but it doesn't hurt as much as it used to. And now I have you. How did I get so lucky?" Derek said with a catch in his voice.

"Luck had nothing to do with it, I suspect. This is the work of the gods, and decided long before you were born." I started to experience that sense of destiny that often accompanied my visions. Suddenly, my body stiffened, and I experienced being transported through many lifetimes. It all started with the birth of my son, then my grandchild and great-grandchild, and on and on through many lives over many centuries to this place and time. And then I was seeing the future, with Derek using magic to help me defend Arthur, in a place I did not recognize.

I heard a voice, as if from a distance, calling my name, and I finally came back into my body. I gasped and blinked, and finally focused on Derek, who was directly in front of me, gripping my shoulders.

"Merlin! What happened? Are you alright?" Derek shouted frantically.

I said hoarsely, "Everything's alright, Derek. I just had a vision spanning a thousand years, and I saw you in the future, using your magic to help me defend Arthur Pendragon."

Derek just stood silently in front of me, wide-eyed and incredulous, until he finally said, "I need a drink."

CHAPTER 23
July 5

W E SAT IN THE TWO comfortable chairs in the reading area with our drinks. Derek was gaping at me, and I was feeling increasingly uneasy under his unblinking stare.

"Well, that's enough of that!" I set the glass down hard on the table, got up and walked over to Derek. I stood in front of him as he gazed up at me in awe, and I grabbed his arms and pulled him out of the chair. "We're going for a walk, my friend. Hopefully some fresh air and exercise will help your mind to re-set itself; if not, by the gods, I will re-set it for you."

I put my keys in the pocket of my shorts, and then propelled my descendant and new apprentice out of the door, locking it behind me. I didn't bother to ward the building as we were coming right back.

"Derek, listen to me. The experience you had when we Looked into each other's beings was beyond anything you have ever known, and your mind is having a hard time translating that knowledge into your everyday reality. Then, when I told you about the vision I'd had, I think it overloaded your synapses," I said as we walked along Main Street.

Confused, Derek asked, "What happened? Where are we going?"

"We'll just walk around the block to stretch our legs and then we'll go back to the shop," I said soothingly.

As I guided him around a group of tourists staring in the window of one of the T-shirt shops, the knowledge that Derek was mine, my own flesh and blood, became a reality in my heart; I was no longer alone. He looked nothing like me, which was understandable after the addition of so many other sets of DNA into the ancestral gene pool, but the connection was there. I felt as protective of him as a parent or grandparent would, and yet I could not treat him as a child—he was an adult. I looked like his slightly older cousin, so that would have to be my role in the eyes of the world. But in my eyes, not only was he my friend, he was my great-grandson.

By this time we had circled the block and were back at The Moab Herbalist. I unlocked the door, escorted Derek inside and sat him down.

"Stay here, Derek," I commanded. I got him a glass of water and helped him to drink it. I then stood behind him and placed my fingertips on his temples, the palms of my hands resting on the sides of his head. I whispered to him, "Relax now, and let me in. Trust in me, for you know that I would never hurt you; *te amo.*"

I felt his natural resistance start to relax as I said, in Latin, 'I love you.' I released a sudden small burst of magical energy, and I felt Derek jerk a little under my hands, then he relaxed with a sigh of relief.

I let my hands drop to my sides and walked around in front of him, reaching down to examine his eyes and check his pulse. He was deeply asleep and I knew that this state could last for a few hours, so I went into the back room to fix something to eat. When I came back out with a plate of sandwiches twenty minutes later, I was surprised to see that he was already awake. I set the plate down on the table.

"Hey, Derek, how are you feeling? I expected you to sleep at least another hour," I said, sitting in the opposite chair and picking up a sandwich.

"Michael, what happened?" He sounded groggy. "I must have fallen asleep. I had a really strange dream about you bein' a sorcerer and me bein' your apprentice, isn't that crazy? And you were really Merlin, and I had magical powers, and..." Derek stopped talking as he finally remembered everything. "It wasn't a dream was it? It's all true?"

"Yes, it's all true," I confirmed, as I bit into my dinner.

"Would you like a sandwich? It's roast beef."

"How can you eat at a time like this?" Derek asked plaintively.

"Because I'm hungry; the events of the past two hours really gave me an appetite." I chewed my sandwich and swallowed. Then I set the food down on a napkin and brushed the crumbs off my lap.

"Derek, I have been alone all this time, never knowing a family, and now I have you. I'm very grateful for that."

"I don't know what to say, Merlin, I'm still feeling overwhelmed. All my life I felt like somethin' was missin' but I could never figure out what it was. I was always drawn to stories about magic and about Merlin—about *you*. Well, you know that, you've seen all my posters, and know about my obsession with Camelot. I could never in a million years have foreseen this happenin' to me..."

"I know what you mean, Derek." I paused for a moment then looked at him slyly. "Would you like to learn a spell or two tonight?"

He laughed delightedly. "You bet I would!"

"Alright, close your eyes and picture a light at the center of your being. Focus on that light until you can see it clearly in your mind. Now open your eyes, and put your right hand out in front of you, palm up. Feel the energy and the light travel through your body to your hand. As you do that, concentrate and say, '*Albus Lux*,' which means *white light* in Latin."

Derek held his hand out, palm up, as I had instructed, and frowned in concentration. "*Albus Lux*," he said quietly. Immediately a small, glowing orb of white light appeared, hovering over the palm of his hand. His eyes widened in excitement as he held his hand steady, admiring the results of his first attempt at magic. He turned to look at me and smiled, breaking his concentration, and the little orb flickered and died. He realized immediately what he had done, and looked disappointed for a moment.

"Well done for your first time, Derek."

"That was awesome, and it wasn't hard to do at all," he exclaimed.

"That's because you were born with the gift of magic, Derek—you inherited it from me. It takes practice and dedication to manifest that magical energy in other ways, but you obviously have a good connection to it already and should progress rapidly," I said. "Let's try something else, just for fun. Concentrate on one of the sandwiches on the plate and picture in your mind the sandwich coming towards your outstretched hand. Say '*Venis ad me*,' which means '*come to me.*'"

Derek stretched his hand out, palm up, towards the plate of sandwiches and repeated the spell. The sandwich underneath the top one struggled out from under it and flew obediently into Derek's hand.

"Well, you must have been eyeing the wrong sandwich if you really wanted the top one, but it doesn't matter, you made your dinner come to you. Good job!" I said. "Now, go ahead and eat the sandwich. Doing magic can deplete your energy just like any activity and you need to feed your body."

"Okay, Grandpa, I'll eat my sandwich like a good boy," Derek said with a smirk. But he ate it anyway, then grabbed a second one when I brought out the beer.

After we finished our dinner, Derek wanted to try lighting a fire using magic, so we went out the back door where I kept my barbeque and Derek tried several times to light the old briquettes, unsuccessfully.

"Why can't I do this?" he complained. "I'm picturin' the flames in my head, then focusin' on the coals, and nothin' happens…"

"Just relax, I think you're trying too hard. Some people have better luck verbalizing a spell, as well as visualizing the result. Close your eyes, take a few deep breaths and center yourself, then visualize the result you want. Now open your eyes, look at the coals with the intention of having them burn, and say '*Adolebit*.'"

Derek did as I bade him, and small flames erupted from the coals, wavering in the evening breeze. "Ah," he breathed, "There it is."

"And it was just last night that you thought it would come in handy to be able to control fire, and now you can," I said quietly, not wanting anyone else to hear me. "Perhaps that is enough for tonight, Derek." I flicked my hand at the coals, quenching the flames.

He did not argue with me but followed me inside, tired but very pleased with himself. As well he should be; not every new practitioner of magic can manage three separate spells the first day.

Deep in thought, I turned to Derek and said, "Actually, there is one more thing. Come with me." We went into the back room and I walked up to an empty space on one wall. I raised my open palm and said, "*Revelare*." The wall seemed to waver and then it disappeared, revealing a sword, a long sorcerer's staff, a crossbow and an assortment of brilliant quartz crystals.

Behind me, Derek gasped, and I recalled how precious these tools and symbols were to me, and knew how extraordinary they must look to him. I stepped forward and grasped my sword, holding it up in the light as memories flowed through me one after another. Memories of another time and place: of Arthur, and Lancelot and Gawain and all the rest. I felt electricity ripple over my body as I held this symbol of my power and my strength of purpose. I do not know how long I stood there immersed in the past, but I finally realized that Derek was saying my name.

"Merlin, oh my God, Merlin. You're...glowin'." Derek whispered, his face alight with amazement and awe.

I slowly lowered the sword, and said to him in a clear, quiet voice, "This is your legacy, Derek. When I am gone from this world, you or your descendants will inherit the tools and symbols of my life's purpose. I told you that I am essentially immortal, but I may some day choose to die when I have been on this earth too long, or perhaps someone's magic may destroy me. It is likely that *you* will be very long-lived, Derek, perhaps as long as 400 years. This sword is not Excalibur, but it was forged for me by the gods. I will use it until it is time to pass it along to you, as my heir." I carefully placed the sword back in the cupboard in the wall, and then ran my hand down the length of the carved staff, pulling it out also. "This staff is my tool as a sorcerer to focus and amplify my magical energy. It was made out of the wood of a 2000-year-old yew tree in AD 436. The wood is strong and resilient and sacred to the gods, and most deadly to anyone who should try to use it with ill intent. This, as well as the crossbow, the crystals and my dagger will be yours one day."

Derek cleared his throat and said emotionally, "I will do my best to be worthy of this great honor, Merlin."

"I know you will, Derek," I said warmly.

I put the staff back as well and murmured "*Celo*," causing the wall to conceal its treasures once more. I turned to look at Derek and said, "It's time to make a plan. Meet me here again tomorrow for more training, and we will start preparing our strategy, which will include obtaining a staff for you to use.

"Oh, and by the way, you asked me if other practitioner's eyes change color when using magic; the answer is 'yes'. Your eyes changed from brown to gold."

CHAPTER 24
July 5

DEREK LEFT SOON AFTER THAT, and I sat in my shop in the dark, thinking about everything that had transpired since the previous day. I was wide-awake despite the late hour. And I needed Emily and missed her sorely. Derek was right, it was time to go to her and reveal myself. She was a part of all this, and I needed her to be aware of everything again. Late or not I was going to her that night. Before she left for Mesa Verde she had felt that something would happen, and had begged me not to give up on her, and yet that is exactly what I had done. I had taken the easy way by allowing her to continue on in ignorance the past few weeks.

As I left the shop I quickly locked the door and activated the warding spell. I hurried to Emily's, the dark streets holding no terrors for me. As I approached her house I realized that she was still awake. Despite the fact that it was close to midnight there were lights on inside; she must not have to work tomorrow. The light was out on her porch so I created my own, just as Derek had done earlier.

"*Albus Lux,*" I whispered, and the orb of light sat in my outstretched palm, bathing everything around me in the soft white light of magic. I closed my eyes and called to Emily from a connection between us that would exist for all time.

Emily, come to me now, love... I sent the message to her from deep within my being, from my heart. A few minutes went by, then I heard the front door open, and there was Emily. She gazed first at the orb in my hand, and then at my face. I heard her gasp in fear and knew that although her soul had responded to my summons, her mind was still blinded by whatever magic had caused this. I did not believe this depth of memory blockage could have been caused by anything other than black magic. The accident Emily had experienced was just the catalyst.

But I would not wait any longer to reunite with her—my sorcery *would* prevail over the darkness.

With my dark hair flowing back in a breeze of magical origin, and with the shadows emphasizing the angles of my face, I'm sure I looked almost sinister to her, but I was determined to be with her despite her fear.

"Emily, invite me inside," I commanded in my Voice, and she had no choice but to obey.

She said, in a flat, strained voice, "Please come in, Michael."

I diminished the size of the orb until it disappeared as I entered her softly lit front room. Emily followed me inside, shut the door, and just stood there, looking at me fearfully.

I couldn't believe that this was the same person I had known intimately only weeks earlier; the fiery spirit that made her what she was had been thoroughly subdued. This situation had to end, now.

"Emily, you must fight this," I encouraged her. "Do you remember when I enchanted you up near Soldier Summit at the end of April, and you reacted so badly that I had to remove the spell or risk you injuring yourself? Do you remember how you felt when you realized I had healed my shoulder when I was injured by the dragons? Emily, it's me, it's Merlin." I hoped that the intensity in my voice would somehow penetrate the layer of blankness coating her memory.

She stood staring at me, her body shaking, and all of a sudden I could sense her fighting to get free.

I made the decision to do the one thing that should bypass the blockage: I would Look into her being, as I had done with Derek earlier, and to hell with the consequences.

Abruptly, I stepped up in front of her and clasped her bare forearms, not bothering to ask her permission as I knew she would refuse. She cried out and tried to pull away, and I spoke softly to her, trying to calm her, "Tis alright my love, I would never hurt you. Please trust me to help you. Look deeply into my eyes, Emily," I said persuasively, using my will to direct her gaze to mine.

Finally, she focused on me long enough that I could begin to connect on a deeper level. I centered myself and tried to Look inside of her...and encountered a dark wall preventing my access. This was the darkest of black magic, to lock a human being's very soul away. I came back to myself and contemplated what to do. I was puzzled—how had I been able to compel her to come outside to me, yet I could not seem to reach her this way. And then it came to me. When I had compelled her, I had reached directly into that deep bond of the heart that had already been forged between us; I hadn't tried to involve her mind.

So I held her tightly in my arms and shut my eyes, feeling that bond on a visceral level, without thought, only feeling, and focused all my attention—and intention—on it, strengthening it by my love and support. I felt a part of me rush into her being through that connection between our hearts, bypassing the black wall and seeing the real Emily behind it, the sweet yet fiery spirit of her that now welcomed me. The love between us expanded until there was no room for the blackness, which silently shattered, releasing Emily from her inner prison.

She took a long breath and let it out slowly, collapsing in my arms as she fainted. I picked her up and sat down on the couch with her on my lap, stroking her hair, touching her face, and gently kissing her lips. Then I sighed deeply, leaned back and closed my eyes. I must have gone to sleep, because I was dreaming that someone was kissing me passionately and stroking my body. I opened my eyes, and found myself staring directly into Emily's beautiful hazel ones.

"Hey, big guy, it's good to see you," Emily whispered, and touched my cheek.

I looked at her, gazing at me with love, and I felt my

eyes well up with tears. "I thought I had lost you," I whispered, holding her against me.

"But I'm back now, and I'll never leave you again, even if I have to come to Avalon with you. Do you think Arthur might need a park ranger in his service?"

"Anything is possible, Emily," I laughed.

We helped each other up off the couch and just held each other until the passion started building; then we kissed and touched, and finally throwing off our clothing, sank down to the carpet. We stroked each other's bodies gratefully, and finally, Emily reached down and guided me home. I entered her slowly, savoring every bit of sensation as she sighed and moved beneath me. I looked into her eyes as we pleasured each other, and I knew that I could not, would not live without her any longer. Long, slow strokes gradually quickened to bold deep thrusts until we both climaxed. Afterwards, I held on to Emily tightly, unwilling to let go of this woman I thought I had lost forever. We finally got up and stumbled into the bedroom, collapsing on her bed.

As I drifted off to sleep in her arms, I realized that I could tell her about Derek now.

CHAPTER 25
July 6

W HEN I AWOKE the following morning I was alone in the bed, sprawled out in abandon. I felt relaxed and satisfied, remembering the previous night.

"Honey, do you want some coffee?" Emily's voice drifted down the hallway.

"I would love coffee!" I called out as I leaped out of bed, more energetic than I had felt in weeks. I walked out into the living room looking for my clothes, and then realized that we had company. Derek was sitting at the kitchen table with a cup of coffee halfway to his lips as he stared at my naked form.

"Uh, sorry, didn't know you were here, Derek" I said, and quickly put on my shorts.

Derek just laughed. "I *have* seen you naked at the gym, and what the heck, I guess it's okay for family members to see each other in the buff now and then, right?"

Emily, who was standing at the kitchen counter making breakfast, turned around and looked back and forth between us, eyes narrowed, "What in the world do you mean by that?"

Derek raised his eyebrows at me and said sheepishly, "Sorry, I didn't mean to let that slip. Can we tell her all of it? I mean, she remembers who you are, right?

I looked at Emily and she looked back at me with questions in her eyes, and I thought, *no more secrets....*

"Yes, she does remember who I am, so let's tell her, Derek." I smiled, wondering how she would react.

"Emily," said Derek excitedly, "I know that Michael is really *Merlin*—he revealed himself to me a few days ago."

Emily looked at Derek, then at me, and said happily, "Well, it's about time! But what's this about family members...?"

"Well that's the interesting part, Emily. We discovered that Derek is my descendant ...and he has magic." I smiled at my great-grandson.

Emily stared at Derek. "Seriously? Merlin...*you*," she looked at me in disbelief, "...are Derek's *ancestor*? That's just plain creepy. How...?"

"In order to connect with Derek on a level deep enough to confirm his magic, I had to Look into his very essence, into his soul. And when I did that, I realized that our essences were very much alike. The only way for that to happen is through blood. My child was his ancestor," I said in a matter-of-fact tone.

Emily said faintly, "I think I need to sit down." She pulled out a chair across from Derek and practically fell into it.

She finally looked up and said skeptically, "About the magic, Derek. You'll have to show me before I'll believe *that*."

Derek grinned. "I would *love* to show you—watch this." And he held his hand out, repeated the spell I had taught him, and manifested a bright orb of light as quickly as if he had been using magic his entire life.

Emily's eyes widened and all she could do was whisper, "Oh, dear God..."

Derek laughed and tossed the orb to me. "Catch!"

We tossed the little globe of light back and forth a few times until I said "Enough, let's have breakfast. *Extinguo*." The orb winked out of existence and I reached for my coffee.

Emily got up and served us the eggs and toast she'd been preparing. "Don't get too used to this, it's your turn next time."

"I've been preparing my own meals for a long time, so I guess I will manage," I said around a bite of egg. I was looking down at my plate as I spoke, but I could sense Emily and Derek looking at each other, and shaking their heads and grinning.

"Whatever you say, old man," Emily said affectionately.

I finished eating and pushed my plate away, ready to get

down to business. As I looked at these two people who had become so important to me, I knew that I had to be totally honest with them.

"I have some important things to say to you, before any more time passes. First of all, I think you know how much I love you both, and I couldn't bear to lose either of you. So you need to be aware of how much danger you are in being associated with me. Emily has a better understanding of that since she has personally seen me fight the enemy. Derek, you have also been present for several attacks, but you were not aware of what was happening. I'm afraid a major confrontation, no, a battle, is soon approaching that will be much worse than what we have experienced so far."

"What are you talkin' about, Merlin? What attacks?" Derek looked puzzled.

Emily answered him enthusiastically before I could reply. "You have no idea what happened to us when we were driving back from the airport in April. We'd stayed at the Best Western in Springville, and the next morning just as we got to Soldier Summit, this whirling screaming darkness hit the car, and Merlin (of course at that time I thought he was Michael) insisted that I pull over to let him out. I thought he was insane, until I saw him do something unbelievable. He threw his arms out and yelled something and this bright flash came out of his hands, and the creature was gone through a rip in the sky! When he turned around and knew that I had seen him use magic, he looked resigned to me either freaking out or rejecting him..."

I wanted to regain control of the conversation.

"Emily..."

"Just let me finish, okay?"

I nodded to her to go ahead.

"And then he tried to enchant me so I'd forget, and it backfired, so he had to reverse the spell, and then I remembered all about his magic including what he'd done in the motel room after we…"

"I don't need to hear about that part, Emily," Derek said quickly, his face turning red with embarrassment.

"Then, everything seemed fine until we turned on Highway 191 towards Moab, and the dragons attacked us," I explained.

"The…*dragons*?" Derek's eyes widened.

"You should have seen him—he was magnificent!" Emily said proudly. "He chanted in another language and used his special Voice, and the dragons just…obeyed him and flew away. But not before one of them slashed him with his claws. It scared me to death, Derek, he was bleeding so profusely."

"My God, what did you do, Merlin?" Derek asked, horrified.

"I did something that apparently convinced Emily who I really was," I said, glancing at her, "I healed myself."

"Merlin, if you can heal yourself, why couldn't you have done that for Emily after her accident?" Derek asked.

"This is another thing you were unaware of at the time, Derek; I *did* try to heal her. I gave her several potions and worked a healing spell, which helped her to heal much faster than normal. Do you remember asking me if I saw the glow around her? That was residual magic from the spell that you were able to see because of your own magic."

Derek nodded. "Ah, I understand now."

But I could see Derek was also thinking about what happened *after* I had left the room. I dreaded having to explain that situation.

"Merlin, *you* caused that 'earthquake,' because you were upset that Emily had forgotten you," Derek said, shocked.

"Regrettably, I did," I admitted, feeling ashamed all over again.

Emily looked at me and said, "You mean the day you both came to see me in the hospital and I thought you were Michael, when everyone was talking about the weird shockwave that had broken all the windows in town? That was *you*? Oh, God, Merlin, I'm so sorry…"

"It wasn't your fault, Em," I said gently, "I couldn't control my emotions, and therefore my magic was out of control as well."

"Look, it's too late to change what happened, so let's move on. Were there any other occurrences I *would* remember?" Derek asked.

"Yes, two," I said. "The day I bought the shop and the truck from Chris, and we drove out to Arches looking for caves and crevices, I was actually looking for portals, Derek. The sandstorm that happened as we were hiking to Landscape Arch was one such occurrence that I had to deal with without your knowledge. Do you remember the shock you received when you touched me? The magic within you was reacting to the energy I had just accessed. And remember the night in the parking lot at Moab Brews when the lights all blew out?"

"I was absolutely clueless, wasn't I? How could I not have known something was going on?"

"There were many times when I caught you looking at me strangely and I was sure you would guess the truth, Derek."

"Merlin, I thought you were more than a little odd, but I never guessed. And then when you finally did tell me about yourself, I was pissed that you had waited so long. Go figure," he said.

"So now that you both are more or less up to speed with what's been happening, I have a few more things to say. Derek, I hope that you will do everything in your power to learn as much as you can, as fast as you can."

Derek nodded in agreement.

"And Emily, sweetheart, there is something that I have to tell you that may shock you to the core of your being, and I am so sorry that there is no easy way to tell you of it," I said.

Emily frowned. "What is it, Merlin?"

"When I connected with you last night to break the spell of dark magic, I saw something within you that confirmed my suspicions—you are not entirely human. Sometime in the past, one of your ancestors mated with a Fae being, most likely an Elf. I'm afraid I can't tell you any more than that without going deeper."

"What? You can't be serious!" Emily scoffed. "That's ridiculous—absolutely impossible."

"Oh, come on, Emily, think about it. You're havin' an affair with a legendary fifth century sorcerer, and you've seen me, whom you've know for years, actually work *magic*. Normally we would think those things were impossible, right? But they're real; Merlin is real. You trust him, and he obviously loves you very much, so if he says you have Elven blood, then you should believe it," Derek said. "And by the way, I think that it's extremely cool that you're part Elf."

Emily looked at Derek, then at me, with a dazed expression on her face, and didn't say anything. I reached over and gently took both of her hands in mine.

"I'm truly sorry to tell you in this way, with no warning whatsoever, but I'm afraid we no longer have the option of withholding information from each other. Another reason I needed to tell you is: you may be able to work magic also—Fae magic."

"Emily and Derek," I continued, "I have no doubt that the gods have all along been aware of the things we have been dealing with: My issues about my father; the fact that Derek is my kin and has magic through his connection with me; that my relationship with Emily has changed my life and possibly the quest; that Emily is Fae and may be able to work magic herself; and that all these strange attacks have been leading up to a major confrontation with a dangerous enemy."

I took a deep breath and said with conviction, "This

journey, this quest, started out as my task alone, but circumstances have changed, and now the three of us are inextricably bound together on this course."

CHAPTER 26
July 6

DEREK HAD LEFT earlier, as he was scheduled to work the late shift, but had promised to meet us at the shop that evening.

Emily was still struggling with the discussions and revelations of the last few hours, and I felt badly that I had not told her about her Fae blood last night. But she and I had just experienced our own crisis, and our reunion had temporarily replaced all other considerations in my mind.

"Merlin, I feel as if my life is suddenly not my own. Everything I have believed to be true is a sham, a dream, and I don't know what to think anymore," Emily said, sounding confused, frustrated and sad. "What if I don't *want* to be a supernatural being, or go to battle; what if I just want my old life back?"

She and I were still sitting at the kitchen table, holding hands. We had been going over and over the same things, and I knew that I could not respond to her concerns the way she wanted me to. I was losing patience. I loved her and didn't want to lose her, but my purpose, my responsibility and my destiny were again foremost in my mind, and I had to move forward.

Finally, having decided on a course of action that would hopefully yield the results I wanted, I stood up, looked down at her, and said things that were probably not what she expected to hear from me.

"When I tried to erase your memory a few months ago, and it was such a bad experience for you, I swore that I would never do that to you again. Are you saying that after all you and I have been through, and with all your talk of devotion, that you want me to erase your memory of the past few months, your memories of me, of what we have shared...forever? Because— and make no mistake, my dear—I am quite capable of doing that *right now,*" I said harshly.

I stalked around behind her and into the living room, allowing bright tendrils of magical energy to surround my body and trail behind me. I heard her gasp in shock. Good, I thought, she needs to feel intimidated. I hated to do this to her, but feeling sorry for herself wasn't helping the situation, and her personality was so strong that drastic measures were required.

I swung around dramatically and faced her, wishing that I was wearing something other than just a pair of shorts, but at least the little bolts of energy flashing around my bare chest looked impressive. I enhanced my appearance to look a little bigger and a little more dangerous, caused my hair to blow back from my face, and then I raised my arms and started to chant in the old language. I was actually reciting a poem, but she didn't know that. I hoped that she would respond. She did.

"Oh, God, no, wait, Merlin, please. I *don't* want to forget you again; I just meant that I feel overwhelmed, and wished that I had time to understand and adjust to this. It's a scary feeling that I'm not in control of my own life," Emily cried, looking at me as if she finally understood who she'd invited into her life—an ancient, dangerous being who controlled unthinkable power.

"I do love you, and I meant what I said about fighting at your side for Arthur's sake, but...I'm terrified," Emily finally confessed.

I immediately let go of my enhanced appearance and allowed some of the energy to dissipate. I sighed in frustration, and my own issues began surfacing. "I know you are, Em. But listen, I have lived like that for *my entire life.* Do you think *I* don't feel fear? Do you think *I* like feeling as if I have no control of my life? What is it that Derek says, oh, yes, '*Join the club!*'" I could feel my emotions escalating as I spoke.

"Do you remember what I said to you a few months ago, that until I met you, I had *never* had a woman's love? I rarely had relations with women and was constantly living for the

King's needs. Try living like *that* for over 1000 years," I yelled, my chest heaving, as my emotions almost broke through my control and my magic strained for release.

"Merlin, stop! I'm sorry I've been so selfish. Relax, honey, please," Emily said softly and lovingly, recognizing that my magic was almost ready to explode. She could feel the pressure that had built up around me, and could see the sparks of energy emanating from my body. Despite her fear, she came up to me and threw her arms around me, kissing my bare chest and stroking my back.

I knew I had to calm down; the last thing I wanted was to hurt her. I barely held back a groan and took several deep breaths. I thought I knew what was really bothering me—I just hadn't wanted to face it.

"My God, Merlin, what in the world is going on? This isn't like you." Emily looked at me with concern.

I began to tell her what I should have said before this. "More than once, you have heard me talk about being the son of a demon, and you may have thought I was joking, or at least exaggerating. What I never told you was this: that day near the movie theater, a couple of blocks from Derek's, a demon actually tried to take me to the Underworld. The evil and the horror were overwhelming. I truly think my father is the god of death: Satan, Beli, he has many names. I have had a difficult time controlling my rage and my fear lately, and it could be that I'm experiencing my *own* heritage. If I am a being like that, it would certainly explain why I never age. Hearing you complain about something as trivial as having Fae blood in your family tree, well, it was just the last straw."

Emily frowned as she heard about my ordeal, and finally said, "I'm so sorry you went through that, Merlin. But I meant what I said before, that I would love you no matter who your father was. I'm totally serious. So I guess I need to step up and embrace my own powers whether I want to or not, so I can go *kick his ass.*"

At that statement by my ferocious Emily, I laughed a little, and as I relaxed, the energy in the house finally dissipated.

I ran my hands through my hair. "I'm sorry, Em, I had originally intended to trick you out of your self-absorption, but instead my own issues took over. I think I should Look again, a little deeper within your being, to see if I can uncover your true Fae nature." I held my hands out to her. "Come, let us hold each other, and see what lies within. You will see your true self, Emily, and it will help you to know me better as well."

She stepped forward into my waiting arms and we gazed into each other's eyes. I Looked deeply, deliberately, into her being, and she Looked into mine, our love and our bond weaving a unique experience, different than anything I had felt before. I went deeper and Saw in her essence a pattern that was only partially human—this is what I had sensed in my encounter with the wall of black magic. I attempted to See into that pattern so that I could uncover her heritage, and found it difficult to decipher. So I magically wove a strand of each of our essences together with the strength of our love and she and I followed it towards a deeper understanding of her being. And there it was, the link to Elven magic and immortality, hidden deep beneath a veil-like separation of the mortal and the immortal in her nature. The secrets to utilizing her magic were there, and I was aware of the moment when she recognized the truth. Our souls rejoiced, and I slowly guided us back to the physical world.

Emily's face was beaming as she accepted her heritage. I gazed at her lovingly, and said, "Do you realize what this means, Emily? We can be together forever. The gods truly brought us to one another. I will guide you in using your magic, if you allow me to, and our powers will complement each other."

Emily looked at me and smiled, and said, "I Saw you, Merlin, and you are *beautiful* inside. There is *no* way that you are the son of Satan. I'm not sure who your father really was, but even if he was a demon god, *you* are not evil. The demon that attacked you must have left behind a spell, and it magnified your fears. Merlin, perhaps your father was a god of light, or an angel; I think *that* would be more accurate."

I was overjoyed by her belief in me. After all the fear and uncertainty regarding my parentage, this news washed over me like a balm from the gods.

I leaned down to rest my head on her shoulder, and closed my eyes while she stroked my back. She leaned her own head against mine. We stood that way for several more minutes, and then I took her by the hand and led her into the bedroom. We removed our clothing and lay down, holding each other close. A kiss and a touch that started out gentle and sweet transformed into a raging torrent of desire. I pulled her under me and she tilted her hips and gasped, *"Now,* Merlin." I drove into her in one long thrust. Our bodies seemed to become one and we moved swiftly to our completion. As we collapsed next to each other, Emily sighed and smiled at me, caressing my cheek, and I knew what should come next...

"I want to get married," I said softly.

CHAPTER 27
July 6

E MILY'S EYES WIDENED. "Right now?"

"That really wasn't the response I expected," I said, perplexed. "Let me say it in another way: I want to marry *you*, Emily, do you want to marry *me*?"

"Yes, I do. When?"

"As soon as possible. Of course, when Arthur returns we should have a formal ceremony but we don't know when that will be."

Emily sat up abruptly, struck a pose, and said in a stilted English accent, "Oh my *God*, I'm going to marry Merlin the Sorcerer, so of *course*, we must have King Arthur perform the official ceremony." She returned to her normal voice. "Since I have no intention of waiting for Arthur, better grab your wand, magic man—we're driving to Las Vegas to get married!"

I laughed so hard that I practically fell off of the bed.

She said indignantly, "Hey, what's so funny, old man?

I grabbed her and kissed her. "*You* are. I love everything about you, you little minx."

Emily, her long hair tangled and her face flushed with excitement, pushed me back down on the bed, threw herself on top of me, and began kissing my face, and then started working her way down my chest. I knew where she was headed, and while I would thoroughly enjoy the results of her efforts, I also knew that we needed to get going if we were driving to Las Vegas today. Although I had never been there, I knew it was at least a seven-hour drive.

"My love, that feels amazing, but I think we should get up and make our plans, don't you?"

Emily abandoned her goal immediately, and a certain part of my anatomy cried out in disappointment. "You're absolutely right. If we leave in the next couple of hours, we might be able to make it to Vegas by eight o'clock tonight." She leaped out of bed with a whoop of excitement and ran into the bathroom. I followed her into the shower, where once again we had to curb our natural inclinations in favor of expediency. We were out and dressed in record time, and it was decided that I would call Derek while she figured out what to wear for our wedding.

"Derek, it's Merlin," I said as he answered his phone. "There's been a change of plans for tonight; Emily and I have decided to drive to Las Vegas and get married. You're family, and we want you to be there with us."

For a few moments there was dead silence, and then Derek yelled so loudly that I had to hold the phone away from my ear.

"Does this mean you approve?" I chuckled.

"Hell, yes, I approve and I am definitely comin' with you. This is the biggest event in history! 'Merlin the Enchanter, the world's oldest bachelor, finally ties the knot.' If I was a reporter, what a story that would make," Derek laughed excitedly.

"I hope you're alone, because that statement could cause some problems," I said, so happy I almost didn't care. Almost.

"Yeah, I'm alone. I'm in the office today and everyone else is out in the field—quite a coincidence if you ask me," Derek said happily. "I'm sure I can take the rest of the day and all of tomorrow off. What time are you leavin'?"

"Emily is busy packing a few things, and I need to go to the shop and pick up Michael's passport and birth certificate, and something to wear. Be here by one o'clock if you can." I ended the call, thinking of the new clothes that I had just bought, not realizing that I would get married in them.

All of a sudden I experienced a rush of anxiety and self-doubt. *By the gods, what was I doing? I was on a quest, we all were, and this seemed to be a huge detour from that path. Wasn't it? Would being married to me put Emily in greater danger?*

Was I being incredibly selfish? My destiny was to bring Arthur back; was marrying Emily the right thing to do? I just stood there, thinking and frowning, and didn't hear Emily until she walked up to me, hands on her hips, her face determined, and said "Hey, old man, what's the problem, having second thoughts? Don't want to dilute the bloodline by marrying an Elf? Time to man up! If I can marry some crusty old wizard—oh, sorry, sorcerer—then you can marry the Fae park ranger, got it? Seriously, Merlin, I know exactly what you're thinking—you're worried that I'll be in more danger as your wife. Not possible. We've known each other for only a few months and I've been in danger every second. You attract trouble like a damn magnet! But I've survived because I'm a strong woman, and because you've protected me and cared for me. Now, thanks to you, I've accepted that I'm, at least to some extent, a supernatural being, and once I start accessing my own powers, I can help *you*, and protect *you,* the man I love. Okay?"

I stood there staring at her, this amazing, powerful woman that I had fallen in love with, and I smiled. "Okay." My life would never be the same.

CHAPTER 28
July 6

BEFORE WE LEFT for Las Vegas, I had managed some time alone to take care of a few things: I put a note on the shop door saying that we would be out of town for a few days, I grabbed my documents and my clothing, and I stopped in at the jewelry store. I found the perfect gold band, upon which I magically engraved special protection symbols for my soon-to-be wife. I made it back to the house just as Derek pulled up. We managed to squeeze ourselves and our luggage into Emily's little car, and we left town in a flurry of laughter and anticipation.

As I had their undivided attention during the trip, I took the opportunity to instruct my two apprentices in the basic use and etiquette of magic. Whomever wasn't driving would practice focusing and creating simple spells. Doing this in the car was definitely risky, but we didn't have time to waste. Emily wasn't having much success and was becoming frustrated at her inability to access her magic. Perhaps the use of Fae magic required a totally different approach. I finally suggested that she spend her time focusing on her inner light, on her Fae self, and just becoming comfortable with it. Also, I instructed her in a few simple techniques of meditation to help her relax and focus inside.

I was careful to monitor both of them, but especially Derek, as he was advancing so rapidly that he was getting cocky. Once, at a rest stop, Derek started a grass fire behind the building, luckily out of sight of others. *"Extinguo,"* I muttered, flicking my fingers at the flames. I knew that he needed more training and practice, out in the open where he couldn't hurt anything as he experimented with his growing powers, but he would have to wait until we found the appropriate spot.

Several times during the trip, I found myself grinning when I thought about our little group; we were on the way to becoming a true family. And I could hardly contain the joy and excitement I felt at the prospect of being married to Emily. But it did feel strange, when I thought about the fact that she was only twenty-eight years old, and I had been alive for almost 1600 years. People saw an unchanging façade, and my body hadn't aged past my thirty-second year, but in my mind, in my thoughts, I sometimes felt my true age. And now I was marrying someone young enough to be my daughter—or my many times removed great-granddaughter. When she looked at me, she saw someone only slightly older than herself, and although she professed to understand my nature, I wasn't sure that she truly did. We had a chance to talk alone during one of our stops, when Derek was practicing a spell in an open area behind the restroom.

I gently caught Emily's hand in mine and we walked to a secluded spot, out of sight of the building and the parking lot. We were standing under a tree at the edge of a grassy area, and the air was fragrant with the scent of pine trees and warm earth. I looked into her eyes and said, "Are you absolutely sure you want to bind yourself to me for all time? I am so much older than you, Emily. When I decided to sleep through the centuries awaiting Arthur's return, I was already in my fifties. Also, understand that the marriage of two beings such as we are will not be the same as for normal people, who may decide later that they cannot make it work and walk away from each other. We will be mated for life in the eyes of the gods. There may be trials such as you have never before experienced. *Please* be sure you can live with this decision." I paused, looking at her seriously, then said, "But know that even if you were to change your mind now, I would still love you forever."

Emily tilted her head and said with a smile, "I Saw your inner being, Merlin. I understand how old you really are, and it makes no difference to me. I also Saw your wisdom, your compassion, and your dedication to Arthur and all that he stands for. I Saw how much you love Derek. And I Saw how much you love

181

me. Yes, there is a place in you that is dark, dangerous, and very scary, but I think that everyone has a dark side to one extent or another. You choose to wield your power in pursuit of an ideal in a way that no one has ever done before. I admire you and love you, and I do want to be married to you, mated with you, for the rest of my life." Her eyes filled with tears as she pledged herself to me.

We suddenly realized that Derek had been quietly standing behind us and had heard everything we'd said, and we turned to him rather self-consciously.

"I think you two just said your weddin' vows. The rest of this trip is just a formality," Derek said quietly.

I nodded my head and did what felt right. I pulled the ring case out of my pocket, took the ring into my hand and slipped it onto her finger. "I take you, Emily, as my wife, in the sight of the gods."

"And I take you as my husband, Merlin, forever." Emily surprised me by putting a ring on my finger also. I hadn't realized that she had one to give me. As I watched, the ring glowed and molded itself to fit my finger perfectly.

As I gazed at the intricately-worked silver and gold ring and sensed the special magic in it mesh with my own power, a feeling of inevitability came over me. "This must have belonged to your Fae ancestor, Emily," I said.

"Yes, I believe it did," she said. "I found it in my jewelry box and I knew it was for you."

We gazed into each other's eyes, kissed each other gently and it was done. We had not planned on conducting our marriage ceremony at a rest stop, and we would still need to observe the formalities in Vegas, but the gods had obviously decided it was time.

And this bond, forged by the gods, was like having a woven strand of gold and steel running between us, heart to heart, ring to ring, invisible to the eye but solid and real nevertheless. No civil ceremony could be more real then the marriage of our souls, witnessed and approved of by the gods themselves.

Without speaking, the three of us walked back to the car, and we continued our journey.

We arrived in Las Vegas around eight o'clock that night, just as we'd planned, and I was immediately overwhelmed by the negative energy being produced in this city of debauchery. The artificial lights turning night into day, the undisguised evidence of crime and corruption, and the general air of unreality made me realize that this place was aptly nicknamed Sin City. I made a concerted effort to center myself, to tap into the peace and harmony in my soul, so that I could focus on the reason we came here—my marriage to Emily Crandall. Neither of my companions seemed to be bothered by this gaudy, unruly place, so I kept my observations and opinions to myself.

As we discussed where we should stay, Derek suggested the Excalibur, and although it would seem a likely choice, I could not abide its pretenses, compared with the real Camelot I had known and loved. I finally made the decision to stay at the Bellagio as it was an oasis in the midst of chaos; quieter and more appropriate for our purposes. Derek and Emily both protested that they couldn't afford such an expensive hotel, but I insisted. "This is where I would like to stay. There is no need for either of you to be concerned about the cost. I will take care of it," I said firmly. I had never revealed to either of them how much money I actually had, but when I paid for our rooms from a wallet thick with hundred-dollar bills, it was obvious that The Moab Herbalist was not the only source of my income.

We settled into our adjoining suites, Emily and me in the larger one and Derek in the other. Having decided that a meal was next on the agenda, we freshened up and changed into our wedding clothes, as we intended to find a chapel and "officially" get married after dinner.

We chose a nice restaurant right in the hotel and celebrated our union with champagne. As we munched appetizers and enjoyed each other's company, we talked about our decidedly unique situation.

"Derek, never in my life could I have imagined that you and I would end up being *related*, in a roundabout way, but I've always felt very close to you—much more than a friend," Emily said.

"I know, I've felt that way about you too, Em."

"I wonder if we really are related. My ancestors and yours came from England. I think I'm going to research it when I have the chance."

"But right now we're here for you to marry your 'knight in shining armor'," Derek said softly.

"Yes, I am." Emily looked at me with her heart in her eyes.

I smiled lovingly at the beautiful woman beside me, and then shifted my gaze to my descendant, whom I cherished. I recognized how truly fortunate I was.

I didn't want to ruin the mood, but I felt it necessary to return to the topic that was uppermost on my mind. "The three of us have a unique destiny to fulfill together, and I'm confident that we will prevail. I just wanted to say that I'm extremely proud of both of you for having made that commitment." We all reached out for each other's hands and gripped them tightly for a moment, acknowledging the bond we shared.

The server approached our table with a large tray, and soon we were enjoying our prime rib dinners.

I took a sip of champagne and looked over at Derek, who seemed perplexed about something.

"Derek, is something bothering you?" I asked curiously.

"Merlin, I feel kind of funny askin', and you can tell me to mind my own business, but where did you get the money?" Derek asked.

I just smiled. To me, money was a tool, to be used to support my life, and now the lives of my wife and my great-grandson, and it was not important to me in any other way. I had noticed that people living in the twenty-first century were so focused on wealth, or the lack thereof, that it controlled their lives.

"Before I entered the Crystal Cave with the intention of sleeping the centuries away, I had to ensure that I would have adequate resources at my disposal in the times to come, so I cached away precious metals and gemstones to be used in support of my future needs, as well as to support the caretakers of my estate. By the standards of this era, I am quite wealthy, but I do not like to advertise that fact, and I do not let that wealth control my life."

Derek looked dazed as he listened to my explanation. "Oh, okay…"

"So that's how you could afford all this," Emily said, indicating the hotel, the restaurant and the champagne. "I don't care how much money you have; I just wondered."

I laughed quietly and said, "Em, I know you aren't marrying me for my money—you just like my magic."

She leaned over and whispered in my ear, "Among other things," and kissed me.

It was late when we went outside to watch the famous water fountains. I loved the show and couldn't resist adding a little extra sparkle to the lights, unbeknownst to the hundreds of onlookers lining the sidewalk. Emily pulled me away after I decided to change some of the lights into glowing animal shapes and people were starting to point and exclaim about the weird phenomenon.

"God, I can't take you anywhere," she chuckled as she scolded me. "Stop with the magic, will you?"

I laughed at her audacity and reached for her hand as we turned to stroll along the sidewalk. Derek stayed back a little to give us some privacy, until a few minutes later when we heard him clear his throat and say, "Look at where we are, you two."

We looked up at the sign in front of us that said Marriage Licenses—with an arrow pointing the way into a well-lit office.

Emily looked at me questioningly. "Ready, magic man? I've got our paperwork in my purse…"

"I'm ready," I said, and we all walked into the building.

We completed the forms, paid the fee, and were given our license; now we just needed to find a chapel. We had removed our rings temporarily so that we could officially slip them on each other's fingers at the ceremony, but until then, Derek had them for safekeeping.

And we found the perfect place in the next block, a little chapel in the shape of a castle. There were flowers available to purchase, which we did, and we stood in front of the minister gazing into each other's eyes, remembering the vows we had already made that had truly bound us to each other.

"You look exceeding beautiful tonight, Emily," I said softly, admiring the sleek, form-fitting dress she had chosen to wear as our lives were joined. It was the color of fresh cream, complementing her hair and skin tone perfectly, and she was wearing simple gold jewelry, creating an elegant effect. Her hair was loose and the golden brown waves flowed around her shoulders. Her make-up was applied lightly and tastefully. She was the most gorgeous woman I had ever seen.

"And you are an extremely handsome man, Michael," Emily replied, letting her eyes roam appreciatively over my body from head to toe. I was glad I was wearing the silvery gray dress shirt and black slacks that I had purchased recently.

"Are the two of you ready to be joined in Holy Matrimony?" The minister asked kindly.

"Yes," we said in unison.

We went through the brief, simple ceremony, accepted the rings from Derek, and carefully slipped them back on each other's fingers. Then, arms entwined, we kissed one another thoroughly. I found myself wishing that Arthur and Guinevere were present to see this confirmed bachelor become a married man.

When the minister said "May I present Mr. and Mrs. Michael Merlin Reese," I felt a quick jolt of disappointment that I had to use someone else's name. But I couldn't very well have given my full real name, Merlin Ambrosius, for the marriage license. At least I had been able to magically insert the name Merlin into the documents before we left Moab.

As we turned away from the minister, Derek raised his phone and took several pictures of us, and promised he would enlarge and frame the best one as a wedding present.

We left the chapel and walked slowly back to the Bellagio. Emily and I still had our arms around each other, and Derek was walking next to Emily.

I could tell that Derek was about to ask yet another question. He'd been reading the old stories again, and I knew from the look on his face that he was pondering the inconsistencies.

"Merlin, I need to ask you somethin'. Accordin' to the legends, Nimue was a young sorceress who was your lover when you got older, and she basically drained you of your powers and then entombed you in the cave. Was any of that true? Could she do that in the future?" Derek asked worriedly.

"I remember Nimue well, and although I did have sexual relations with her once when I was very young, we were never *lovers*. Derek, you see me today as I appeared then—I never 'got older,' at least in appearance. Nimue possessed powerful magic as a priestess of the old religion, and she did turn it against me, but as I'm sure you have noticed, I still have my powers. And I have never been entombed, except by my own hand. She will never again be able to hurt anyone. She is dead."

"What happened to her?" Derek asked, still curious.

"I would rather not say. It's an unpleasant story, and I do

187

not wish to tarnish tonight's happiness by talking anymore about it now. I promise that I will tell you as we drive home, because you do need to know about her."

"Alright, Merlin, I can respect that. And I apologize for bringin' up such a disagreeable topic tonight. I'll wait to hear what you have to say when we're on the way home," Derek said with a smile.

We continued to walk and apparently he was appeased, at least temporarily, as there were no more questions forthcoming. I was grateful for that, because even mentioning her name caused shivers of dread to snake down my spine, and this special night was not hers—it was mine.

I kissed my wife's cheek and she leaned against me as we walked, fitting perfectly under my arm.

CHAPTER 29
July 6-7

WE FINALLY REACHED the hotel and went up to our rooms. Tired, but feeling a glow of happiness as I held Emily's hand, I suggested that the three of us meet for breakfast in the morning in the hotel restaurant. We wished Derek a good night, and closed the connecting door, anxious to celebrate our wedding night.

And then we were alone for the first time since the gods had united us. I was struck by the fact that this wonderful young woman, whom I had known for such a short time, was now my wife. The thought that I would not be living in the Crystal Cave in the future gave me a slight feeling of loss, but I realized that it would still be available should the two of us ever need it for sanctuary.

An unexpected thought suddenly occurred to me: She would be the mother of my children. Then I felt a moment's uncertainty—would she *want* to have children with me? And I wondered if she were with child at this very moment. For some reason, I had not even considered the possibility that our intimate activities could have already created a new life.

I must have been staring at Emily with a startled, confused expression on my face, because she looked back at me with concern.

"Merlin, are you okay? You just got very pale all of a sudden. Why don't you sit down, honey?"

"I... I'm all right, Em, I just realized that we could have already started a family. Do you think that you are...?"

"Pregnant? No, I'm not pregnant, Merlin. We've had sex *many* times since we met, but you never asked me about it before. We have very reliable contraceptives in this century and I've been on birth control pills for about six months." She paused and said reassuringly, "I *would* like to have kids someday, though."

I was disappointed, but at the same time, relieved. It could be very difficult to continue with our quest if Emily was currently carrying our child. When the time was right, perhaps we would have a child together, but that time was in the future and in the hands of the gods. Right at this moment, it was time to celebrate our marriage.

I looked into my wife's eyes and smiled. "I will love you, Emily, even if we never have children. Being with you is all I really need." And I reached for her, kissing her gently, and began unfastening her dress. I slipped it off of her shoulders, then unhooked and removed her lacy bra, freeing her large, firm breasts.

"Oh, that's much better," she whispered as she stepped out of her dress and removed her panties, and then began unbuttoning my shirt. She got halfway through them and became impatient, pulling the shirt apart so the rest of the buttons flew off in all directions.

"Em, that was my new shirt," I complained half-heartedly.

"Fix it later with magic. Right now it's time to get naked, handsome," Emily murmured.

The rest of my clothing came off quickly and we stood together, holding and caressing each other.

"Merlin, I would like you to make love to me with your magic."

My eyes widened. "I don't know if I can do that without hurting you."

"I think you'll figure it out." She smiled mysteriously as she began running her hands over my chest, and a faint humming emanated from her throat. A soft glow and a slight tingling sensation came from her hands as she continued to caress me. There was magic in her touch and I gasped.

"You have accessed your powers," I said, feeling as if a thousand tiny ripples of sensation were racing across my skin. I groaned as the pleasurable sensation traveled downward to my groin.

"I felt it when we got married tonight—it's as if the official ceremony binding us together released my magic. I don't think I need spells to use it, at least for *this*." She took my hand and led me over to the bed, and we lay down, entwined in each other's arms, kissing and touching. We took our time, knowing that we had all night if we wished.

As I became more and more aroused I felt my own magic stir as well, and instead of keeping it in check as I would have done in the past, I allowed some of that energy to manifest on my bare skin. I pulled Emily beneath me and kissed her mouth, her neck, her shoulders, and with every contact tiny sparks danced. She stopped humming for a moment as she gasped, moaning with pleasure as she felt my magic caress her breasts and her belly; in fact, every place our bodies touched. Then she reached down and kneaded my buttocks, causing a jolt of energy to flow through my body. It felt so good I inhaled sharply.

Emily started humming again, slowly increasing the volume until it almost sounded like she was singing, and the intensity of our passion reached such a point that waiting was not an option. My erection was almost painful I was so aroused, and I said to Emily hoarsely, "Open for me now, Em." She did, and I pushed slowly inside her until I was buried to the hilt. "Ohhh!" she gasped, as she stiffened and quivered with excitement.

I remained still inside her, maintaining that small amount of magical energy throughout my body. I had never done this before, but it seemed almost as natural as breathing to combine it with lovemaking.

The experience went far beyond anything I had ever known, and I could tell from the look of ecstasy on Emily's face that she was feeling the same way.

Finally I started to move, one long stroke after another, until we approached the pinnacle together and went over the top, and as we both climaxed, we literally generated fireworks. Our bodies glowed with light, and so much magical energy was released that we had a repeat performance of our first time together, only with more intensity. Everything in the suite made of glass shattered, belongings flew out of drawers, chairs crashed against the wall...and our joined bodies floated into the air.

We heard Derek frantically pounding on the door adjoining the two suites, but neither of us could speak.

So I communicated with Derek in a fashion that I had not done since Camelot: I projected my thoughts directly to his mind. *Derek, we're all right—just experiencing an overload of energy. We'll talk in the morning.*

He must have received my message, as the noise stopped immediately.

"Did you just do what I think you did? Did you send Derek a message telepathically?" Emily asked.

I grinned and projected to her, *Yes, I did.*

"Oh, my God, that is so absolutely awesome," she said excitedly. All of a sudden Em realized we were floating in the air above the bed.

"What the heck?" She was shocked to see the ceiling not far above my head.

I laughed, impressed at our combined skill, initiated subconsciously during our passionate interlude.

"Uh, honey, can you get us down please?"

I murmured, *"Descendere,"* and still joined, we descended gently to the bed below.

"Did your magic do that, Merlin? Levitate us, I mean?" She asked as we lay on our sides facing each other.

"Not entirely. You did at least *half* of the magic we just experienced together, without any training, just by using your intuition. You're amazing."

I gazed lovingly into her shining eyes. She grinned happily, relaxed and satisfied by our first joint magical experience, and the most incredible lovemaking we'd ever had.

"I like my new powers," Emily said softly as she sat up and leaned against the headboard. "I just feel what I want, and hum, and it happens."

I smiled, thrilled that my wife was so talented. I kissed her gently and got up off the bed, calling forth a light orb to illuminate the room so that we wouldn't step on the broken glass. I gave a flick of my wrist and started cleaning up the mess. "Think we'll have to forfeit the deposit on the room?" I laughed.

"Wait, Merlin, let me try," Emily said as she moved over to the edge of the bed. She looked at the broken glass near the bedside table, and then at the wastebasket, hummed that unusual sound, and glass fragments began to float obediently into the bin. When the glass was cleaned up, she looked at me and shook her head. "Why did I not want this?"

I glanced down at her. "Emily, I learned that I had magic when I was a child, and long ago accepted that it was a part of me. Less than three months ago, before we met, you did not know that magic even existed, let alone that you had magic yourself. You had no idea who you really were. So it's not surprising that you were afraid and resisted the unknown. And now, sweet woman, whether you are ready for it or not, your life has changed forever." I used magic to finish righting the furniture and to put away our things, and then sat back down on the bed next to Emily. The orb I had created continued to float above us, emanating a soft glow of light, and I noticed her looking at it speculatively.

"I expect you can do the same," I said. "You may not even need a spell to do it—technically *I* don't really need to use a spell either, it's just habit. Perhaps you can use your will, and hum or sing it into existence."

"I'd like to try it," she said, and closed her eyes, her forehead wrinkling slightly as she concentrated.

I was fascinated. I had never spent any time with a Fae being, and now I was married to one. Although Emily's connection was very distant, it was obviously enough to enable her to wield the Elven magic.

She began to speak in a Voice and a language I had never heard before; it had to be that of the Elven people. I was mesmerized—how could she know it? Could she have obtained it from her inner link to her heritage? Could she have learned it solely through her intuition?

She slowly opened her eyes, which looked like liquid silver in the soft light, and then a glow appeared suspended in the air in front of her, casting a myriad of colors across her face. It almost looked like her ears had changed shape just a little bit.

She gently waved her hand and the glowing rainbow moved to hover over the lamp.

"Well done, my dear," I said proudly.

She calmly looked over at me, then grinned happily. "Hot damn, that was *fun.*"

I smiled. "Now our work can truly begin. Both you and Derek have magical abilities that you are learning to control. You and I are united by marriage, in the eyes of all, and together it is possible that our powers will be magnified."

I leaned over and brushed a few strands of hair away from her face, then gently caressed her cheek and kissed her full lips. "I love you, Emily," I said, my voice thick with emotion.

"I know you do, magic man, and I would do anything for you," she said softly.

"You may have to," I said solemnly.

CHAPTER 30
July 7

THE NEXT MORNING at breakfast Derek confronted us about our energetic activities of the night before.

"I thought you didn't appreciate hearing all of the details of our love life, Derek," Emily teased.

"No, I don't want to hear the details of *hmmm*, certain...*ah*, things, but I do think I deserve to know why I was so rudely awakened by chairs bein' flung against the walls and the sound of glass breakin'," he said self-righteously, although I heard the humor in his voice.

"I don't think you could have gone to sleep that quickly, Der. But, let's just say that when we included a little magic in our lovemaking, we didn't realize how powerful our combined energy would be, or we would have tried to tone it down a little," Emily smirked.

"You know, that is way too much information," Derek complained.

"Well, you asked."

"Listen, you two, I have an idea. Why don't we find a suitable spot for you to practice your magic for a couple of hours before we arrive back in Utah? You can work on the spells that include fire and wind; spells that we definitely don't want anyone to see you practicing. Perhaps in that corner of Arizona that we drove through on the way down?"

They agreed that it sounded like a good plan, and we headed out of Las Vegas happily chatting about various spells and other magical topics. We drove on until we reached just the right location and piled out of the car. We found an area that was blocked from view of the highway and started working.

Some time later, we concluded a successful training session, during which I taught both of them how to extinguish their own flames, and put an end to an out-of-control whirlwind, among other things.

As we were walking back to the car I happened to notice an old oak tree that recently had lost a large branch. I found a suitable length of wood and trimmed it with my dagger, feeling sure that this would be appropriate for Derek's staff. The fact that this was not the type of terrain that normally supported oaks led me to believe it was special and we were meant to find it. We wedged the staff into the car and continued on our way.

We had been back on the road for some time and I was driving, when a curious feeling came over me. I had been thinking about the wonder of our wedding night and the joy of being with my wife, and I could not imagine why I was feeling so strange and light-headed. It was not the feeling of dread and doom that I had become familiar with when an attack by the dark practitioner was imminent, but more like a dizzying feeling of inevitability and expectation; not unlike the feeling I've had just before experiencing a vision of some magnitude.

Derek happened to look over at me as I was close to passing out. "Merlin, pull over *now*."

I immediately pulled off the road, and was barely able to stop the car and turn off the engine before the blackness overtook me. Faintly, I could hear both Derek and Emily calling to me urgently, and I could feel Em's hands on me, then all sensation ceased.

As if from a great distance came a familiar voice, one that I had not heard for more than 1500 years.

"Merlin, listen now, the time is soon approaching when you will come to me, and together we will create the new Albion, a new nation for all the people of the world, not just Britons."

As the voice continued, a face gradually materialized, then an entire form, so dear to me that my heart swelled with joy.

"Arthur, my friend, I have missed you so," I said, as we seemed to stand together in a soft white light that emanated from everywhere at once. A red dragon emblazoned upon Arthur's chest, shadow armor encased our "bodies" lending an even more surreal aspect to the encounter.

"And I have missed you sorely as well, old friend," Arthur said.

"Where are we, Arthur?"

"I am still in the Fae realm at Avalon, and physically, you are still in the mortal world of the twenty-first century. Together, our spirits are in the Other World while we have this brief conversation. And brief it must be, for the Fae have warned me that because of your unique nature, being the son of the Welsh god Llyr and a mortal woman, your spirit must not be separated from your body for long. Too long a separation and you would be unable to return, and thus you could not serve me, nor aid the mortal world.

"Listen carefully, Merlin. You are going to experience more severe and frequent attacks by your nemesis, and these attacks will affect the people you are now connected to: Derek, Emily and others who will soon join you in the quest, others you have known in the distant past and who have returned to serve you. They are in great danger. I wish I could tell you who this foe is, but it is not within my power to do so. I can say one thing more—this is an enemy with two faces; one you thought you had vanquished long ago, and one who will seem familiar to you but whom you have never met. Be warned, and be most careful. I must go now Merlin, my loyal friend. Until we are together again, be well, and may your marriage be all that you have wished for."

And with that statement, Arthur's glowing image faded away, as did the ethereal light.

I was left in the darkness, alone, and I realized that I

couldn't breathe.

Suddenly I was retching and coughing, taking great gulps of air as I heard cries and shouts near me. My eyes flew open and I realized that I was lying on the rough ground of the road shoulder, next to the open car door. Derek and Emily, pale and frightened, were on the ground next to me and had been trying to revive me. They helped me sit up and both held me close. Emily sobbed, "Merlin, we thought you were *dead*!"

I blinked, took a deep breath and let it out slowly, then gathered my wife in my arms to comfort her. "My love, I'll be all right, I'm not dead. You need to stop worrying about me so," I said gently, as I stroked her back and then wiped her tears with my shirt. She began to calm down as her natural resilience enabled her to recover from this traumatic experience, and she helped Derek to get me up off the ground. I finally started feeling normal again and was able to stand by myself.

I was afraid that other vehicles would soon be stopping to see if we needed help. "We should get back in the car quickly and leave this place. We cannot draw too much attention to ourselves, especially now." I instructed Derek to take over the driving as I walked carefully around to the passenger seat, asking Em to sit in back as I did so.

Derek glanced at me as he prepared to merge back onto the highway and said, "You scared the crap out of us, Merlin. What the hell happened to you?"

"I thought I was going to be a widow before I had a chance to be a wife," Emily said with a catch in her voice, as she reached over the back of the seat to smooth my hair and touch my shoulder. I patted her hand, then squeezed it gently.

As we joined the northbound traffic and Derek set the cruise control, I decided not to wait any longer to share my experience. I wondered if they would believe me. Over and over again in the past few weeks I had been pushing them too hard, and I couldn't help but feel that they both had reached the limits of their acceptance.

"I'm sorry that you both were frightened, but I had no control over what happened. My spirit was called from my body, drawn to the Other World at the behest of King Arthur, who had information to impart to me. We will be called to the quest very soon, and in the meantime, we have been warned most urgently to beware of future attacks, which will increase in both frequency and strength."

Neither Emily nor Derek had responded, and as I glanced from one to the other I saw the astonishment and disbelief on both of their faces. And it occurred to me how young they were, how many changes they had both been through lately, and how ill-prepared they were for this quest. War was brutal and they had no idea what was coming or how to handle it. How could I have thought that a few days or even weeks of training in the magical arts would be enough to enable them to survive, both mentally and physically?

I closed my eyes, suddenly tired and a little discouraged. "You don't believe me, do you?"

There was dead silence. It dragged on a moment too long.

"Yes, of course we do, Merlin, but I think both Derek and I need to feel more connected to this quest before it truly becomes real for us. Right, Derek?"

Derek took his eyes off the road for a moment. "Pretty much. I'm sorry, Merlin. I hope you're not too disappointed in us."

I opened my eyes and glanced back at Derek, then looked over my shoulder at my young wife. Both of them had worried looks on their faces, and it was obvious that they both felt guilty for "failing" me.

Oh, gods, compared to my age and experience, they were both children. I was the one who had let *them* down by not preparing them more thoroughly. Their disbelief could be a way to cope with something they couldn't comprehend.

"No, this is not your fault; it is entirely mine, and I am going to rectify the situation, if I can. Why don't you pull off at the next rest area, Derek, and I will take care of *part* of the problem right away."

"What are you going to do, Merlin?" Emily drew back from me, a little frown of apprehension on her face.

"Emily, are you and Derek...*afraid* of me?" I asked incredulously.

"Merlin, you're my husband and I love you, but sometimes you can be one scary dude." Emily gave me a quick grin, but there was anxiety in her voice.

"I think it's more like having a healthy respect for the most powerful bein' in the world, even if he is a relative," Derek said seriously.

I hardly knew what to say that could convey my feelings adequately. "I am sorry that *I* have failed *you*, and it won't happen again. I have been so self-absorbed that I haven't taken into account that you don't have the knowledge or the experience to deal with this." I felt terrible that I had not realized this before, and yet they had trusted me enough to continue forward blindly even so.

"Hey, Merlin, there's a rest area up ahead and it looks like we'll have the place to ourselves," Derek exclaimed.

"Good, then that's where we'll stop."

We sat at a picnic table under the trees as far from the parking lot as possible, just in case other travelers arrived. I glanced back and forth between Emily and Derek. "First of all, I think I have figured out who the dark practitioner is. I can't tell you what her ultimate goal is yet, but I will discover the answer soon, I promise you."

"The dark practitioner is a woman?" Emily looked surprised.

"Yes. I firmly believe that our nemesis is Nimue. Derek

asked about her the other night and it is time for me to relate that story." I swallowed and closed my eyes for a moment, preparing myself to relive a part of my past that still haunted me.

"She was the bane of my existence for years. The tales about her that have come down through the centuries have been distorted so much that her true nature has never been accurately recorded. As with many myths and folk tales, the truth has been subverted to make the stories more acceptable for families and for children, when in reality she was so evil that no sane person should want to hear of her. Nimue was physically the most beautiful woman I had ever seen, tall and voluptuous, with rich brown hair and blue eyes, and like many men before me, I had been drawn to that physical beauty, only to discover that beneath the surface was a monster. Not in the sense of a supernatural creature, but a being who chose to thrive upon the pain and suffering of others. She was a sorceress, perhaps partly human, most likely the offspring of a cruel god. I had met her when I was in my fifteenth year and she was in her twentieth, before I had started serving Arthur's father, Uther Pendragon, and both my passion and my magic were highly volatile. The fact that we both had powerful magic had drawn us together as much as the sexual attraction, and she was able to hide her ugliness from me at first. I had never had relations with a woman, and when it appeared that she wanted me as much as I wanted her, despite the difference in our ages, I did not think, I just reacted. It was an exciting experience at first, but as soon as my ardor cooled, my magical senses showed me the truth, and I could not leave her fast enough. My rejection triggered a hatred so deep in her that for many years she tried to take her revenge. Even though there had never been any commitment spoken between us, she could not forgive me for what she saw as a betrayal. She pursued me relentlessly for years, during the time I served King Uther and into the years I was with Arthur. Finally, one day when I was visiting my old teacher, Gaius, she caught me with my guard down and almost killed us both. She tried to steal my powers, but somehow I was able to recover enough to use them against her, calling down a bolt of lightening that killed her. At least, I *thought* that I had killed her." I sat staring into the distance, lost in thought, then roused myself to finish the tale.

"About a month ago—in fact it was the night we returned from seeing Emily in the hospital—I went to bed and had a disturbing dream about Arthur, which would not have been that unusual, except that at the end, a voice said 'You will not escape me this time, Merlin...'"

"And that's when you realized who it was?" Derek asked.

"Not at first. I had been so certain that I had killed her that I just couldn't entertain the notion that she was still alive. But there can really be no other explanation. I have thought about every one of the attacks that has occurred since I awakened. Every time there has been a small but recognizable 'signature' that points inexorably to Nimue: the style and execution of the magic definitely points to her, as well as the sheer doggedness with which she has pursued me. She has played with me like a mountain lion with its prey." Gods, I could not believe it had taken me so long to realize the truth.

"Of course, I have not really worked out all the details, such as how she escaped being destroyed by a bolt of lightning, and what her ultimate goal is, but I no longer have any doubts that she is our true enemy."

"Okay, this information does help to clarify things, but I think what Derek and I need most is to learn more about Arthur, and what really transpired when you were...*uh*...unconscious for so long," Emily said carefully.

Startled, I stared at her. "But I was only with Arthur for a few seconds, a minute at most."

Derek traded glances with Emily. "Merlin, you weren't breathin,' man. We'd been trying to resuscitate you for at least twenty minutes. That's why Emily was so upset—you were *dead!* And then you came back to life…"

My heart was pounding in my chest as I finally let go and accepted the truth that had been in the depths of my being all along: I was the son of a god and I truly was immortal. Even if I died, I would come back and live again and again. Forever. My inability to totally accept my true nature had always been my weakness and Nimue had known this. Well, time to face the reality that Emily and Derek already suspected—I had special gifts because I had inherited them from a god. They had both Seen what I truly was but could only interpret that information through their own limited experience. Every time I retreated into that white light inside of me, I was with the gods *because I belonged there.* And now that I was no longer trying to deny my real self, I knew that I would start remembering everything.

I closed my eyes and saw, just for a second, a wise face that looked remarkably like my own, smiling. And I knew that I had just seen my father. Finally, I opened my eyes and smiled at Emily and Derek, who must have thought I was demented, as they had just informed me that I had died.

Emily frowned suspiciously and said, "Honey, what in the hell is going on?"

"Touch me," I said gently but firmly, and held out my hands to them, "I will show you what I experienced while I was 'dead,' and what you need to see and hear for yourselves. Close your eyes, and open your minds and hearts to me now."

The three of us held each other's hands tightly in as much of a circle as we could create while seated at the rough picnic table. It didn't matter—it was enough. I could feel the energy humming through us as the marital bond I shared with Emily, the ancestral bond I had with Derek, and the bond of friendship we all had with each other created a magical connection that surged between us. I closed my eyes and took control of the flow of magic and directed my memories into their minds. I could feel their amazement and awe as they experienced the meeting with Arthur, and heard his words confirming my heritage. They knew that he truly existed in the Other World, in the realm of spirit, and that someday he was destined to return to the human realm, uniting all people in a global Albion.

I finally released the connection and relinquished their hands. I opened my eyes to see the stunned looks on both of their faces. All three of us had tears in our eyes from the intensity of emotion involved in the experience.

"Merlin, you're actually the son of the god, Llyr?" Derek asked as he self-consciously wiped the tears away.

"Yes, the Welsh god of magic and healing is my father," I said, marveling that I could say it so easily.

"In Greek mythology, the offspring of a god and a mortal is called a demi-god. That must be what you are, Merlin," Emily said, as she tried to make sense of what she had witnessed.

"I suppose you are right, Em," I said. "And I had a vision of my father; I look just like him."

"I hope some day I can meet him, Merlin. You know, this makes *so* much more sense than your father being a demon! I'll bet you anything that Nimue is the offspring of the demon god, and that her influence caused you to fear that *you* were."

Emily was very perceptive, and it seemed logical that at some point Nimue had begun to poison my thinking, undermining my entire belief system. And I thought I knew when it had started—it was the day she almost took my powers from me. To get them back I had to literally pull them out of her, apparently with some of her thoughts and memories attached. All the times I had succumbed to a bitter anger and thought myself the offspring of a demon, were of her doing.

I arose from the bench and stretched, throwing my head back and breathing a deep sigh of relief. I felt as if I'd put down a heavy burden, one that I had carried unknowingly for most of my life. My spirits soared and I thought, *Perhaps I **can** fly*.

I heard Emily walk up behind me, and I smiled. I turned and slipped my arms around my lovely wife, and she tilted her face for my kiss, which I returned passionately. Had we been alone and out of sight we might have continued on to the obvious conclusion. But we were not, and it was time to drive on.

CHAPTER 31
July 7

WE FINALLY ARRIVED in Moab after seven o'clock that evening, tired and hungry. We decided on Pasta Ray's for dinner, so we parked the car in front of the restaurant, went inside and waited for the hostess to seat us.

Immediately, the noise level dropped as all eyes turned towards us. This was most alarming, as the three of us should not have attracted undue attention simply by entering the room. Emily said silently, knowing that I could hear her thoughts, *I think that people are looking at* you *Merlin. You just came back from the dead a few hours ago, and you seem to be glowing a little bit.*

I looked down at myself and noticed that my aura was indeed brighter than normal, although I was surprised that all the patrons in the restaurant would notice it at the same time. I reached inside myself and deliberately dampened the glow so that it would be visible no longer. Then, I carefully glanced around the room and realized that people's attention had already drifted back to their plates and to their dinner companions. Except for one individual in the corner.

As the hostess came to show us to our table, I was able to glance in his direction without staring directly at him. His eyes followed me as we walked to our table. I sat down where I could watch him, as I had no idea what to expect. I sensed no magical threat, no underlying power, although he did look vaguely familiar to me, perhaps from one of my sessions at the shop. Quite muscular and fit, the fellow had shoulder-length blond hair, and he appeared to be about thirty-five years of age. He looked tired and careworn, as if he had known a hard life, but his eyes were bright with hope and unanswered questions.

After our server had taken our orders and walked away from the table, I said quietly, "I have a feeling that before the night is out, we will be welcoming someone new to our circle. Remember, Arthur indicated that there are others whom I have known before who are meant to join the quest, but who may not be consciously aware of it. I had not considered the possibility before, but what if the Knights of the Round Table have been reborn in this century?"

Emily asked, "Would they even remember their true identities?"

"I don't know, Emily, but I think we will find out."

A few minutes later, I looked up to find that the man from the corner was walking towards us with a determined smile on his face.

I smiled politely back at him. "We are about to have company," I said to Emily and Derek. I deliberately avoided making prolonged eye contact, but I was beginning to sense something special about him and wanted to know more.

"Uh, hello, I apologize for interrupting, but I felt that I should come over and introduce myself. You're Michael Reese from The Moab Herbalist, correct? My name is Ryan Jones, and I've attended your evening storytelling sessions a couple of times." Each word was an effort for him, as if he wasn't comfortable talking to me. But something inside of him made him continue. "Each session is very...entertaining, and I can't help but feel that you and I have known each other before...or something. It's the strangest feeling, like déjà vu." Ryan was clearly distressed but driven by a need he didn't understand.

"You're welcome to join us for dinner Ryan, if my companions have no objections. This is my lovely wife Emily and my cousin Derek Colburn," I said, introducing the two of them.

"It's nice to meet you, Ryan. We would be happy to have you join us," Emily said pleasantly.

"Yes, please do," Derek said, but I could tell he wasn't particularly interested in having a stranger sit down with us.

"It's nice to meet you both, but I've already eaten, thank

CARYL SAY

you anyway." Ryan was a little flustered, as if he was wondering what in the world he was doing. "I just wanted to say hello and to thank you for making my life a little brighter; especially the night you got so involved in your story that you began speaking in—what did you call it?—old British. I was amazed that you could be so fluent in what must be a dead language. But the funny thing was, it sounded *familiar* to me, I don't know how—*I'm* certainly no scholar. Anyway, it looks like they're bringing your food out now, so I'll let you eat in peace." Ryan started to walk away, but I decided we needed to speak with him away from the crowded restaurant.

I stood up and said, "Ryan, I'm pleased that you've enjoyed my evening sessions. I know it's late, but we're having a meeting at the shop in about an hour and hope you can join us. We think you'll be interested in what we have to say."

By this time the food was on the table, and I could see that both Emily and Derek were wondering what I was up to.

"Sure, I can be there about nine o'clock, is that alright?"

"That's fine, Ryan, see you then," I said, giving him a wave as he turned to leave. I sat back down and started eating my dinner. I was starving. The whole process of dying and coming back to life had most definitely affected my appetite.

"Merlin, what's up?" Derek said quietly. "Do you think Ryan could actually be one of King Arthur's knights?"

I swallowed some wine and used my napkin before answering. "I feel very strongly that he is, but I have to be able to touch him and look into his eyes, which I could not do in front of all these people," I said, excited at the possibility of reconnecting with one of my old friends.

Emily looked at me thoughtfully, as she took a sip of her wine. "You know, we could end up with a veritable army, Merlin."

"Yes. An army such as this century has never before seen."

208

CHAPTER 32
July 7 Evening

A FTER WE FINISHED EATING and I had paid the bill, we left the restaurant and headed for The Moab Herbalist, which was only a block away. Emily and Derek hadn't commented on the fact that I had paid for dinner again. They were getting used to it, I thought wryly.

The night was warm and the sidewalks were crowded with tourists looking for the perfect gifts for their friends and family at home.

As we neared the shop, we heard tires squealing and a car engine racing. Someone yelled frantically, "Watch out!" and I realized that a vehicle was out of control and coming right at us. If I didn't do something immediately, we, and all the other people on the sidewalk with us, would be crushed.

Instinctively, I summoned my power and slowed time, simultaneously creating an invisible shield in front of everyone that was in the path of the oncoming car. As I held the shield in place with my right hand, I extended my magic inside the car to surround the terrified occupants with a protective cushion of air.

As I allowed the flow of time to return to normal, the car hit the shield barrier, and the cushion of air buffered the force of the blow for the people in the car. I grabbed Derek and Emily and suddenly, we were inside the shop, having passed right through the wards and through the closed, locked door. As I stood with one hand on each of them, I felt exhilarated, having utilized my powers as never before.

As I let go of their arms, they both stared at me, and Derek exclaimed, "Holy shit! One second the car was almost on top of us, and the next, it was stopped, and no one was hurt. Merlin, you must have done that, but how? I didn't see you move. And how did we get in here without openin' the door first?"

209

"I slowed time and worked my magic in different ways simultaneously. And then I...teleported us into the shop," I said slowly. The magic that I had just performed felt familiar, and right, and yet I didn't remember having accomplished those particular feats previously.

"You did what?" Emily gasped, finally finding her voice.

"Dude, I didn't know you could do any of those things," Derek said admiringly.

"I didn't either," I said in amazement. And then I felt something happen in the depths of my being as the powers I had inherited from my father began to shift and grow. I stiffened as a stream of raw power rushed through me, then groaned aloud as an indescribable, almost painful sensation seemed to alter my consciousness. I went down on my knees, holding my head and gasping for breath.

"My God, Merlin, what just happened? Are you alright?" Emily exclaimed as she helped me to my feet.

"I think my magic is...evolving, now that I've unconditionally accepted my true nature," I said roughly. "And I think that what just happened on the street was a test, to force me to utilize those new powers."

Just then there was a knock at the door, and I realized it must be Ryan, coming to see us as planned.

"Em, start some coffee if you would, please, and Derek, turn on the overhead lights." I walked over to the door and released the wards before opening it.

"Hello, Ryan, please come in," I greeted him, and then closed and locked the door behind him

"Did you see what just happened right out in front of your shop? The brakes must have gone out in that car, and the driver lost control. It almost mowed down a group of people on the sidewalk!" Ryan exclaimed as he walked into the room, thinking about what he had just seen and totally unaware of the power that was pulsing through my body.

Covering with a lie, Derek responded, "Yeah, we heard a commotion outside but decided we'd better stay out of the way."

I led Ryan over to the comfortable chairs in the reading area, and we sat down. I was impatient to find out his true identity, but I did not want to frighten him.

"Ryan, we're happy you were able to join us. We know it's a little late in the evening but there's something we'd like to talk to you about."

Ryan looked around and realized that he was the only one there besides the three of us. I could tell he was starting to feel nervous.

"Would you like some coffee?" I asked, as Emily poured a cup for herself and one for Derek.

"Uh, no thank you, Michael. I wouldn't be able to sleep tonight if I had caffeine now," he said.

My wife raised an inquiring eyebrow. "I think I will decline also, Emily, but thank you," I said, smiling at her as she looked at me suspiciously. I never refused a cup of coffee, but I had a rather intense headache that appeared to originate from the power surge I had experienced.

Ryan looked at me anxiously. "Where is everyone? I thought you said you were having a meeting?"

"There is no one else coming, Ryan—this meeting is for you alone. Please don't be nervous. I will explain everything, but first I would like to ask about the comment you made at the restaurant. During my story about King Arthur and his Knights of the Round Table, when I began speaking old British, you felt a sense of familiarity about the story and the language. In other words, you had a feeling of déjà vu. What if I told you that this tale, along with many others I've told during my reading sessions, was true?"

Ryan looked dumbfounded. "Excuse me? How do you know?"

"Because I was there," I said. "And I believe you were there also, Ryan, in Camelot, in a previous life."

"What do you mean?" He said, alarmed. "This is crazy! Who the hell *are* you?"

He started to glance towards the door as if he intended to bolt. I knew I had to tell him now, or risk losing him altogether.

I asked, "My real name is Merlin."

"Your name is really Merlin, like King Arthur's Merlin?" Ryan said, confused and distressed.

"Ryan, I *am* King Arthur's Merlin, the sorcerer of his court, and it is possible that you were one of his knights."

I noticed Emily and Derek looking at each other smugly and I smiled, remembering their reactions when they found out who I was. I glanced at Ryan, who was staring at me in shock and confusion. I extended my hand to him and said, "Come, let us discover the truth together." His eyes were wide and frightened, and as he looked at my outstretched hand he said suspiciously, "I was a Knight of the Round Table? And you are the *original* Merlin, the same person who was alive all those centuries ago?"

"Yes, Ryan, I am he, and I have the ability to see into your past lives, if you will allow it," I said gently.

"I, uh, well, I guess." Ryan was so nervous he was shaking. "This is not what I expected to happen tonight. I feel like I'm dreaming...Merlin, how can you still be alive?"

"I am immortal, Ryan, but that is another story. Give me your hands, and we will determine who you once were. Please trust me, my friend."

Finally, Ryan reached out to me, and with both of his hands firmly clasped in my own, I Looked deeply into his eyes, and we began our inner journey. We traveled back through his past lives, one after the other, until finally we reached that very first spark of life, that defining moment of his soul's first adventure in human form. Together we witnessed his birth, his childhood, his adolescence and then his adult years as both friend and betrayer of King Arthur, lover and protector of Guinevere, and loyal knight and friend of mine… Lancelot.

And Ryan/Lancelot experienced *my* unique beginning, a childhood of confusion and magic as I grew up fatherless, eventually being brought before Vortigern to be used as a sacrifice. He witnessed my involvement with Nimue, then my service to Arthur's father Uther Pendragon, and on through the years with Arthur in Camelot. He also Saw my periods of waking and sleeping in the Crystal Cave, my arrival in Moab, my relationships with both Emily and Derek, and most recently, my encounters with Arthur and with my father, the god Llyr.

I slowly brought us back to our current selves and we stood looking at each other quietly for a moment. Then we came together with a shout and a hug and several comradely slaps on the back.

Like the sun emerging from behind a cloud, Lancelot's face shone as Ryan's persona fell away. "By the goddess, Merlin, my old friend, it is a wonder seeing you again! You look *exactly* the same as I remember, and now I know why. Gawain and I always thought that there was something different about you, other than your magic of course, but we never realized what you truly were."

"Yes, immortality does seem to be linked to being the offspring of a god," I said wryly, "although, since I have never met any others of my kind, I have no way to confirm that. You certainly look different in this incarnation, as Ryan Jones—I would never have known you without our journey together."

"That is true, Merlin, but my mind and my soul are the same, are they not? I live in this century as Ryan Jones, but I now remember who I really am: Lancelot."

I just smiled and turned to Derek and Emily, who were waiting impatiently for me to acknowledge them, and beckoned them closer.

"You met these two in the restaurant earlier, as Ryan, but now through our journey, you Saw who they really are. Emily and Derek, meet Lancelot, daring Knight and Champion of the Realm."

"Having had the privilege of seeing you through Merlin's eyes, I feel as if I've known you for many years," said Lancelot, as he smiled and graciously acknowledged them.

He glanced at me and then at Derek, and said, "The other knights and I had despaired of Merlin ever bedding a woman; we thought he was abstaining to protect his magic powers. But it seems that we were wrong, if you are indeed his descendant. Well met, sir! And it appears that you have inherited some of his magical abilities."

Derek grinned. "It's an honor to meet you, Sir Lancelot, and I look forward to standin' beside you in this battle, and on this quest for Arthur."

"The honor is mine, Derek," Lancelot said, then turned to Emily. "Finally, Merlin has married, and to the loveliest maiden I have ever seen. It is certainly an accomplishment, Lady Emily, for you to have captured the heart and soul of the greatest sorcerer who has ever lived—the immortal Merlin. I commend you, my dear." Lancelot reached for Emily's hand and raised it to his lips in a courtly gesture.

Emily blushed and smiled shyly, a testament to the power of the knight's charming ways.

"I'm pleased to meet you, Lancelot," she said.

Reluctantly, Lancelot released Emily's hand and after bowing to her, he turned to me and said, "Now, how may I serve you, Lord Merlin? Without magic at my beck and call, I am not certain exactly what I can do to help you in your time of need. But please be assured that I am at your service. I have gained many fighting skills over the course of my lifetimes, and I will use those skills to serve and protect all of you, in any way that I can. In my current life, as Ryan Jones, I have been trained in hand-to-hand combat—and I own firearms as well as a collection of old swords and crossbows, so in that way I am prepared to fight for you."

"The gods alone know what role any of us will truly play in the coming battle. We can only hope that we will be victorious, and guided truly in our quest to bring about Arthur's return," I said.

He gave me his cell phone number and said his good-byes, assuring us that we'd meet again soon. I turned slowly to Derek and Emily, knowing that they would undoubtedly have questions about what happened earlier. I realized that my headache had subsided, but I still felt the pressure of my new powers expanding inside my being, and it felt...unusual.

The two of them were now looking at me with varying degrees of excitement and awe, as if I had suddenly increased in stature in their eyes. And I admit to experiencing a certain amount of awe myself at my gift from the gods.

"Merlin, you are very different now than you were even two hours ago. This may sound strange, but it's as if you've suddenly become a superhero," Emily said as she walked up to me and put her hand on my chest, gazing adoringly into my eyes.

I stood still, looking at my wife's face shining with love and pride, vowing that I would be the hero that she saw in me.

Derek spoke up, "What you did with that car outside— that was freakin' *incredible*. You definitely seemed to have moved into a higher level of magic, and I'm afraid that it'll be impossible for me to keep up with you."

"Just stay true to yourself Derek, and always do your best, and no one can fault you for that," I said sincerely. "I don't know how to explain to you what happened earlier. As we were walking along, I heard the noise and saw that the car was out of control, and I intuitively knew what steps to take: Slow time, create a barrier and protect the people in the vehicle, then grab you two and get inside the shop as fast as possible. I never had to think about how to accomplish those things, and I never even thought about or verbalized any spells. The gods have bestowed upon me more power than I could have imagined, or perhaps they are helping me realize the depth of the powers I already had. Obviously I can now teleport myself and anyone that I am touching, just as I did earlier."

"I can hardly believe it, Merlin." Derek said. "It's amazin'."

Emily turned to Derek. "Yes, but it isn't any more unbelievable than the other things he's capable of, right?"

"That's true, Em. God, my mind is just reelin' and I think I need some sleep," he sighed as he collapsed into a chair and rubbed his forehead.

"I know, Derek, I feel that way too, and I'm married to him," Emily said.

"I know these last few days have been particularly intense, but you cannot let any of these events overwhelm you. I had no control over what happened to me, and I suspect things will only escalate from this point on, so please, have faith—in our quest, in King Arthur, in the gods, and in me!" I exclaimed. "Emily, my dear, earlier today you called me a demi-god, and it is true. A demi-god possesses some of the powers of the god but not all. I am still half human. It is obvious that you both perceive me differently now, but please believe me, I am the same man I have always been. I am your husband, Emily, and Derek, I am your kin. I love you both and that will never change."

As I concluded my impassioned speech, I gazed into their eyes and saw acceptance, love and trust, and I could not ask for more than that. I also saw exhaustion on their faces. For hours I had been feeling the power of my father inside of me, but now I also felt the bone-deep weariness of a mortal man. I took a ragged breath and said, "Let's go home."

CHAPTER 33

July 7 Night

WE TURNED OFF THE LIGHTS and the coffeemaker, and left The Moab Herbalist the conventional way, through the door. I checked the wards to ascertain that all the energy going through them hadn't disrupted the effectiveness of the spell. Everything seemed to be alright.

As we headed back to Emily's car, which was still parked at the restaurant, I noticed that the vehicle I had stopped had been towed away, and there were very few tourists in sight. It was nearly midnight, and I realized with a shock that it was just last night that Emily and I had been married in Las Vegas. This had been a very long day for all of us, and I could tell that my bride was having a hard time walking she was so tired. I reached down and swept her into my arms, holding her close. She blinked sleepily, then smiled and slipped her arms around my neck.

Derek glanced at me and just shook his head, "I don't know how you do that, Merlin; she's five-foot-nine and weighs at least 140 pounds, and yet you pick her up as if she weighs next to nothing!"

I grinned and whispered, "It's magic."

"Very funny," Derek said, rolling his eyes.

We finally reached the car and he started to get the key out of his pocket that Emily had entrusted to him earlier.

I just laughed and used magic to unlock the car doors. "That's your next assignment, Derek. Learn to manipulate the locks on doors using your magic, with and without a spell."

"Tomorrow," Derek promised.

Finally, we arrived back at Emily's place—mine now also, I realized. Derek threw his bag into the back of his truck, waved in my direction, then climbed into the cab and went

CARYL SAY

home. I unloaded our suitcases and the branch I intended to carve for my apprentice's staff, then lifted my sleeping wife into my arms and carried her into the house. As I set her down on the bed she began to stir, and as I undressed her she gazed up at me and smiled, grabbing my hand and placing it on her breast. I leaned down and kissed her as I gently squeezed the sweet globe under my hand. We were both tired and needed a shower, but neither of us could resist the other. I threw my clothes off and lay down next to her, pulling her tightly against me. Emily kissed me and ran her hands down my back to my buttocks, then reached between us and gripped my erection, causing me to gasp in anticipation.

"Merlin, I want you, take me now," Emily whispered in my ear as she opened her legs and invited me inside. I slowly entered her as we lay on our sides, and she rested her leg on my hip. I steadied her as we moved together, and I directed a small amount of magical energy into the movement, causing us both to gasp with pleasure. We looked deeply into other's eyes until we Saw each other, increasing the feeling of intimacy as our souls as well as our bodies were joined. We felt each other's explosions of ecstasy and clung together, finally relaxing into sleep in each other's arms.

And then I was with my father.

My son, I commend you for following your Heart and seeking the Power as I had bid you. Continue on your quest, however, for your journey is far from its completion. Also, I am pleased that you are now learning to use the powers you have inherited from me, but you must be diligent to keep them hidden from mortals, for they would not understand, and would turn on you if they knew who you were. If it should come to pass that you must use your powers to protect the weak, as your nature re-quires of you, then so be it, but do so quietly, secretly.

218

I was standing below a raised platform upon which were many bejeweled thrones and couches. I realized that I was wearing my best robe trimmed in ermine, which was appropriate for being in the company of the gods occupying those seats. My father was directly in front of me on the dais, tall and regal, with long, dark wavy hair and brilliant green eyes; his features so similar to my own that it was like looking into a mirror. My hair was blacker and straighter, apparently inherited from my mother, but otherwise we looked the same. My heart swelled with gratitude and happiness, and I knew that my heritage was something to be proud of.

He was just about to speak to me again when suddenly I heard a distant scream and was pulled away from him…

I came back into my body with a jolt as Emily screamed again. I immediately sensed an evil presence in the bedroom and realized that it was trying to take my wife. She was fighting valiantly, but seemed unable to access her magic. I quickly grabbed Emily and teleported to the apartment above the shop. I stood in the middle of the small room holding her in my arms, wondering if *it* could follow us here. Emily started shaking, from fear I thought, because she couldn't possibly be cold, could she? After all, it was July, and we were standing in a second floor room that had been closed up for several days. But the room *was* surprisingly cold, and other things were different as well. The bedding had obviously been slept in many times without benefit of laundering, if the smell and the dirt were any indication. Cobwebs festooned the corners of the ceiling and dust covered the floor. Normally, the street lights would shine into the apartment when the curtains were open as they were now, but there was virtually no light coming through the windows.

A frisson of fear and dread ran down my spine and I thought, *What, by all the gods, has happened?* Then I realized what I must have done: Not only had I teleported us physically away from danger, I had, in my haste to escape, transported us in time as well.

I needed to figure this out, but we were both naked and cold and it was imperative that I find some clothing to cover our bodies. I hoped that some of my things were still here in the room. I quickly created an orb of light and directed it to the ceiling for maximum illumination.

"Merlin, what...what's going on? I was asleep, and the next thing I knew I was fighting for my life. Then you grabbed me and...we're in your apartment?" Emily said as she tried to make sense of the last few minutes. "And why is it so damned *cold* in here?" She was shivering and had wrapped her arms around her upper body trying to retain some warmth.

I finally found a few odd items of discarded clothing in the back of the closet. I handed Em an old Moab sweatshirt that had seen better days, and an old pair of sweatpants that were too short for me, then I put on a ragged long-sleeved T-shirt and a pair of dirty, threadbare jeans while I tried to think of what had occurred.

"Em, I believe I must have transported us in time," I confessed.

"*What did you say?*" Emily asked in astonishment, standing as if frozen with the clothes in her hands.

"It seems you have married a sorcerer-turned-time traveler," I said sheepishly.

"Holy crap, magic man, really?" She quickly pulled the clothes on. Her shock soon turned to curiosity and she asked, "What year do you suppose this is, anyway?"

"Unfortunately, I don't know, but I'm fairly certain it's the future, not the past, and it does not look good," I said, indicating the view from the windows.

Emily looked up and down Main Street as far as she could see in the pre-dawn gloom, and whispered, "My God, the town, it's...abandoned or something. There should be some activity, some traffic, and there's absolutely no one around, no lights, nothing; in fact it kind of looks like a war zone. What *happened* here?"

"I don't know, but we need to find out. I don't think I can get us home unless I know what year this is," I said from the back of the closet, as I was trying to find some kind of footwear for us.

Just then Emily said, "Shh, I think I hear someone downstairs!"

I tossed an old pair of flip-flops at Em and put a worn-out pair of Teva sandals on my own feet, then gently opened the door. I extended my senses and Listened carefully to the quiet voices downstairs.

"Ryan, we can't hold out much longer without makin' a run for food and drinking water," a familiar voice said.

"I know, but the trolls and the vampires are still out in force, so we'll have to wait until the sun is up. By the way, we need to find a way to open that hidden cabinet of Merlin's. We could really use his tools right now. You inherited them when he died, didn't you? Obviously I can't use his staff, but *you* can, and Gary and I could certainly use the crossbow and sword; we're running out of ammo."

Lancelot seemed to have reverted to his twenty-first century persona. And why would he think that I had *died*? He knew that I was immortal. I wondered how he knew about my tools; I had not mentioned my concealed cabinet to him. And who was Gary?

"Yeah, I could use his sorcerer's staff, but it feels sacrilegious somehow. I have no idea what happened to the one Merlin was goin' to carve for me. I still don't think either of them are dead, Ryan. We never found their bodies after the fire at Emily's place. They simply disappeared. Besides, Merlin is immortal, remember? And because they're married, I think Emily is immortal also. I don't know why you're so eager for them to be dead and gone!" Derek shouted impatiently.

"You ass, I'm just being realistic. We haven't seen them for years," Ryan growled.

I had heard enough, and Emily and I started down the stairs as quietly as possible so as not to startle them. I'm sure that they each had a weapon and I didn't want either of us to get shot. If we died we would come back to life, but it would hurt like hell and take time to heal.

"We are alive and well, gentlemen," I said, as Emily and I walked out of the back room hand in hand.

"What the *fuck*?" Ryan and Derek exclaimed in unison.

"Where have you been all this time?" Derek demanded rudely, looking bitter and hardened and much older than when we had seen him just a few short hours ago. He was dirty, his clothes were ragged, and he seemed to have developed a nervous tic. And despite having just defended us to Ryan, he was surprisingly unfriendly.

"What's the date?" Emily asked, looking worried.

"It's the winter of 2016, and you both have been missing and presumed dead since that night in July when you showed me I was Lancelot," Ryan offered, sounding tired and discouraged.

"We just arrived here. A few minutes ago we were in bed that same night, and we were attacked. I teleported us to the apartment upstairs, and apparently transported us through time as well," I said.

"Merlin, because you disappeared, and weren't here to defeat the initial attack, every sort of evil you can imagine has taken over—not just here in Moab—but across the entire country. We're in a war; a war we can't possibly win. It's the humans, and those of us with some degree of magical power, against a supernatural horde of creatures unleashed by your old nemesis," Derek said bleakly. "Thousands have died and will continue to die unless you do somethin'."

"Derek, I am so sorry that you and Ryan have had to

THE HEART OF MAGIC

face this horror without me and..." I was interrupted before I could finish my sentence.

"Derek, *qué pasó*? What's going on?" A dark-eyed woman with tangled hair and torn, too-large clothing got up from where she had been sleeping in one of the chairs, and walked over to stand beside him. I recognized her as the server, Maria, from Moab Brews who had waited on us when we had returned from Cortez in June.

"Merlin and Emily, this is my wife, Maria. She knows about the magic, and with the state the country is in now, there's no point in hidin' the truth any longer anyway. Everyone with magic has had to come forward to help fight the enemy." Derek turned to Maria. "This is Merlin, the sorcerer I told you about, and his wife, my friend Emily. They are the ones who disappeared just before all hell broke loose."

She just nodded gravely, barely acknowledging us, and as she started rubbing her protuberant belly, I realized that she was with child.

I just stared at the three of them, so damaged by their experiences. I turned quickly and guided Emily into the back room.

"Em, we have to go back and make sure that this future does not come to pass," I whispered urgently. I could see Derek, Maria and Ryan out front, staring at me, while Emily stood quietly at my side waiting for me to make a decision. Suddenly, I knew this was all wrong.

None of this was real; it was a vision.

I squeezed my eyes shut, blocking out the sights and sounds of this bleak future world, and concentrated on what I knew to be true: My heritage, my marriage to Emily and my love for Derek, my reunion with Lancelot, my devotion to Arthur, and above and beyond even those precious things, the light and love that resided in the depths of my being.

And all of a sudden, I realized I was still standing in the

presence of my father, Llyr, in the realm of the gods, and he nodded approvingly. Emily had not been attacked, nor had I transported us into that desolate future. It had been a vision of startling magnitude and complexity, of an event that *might* yet occur. And I swore to myself that it would never happen, even if it meant my own destruction.

Merlin, your intellect is beyond any mortal man's, and yet you still do not realize the extent of your powers. You can never be destroyed by any normal means; you will always exist, in one form or another. And you will never be alone, because I will be watching over you, and I will come to you at your summoning if you ever find yourself in dire straits. Now go back to your life, to the Elven woman you have married. And be aware that the Fae, whose strength and loyalty are well-known throughout the realms, are now bound to you through your mate. And though your mate has gained a certain immortality through her heritage, she also shares your immortal status through the bonding of your hearts. Go back, Merlin, and wake to a new day that will find you closer to your goal.

And my father slowly faded from my sight…

CHAPTER 34
July 8

A BIRD CHIRPED OUTSIDE of our bedroom window, and I opened my eyes to see the early morning sun shining through the gap in the drapes. I turned my head and saw Emily watching me with love in her eyes.

"Good morning, husband," she said softly, while stroking my hair.

"Good morning, wife," I replied as I reached out and wrapped my arms around her, marveling that the entire experience of the future had been essentially a dream. "I have some interesting news for you, Em."

"Mmmm, and what's that?" She began kissing my neck and shoulders in a leisurely fashion.

"I was with the gods last night, my love, and Llyr has confirmed that you and I will be spending a very long time together. Your status as an immortal being has been guaranteed as your birthright, as well as through your bond with me," I said, as I held her close.

Emily lifted her head and looked into my eyes as she gasped, "I thought true immortality was strictly for full-blooded Fae. But you're saying that through my distant link to the Fae, *and* because we are bonded, I'm guaranteed immortality?"

"Yes, Em." I smiled at the awestruck look on her face.

"Merlin, this is an amazing gift. I don't know what to say." Tears welled up in her eyes and she buried her face in my neck.

"It's alright, sweetness, you deserve it," I said gently, kissing the top of her head. "And there is one other thing I wanted to talk to you about. I have more than enough money to support us, so if you ever want to stop working, you are welcome to do that," I said, hoping that she would give up the Park Service job. It was one thing for Derek to be working as a law enforcement ranger, but I hated to see Emily in that position. In this century, I knew that women prided themselves on working in a field traditionally dominated by men, but Emily now had a different role to fulfill.

She pulled back from me, wiping the tears from her cheeks. "Merlin, I appreciate the offer, and at some point I'll probably take you up on that, but right now I want to keep working for the Park Service. It suits me. I know it bothers you that I work as a ranger, but I can't just stay home and keep house—I'd be bored. Can you understand and accept that?"

I nodded. "I do understand, but I hope that when it becomes obvious that your destiny lies elsewhere, you will accept the inevitable." And I started caressing her naked body, hoping that she had time to...

"I promise I'll keep that in mind," she said, interrupting my train of thought. "Now, as much I would like to do lovely, naughty things with you, I need to get up and go to work. And I seem to recall that we made love quite thoroughly last night." She gave me a quick kiss and eyed my body longingly, but got out of bed despite her obvious desire. I watched her as she got dressed, grinning when she bent over to retrieve a shoe and her uniform pants pulled taut over her sweet backside.

After Em had left the bedroom, I lay there for a few moments thinking about all that had transpired in the previous couple of days, and then I decided to get up also. After all, I did have a business to run and an enemy to find and destroy.

I dressed quickly in jeans and a T-shirt and walked into the kitchen looking for coffee. Emily had just started a pot and I got the cups out. I loved this beverage and drank at least six cups a day, so I was glad that the caffeine seemed to have no negative effects on me.

Emily and I had a few minutes to sit and drink our coffee together, and we chatted about how well the herb shop was doing. I knew that I needed to talk to her, and to Derek, about my disturbing vision, but I was reluctant to share anything with them until I'd had some time alone first.

Minutes later Emily ran out the door in her usual hurry, and I decided I needed to leave also. After pulling on my boots, I walked swiftly to the shop to get my truck, and drove to Arches National Park. I showed my pass at the entrance booth and continued up the park road, expecting to see Derek's work vehicle, but it wasn't in sight. I decided to hike up to Delicate Arch as I hadn't been there in a while and I wanted to look for portals in the area. As I drove, I thought about the fact that I'd left my sorcerer's staff back at the shop; I hoped I wouldn't need it.

I parked in the designated lot, reached for my water bottle, and discovered that it was empty; I'd forgotten to fill it earlier that morning. For a moment I was irritated with myself, then remembered that I could use my powers to fix the problem. I concentrated for a moment and magically filled the bottle with cool water.

"Nice," I murmured, relishing the ease with which my augmented powers flowed through me. I grabbed the sunglasses I probably didn't need anymore and was ready.

The day was bright and clear and already warm, despite the early hour, but I was not too concerned, as I knew that I would be able to regulate my body temperature later when it got too hot.

With all these changes I was experiencing, I hoped that I wouldn't forget my human side....

I strode up the trail until I reached the sandstone ridge leading up to the arch, whereupon I stopped and cast my senses out, seeking the power signature indicating a portal. Nothing yet, so I continued up the slope, admiring the intense, deep blue sky above me and the red rock under my feet. After hiking for another thirty minutes or so, I came to the end of the trail and saw Delicate Arch ahead of me.

What an amazing natural structure, I thought, admiring the work of the gods. And then I started to feel the power pulsing from the center of the open space below the arch.

I felt uneasy that the tourists were scrambling around right next to the portal, and wondered why people were not being sucked into what seemed to be an energy vortex.

I decided I needed to be alone up here, and the easiest way to persuade people to leave the area was to create an enchantment that would blanket the entire area.

I quickly summoned energy from the rocks until it filled me, then with my mind I cast a "net" of magical energy over the ridge, the arch and down the hill on every side, including the arch viewpoint area, and said *"Abscedere."* The enchantment drifted down over the hikers, who began to feel the urge to avoid the area, and caused them to walk away from Delicate Arch and back down the way they had come.

I stayed quietly in the background until I was certain I was alone. Then I teleported to the top of the arch and stood gazing at the slopes, which were now empty of people. From my vantage point, I would be able to sense other portals as well. Just as I was preparing to use the spell to light the portals, I was interrupted.

"Hey, you on the arch, get down from there, *now*." I heard a voice say with authority, and I looked down at two park rangers standing where I had been only seconds ago.

Bollocks, I thought, preparing to use my forgetting spell.

"Merlin, it's me," the other ranger called out. "I'll take care of it!"

And I saw my apprentice turn to the first ranger, look into his startled eyes, and wave his hand as he intoned a spell. As the man slowly crumpled to the ground, Derek made sure he did not hit his head.

I teleported over to Derek to check his work. He had

combined my forgetting spell with a sleeping spell and it had worked perfectly.

"Congratulations, my friend," I said.

"Thanks, I had hoped it would be effective, it's the first time I've used it," Derek explained. "What were you doin' up there?"

"I was looking for portals, as usual. I had just arrived and sent the tourists away when you two appeared. Why are you up here?"

"We had a call about someone lost in the vicinity, and then of course we saw the mass exodus of hikers and became concerned that there was a mountain lion in the area. Everyone was actin' strangely, very distressed, and hurryin' back to their cars. What did you do?"

"I created an enchantment that covered the whole area in a feeling of unease, and basically just told them to go away, to avoid the area." I paused as I thought about my apprentice's progress. "You have become proficient very quickly in using spells, Derek. It has only been a few days since you discovered you had magic."

"I think about it all the time, and I practice simple stuff whenever I get a chance. Last night you told me to practice lockin' and unlockin' things with and without spells and I can do that now. I got up early this morning and worked on it for several hours," Derek said.

"I am impressed. You have already surpassed my expectations," I said.

"Thanks, Merlin," Derek said. "Before my partner comes to, maybe we could try to sense the person who is supposedly lost, and then I can get him back to the office. How do I do it?"

"Concentrate and imagine your senses—your sight, your hearing, your sense of smell, and your intuition—flying out in all directions, and bringing back the information you seek. This is something you can practice anywhere, but just realize that it's best if you're alone at first. Otherwise people will look at you strangely and wonder what you're doing. Ready? Let your senses fly…"

We both stood there and sent our senses out to hopefully find this lost individual. Derek had closed his eyes to concentrate more effectively.

I realized long before Derek did that there wasn't anyone lost out here. There were several people walking on the Viewpoint Trail on the other side of the gully who had encountered my avoidance spell and had turned back, and there was a mountain lion about a mile away heading north. Otherwise, everything was peaceful.

Derek opened his eyes and confirmed my findings, and I praised him again for his magical accomplishments. Just then his partner started to wake up and I winked at Derek and whispered, *"Invisibilis."*

Derek winked back as I vanished, and he leaned over his partner, saying, "Hey, Ken, you okay? You just collapsed…"

Ken opened his eyes and sat up, confusion evident on his dark face. "I…don't remember what happened, Derek, what's going on?

"We hiked up here lookin' for a missing person, but we didn't find anyone. We'd decided to head on back to the vehicle when you suddenly passed out. Here, have some water; maybe that'll help you feel better." Derek handed him his canteen and helped him take a few swallows.

Ken stood up, and he and Derek slowly started walking back down the trail, chatting about what they still had to do before they were off work. Derek casually glanced over his shoulder and grinned at me; even though he couldn't see me, he evidently could sense where I was standing.

When they were out of sight, I released the invisibility spell. I turned and looked toward the portal under Delicate Arch.

It was gone.

CHAPTER 35
July 8

"WHAT THE HELL?" I exclaimed. Where was the portal that I had both seen and sensed earlier? It couldn't have just disappeared! It was real, not an illusion, and I immediately suspected magical intervention of some kind.

I cast my senses carefully towards the spot where I had originally seen the portal and I felt a wall of some kind blocking me. *How is this possible?* I thought. My recently enhanced powers should allow my senses to go through the wall like a hot knife through butter, and yet I was stopped. The only person I could think of who had similar powers to mine, and who hated me enough to do anything to stop me was...

Nimue, immortal daughter of a god. Suddenly everything made sense. I hadn't actually killed her with the lightning bolt all those centuries ago; I had merely stopped her temporarily, just as I had suspected. She was able to block my powers because she had similar ones. This portal could be her own personal entrance to the Other World, or to another land where she could reside without being found. Or it could be a clever decoy.

She wanted to prevent Arthur's return, so that she could impose her own rule. And not just upon our homeland, but upon the entire world. The future that I had experienced in my vision would come to pass if I did not prevail. And she was hoping that I would lead her straight to the Avalon portal...

Llyr had assured me that I could not be destroyed—by any *normal* means. Would that hold true for Nimue as well? If so, how could I possibly stop her?

I needed to consult with my father, because I had no idea how to handle this disastrous situation. I sat down on a boulder and went deep inside myself, into the light at the center of my being, seeking entrance to the realm of the gods. I was denied over and over again, until I gave up and opened my eyes, puzzled and disturbed by this turn of events. I had never been denied entrance before—that I could remember. I considered summoning Llyr, but was not at all sure that he would consider this situation dire enough. Was there a battle going on in the realm of the gods as well?

I must keep searching for the Avalon portal, I told myself, but I knew I would have to shield my efforts with magic to deflect Nimue's awareness. Obviously she knew exactly where I was and what I was doing, as evidenced by the veiling of the Delicate Arch portal.

I drank a large portion of my water, realizing as I did so that I had not yet eaten, and no amount of conjured fruit was going to satisfy my hunger. I decided to teleport home to eat lunch, leaving my vehicle in the parking lot below, and then I could continue my search within the park later in the afternoon. I needed to think. Although I could see hikers again toiling up the hill towards me, they were still far enough away so that there were no witnesses to my sudden disappearance.

I found myself in the living room between the couch and the coffee table. I told myself that I'd better learn more about my teleporting ability before I ended up in the middle of a piece of furniture, or a wall, as did the men in *The Philadelphia Experiment*. Derek and I had watched that movie recently, and I kept thinking about it in relation to my recently discovered, or rediscovered, power to teleport. As a child I used to dream that I could move through space and time. Perhaps it hadn't been a dream at all. But why had I forgotten about it?

I walked into the kitchen and poked my head into the refrigerator to see what there was to eat. Enough food to make a sandwich, but one of us would have to go shopping before long. As I prepared my lunch I shook my head in wonder at my acceptance of twenty-first century life. I'd only been here about three months, but I felt as if I'd been here for years.

I carried my sandwich outside and sat on the steps as I often did, and wondered where the cat was that had been around when I'd first arrived in Moab. Then, as if I had summoned it, there it was sitting at my feet staring at me intently. *I am here*, I heard faintly in my mind.

Startled, I stared back at the animal. *Did you just speak to me?*

The cat cocked its head and blinked at me. *Yes. You are Merlin, son of Llyr.*

I am, but how does that enable me to understand you? I was amazed.

You are the only one whose magic is strong enough. You are the only one I will serve. The cat stretched lazily and rubbed against my legs.

I am truly honored. I stroked the cat's head and back. *What shall I call you?*

The cat just blinked. *Just think of me and I will come. You will know my name in time.*

The cat left as quickly as it had come, leaving me astonished and wondering if there was anything I *couldn't* do. And it wasn't lost on me that the cat had black fur and green eyes...I just wasn't sure what it meant.

After lunch, I teleported back to Delicate Arch, then hiked back down to the parking lot, trying to make sense of everything that had happened. My father had said that this day would find me closer to my goal, but I didn't feel that that was the case at all, although I'd had an experience with a talking cat. And I still hadn't been able to enter the realm of the gods.

I noticed that the temperature had soared in the previous couple of hours to well over 100 degrees, but my body was automatically compensating and I felt perfectly comfortable. However, I noticed that my jeans were a bit tight for hiking and vowed to put the long pants away for the summer in favor of my cargo shorts.

Hours later, having exhausted the possibilities in another section of the park, I decided to go home. I knew I had to open up the shop the following morning, as I should have done earlier this day. Having been gone for several days in a row now, there would be a lot of things to catch up on.

Of all the things that had happened to me since I'd seen Emily this morning, my encounter with the cat would be the hardest to explain.

CHAPTER 36
July 8 Evening

NEITHER EMILY NOR I FELT like shopping or cooking, so we decided to go out to eat, then we were to meet Derek and Ryan at the tavern for a game of pool and a beer or two. Ryan had contacted me earlier and suggested that we get together and I had concurred that it was an excellent idea. All of us could use an evening of relaxation.

We chose to eat at the City Diner since it was right next to the tavern and we didn't have to drive. As we took our seats, I sighed and brushed my hair back from my face. I took my headband out of my pocket and put it on. Better.

"You seem distracted, Michael, what's wrong, honey?" Emily asked, careful not to call me Merlin since the Diner was fairly crowded this night.

"Well, it has been a strange, crazy day, which I will describe in detail when we're alone later. I rushed out of the house as soon as you left for work and drove out to Arches. I saw Derek up at Delicate Arch along with his partner, and let's just say that he has accomplished some things in the past few days that are truly remarkable for such a young...practitioner. It's incredible, how fast he has learned his craft, if you know what I mean. And I was wondering how you would feel about adopting a cat?" I said, finally winding down.

Emily looked confused at my meandering monologue, especially when I mentioned the cat, as I had never before expressed any interest in having a pet. She read the menu, trying to figure out what she wanted to eat, then closed it and pushed it aside.

"I think it probably *would* be best to wait until we get home to talk about your day, because what you just said made very little sense to me," Emily said. "But my day wasn't any better, in fact, it totally sucked. I was informed that my job is being eliminated due to budget cuts. I don't have a termination date yet, but it could be tomorrow or at the end of the month." She looked at me suspiciously. "You didn't by any chance talk to your father about this did you?"

Just then the server walked up to take our orders. I hadn't even looked at the menu, so I randomly chose the burger platter and a dinner salad. As soon as the man took Emily's order and walked away I leaned towards her.

"No, I didn't. In fact, I tried to contact my father all day with no luck. I'm truly sorry, Em—I know you really love your job. But the gods work in mysterious ways to put us where we're supposed to be."

She frowned. "I know, but it was kind of a shock, especially since it happened the same day you offered to support me."

"You can work with me at the herb shop and I can teach you how to make potions," I suggested hopefully.

"Huh, that's true, I could do that. I'll think about it."

We sat thinking our own thoughts until our food was served, and then we were too busy eating to talk any more about it.

After dinner, we walked hand in hand next door to Moody's Tavern and joined Derek and Ryan, who had arrived earlier and had already indulged in several beers as they played pool. I noticed that the two men were being extremely competitive, baiting each other constantly. Derek was normally so easy-going that this seemed out of character. And I didn't remember Lancelot being so aggressive either, but this was Ryan's lifetime and he'd had experiences this time around that he'd never had as Lancelot.

Emily had walked over to the bar to get our beers when I noticed an altercation starting in the corner of the room. One man with brown wavy hair and neatly trimmed facial hair had obviously had too much to drink and was picking a fight with a man quite a bit taller and heavier than he. This could end very painfully for the shorter man, I thought, and wondered if I should intervene with a little magic. As I looked closer, I thought I knew him, he looked so familiar. My eyes widened as I recognized someone that couldn't possibly be here in this time.

"Ryan!" I pointed to the man in the corner. "Does he look familiar to you?"

Ryan glanced over in the direction I was pointing, and exclaimed in shock, "It *can't* be!"

We looked at each other and nodded, then hurried over to the man about to get beaten, and dragged him outside. Derek and Emily watched us go out the door, and I heard in my mind, *What's going on?*

Meet us at the shop as soon as you can, I said.

The man we had removed from the bar was fighting us and cursing in a language Lancelot and I both recognized—it was the old British language we had all spoken centuries ago in Camelot. It wasn't possible, and yet the person struggling with us was none other than Sir Gawain, former Knight of the Round Table.

I shook the man and said, in the old language, "Hold still, will you? We are trying to help you, you stubborn fool."

"I am no fool, and I will fight any man who calls me such. Where is my sword?" Gawain said furiously.

"Most likely back in Camelot, Gawain, now stop fighting me; 'tis Merlin!" I hissed, hoping no one walking by had heard me.

"Be easy now my friend. I, Lancelot, am here also," Ryan said, quietly.

"Merlin? Lancelot? How can you be here? I must be dreaming," Gawain said loudly.

"Shh! Be quiet now, Gawain!" I said. People walking up to the front door of the tavern were glancing in our direction.

"Ryan, we need to take him to the shop. Help me get him across the street."

"What about Derek and Emily?" Ryan asked, frowning.

"Since the three of us are linked telepathically, I've already told them to meet us there," I said.

"Uh...what's that?" Ryan asked, disbelief in his voice.

"The three of us are bonded through our ties to each other, of friendship, love, blood, and marriage. Derek and Emily cannot yet communicate with each other through their thoughts, but I am able to hear and project to both of them."

Ryan shook his head and grinned, then got on the other side of Gawain.

When we finally reached the The Moab Herbalist, I deactivated the wards, then unlocked the door with the key in the normal way since the sidewalks were teeming with people, despite the late hour.

Gawain was nearly unconscious, so we put him down in one of the chairs while I started some coffee and chose a potion from the shelf that, along with a spell, would help to alleviate his drunken condition. Wood betony really should be taken *before* getting drunk, but I knew I could make it work.

I removed the stopper from the bottle and tipped it into his mouth. He automatically swallowed, and I placed my right palm on his chest and said, *"Sanare."* I stepped back and watched as he slowly regained his sobriety.

Gawain blinked and looked around, noticing me standing over him, and Ryan leaning against the counter, as the coffeemaker gurgled and spit coffee into the pot.

"What....who are you? Where am I?" Although he was still a little groggy, he spoke modern English.

Ryan and I looked at each other, and I said, "He doesn't remember who he really is when he's sober."

"Interesting..." said Ryan, a thoughtful look on his weathered face.

Just then, Derek and Emily rushed through the door.

"Michael, what are you doing? Who is this?" Emily asked.

I looked at Gawain, who obviously remembered nothing of his actions at Moody's, and then at Emily and Derek, and said, "Well, we have here one of Arthur's most gallant knights, and he only knows his real identity when he's under the influence of alcohol."

Gawain stared at all of us and said belligerently, "I don't know what any of you are talking about! My name is Gary, and I don't know anybody named Arthur. I demand to know why you are keeping me here."

Hearing his name, I suddenly remembered my vision from the night before. Gary had been a part of that future world that could not be allowed to come to pass.

"You are about to have the experience of a lifetime, man," Ryan said. "And when this guy..." he pointed at me, "...is through with you, you'll be happier than you've been in a thousand years."

"You're all insane and I'm leaving!" Gary spat, starting to get up.

"I'm sorry, but you need to stay for a while longer," I said softly. I put my hand out, and with a slight surge of power, pushed him gently back into the chair.

His familiar face registered shock as he realized that I was holding him in place without physically touching him.

"Gary, you are not who you think you are, and I would like to help you discover the truth. This man beside me..." I gestured towards Ryan, "...was one of your best friends in a past life long ago. His name then was Lancelot. I, Merlin, the Sorcerer of the Realm, was also your friend, and we all worked together in the fifth century to build one nation under the rule of Arthur Pendragon of Camelot."

Emily and Derek stood to the side and watched as if

mesmerized while I talked to Gawain. It never failed to amuse me that the pair were so easily impressed by my theatrics.

I gazed into Gawain's eyes and kept him from moving as I walked toward him, then reached down and gently pulled him to his feet. At five feet ten inches tall, Gary was enough shorter that I seemed to loom over him, and he tried to back away, gasping in fright. I grasped his wrists, and said to him kindly, "Do not be afraid, my friend, this will be a good experience, I promise. You will be able to remember who you really are without having to get drunk."

Finally, his eyes met mine and I Looked deeply into his being to discover his soul's beginning.

A few minutes later, we came back out of that inner well of discovery, and I saw the sheen of tears in my friend's eyes.

"Merlin, how can I ever thank you for this gift? As you just witnessed, I have been tormented for centuries by memories of my life in Camelot. I was only aware of those memories in dreams, or when I had had enough to drink that my mind could roam free. I have never been satisfied and have always searched for... I knew not what," Gawain said, his voice rough with emotion. "And it is obvious to me now that this has been my purpose, to live again at this time when you and Arthur need me the most. How may I serve you, my lord?" And he kneeled in front of me with his head lowered in obeisance.

I looked down at his bowed head and although I felt the intensity of his devotion, which bordered on worship, I also felt somehow detached, as if I was accepting his loyalty as my due. Was this how it felt to be a god, to be above and separate from everyone else? If so, I didn't like it. A demi-god I might be, but I did not ever want to lose my humanity.

"Get up, Gawain, please. While I appreciate your loyalty and your help more than I can say, there is no need to bow before me like this," I said quietly, as I reached for his hand to pull him to his feet.

"Merlin, your father is a *god*, and you have powers no one else has. How can I not bow before you?" Gawain said.

"Because *I* am not a god. Gawain, look at these three people, one of whom you know better than anyone. They can tell you how human I am and how ungod-like my behavior can be. Now, if my father was here, that would be a different story, and we would *all* be on our knees before him," I said wryly. I glanced over at Ryan who was waiting for my signal. "Lancelot, aren't you going to welcome our old friend?"

Ryan immediately crossed the room and gave him a bear hug. "I am most pleased to see you, Gawain."

Gawain grinned at Ryan as he hugged him back. "I would not have known you, Lancelot, had I not seen you through Merlin's eyes. You are much larger in this lifetime, and your coloring is different."

"And you look the same—how is that possible? We know that Merlin has had one body and one lifetime all these years due to his immortality. But your body looks the same as it did in Camelot. In all of your past lives have you been born like this?" Ryan asked.

"Apparently I have, although I was not aware of it until Merlin showed me," Gawain said with a shrug.

"I did not notice any sorcery involved as we journeyed through his lives, so perhaps it was just his destiny," I conjectured.

We continued to banter back and forth, just as we had in times past. Bottles of beer were brought out from my refrigerator in the back room, and as we drank we got a little noisy.

I noticed that Emily was curled up in a chair reading a book, and Derek was nursing his beer while leaning on the counter, a scowl forming on his normally easygoing face.

"So Gawain, what are you doin' in Moab? That is, what brings *Gary* to Moab, huh?" Derek interrupted our conversation rudely and impatiently, his skin starting to glow and to emit bright sparks.

"Uh, Derek, do you realize what you're doing?" I asked, seeing my apprentice becoming a full-fledged sorcerer right before my eyes, with little knowledge of how to control the power that he was unconsciously tapping into. I was amazed at the change in him—in less than a week—from someone who didn't even know himself into someone who could prove to be extremely powerful and dangerous.

Hearing my tone of voice, Emily looked at Derek and became alarmed. "Merlin, why is he doing that?"

"I don't know, Em. That's what I'm going to find out. Stay with Ryan and Gary, please." I grabbed Derek's arm and teleported us to the top of the Rim, below which I could see the bright lights of Moab, and above, the myriad stars in a velvet blackness.

"Whoa, Merlin, why did you do that?" Derek was startled to find himself suddenly outside and a thousand feet higher than he was a moment ago. His attention diverted, he had ceased drawing in power and had released some of the energy he had been holding onto.

I just looked at him for a moment and suddenly realized what was wrong. He was jealous of the attention I had been giving Ryan and Gary. He didn't see what I did—two old, dear friends from Camelot—he saw two strangers taking my attention away from him. It was childish, yes, but Derek was still a boy in some ways. Only a few days ago his hero had come to life and fulfilled all his dreams, and he wanted to keep that hero all to himself.

I sighed and pulled my friend into a hug, holding onto him tightly. "Derek, you are so important to me that I can't even express how much I care about you, how much I *love* you."

Derek just stood in my arms, and then finally hugged me back and I could feel him relaxing. "Merlin, I'm so sorry, I guess I'm jealous of them; maybe even of Emily a little bit." Then he stepped back and looked startled at his own admission. "Uh, I didn't mean I wanted to, uh, you know…never mind, okay? I'm fine."

"I think you need to experience some of my memories of Camelot, to give you some perspective about my attitude towards Lancelot and Gawain," I said, and held out my hands.

Derek reached out and we gripped each other's forearms as we had done only a few days ago. Looking into his eyes, I called up and shared memories of the knights and myself with Arthur, during battles, during hunting expeditions and during relaxing evenings in the tavern with pints of ale.

Derek's breathing grew labored and his body tensed as he experienced the battles, and he relaxed and smiled as he felt the camaraderie we'd shared during less stressful times.

When we stepped apart, he took a deep breath and said, "I had no idea, Merlin. I'm grateful that you shared your memories with me. It helps me to understand the bond you still have with them. You and I have a different bond, but it doesn't mean that it's any less important to you; I get that now. Thank you for helpin' me to see the truth."

"Now, we need to talk about what you were doing just before we left the shop so abruptly," I said, hoping to convey to him the seriousness of his actions. "You were gathering energy from outside of yourself, and filling your being with so much power that you couldn't contain it. It was spilling out of you so that your body was glowing and you were emitting sparks. It's commendable that you are able to do that but it's obvious that you had no control over it."

And I proceeded to teach him some things that a sorcerer needed to know, for he was already beyond the wizard's level of power that I had originally envisioned him having. I had come to the conclusion that the difference between a wizard's powers and a sorcerer's wasn't so much whether either practitioner was "good" or "bad." It was a matter of how his or her magical powers were accessed: A sorcerer's magic was a gift from the gods, and the use of it was intuitive and automatic, whereas a wizard needed intensive training and had to focus on spell-casting to access his or her magic. And a wizard was never quite able to reach the depth and breadth of power wielded by a sorcerer.

Over an hour later, we appeared back in the shop. The lights were dimmed and the coffee pot was turned off, and Ryan and Gary had apparently left, for home or for the tavern. I heard someone moving around upstairs and received a picture in my mind of my wife undressing.

"Derek, I think we're done for tonight. We still have a lot to talk about, so we need to meet tomorrow sometime. Why don't I call you in the morning?"

"Sure, that's fine." Derek started to head for the door, but stopped and turned towards me. "Merlin, thanks for everythin'…" He said, blinking his eyes as they threatened to overflow.

"You are most welcome, Great-grandson," I said softly, as Derek departed.

CHAPTER 37
July 8 Evening

I LOCKED THE DOOR behind Derek, and activated the wards, then headed into the back room, and up the stairs. I was glad that Emily had decided to stay here this night.

"Em?" I whispered, hoping that she would want to make love.

"In here, honey." A low sultry voice came from the small bathroom, and I realized she was getting into the shower. I stripped my clothing off quickly and joined her, despite the fact that there was very little space to move in the stall shower. Of course, this caused us to be rubbing against each other, which was a most pleasant experience. I molded myself to her back and wrapped my arms around her, fondling her breasts and running my hands down her belly to her hips and thighs. I manifested liquid soap in my hands and starting washing her body, the slippery sensation causing her to gasp and push herself back against my burgeoning erection. Emily turned around in my arms, wiggling against me, sharing the soap and causing all manner of erotic images to flash through my mind. As the water cascaded down our bodies, rinsing the soap away, I lifted Emily up, braced her against the side of the shower, and as she wrapped her legs around me, I pushed into her. We kissed hungrily and moved together, the water running over our straining bodies like a waterfall. Emily hummed a little of her magic and I released a bit of mine, and we experienced that exciting tingle throughout our bodies.

I was panting with the effort of holding her up in the small space, but we were both so close to coming that I kept moving, thrusting into her. She moaned and started to climax, which caused the same reaction in me, and we both soared in passionate release. Afterward, I closed my eyes, rested my forehead against hers and felt again that oneness of our bond. Gods, I loved her so much.

"Merlin...open your eyes and for God's sake, *don't move!*" Emily's voice sounded strange and tense.

I slowly opened my eyes...to darkness and the feeling of rough, cool sandstone under my bare feet. I was standing on the edge of the cliff overlooking Moab, Emily still in my arms.

Carefully, I put her down, and we deliberately stepped back from the edge. I realized this was the same spot where Derek and I had stood only an hour earlier.

"Huh," I said as I gazed down upon the lights of Moab a thousand feet below us.

"Seriously? That's all you have to say?" Emily crossed her arms over her chest in annoyance as she stood naked and still wet from the shower, the breeze blowing her tangled hair around her face.

I lifted my eyes and met Emily's smoldering gaze. She looked magnificent.

Seconds later we were back in the apartment above the shop. I must have had a guilty expression on my face, because Emily put her arms around me, kissed my bare chest, and sighed. "Oh, magic man, what am I going to do with you? Really, you're going to have to figure out this teleporting thing. I *know* that we're immortal, and even if we'd fallen it wouldn't have been the end of us, but I was *terrified* when I opened my eyes and we were on the edge of the cliff.

"And by the way, last night I dreamed that you not only teleported us from our house to the apartment, but we time-traveled to the future as well."

I was speechless as I realized that she must have seen my vision through our bond. I should have known that the bond would create a shared experience, and I should have discussed it with her this morning, but instead I badgered her about quitting her job.

And then tonight after loving her, I teleported her unexpectedly—wet, naked and vulnerable—to the Rim. It is true that if we'd fallen I could have either teleported or levitated us to safety, but I had truly frightened my wife. Oh, gods, what had I done?

I sighed. "I guess I need some lessons on being a good husband."

Emily just shook her head and smiled. "I doubt there is a marital guidebook for sorcerers or demi-gods, but I know there is *one* thing that you do *perfectly...*" And she rubbed against me provocatively.

I desperately needed to talk to her, but my traitorous body had other ideas. I groaned and kissed her, backing her towards the bed until we collapsed on it. Already hard, I impaled her in one long thrust tempered by magical energy. She cried out, climaxing immediately, and I followed soon thereafter.

"Oh, my *God*, Merlin!" Emily sighed in complete contentment. "As I was saying, absolutely *perfect*."

"*You* are absolutely perfect, wife." I lay stretched out on the bed, already half asleep as I mumbled, "I certainly won't need to go to the gym for awhile."

By the time we had roused ourselves to clean up and brush our teeth it was very late, but there were so many things I needed to say to her, not the least of which was to apologize, that I didn't want to wait until morning.

I asked her to sit next to me on the bed, where I took her hand in mine, and told her how sorry I was for scaring her, for lecturing her about her job, and for neglecting to mention that horrifying vision of the future. I told her that I would try hard from now on to communicate better, so that she wouldn't regret marrying me.

Emily was silent for a few moments, holding my hand tightly, then she looked into my eyes. "Merlin, I've loved you from the first moment I heard your voice, before I even knew who you were. I love everything about you—you're the sexiest, smartest, kindest man I've ever met. You're humble even though you're a demi-god and the most powerful sorcerer in history. Because of you, I have discovered who I really am. You are my dream-come-true, magic man, and there's nothing you could *ever* do to make me regret marrying you." She framed my face with her hands and kissed me sweetly.

I held her against me and thanked the gods for bringing us together. "I forget sometimes that our bond is not only one of heart, it is one of mind as well. We have only just begun exploring the extent of the communication that we have through this connection. When you experienced the vision I had, did you feel as though you were living it, or watching it happen? And did you experience being with me in the company of the gods—did you see my father?" I asked Emily this hoping that she'd seen what I'd seen.

Emily thought for a moment, then said, "When I started seeing the vision it was as if I was actually there with you, living it, not just watching it. And yet, I also knew I was home in bed, so I thought I was dreaming. Then, I remember seeing a bright golden light and a man who looked remarkably like you, wearing a jeweled robe and standing on some sort of a dais. That must have been your father; you look just like him, although he appears to be much taller than you. I got the feeling that he is much larger than a normal human being."

"I think you're right, Em. He has to be at least six feet seven inches tall, perhaps even taller," I speculated.

In the midst of our conversation, a strange feeling came over me and I realized that time had stopped; Emily sat unmoving, her mouth slightly open as she started to speak. I glanced towards the windows and saw that someone was standing there, someone I had not expected to see in this realm: Llyr. I was startled and amazed that he would come to *me*, and I immediately got down on my knees to bow to my god.

"You may get up, Myrddin Emrys, there is no need to bow before me, especially in this setting. Leave the rituals for the other realm." Despite the fact that he used my Welsh name, the tall man in twenty-first century clothing spoke to me in perfect, unaccented English.

"Father, what are you doing here?" I stammered as I got to my feet, looking into his eyes and seeing an eerie reflection of myself in him. He stood about six inches taller than me, and was proportionately larger in frame, making me feel small by comparison. He was wearing denim shorts and a polo shirt, with sandals on his feet. It was the most incongruous sight I'd ever seen.

"And why should I not visit my own son?" Llyr said, looking into my eyes.

I started to smile and stepped towards him. He laughed and drew me into a hug—the first time in my life that I could remember being in my father's arms. Suddenly I was enveloped in such a feeling of love that I started to weep, letting go of more than a thousand years of pain, rejection and loneliness.

Finally, he and I pulled away from each other, and I swiped at my streaming eyes. I had to ask him the question that had been present in my mind since I was a child. "Why have you never visited me before? I have spent centuries being terrified that I was the son of a demon. Why would you not tell me the truth?" I hated that I sounded so accusatory, but I had to know.

"Merlin, you do not understand the situation in the realm of the gods; it is not that simple. Here in this realm, human politics runs the entire mortal world. In my realm it is a similar situation, but it is much more complicated. Until you were strong enough to recognize and overcome the magical influence that Nimue had placed on you so long ago, I was powerless to act. There are exceptions to the rules, but mostly we are forbidden to interfere in the affairs of our children in this realm. I am very sorry, my son." Llyr looked at me with compassion on his unlined face. It was strange to realize that he must be seeing me in much the same way that I saw Derek.

"But what about during the first fifteen years of my life, before I'd even met Nimue?"

"Merlin, I *was* there for you many times when you were a small child, when you were accused of being demon spawn. I am truly sorry that you do not remember that."

"What?" I was aghast, and realized that Nimue must have stolen those precious memories from me.

Llyr looked pensive for a moment, and then appeared to make a decision.

"Merlin, your existence is so much more than you know. You feel that the span of your life has been an extraordinarily long time, but you do not realize that before you had a human body, you had already been alive in spirit form since the dawn of time, waiting for the opportunity to live in the mortal world and so be able to affect the destiny of the entire human race. I volunteered to be your father..." Suddenly he stopped talking as if unable to continue with his sentence.

"I have said too much and am being summoned back to the realm." As he began to fade from my sight, he looked into my eyes and said, "I love you, Merlin. Take great care..." And then he was gone.

"Father, please come back..." I implored him.

"Merlin? What's wrong? Who are you talking to?" Emily looked up at me in concern as I stumbled towards her. She jumped up off the bed and came into my arms, which I tightened around her as I sought her comfort.

"My father was here, and..." I choked and couldn't speak, so I looked into her eyes and shared the memory with her.

"Oh, my God, Merlin," she gasped, "this is *amazing*! I wish he would have allowed me to see him," she finished, wistfully.

"I'm sure we will see him again, wife. Let's go to bed. It's very late and you have to go to work in a few hours."

"Yes, but I have decided to quit my job tomorrow, Merlin. I've been thinking about it. Being a park ranger has been my only focus for years, but now, well, I'm through with that part of my life; I'm moving on. You were right. Somehow it just doesn't seem that important anymore. Besides, they're going to let me go in a few weeks anyway. And it's obvious that my life with you, and with the kids we'll have some day, will keep me busy and will *never* be boring," Emily said.

"Are you sure, Em?" It seemed a sudden turn-around from her previous attitude, but I didn't care, I was just glad she had changed her mind.

"I'm sure, husband." She grabbed my hand and led me to the bed. We climbed under the covers and immediately succumbed to sleep, awakening only when the morning sun came streaming through the east-facing windows.

CHAPTER 38
July 9

WITH THE DAWNING of a new day, I bounded out of bed, feeling renewed, despite having slept only a few hours. I attributed my feelings of elation to having been with my father.

Emily was still sleeping and although I didn't want to wake her, I knew she would be upset if I didn't.

"Em, love, you need to wake up so we can go home and you can get dressed for work." As she stirred and opened her eyes, I asked curiously, "Did I hear you correctly that you are planning to quit your job today?"

"Yes, you did hear me correctly, and I hope that you're not going to gloat about it," Emily said in a sleepy voice.

"No, I would not think of doing so, but I hope I am allowed to be pleased about your decision?" I asked, grinning widely.

Emily chuckled, "I hereby give you permission to be pleased about my decision, old man."

"It's ironic that you would call me that this morning, because Llyr actually admitted that before I was born into this body, I had been 'alive in spirit form since the dawn of time.'" I was a little worried about how Emily would receive the news.

"You shared your memory with me last night, but I don't remember that part. That's incredibly intimidating. It…it means that you're as old as your father, which means…" Em jerked into a sitting position and her eyes got really big as she whispered, "Holy shit, Merlin, *you're one of the gods.*"

I closed my eyes as the truth sank in, and I groaned, "Bollocks, that complicates *everything*. No wonder Llyr wasn't supposed to tell me."

Emily just sat there staring at me, and said, "You know, I haven't talked to my parents for years, and I'm sure they think

I'm a complete failure. I am tempted to call them and say 'Hey Mom and Dad, by the way, I'm married to a god; how do you like me *now*?'"

I frowned in confusion, since she had never talked about her parents, and I didn't understand the significance of that last sentence.

"Don't worry about it, honey. I'm just being my usual off-the-wall self, feeling a little strange that I'm married to a god. Oh, well, I guess it's only a step up from being the wife of a demi-god, right?" Emily said, her voice shaking slightly. She grinned at me but I could tell she was upset.

"Sweetheart, nothing has really changed," I assured her. It was amusing really. I had been so concerned about being a demi-god, and now it seemed that I was one of the gods, in human form because one of the other gods had volunteered to be my father. I just wished I could *remember*.

Emily quickly and silently put yesterday's clothes back on, and I donned clean ones since most of my clothes were still in the apartment. We swiftly walked the four blocks to the house and I fixed breakfast while Emily changed, for the last time, into her uniform. As she sat down to the coffee, eggs and toast that I put on the table in front of her, she called her supervisor and apologized for being late. She then explained that she had decided to be a full-time wife (as she said this she looked at me and winked) and was terminating her employment today. We hadn't spoken more than a few words since we left the shop, but I assumed Em was thinking about everything that had happened lately. After she ended her call she ate a few bites of her breakfast, drank her coffee, and then went into the bathroom to brush her teeth.

I was very proud of her for realizing the importance of her role in our quest, and in our family. After all, at some point in the future she would have our children to raise, and as they would undoubtedly be magically inclined, she would not have

254

time to work outside of our home, wherever that might be.

After Emily left the house, I called Derek and told him what had transpired last night after he left, minus an account of our marital activities.

There was complete silence for a few moments, and then he said calmly, "You're a *what*?"

"I'm a god. At least I think I am."

"Okay, I'll bite. Which one?" Derek asked, still calm, but starting to sound a little bit sarcastic.

"Well, I'm not sure, but I think that I'm the god of magic and healing. I think Llyr was the god of the sea until I left and he had to take over my responsibilities," I explained.

"I'm comin' over in a few minutes, Merlin, so we can talk. I'd appreciate it if you could make us a pot of coffee."

I prepared more coffee, and then spent the rest of the time until he arrived trying to make room for my things in the bedroom. It was a good thing we had the apartment for storage, because there was no room to spare in this small place. *We need to look for a bigger house*, I thought, forgetting for a moment that we might all be going to Britain once we brought Arthur back from Avalon.

I was sorting through some cupboards when I heard Derek walk through the front door without knocking. *Hey, where are you, Great-grandfather the god?*

I'm in here, Derek. Don't get too cocky; you still don't know what I'm capable of.

Yeah, but you love me, so I don't think I have anythin' to worry about, he responded.

I headed into the living room, enjoying the mental sparring. I hadn't realized that Derek had progressed to the point that he could contact me telepathically and I was most impressed.

We came together in a hug, and then thumped each other on the back in true masculine style.

"Derek, your progress astounds me," I said.

"Apparently, I've inherited more from you than either of us anticipated. When I walked in just now, it seemed the most natural thing in the world to communicate that way. Your thoughts are like a beacon in the darkness, and my thoughts are drawn to yours like a moth to a flame. It's pretty cool, actually," Derek commented. "It must have been strange when Llyr showed up like that—what did he say, exactly?"

"It would be more effective just to show you," I said, and Looked into his eyes, projecting the memory of my time with my father directly into Derek's mind. We were so connected now that I didn't even have to touch him.

Derek exclaimed, "Holy shit, Merlin!"

"That is exactly what Emily said." I sighed and rubbed my forehead. "I told her that it doesn't change anything, but I'm afraid it does. It will change how all of you treat me; how you talk to me, how you act around me. I can't have everyone kneeling before me, it makes me uncomfortable. If I am a god, it explains why I have the powers that I do. I doubt a mere demi-god can affect time, but a god can. However, I can always hope that I misunderstood what Llyr told me."

Derek looked at me sympathetically. "You know, it makes no difference to me if you're a god or a demi-god, Merlin. You're my friend, first and foremost. And you just happen to be a freakin' powerful sorcerer, who also happens to be my umpteen times removed great-grandfather. And, uh, I've always kind of idolized you, so nothin's changed there." I rolled my eyes as he said this, even though I knew he was serious. Derek continued, "*Maybe* you misunderstood Llyr; although he *did* clearly say that you have been around since the dawn of time. Which pretty much puts you in a whole different league than the rest of us, doesn't it?"

I groaned, closed my eyes for a moment, and then glanced at Derek with a half-hearted smile. "Well, I've *always* been different than anyone else, so in *that* way, nothing has changed."

"How did Emily react to you bein' a god?" Derek asked.

"Not well. She's been so accepting of everything that's happened, and she swears that nothing will cause her to regret marrying me, but I don't know how many more shocks she can take. She's at work for the last time today. She's quitting to be a full-time wife and an active partner in this quest."

"Is she pregnant?" Derek asked, with a shocked look on his face.

"No, I don't think so. We're not ready for children yet. She's going to work with me at the shop for now, and I hope she'll be satisfied with that. Derek, I can feel the changes happening in this realm, and I'm afraid that the battle is imminent. I haven't had time to tell you about it, but the other night I had a vision..." I went on to describe what I had experienced in that possible future, so that he would be aware of what could happen should we fail here in this time.

We talked through the morning, drinking coffee and discussing possible strategies, the major problem being that we still had no idea from whence the attack would occur. I should have asked Llyr about Nimue last night, but he probably would not have been able to say anything else without alerting the other gods, particularly Nimue's father.

Shortly before noon, Derek left to take care of some errands, and I sat down to make a list for grocery shopping. Before I had written even one item, I heard Emily's car and walked out to greet her, hoping that she would talk to me.

"I saw no point in staying the rest of the day, so after I finished the paperwork I left and went to the store," she said brightly as she pulled sacks of groceries out of the back seat and handed them to me, not meeting my eyes. "I'll bet you're hungry; why don't I make some lunch?"

"Sure, that would be nice," I responded, my heart feeling like lead in my chest when she wouldn't look at me.

We went into the house and put the groceries away in silence. Finally, I couldn't stand it any longer and gently pulled her into my arms. She clung to me for a minute before she dropped to her knees in front of me, and gently kissed my sandaled feet. I was horrified that my wife felt she had to prostrate herself before me, and I reached down to help her stand up.

"Emily, please, you *never* have to bow to me like that. Even if I *am* a god, I don't remember it, and I would certainly not require anyone, let alone my wife, to kiss my *feet!*"

"Merlin, how can I help you to understand the way I feel? I love you so much, and sometimes I'm really in awe that *you* want *me*. It has always been a little difficult to comprehend what you are—an immortal sorcerer, a demi-god—and then to be faced with the reality that *my husband* has been around since the beginning of time itself; that he is a *god* walking around in a human body that he *asked* for so that he can save the human race...I..." Emily started crying softly and I held her against me, kissing her hair as she whispered, "Expressing your devotion to someone you worship with all your heart and soul is not a bad thing, Merlin, it is a privilege." As she looked up into my eyes, I Saw directly into her soul, and I was humbled beyond measure.

"Gods, Emily, I... I don't know what to say," I said softly, my love for her soaring to greater heights. I held her against me, feeling the beating of her heart and the sigh of her breath as she inhaled and exhaled. I thought our bond, our marriage, was the most amazing thing I had ever experienced, but this incredible woman had just offered her very existence to me in devotion, and it was the most precious gift I had ever received.

Emily finally pulled away from me, collected herself and said with her usual spunk, "Well, magic man, where do we go from here? I'm not sure how much more my poor little Elf being can stand. And don't worry, there won't be any bowing or foot-kissing in public. If I feel the urge coming on I'll make sure to keep myself in check until we find a private spot, but then all bets are off. Have you told Derek about your new status?"

"Yes, we talked all morning, and I don't think he's anywhere near as impressed as you are. In fact, *I* was impressed with *him*—he seems to have mastered telepathic communication already. When he first came over this morning, Derek walked right into the house and projected into my mind, 'Hey, where are you, Great-grandfather the god?'" I just shook my head in wonder at his boldness, and realized that I was incredibly proud of him.

"That's an amazing accomplishment. How did he learn to do that?" Emily asked as she fixed a salad and heated some soup.

I thought back to my childhood when I was exploring my magical gifts, and remembered that until Gaius took me under his wing and mentored me, I had used magic instinctively. Telepathy had come automatically to me; no one had taught me how to do it. Gaius had guided me in honing the skills I already had, and taught me many of the spells that I'd used over the centuries.

"As you are undoubtedly aware, having started to learn about your own magic, it's instinctual first of all. When I taught Derek his first three spells, all I did was show him how to focus on the power inside him in such a way that it could be translated to the physical plane. He is much stronger than I had ever imagined. In fact, he's almost strong enough to be my *son*, not a centuries-removed great-grandson."

"Merlin, that sounds even stranger than when you first told me he was your descendant. I mean, there's no way he could be your son," Emily insisted. She put the food on the table and gestured to me to sit and eat.

I looked at her suspiciously, hoping she wasn't going to start bowing and kissing my feet again. She glanced at me with a twinkle in her eye and sat down, handing me the salad dressing and a thick slice of French bread.

CHAPTER 39
July 9

W E HAD JUST FINISHED eating when I felt dark magic insinuating itself into my consciousness. I dropped my fork instantly, raised my hand and created a protective shield around us. Emily jerked her head up and glanced around, sensing the energy of the shield, and looked at me questioningly. *Merlin, what's going on?* Although she was not yet strong enough to initiate contact, she knew I could hear her.

A very dark power is attempting to invade my being. It must be Nimue, but I'm not sensing exactly the same identifying signature. It *was* similar to Nimue's. Were there two dark magic practitioners? Who was the other one?

I thought back to all of the attacks and minor events that had occurred over the past couple of months and came to a disturbing conclusion: There definitely were two separate magical signatures. The differences were subtle but present nonetheless. Could Nimue have a son or a daughter to whom she had taught all of her techniques? Gods, I hoped not, I thought glumly.

As I felt the strength of this current assault increase, I closed my eyes and pushed back with all of my power, sending the darkness back to the perpetrator. Deep within my being, I sensed an agonized cry and felt someone's intense pain. It wasn't Nimue. I felt shaken. How could I have felt that pain on such a deep level unless...Oh, gods...I choked back a cry of my own and felt such heartache that I groaned out loud.

"Merlin, what's wrong?" I heard Emily's voice and dragged myself out of the depths of my despair. I opened my eyes and looked sadly into hers. "Emily, the other dark practitioner is Nimue's daughter."

"I don't understand what the problem is," she said, confused.

I sighed. "She's also my daughter."

Emily gasped and her eyes widened in horror.

"I felt her pain when I pushed the dark magic back at her." I got up and started pacing.

"The other day when I talked about Nimue, I'm sure I mentioned that I had bedded her only once, but she apparently had conceived. I never knew she'd had my child. No wonder she was so angry, and so obsessed with me when I rejected her." I paused, deep in thought. "Our child must be very powerful: Her parents both sorcerers, both grandfathers gods." I shook my head in disbelief.

"Or perhaps some of that power by-passed her altogether, Merlin. Otherwise, why wouldn't she have been more forceful? She could have destroyed you, or at least those around you—Derek, me, the knights—long before this if she'd that kind of strength," Emily said, levelheaded and practical as usual.

I looked at her doubtfully. "Not very likely, but possible, I suppose. In any case, how can I oppose her, stop her? Gods, how can I *kill* her?" I was in agony at the thought of what I might have to do.

"Merlin, my love, I don't know, I truly don't. And she may be immortal like you, so how could you destroy her anyway? But whatever happens, Merlin, I'm sure that you will do the right thing," she said, holding me in her comforting embrace.

I've always eschewed detachment, but this was one time when being detached from human emotion would be helpful, I thought with wry humor.

"What's her name, Merlin?" Emily asked curiously.

"Adrestia," I said grimly. "Nimue named her after the Greek goddess of revenge." I was furious that she had raised our daughter to be an instrument of revenge against me. I swore that I would try to save her if at all possible, but Nimue, the epitome of all evil, would be utterly destroyed—I would see to it.

CHAPTER 40
July 9

"HELLO, ANYBODY HOME? Em? Merlin?" Derek called out as he walked through the front door.

"Oh, there you are," he said as he noticed us in the kitchen. I saw him stiffen as he saw the look on my face. "What's wrong?" he demanded, ready to jump to my defense.

"It's alright, Derek," I said calmly, "there's nothing you can do. I have to deal with it." I got up and took our dishes to the sink.

"Deal with what, Merlin?" he insisted.

I smiled wanly. "I appreciate your loyalty, Derek, but this situation, our battle with Nimue, has just become infinitely more complicated." And I told him what had just occurred here, and what it meant.

"Oh, my God! You have a daughter? With Nimue?" Derek's voice rose several octaves.

"Shit, this just gets better and better," he muttered, crossing the room and throwing his arms around me. "Merlin, I'll do anything to help you! If that bitch Nimue lays one finger on you, so help me I'll kill her myself," he swore, ferocious and protective as a mother bear. His magic flared brightly, out of control for a moment, until he took a deep breath and curbed his emotions as I had taught him.

At that moment I sensed rage in him, and a potential for such raw power that I knew we needed to have another talk, very soon. As much as I appreciated his love and his loyalty, Derek's incredibly fast acceptance and instinctive use of his magic was making me a little nervous. His potential for causing untold destruction was approaching a critical level. In the three months that I had known him, Derek had always hidden his temper behind an easy-going demeanor, but since wholeheartedly embracing his sorcerer's abilities, his confidence—and temper—had soared almost overnight.

But if he would submit himself to my lead, and not attempt to access his untried potential too soon, we could prevail over the darkness. I decided to test him. I pulled out of Derek's embrace and calmly started walking across the room, shielding my thoughts from him. Derek had turned away to talk to Emily, when suddenly, unexpectedly, I turned back to him. "Derek, look at me, now!" I demanded.

He complied immediately, gazing with the utmost trust into my eyes as he surrendered his will to mine, without hesitation.

Good, I thought. *Very good, Derek! Immediate obedience is essential if I am going to be able to meld our powers when necessary. And it will become necessary sooner than we would like.*

Just before I broke our telepathic connection, I showered him with all of the love I felt for him, not just as a distant relation, but as a son, or a grandson.

He was still looking deeply into my eyes as he felt the gift of my love, and I could see his eyes widen and then close, tears of joy running freely down his cheeks.

I gave him a few minutes to compose himself and then I suggested that the three of us seek guidance and reassurance from the gods, my father in particular. "Why don't we sit together on the couch and go inside to the inner light. We could all benefit from this calming effect," I said quietly. I sat down with Derek on one side of me and Emily on the other, and we clasped hands to connect us more completely.

Almost immediately I heard my father's voice, and I silently requested that he share his message with both Derek and Emily, so that we would all experience the hope and confidence he provided.

Some time later there was a knock on the door, and I

sensed that it was the knights, whom I had contacted earlier. I bade them enter and they walked into the room, their eyes immediately seeking mine for instructions. Both of them kneeled down before me.

"I am here for you, Merlin—how may I serve you, my lord?" Ryan was obviously ready and willing to do whatever I asked of him.

"Lord Merlin, I am yours to command and would gladly lay down my life in your service," Gary declared solemnly.

I rose to my feet and looked down upon their reverently bowed heads. I sighed to myself, then reached out and drew them both upright. "I accept your fealty, worthy knights, but I do not require that you bow to me," I said. "Please sit for a moment. I need to talk to all of you."

I stood in front of these four people who would gladly give their lives for me and I was properly humbled. "We need to recruit anyone who has magic and is fairly proficient at it. The stakes are high. The entire planet may be at risk, with two practitioners of dark magic actively opposing us. Nimue, whom I thought I had destroyed centuries ago, is one of those practitioners. Adrestia, her daughter, is the other. The challenge will be to kill Nimue but not her daughter. I cannot condone killing Adrestia, as she is also my daughter, and she has been an unwitting accessory for her entire life." I noticed that both Ryan and Gary were clearly aghast at this turn of events.

"Derek and I will be using our sorcerer's senses to search for those with magical skills, but if anyone here intuitively feels that someone could be a candidate to assist us, please call me, or Derek, and let one of us approach the person. I will be at the shop tomorrow if you feel the need of my help or my company. I will be working towards a plan of action that has heretofore eluded us."

I continued with heart-felt intensity, "The time fast approaches when we will be fighting not only for our lives and the lives of the people here in Moab, but for the continuance of life on this planet. Whatever deity you pray to or commune with, please do so. We need any and all assistance that may be offered to us."

And then I felt my god-self take over: my body started glowing and from deep within me, in a resonant voice, came the words: "Have faith in me." I must have visited the gods again, because I was unaware that I had been carried into the bedroom until I opened my eyes and saw Emily sitting beside me, stroking my hair.

"Hi," I said faintly.

"Hi, yourself," she said, raising my hand to her lips. "Were you with Llyr?"

"I must have been, but I don't remember," I said, confused about the time I had been unconscious. This seemed exceedingly strange to me, as I should have been able to access the memory easily. Perhaps the gods had blocked my recall for some reason.

I sat up on the edge of the bed and looked at Emily, grateful that she was bound to me forever. She gazed back at me with a love I could never have imagined, and we reached out for each other, content for the moment just to be in each other's embrace.

I eased out of her arms and stood up, stretching. "I should go to the shop, Em. What time is it? When did the others leave?"

"It's almost four o'clock, so they must have left over an hour ago. Derek would have stayed, but I told him you would call if you needed him. He loves you so much he would do anything for you, Merlin, and I'm starting to be a little afraid of his powers; I don't know if he can control them."

"I know exactly what you mean, Emily, and if you had been able to sense what I did earlier, you'd be even more concerned. The only thing that will keep him from totally losing control is his love for me, and submitting to my will instantly is the only thing that will save him," I said.

I walked into the bathroom to splash my face with cool water. Em leaned in the doorway watching me. "Would you like me to go with you? I could start learning how to run the shop," she said as I toweled my face dry.

"Sure, I'd love the company. I haven't been keeping regular hours for a few days now and I should at least unpack the last shipment of books, and perhaps do some paperwork. I can show you how to mix some of the potions also, if you like." I was quiet for a few minutes as I brushed my hair and put my headband back on, and then I turned to my wife.

"Emily, Nimue will be coming for me any time now, I'm sure of it. I have to spend some time in deep meditation to attain the insight necessary to discover from whence she'll attack. All of us need to spend time coordinating our strengths and practicing with various weapons that match our fighting styles. I never was as competent with the crossbow as Gawain, so he can use mine. And as far as I know, Lancelot, er, Ryan, has guns, as well as swords, crossbows and longbows, and has considerable expertise with all of those weapons. Derek has his Park Service weapon and of course, his magic. My magic is by far my greatest asset, and if I can access them at will, my god-powers. I am a competent swordsman using the one that was forged for me by the gods, but it isn't a good use of my time and efforts."

Emily was acting a little annoyed so I asked her what was wrong.

"Merlin, you haven't mentioned me at all, but let me tell you something. I can shoot as well as Derek—maybe better— and although I had to surrender my Park Service weapon, I still have my own gun. My magic's not as strong as Derek's, or yours of course, but it could surprise us all in the long run."

"Em, I'm sorry to again seem to be disparaging your talents. Of course, you must train with everyone else, and I do consider you my partner in all things." I kissed her soundly and we both enjoyed every second of it.

We walked out the front door and headed for the shop on foot as usual. Emily reached for my hand and clasped it tightly, glancing at me slyly out of the corner of her eye.

"What is it, Em?" I said, looking at her questioningly.

"I was just checking to see if you looked any different than before you realized you were a god," Emily admitted.

"Do I?"

"Yeah, your feet look really kissable," she snickered. She turned, laughing, and ran the rest of the way with me in pursuit.

We arrived at the door of the shop breathing hard and overheated but feeling more light-hearted than we had in days.

I unlocked the door and removed the wards, and we entered the main room. It was hot and stuffy, so I turned on the cooler and looked around. We were just here this morning, but it seemed like a long time ago.

We didn't bother opening the shop to the public as it was so late in the day. We did some light cleaning and unloaded boxes of books and herbal supplies, pricing items before we shelved or packaged them. Emily was a quick study and seemed to enjoy working side by side with me. I knew she had made the right decision to quit her job, but I wasn't sure if she might feel some remorse. After all, the Park Service had been her life for many years. And then she met me and her life changed forever.

We had been working steadily for about three hours when I decided we had done enough for the day. It was time to go home.

Part 4:

Resolution

CHAPTER 41
July 10

THE DAY AFTER ADRESTIA'S ATTEMPT to overcome my senses with black magic, I intended to create a plan of attack utilizing all of our strengths. Both Gawain and Lancelot had pledged to protect the rest of us with their lives, but the truth was that we would probably end up protecting them. They had fighting skills remembered from long ago Camelot, and more recently, Ryan had martial arts training as well as hand-to-hand combat and weapons training from his days in the military. But it remained to be seen whether those skills would be enough to stand against powerful magic and supernatural forces.

I had spent some time in meditation that morning but was no closer to solving our dilemma. I had just opened the shop for the day when the chimes tinkled their usual melody and Derek came in with a tall, thin young man whom I did not recognize. Since my friend was supposed to be at work, I wondered what was going on. It had to be important for him to leave the park during his shift.

"Hi, Derek, what are you doing here?" I asked.

"Mer...uh...Michael, I wanted you to meet my new friend, Adam Gonzalez. We met out at Arches earlier today, and we found that we have somethin' interesting in common," Derek said. "Adam, this is Michael Reese."

The young man held out his hand, and as I grasped it firmly with my own, I experienced a warm, tingling sensation and knew that Adam had magic.

"Well, well, what have we here?" I murmured, intrigued as I looked at this stranger, noticing that he was several inches taller than me.

Adam grinned, acknowledging that he had also felt the telltale sign of magic from me, and said, "It's nice to meet you,

Michael. You can imagine my surprise when I ran into Derek and discovered a kindred spirit. He told me about you, and I persuaded him to bring me here to meet you."

"Oh? And what exactly did Derek say about me?" I glanced at him, hoping he hadn't said too much. We did not know this wizard, and it was possible that he was in league with our enemy.

I don't think so, Merlin. And I didn't tell him very much. Derek's thoughts were clearer than ever as he contacted me telepathically.

"He just said that you were his best friend as well as a relative, and that you owned an herb shop. And that you have magic, of course," Adam explained.

I nodded at Adam while addressing my thoughts to Derek. *Good work, Great-grandson!*

You know it sounds weird when you say that, don't you?

I know, but I don't care—I feel very grandfatherly, even fatherly, towards you sometimes as you well know.

Yeah, but you still look more like my cousin, Great-grandfather, Derek countered.

I just shrugged and smiled at him.

Adam, who was expecting me to speak to him, looked between Derek and myself and frowned in confusion.

"What, are you guys telepathic or something? I didn't know that was part of the magical gig."

It may have been a mistake to reveal our telepathic connection since he was an unknown factor, but it gave me an idea. I'd do some careful probing and see if I could sense to whom he had promised his allegiance.

"I'm sorry, Adam, that was rude of us. Derek and I have a close bond between us, and we've discovered that we can communicate with each other without words. But, please, tell us about yourself, and about your family. We can sit over here in my reading area and get to know each other. Would you like coffee, a soda, a glass of water?" I played the genial host, hoping that this tactic would put him at ease and help me to sense his intentions. As I waited for Adam to reply, I glanced around casually, confirming that the shop was empty of patrons, which was a good thing with Adam there, speaking openly about magic.

As he slouched down in one of the armchairs, Adam finally answered my question, "Uh, well, water I guess."

I held my hand out to him and manifested a glass of ice water, which he took from me with a startled look and quick nod of thanks.

He drank deeply from the glass before putting it down. Then he leaned back, stretched his long legs out in front of him, and began to speak. "Yeah, about my family; it's a long story, so I'll just give you the short version. My parents met in Los Angeles about twenty-five years ago. My dad, Guillermo, had just come from Mexico, and my mom, Leslie, had moved to California from England, and when they met and realized they both had magic, well, sparks flew."

I grinned to myself as I thought about the sparks that happened between Emily and me.

Adam continued, "They married and had three boys— I'm the youngest—and all of us have magic. I guess we're pretty lucky, because our parents helped us learn how to use and control our powers, and..."

I watched his face as he talked about his family and his upbringing in a household of wizards, and on the surface at least, it seemed that he was telling the truth. I noticed that Derek was fascinated by the story, obviously wishing that he had experienced his own magic as a child. I could tell him that he was fortunate to have had a normal childhood. I had been known as the boy without a father, and even worse, I was suspected of being the child of a demon, which resulted in being shunned and regarded with suspicion and fear. It was not a pleasant time for me. Now, of course, I knew the truth: Llyr had been there for me, time and again, but I had no memory of it.

I turned my attention back to Adam and very carefully reached into his mind. His thoughts indicated that he was a very young wizard, no more than eighteen years old, very cocky yet competent, but far below my level of ability. In reality, being the son of a god and, if I'd understood Llyr correctly, a god myself, I had an entirely different and more complex range of abilities, so Adam had no way to prevent me from accessing his thoughts. However, if I wasn't subtle, he might realize what I was doing.

Again I reached out to Adam and felt his innocence, his lack of guile, and his proficiency in using magic. I almost felt guilty for invading his privacy, for the only other things of importance that I discovered were his intelligence, his love for his family and his loyalty to his friends, which now apparently included both Derek and me.

His parents were no more than mid-level wizards, but had taught their children all the basic magical skills and, most importantly, they had taught them integrity. Also, I sensed that the family worshipped one of the old gods. The image in Adam's mind was not clear but looked rather like my father—or like me, for that matter. And I wasn't willing to delve into *that* subject just now.

While I was a little hesitant about immediately including this boy—and perhaps his parents and brothers if they were willing—in our circle, I knew we needed the magical assistance as soon as possible.

"Adam, are you here with your parents, or by yourself?" I asked, hoping he would confirm what I already knew from my exploration of his mind.

He looked at me questioningly for a moment, and then admitted that he was here with his parents, visiting the Utah national parks during his summer vacation. He had just graduated from high school and hoped to go to college eventually, but he'd wanted to take some time off before committing himself to any particular field of study.

I considered my words carefully. If he decided to help me, it could change the course of his life forever. "Adam, there is a situation that is rapidly becoming critical, that could affect not only this area, but the entire planet. I need the help of as many competent practitioners of magic as possible, but they need to understand what is at stake and to accept my leadership without question."

Adam listened quietly to what I had to say, but it was obvious he was confused. "Michael, I'm sorry, but I don't understand what this is about, or why you're involved."

Derek had been observing until this time, but now he thought, *Merlin, I don't know if we can convince him without revealin' who you are. Do you really think Adam and his folks would be of help to us?*

I turned and looked at him. *Yes, it is certainly possible. And you were right Derek, he's not in league with Nimue or any of her min...*

Please, don't say minions, Derek interrupted.

I smiled. *All right, associates. We need help from as many practitioners of magic as we can find. I'm hoping to persuade the three of them, and perhaps Adam's brothers, to join us, and to convince them to contact their friends who have magic.*

Our interaction had taken only a few seconds, but I could tell that Adam was feeling left out and impatient. I didn't have to know exactly what was in his mind at this moment. His uncontrolled emotions were obvious.

"Adam, I appreciate your patience," I said evenly, as I heard a sarcastic, *Yeah, right,* in my mind. "Derek and I needed to confer a moment about something important. I know it is asking a lot of you, but we hope you'll be willing to wait for a few hours longer for the answers to your questions. The reason for the delay is to gather the rest of our group and introduce them to you all at once tonight. We hope that you can come back, with your parents, perhaps around eight o'clock, and I promise that the information we will impart to you will be sufficiently startling to make it worth your while. At that point, we would be happy to answer any and all of the questions that you may have."

Adam calmed down as he thought about my proposal. "Okay, I'll come back later and I'll bring my parents along. I'm sure they would like to know that there is a community of wizards here in Moab. We'll be here at eight."

Neither of us corrected him; he'd find out soon enough. As Adam and Derek walked out the front door, Derek thought, *Little does he know that our 'community of wizards' consists of two sorcerers, one Elf, and two knights without magic! This ought to be interestin'...see you tonight.*

Be here at six-thirty for beer and pizza—I need to talk to everybody before the Gonzalez family arrives.

Got it. See you at six-thirty Great-grandfather—or should I say 'Dad?' Derek looked back over his shoulder at me and winked.

I grinned wryly and shook my head. When I had given him my love the day before, he had tearfully accepted that gift with his entire being. But today, he was determined to make light of it. Despite the fact that he was still vastly untried and potentially dangerous in regards to his powers, I was still as proud as a father that Derek would be a first-class sorcerer in the not-too-distant future. The fact that he had the confidence to refer to himself as such told me that he was already aware of his strength.

I watched thoughtfully as the two young men left the shop, intrigued that Adam had no experience with telepathy. It could be that this ability—or lack thereof—was one of the differences between wizards and sorcerers; something to delve into later.

I had just returned my gaze to the document in front of

THE HEART OF MAGIC

me when the chimes tinkled again, and one of my regular customers entered and greeted me. I responded with a smile and a nod. However, my thoughts were elsewhere. I would need to call everyone immediately. I had already made it clear that a summons from me overruled personal plans, so I knew that they would all be here without fail.

I had an idea about how to most effectively introduce everyone to Adam and his parents. I did not know anything about them except what the boy had mentioned, and of course what I had experienced in Adam's mind, but I realized that the young man's cockiness needed to be addressed. I intended to make it clear to all of them that I was the undisputed leader of the group.

At six-thirty that evening, everyone in our circle was present. Emily had just arrived with the pizza and Derek accompanied her carrying the beer. Together they efficiently set everything out on the counter.

We all helped ourselves to the food, and as we ate, I recounted my experiences of the past few days. The most difficult thing to talk about was my vision of a horrific future world. I had to make everyone understand that we must prevail over our enemy, to prevent that future from happening. I expressed my hope that we could overcome any differences that we might harbor amongst ourselves, because those things would weaken us, make us vulnerable. We must be strong, and support each other at all costs. I described the realization I'd had about Nimue, and mentioned my experience at Delicate Arch with the vanishing portal and the invisible wall that had blocked my access to it. I also mentioned my suspicions that there was a battle raging on another plane of existence, in the realm of the gods. However, I did not tell Lancelot and Gawain about my experience with Llyr, in which he had essentially revealed my origins—they would probably realize the truth before the evening was over.

I discussed with everyone the way in which I planned to

introduce us to the newcomers, the intent being to impress upon them that our group would be the guiding force in this unusual situation.

I also prepared a few spells in case I felt the need to show off a little.

Around eight o'clock the door opened and Adam and his parents came in. I noticed that the parents were in their forties, fit and healthy and tall.

"I'm glad you could come, Adam," I said. And then I turned to his parents. "Hi, I'm Michael Reese. And you must be Guillermo and Leslie Gonzalez. I'm pleased to meet you."

As we shook each other's hands we all recognized in each other the tingling indicative of magic, and I smiled, welcoming them to my humble shop.

"First of all, I would like to mention that none of us are wizards, as your son may have mistakenly told you, and we apologize for any misconceptions. Actually, Derek and I are sorcerers. I hope that is not going to affect our future relationship."

I knew there was often a certain enmity between wizards and sorcerers and wanted to bring that possibility out in the open right away.

The Gonzalez family seemed a little wary and tense after my announcement. Did they assume we would try to coerce them with black magic? In the past, many people had assumed I was evil when they discovered that I was a sorcerer.

"No, of course not. I'm sure we will all get along fine," Leslie said diplomatically.

"Good. Now I would like to introduce and showcase each person's particular talent. First is the beautiful woman who happens to be my wife, Emily Reese. She is a Fae being, an Elf, with her own form of magic," and I gestured to her to reveal her glowing skin and silvery eyes. She smiled and held her head high as she stood a little apart from everyone else.

"Next is Ryan Jones, who is the reincarnated soul of Sir

Lancelot, a Knight of King Arthur's Round Table," and I triggered a spell which revealed Lancelot in his original body, complete with armor and sword, standing between Gary and Derek.

"And this is Derek Colburn whom Adam met earlier today. He is my many-times-removed great-grandson and an able sorcerer." As I nodded to Derek to present himself, I noticed out of the corner of my eye that Adam's parents looked startled at my announcement and began glancing at me suspiciously. It was possible that they had guessed my identity.

Derek didn't disappoint me. He closed his eyes and raised his arms, energy pouring out of him in a controlled display of power that crackled and flashed around him, raising the hair on his head and causing his skin to glow. He slowly opened his eyes and crossed his arms, then quietly used my spell, *"Levo."* He rose a foot in the air, then descended smoothly, looking solemn but pleased.

I glanced at Adam, Guillermo and Leslie, and saw that their eyes were wide with astonishment. They had expected wizards like themselves and they were meeting sorcerers and knights—and an Elf.

"And this is Gary Gardner, who has reincarnated over and over again looking exactly the same as he did in Camelot when he was Sir Gawain, a truly dedicated knight." And I showed Gawain also clad in armor and wielding a sword.

Now Derek took over to introduce me: "Adam, Guillermo, and Leslie, now meet the one to whom our lives are bound. Although he goes by the name Michael Reese, he is actually Merlin, also called Myrddin Emrys, former Sorcerer of the Realm for both Uther and Arthur Pendragon, and son of Llyr, the Welsh god of magic and healin'. And he *is* my ancestor." I revealed myself in my deep blue Camelot robe trimmed with gold and ermine, with my hair and beard down to my waist, skin glowing with energy, golden light arcing over my head. I levitated up toward the ceiling and floated there for a few moments before I smoothly descended to the floor below.

All three members of the Gonzalez family were awestruck and humbled, which is exactly the reaction I wanted to see from them. I casually flicked my wrist at Ryan and at Gary and removed the spells, and then Derek and Em each let go of their own "special effects."

I held onto my guise the longest and walked slowly over to Adam and his parents, all three of them promptly sinking down on their knees, looking up at me in disbelief. I gradually allowed my normal appearance to return, looking each one in the eye as I did so. I gazed at each person just until it could have become something deeper, then looked away. I was establishing myself as the undisputed leader of this group. Perhaps it was ridiculously overdone, but I wanted all of them to realize that although I respected their magic, none of them had seniority here.

Then they sank even lower, bowing their heads to me in obeisance, much the same as Gawain had done the other night.

I began to regret my theatrics as the Gonzalez family remained on their knees, tears streaming from their eyes. I was afraid they were going to kiss my feet.

"Please, you may rise now, for I am not King Arthur, nor am I my father," I said kindly but firmly.

Adam looked up at me and said earnestly, "Oh, my lord, you don't understand. My family has always *prayed* to *you*, Myrddin Emrys, and I was taught that *you* were the god of magic. And now we are here in your presence—*you're real and you're alive."* Adam stood up before me with his countenance glowing with adoration, and tears coursing down his cheeks, while his parents just remained on the ground, worshiping me, their foreheads resting on my feet.

To say that I was astonished would be an understatement. I looked at Emily and Derek expecting to see that they were as surprised as I at this turn of events, only to see a similar look of adoration in their eyes as they looked back at me.

THE HEART OF MAGIC

Merlin, they obviously worship the ground you walk on, Emily said silently. I saw tears of devotion in her eyes. *As I do...*

Derek was emotional and a little embarrassed as he projected to me, *Merlin, you already know how I feel...kinda like they do.*

Well, Merlin, now you've done it, I thought to myself, *you've just confirmed that you are indeed their god.*

Suddenly I was dazzled by a memory of brilliant light: I remembered my true form, a being of light and spirit, and I remembered living in the realm of the gods among other beings such as myself. Finally, I recognized the truth: I was the god of magic and healing.

I felt an abrupt change in the stream of time, and everything stopped. Llyr stood in front of me, a troubled look on his face. "Merlin, I blame myself for what you have just done. I encouraged you to remember your true self, and you have revealed too much to these mortals. It was too soon for this to happen. Human beings are not ready to know that a god walks amongst them, and you are not ready for the consequences of that knowledge.

"The one God, who governs all and is supreme over even the realm of the gods, has decreed that you have upset the balance in the universe by your actions this day. However, because of who you are, and because you are important to this world, you have been granted leniency.

"You have two choices, Myrddin Emrys: I will remove the memory of your actions here tonight from everyone in this room. No one, including you, will remember that you are in reality the god of magic and healing, on this earth in human form. When the right time comes for you to reveal yourself, your memory shall be returned to you.

Or, you alone will be allowed to keep your memory, but will be unable to speak of it, or to access your god powers, until

God allows it. The choice is yours, my son."

I was stunned by this turn of events, although it should not have surprised me. I had, due to my ego and love of theatrics, caused everyone in this room to make the connection between Merlin the Sorcerer, son of Llyr, and Myrddin Emrys, the real god of magic and healing. I had known in my heart that I was making a mistake, and I did it anyway; a failing of my current partially human state.

"Father," I said ironically, for Llyr was my friend and fellow deity long before I took human form. "I truly apologize. I allowed my ego and my desires to dictate my actions. But I beg of you, please allow these people to remember everything *except* that I am a god. I believe it is imperative for them to realize that, as the son of Llyr, I have special powers and leadership over them for purposes of this upcoming battle with Nimue. And please, allow me to keep my memories. I have wondered for so long who and what I am, that I... *need* to remember, even if I'm not allowed to speak of it or to access my higher nature or my god powers."

Llyr stared at me for a moment, and then his mouth twitched with barely suppressed humor as he nodded solemnly. "You always were the smartest of all of us, my friend, and the most motivated to involve yourself with the human world. Very well then, it shall be as you have requested."

I prepared myself for the change about to occur; I knew that Llyr would turn time back to earlier in the evening.

I presumed that Emily and Derek would also lose their memories of what had transpired between us regarding my god status, and I was momentarily saddened that Emily would lose that intense feeling of devotion she treasured. But it was for the best. I hoped that I had made the correct decision for myself.

As Llyr faded from my sight and the flow of time resumed, it was apparent that it was again time for pizza.

CHAPTER 42
July 10 Evening (again)

A T SIX-THIRTY THAT EVENING, everyone in our circle was present. Emily had just arrived with the pizza and Derek accompanied her carrying the beer. Together they efficiently set everything out on the counter.

We all helped ourselves to the food, and as we ate, I recounted my experiences of the past few days. The most difficult thing to talk about was my vision of a horrific future world. I had to make everyone understand that we must prevail over our enemy, to prevent that future from happening. I expressed my hope that we could overcome any differences that we might harbor amongst ourselves, because those things would weaken us, make us vulnerable. We must be strong, and support each other at all costs. I described the realization I'd had about Nimue, and mentioned my experience at Delicate Arch with the vanishing portal and the invisible wall that had blocked my access to it. I also mentioned my suspicions that there was a battle raging on another plane of existence, in the realm of the gods. However, I did not tell Ryan and Gary about my experience with Llyr, in which he had essentially revealed my origins.

This time when I discussed introducing ourselves to the Gonzalez family, I did not mention any overt show of special powers. I asked Emily and Derek to tone down any introduction of their powers they might have been planning. And I would not allow any extreme introduction of myself unless they didn't believe I was Merlin.

And this time, I did not prepare any spells for showing off. Who was I kidding? If I really wanted to show off, I wouldn't need a spell.

Around eight o'clock the door opened and Adam and his parents came in. I noticed again that the parents were in their forties, fit and healthy and tall.

"I'm glad you could come, Adam," I said. And then I turned to his parents. "Hi, I'm Michael Reese. And you must be Guillermo and Leslie Gonzalez. I'm pleased to meet you."

As we shook each other's hands we all recognized in each other the tingling indicative of magic, and I smiled, welcoming them to my humble shop.

"First of all, I would like to mention that none of us are wizards, as your son may have mistakenly told you, and we apologize for any misconceptions. Actually, Derek and I are sorcerers. I hope that is not going to affect our future relationship."

I knew there was often a certain enmity between wizards and sorcerers and wanted to bring that possibility out in the open right away.

The Gonzalez family seemed a little wary and tense after that announcement. Did they assume we would try to coerce them with black magic? In the past, many people had assumed I was evil when they discovered that I was a sorcerer.

I knew that at least Leslie would not object, but I would have to wait for her to verbalize it.

"No, of course not. I'm sure we will all get along fine," Leslie said diplomatically.

"Good. Now I would like to introduce my friends. First is the beautiful woman who happens to be my wife, Emily Reese. She is a Fae being, an Elf." She just smiled and silently stood a little apart from everyone else.

"Next is Ryan Jones, who is the reincarnated soul of Sir Lancelot, a Knight of King Arthur's Round Table." Ryan bowed briefly but did not speak.

"And this is Derek Colburn whom Adam met earlier today. He is my many-times-removed great-grandson and an able sorcerer." Derek just nodded and smiled and showed no outward sign of power.

I looked at Adam, Guillermo and Leslie, and saw that

their eyes were wide with astonishment and a dawning realization of my true identity. It was obvious that they were not as affected as the first time when they witnessed the "special effects."

"And this is Gary Gardner, who has reincarnated over and over again looking exactly the same as he did in Camelot when he was Sir Gawain, a truly dedicated knight." Gary nodded briefly in acknowledgement.

Now Derek took over to introduce me: "Adam, Guillermo, and Leslie, now meet the one to whom we owe our allegiance. He is known here in Moab as Michael Reese, but he is actually Merlin, former Sorcerer of the Realm for both Uther and Arthur Pendragon, and son of Llyr, the Welsh god of magic and healin'."

All three members of the Gonzalez family were pleased and impressed, which is exactly the reaction I hoped to see from them, rather than the extreme reaction I witnessed the first time.

I wanted all of them to realize that although I respected their magic, none of them had seniority here, and it appears that I accomplished that.

The three of them kneeled before me, their heads lowered in obeisance, much the same as Gawain had done the other night.

I realized that there would be no scene, no worshiping at my feet, no declarations of devotion such as happened the first time, and just for a moment, I was disappointed. Was it in my true nature to expect obeisance from mortals? I truly hoped not.

"Please, rise. You do not have to be on your knees before me. I'm half human and far from perfect," I said, kindly but firmly.

As Leslie slowly stood up, I noticed that she still looked at me with worship in her eyes. And Guillermo countered, "But Lord Merlin, you are immortal and a demi-god, are you not?"

"Yes, I am those things, but..."

"Then to me and my family you are precious, and you

285

are the one we will serve until our last breaths, as we have striven to serve your father, Llyr, all our lives," Guillermo assured me in a deep voice. This was different from the first time, and I realized that Llyr had altered their memories so that it wasn't me they had worshiped.

And the Gonzalez family, with that solemn pledge, joined our circle. They promised that they would immediately contact their other two sons, and would alert all the wizards they knew from here to California to come and support our cause.

When I began to speak again, I knew that the gods were now dictating my words and controlling my breath. "A change is coming; it vibrates throughout the very heart of this mortal realm. I see the shadows of darkness eventually consuming every living thing on this planet unless the forces of good prevail. The purest and noblest of hearts stand ready, in this room, to vanquish the evil that has been stalking this earthly realm for over a thousand years. I, Merlin, son of Llyr, swear to you that the courage and love living in your hearts is stronger than you can know, stronger than that evil. This place and this time may well be the turning point in a war that started long ago."

An hour later, Emily and I were left alone in the shop amid dirty coffee cups and garbage bags emitting the faint order of tomato sauce and garlic.

CHAPTER 43
July 10 Night

I WAS INTROSPECTIVE, REALIZING the magnitude of the memory I had experienced, and the finality of the judgment against me for having caused an imbalance in the universe. I hadn't known, or hadn't remembered, that the gods were governed by the one God, and I was aghast that my actions had brought disruption to both the realm of mortals and to the realm of the gods.

"You're awfully quiet, magic man," said Emily thoughtfully, walking up behind me and rubbing my shoulders.

"Just thinking. Ohhh, Em, that feels wonderful," I sighed, closing my eyes in appreciation. Had I been a feline I would have purred. "Have I told you today how much I love you?"

"No, you haven't, but I always feel your love through our bond, Merlin, and I love you, too, endlessly," Emily said softly. She finished the shoulder rub and came around and knelt in front of me, laying her head on my lap.

"It didn't work, you know," she said after a moment's silence.

"What didn't?" I asked, stroking her silky long hair.

"Llyr's plan to remove my memory that you're the god of magic and healing."

I was quiet for a minute then chuckled. "He should have known that it wouldn't work. Our bond is so strong, our connection so complete, that even if you had forgotten, you would have sensed the truth again anyway."

I cradled her face in my hands and leaned over to kiss her tenderly. I gazed into her eyes and said in a voice deeper than my normal baritone, "It was destined from the beginning of time that I would marry you—I know that now. You're the best thing that has ever happened to me, my love."

"Merlin, you're a god, how can you say that? I'm not *that* special."

"You are unique in this entire universe, and you have always been meant for me. I have been waiting for you literally since time began," I said, my god-self speaking through me. I Looked deeply into her eyes, and Emily saw what I Saw, and felt what I Felt; she experienced the truth of it. I could tell she was awed and overwhelmed and I quickly brought myself out of the trance-like state.

"Emily, I'm sorry." My voice had returned to normal. "I'm not yet used to keeping the infinite part of myself held back in this physical plane." And then I realized that I shouldn't have been able to talk to her about that part of myself, nor connect to that god-state at all. *Had Llyr not been able to affect me? Am I the stronger of the two of us? Or has the one God allowed this?*

"It's okay, Merlin, it's actually very exciting. You're glowing like crazy and radiating so much love that I'm feeling very high right now," Emily giggled. She bounced to her feet and then sat in my lap, kissing me provocatively.

My body responded quickly and I groaned in anticipation. I held onto my wife and teleported the two of us upstairs. It seemed that we had spent more time in the apartment bedroom in recent days than at home.

We frantically ripped each other's clothes off and threw ourselves down on the bed, caressing each other as we felt our magic building and coursing through our bodies. When I entered her she gripped me tightly inside and sent her magic humming through me from her center. We moved together rhythmically to a tune only we could hear, a song originating from our souls. We were nearing that ecstatic state of completion, and when we soared, our combined consciousness would have left our bodies if I hadn't held tightly to this mortal realm.

Emily finally opened her eyes and seemed surprised that

we were still in the apartment.

"Oh, my God, that was out of this world, Merlin! What did you do?"

"We almost left our bodies behind and I had to hold us to the physical plane."

"But what did you do before that? It felt like we took a ride on the god train," she said breathlessly.

I just laughed, because that was exactly what had happened.

We lay entwined for a time and just stared at each other.

"Emily, I feel so strange right now, as if I am two separate entities: The man named Merlin who I have always been, and the being of spirit and light that has existed since the creation of the universe. Perhaps I should have had Llyr take this memory away for now. It's almost too much, too beautiful, to bear."

"Merlin, you've waited so long to know the truth that it would be a crime to take that realization away from you." She sat up and started to reach for my feet.

"Em, you're not going to kiss my feet again, are you? Please don't do that. The god in me seems to enjoy it, but it makes me, Merlin, feel really uncomfortable. Your devotion is very precious to me, but the foot-kissing—*Gaah*!"

Emily laughed. "Merlin, I was just going to rub your feet. Sheesh, you gods are so touchy!"

She started rubbing my right foot, which felt amazing. But as she continued on to the left foot, Em grinned slyly and kissed that one quite deliberately.

I rolled my eyes, feeling more like Merlin again. I would have to learn to keep the god in me under control, because I certainly couldn't live normally in Moab, glowing and slipping spontaneously into a trance while I was at the grocery store, or even at my shop. I would certainly reveal myself, which could obviously cause major repercussions since I was not supposed to be able to use the god powers.

All of a sudden I wanted to get away; I was feeling restless for some reason.

"Em, let's go somewhere! It's not that late, maybe we could teleport to the Bahamas or someplace and walk on the beach."

"Okay," Em said, obviously feeling as restless as I did. "I don't have to work tomorrow since I quit my job, and you could always tap into some infinite energy source if you get tired at the shop tomorrow. So sure, why not?" Excited, she started dressing.

I pulled on my shirt and pants and slipped my feet into sandals. "I just want to be alone with you, away from here, even if it's just for a few minutes. I really wish I could take you to my cave back in Britain."

And instantly, we were there, in the Crystal Cave, and I had the feeling it was no longer the twenty-first century. I was afraid to see if my previous self was unconscious on the bed.

"Whoa," breathed Emily, blinking at the sight of all the crystals around us and starting to shiver in the cool damp air. She hadn't had time to put her shoes on and she curled her toes against the cold rock floor.

I was absolutely speechless. Was this real or just another vision? It certainly felt real, and it went beyond mere teleportation. I had wished to be here and instantaneously, we were here. My higher self had evidently done this. I needed help—this was beyond me.

"Father, Llyr, please come to me," I called. Llyr materialized in a robe of silk and gold and silently regarded our two stunned faces.

"Well, son and daughter-in-law, what have you done now?" His deep, echoing voice stirred Emily, and she scrambled to kneel at the god's feet.

I bowed briefly, no longer feeling as awed by him, and

then straightened. "I do not know how we came to be here. I was not aware that I still had access to all my powers as a god, and yet I wished us here. I'm a bit startled, I have to admit."

"Merlin, when you chose to keep your memories of your true nature, that was *all* you were supposed to keep. Somehow, you are much stronger than I anticipated and you held onto the powers that were supposed to have been denied to you.

"I will return you to your home in Moab and you will remember everything, as I had promised, but the only powers you are allowed to use are the ones that were yours *before* you remembered your true nature. I am sorry, but you have forced my hand," he said sternly. Emily was still kneeling before him.

"You may rise, my child." Llyr looked down from his great height and smiled at my lovely wife, and then he turned to me. "Oh, yes, she is indeed the one, Merlin."

"Now, both of you, close your eyes," he said, as if to recalcitrant children. We obeyed, and immediately felt the change as we suddenly were back in the apartment above the shop.

"Did that really just happen?" Emily asked uncertainly.

"Yes, Emily, it did." I searched my memory and was relieved that I still remembered I was a god, but when I tried to access that infinite being of spirit, I failed. Llyr had finally succeeded in blocking access to my higher self. I could still go into the light as I always had, but not into that special place I had barely had time to explore. After having been aware of it, and having basked in that higher energy and reality, I felt bereft, as if a part of my body had been amputated.

I cried out in anguish, "No!" I dropped to my knees and covered my face with my hands, tears of sorrow overflowing from my eyes.

"Oh, Merlin, I'm so sorry," Em cried as she experienced my pain. I could feel my wife's arms around my shoulders and her embrace warmed my soul through my despair. Being able to remember something I could no longer experience was torture, but I knew I had brought this on myself.

Merlin, you still have all of your powers as a demi-god. Enjoy and use them as you have always done, and let the memory of your real self be there to comfort you, not to remind you of what you have lost. You are the same being you have always been; courageous, unique, selfless. My friend and my son, I will always be with you and you with me, as it has always been, and will always be until the end of time...

CHAPTER 44
July 10 Late Night

A S LLYR'S VOICE FADED, I felt a great weight lift from my heart. I took a deep breath and exhaled, letting go of the pain and sadness and feeling whole again. I looked into Emily's worried eyes and rejoiced that she was part of my life. I smiled. "It's okay, love, I'm back."

"Well, thank God, because I've had enough drama for one night. At least I got to see your cave—for two seconds—and I finally met your dad. I think he likes me," Emily said.

"Oh, he definitely likes you, Em," I said reassuringly.

Suddenly the events of the past twenty-four hours seemed to catch up with both of us.

"Merlin, can we go home now, please?" She sighed, sounding fatigued.

"Yes, I'm ready too. I'll lock up properly and set the wards, and then I'll take us home."

"Let's just walk, okay? I'm tired, but I need the time to unwind and stretch my legs."

"Alright, wife, we can walk home if that's what you want."

A few minutes later we were strolling down Main Street, hand in hand, looking in the store windows and enjoying each other's company. As we traveled farther from the shop and turned down the side street, then along the path past the creek, the street lights became few and far between, and it was very dark under the trees. Normally, I loved the warm summer nights in Moab, but this night having been fraught with emotion, I was a little more sensitive to the energies around me. And something seemed off, dangerous. I looked at Emily and she seemed to feel it also—she was tense and alert beside me.

Suddenly a tall form burst from the shadows and

growled in an archaic British accent, "Stop there, and give me your valuables, posthaste!"

"Seriously?" I said incredulously, as I readied my magic and surreptitiously created a protective shield around us. Emily had already stepped close to me as she had sensed my intention through our bond.

"Do not act the dunce, or I swear I will cut you," the man threatened, brandishing a wicked-looking dagger.

"You would be wise to let us pass," I warned him, knowing he could not breech my shield, but I was in no mood for this.

As the man came towards us, furious at my unwillingness to submit, I raised my right hand and said, *"Desino,"* and the attacker was stopped, motionless, the hand wielding the dagger thrust out towards us.

"If you knew what we have been through this day, you would run screaming from this place." Impatiently, I created a small orb of light, the better to see who had the audacity to threaten us. The soft light of magic highlighted a handsome face currently twisted in a ruthless expression, eyes wide with fear as he heard my words and witnessed something he had not expected to encounter.

As I looked more closely at this man, about my height but heavier, more muscular, I thought I recognized him as someone from my past, another person I had never expected to see again.

"What is your name, brigand?" I demanded as I released enough of the spell to allow him to answer; to confirm what I suspected.

"Percival," the man answered belligerently.

"So, Sir Percival, how came you here, when you obviously have no business in this town, nor in this century, for that matter?" I spoke harshly in the old British language.

"What? Who are you? By the goddess, is that you, Merlin?" Percival asked in disbelief, also speaking in the old tongue.

Emily looked at me in shock. Though she didn't under-stand the language, she did hear the would-be thief call me by name. "How does he know you, Merlin?"

I stared grimly at the disreputable figure held fast by my spell. "How he came to be here is not clear to me, but this man seems to be Sir Percival, one of Arthur's knights. Once honora-ble, he is now a thief and possibly a murderer."

"Nay, I have *never* killed except in battle, or out of dire necessity; as you are well aware, sorcerer!" Sir Percival said ve-hemently in modern English, still unable to move.

Emily started to speak, but I stopped her while I made sure that the shield spell would enable us to speak privately. I then indicated to Emily that she was free to speak her mind.

"Merlin, I don't understand how he can be here, speak-ing modern English. It's as if he was just transported here from the past and is under some enchantment."

"It certainly seems that way, doesn't it?" I said thought-fully.

"Why is he so angry with you? I thought you were friends with all the knights?"

"No, not all of us were friends, although I could have sworn that Percival was not among those individuals who wished me ill. After Arthur died and was taken to Avalon, many of the knights who survived the battle at Camlann, in their grief blamed me not only for what happened to Arthur, but for everything. They apparently felt that I should have predicted the battle, which I did, and that I should have been able to prevent it, which I could not. They felt I should have been able to save *all* the citi-zens of Camelot who fell that day, which was not possible. Call it destiny or fate—that is something I cannot control." I closed my eyes and tried to obliterate the harsh scenes of the battle from my mind. It had been centuries since I had been faced with those images and I truly wished that I had not been reminded of them.

I opened my eyes and stared at Sir Percival, attempting to sense his thoughts, but I could not. Was this block due to black magic or did he have an inherently closed mind, requiring physical contact to penetrate the blockage? I really did not want to touch him, or to initiate any kind of Sight that would enable him to See into my being. I didn't trust him and it seemed the feeling was mutual.

I decided to talk to him, and if he should be able to explain himself, all the better. Again I released the shield enough to communicate. "Sir Percival, I will ask you once again. How came you here?"

"That is a very good question, Merlin," he said sarcastically. "Unfortunately, I cannot answer it, for I know not. One moment I was in the tavern in Camelot throwing dice, and the next moment I was here—alone, friendless, speaking a strange tongue that I had never learned. Not knowing from whence my next meal, or my next lodging, would come."

Emily thought, *Could Nimue have done this? But why would she? Maybe the gods brought him from the past. But if that is the case, you would think they'd have chosen someone that actually liked you.*

I agree, neither option seems logical, I projected back to her.

"It seems that you have been drawn into a struggle that is not of your making, nor was it your choice to come here. Therefore I will free you." Reluctantly, I released the spell and the protection shield, and simultaneously took his dagger from him. Percival stumbled slightly as he regained his balance.

"It appears that some sort of magic has transported you from the past to the twenty-first century, Sir Percival," I said unhappily. Under different circumstances I would immediately welcome him to our group, but I was unsure of his intentions.

"Twenty-first century?" He shook his head in disbelief and muttered, "Well, that would explain why I did not recognize my surroundings."

"It is indeed different from the fifth century, and from our homeland."

"Yes, it is, sorcerer."

"Merlin, I think we should go to the house and get Percival something to eat, and save the reminiscences for tomorrow. It's really late," Emily insisted.

"I'm sorry, wife. Yes, you're right, let's go home," I agreed. "Come with us if you wish, Percival. Let us suspend hostilities, at least for tonight." I was willing to do this for Emily's sake but I would watch him closely while he was in our home.

"Agreed," Percival said sullenly. Then he realized what I had called Emily and he gazed speculatively at the both of us. "Did you say wife? You married? *You?* Pardon me if I seem overly surprised. I thought sorcerers never wed."

"You are correct, sorcerers do not usually marry. But I am not just any sorcerer. The gods led us to each other and it was our destiny to fall in love and marry," I explained as I extinguished the orb, and we began to walk towards the house.

"What do you mean?" Percival asked insistently.

"I am the son of a god, Percival; I am immortal. How else could I still be alive after sixteen centuries, looking the same as I did in Camelot?" I said impatiently, wishing I had just kept quiet.

Percival looked skeptical. "I thought you had been transported here as I had been."

"No, I was not." I abruptly ended the conversation. Emily looked at me, puzzled, but said nothing, and we walked the remaining two blocks in silence.

When we entered the house, Emily turned to me. "Please introduce me properly to Percival, Merlin."

I looked at her and realized what she intended to do. *As you wish, my love.* I then spoke aloud in a formal tone, "I do apologize for being negligent. Emily, may I introduce Sir Percival, previously a Knight of the Round Table for King Arthur in Camelot. Sir Percival, may I present my wife Lady Emily, descendant of warriors and kings."

"My lady." Sir Percival bowed low to her, and she nodded, accepting the homage as her due.

"Sir Percival, I would say that it is a pleasure to meet you, but your initial greeting at knife point was far from courteous," she said coolly. "However, you may call me Emily if you wish."

I smiled to myself and felt very proud of her. As my wife, she should receive at least the courtesy extended to someone of my station, and she instinctively responded appropriately.

"Lady Emily, I apologize and assure you that I will not take up arms against you or Lord Merlin again," Percival pledged on one knee.

"I accept your pledge, Sir Knight," Emily said. "Merlin?"

"I accept your pledge, conditionally. Should you decide to renege on that promise, for any reason or to any extent, you will not enjoy my response overmuch," I said mildly, but managing to convey a real threat.

"I understand completely, Lord Merlin," he responded quickly.

I knew that he really did not understand who I had become. He remembered a younger, less experienced Merlin and assumed I was the same person.

As Emily started into the kitchen to prepare a quick meal for our unwelcome guest, I informed her that I was going to take Percival to the shop momentarily and find something clean for him to wear. "I still haven't brought all my things back here, so there should be something that will fit him well enough."

"Okay, but please be back soon. I'd really like to go to bed—I'm exhausted," she said from behind the open refrigerator door.

I clamped my hand none too gently on Percival's arm and transported us to the apartment. Percival looked shocked and sickened by the abrupt movement and the sudden change of venue. I did not give him a chance to recover before I called upon my magic and changed my appearance to be as Emily had seen me before we left for Las Vegas; larger than normal and seething with power. But this time I was absolutely serious. My body glowed and increased in size until I towered over Percival. I growled, "If you ever threaten me, my wife or anyone I care about ever again, in any way, you will disappear in a blast of fire so intense there will be nothing left but ash."

Percival was so frightened that he threw himself flat on his stomach, groveling in front of me. "Gods, please have mercy, my lord, I am truly sorry."

Suddenly I heard Emily's voice. *Merlin, stop it, please! I can feel your rage. You want to punish him, and in a way I don't blame you. But I'm asking you to give him another chance.*

I closed my eyes and breathed deeply several times, trying to calm down. I could feel the sparks and the glow subsiding, and I returned to my normal size. I had not lost my temper for quite some time and it sickened me to do so. But I could understand the concept of a vengeful god—I had almost allowed myself to become one. Emily could feel me returning to normal, and I let her know that I would give the brigand another chance.

I slowly opened my eyes and looked down upon Sir Percival, who by this time was up on his hands and knees, scrabbling backwards across the floor to sit against the wall, shaking.

I sighed and rubbed my eyes, suddenly weary. It seemed that it had been one thing after the other for days now, and I just wanted a little peace and quiet. I walked over to my dresser and pulled drawers out, rummaging through my clothes until I found pants and shirt that were a bit too large for me, and I tossed them to the fearful knight.

"Here. Please go bathe and change, and then we'll go back to my house and you can eat." He didn't respond.

Percival climbed to his feet but continued to act terrified of me. Well, he should be, I thought to myself. Even though Em was now immortal, it still infuriated me to think of anyone hurting her.

"I'm sorry that I lost my temper, but I would gladly kill anyone who would attack my wife," I said.

"Yes, Lord Merlin, I understand. I will go bathe now if you will show me where the water is," he said subserviently.

I pointed silently to the bathroom, and Percival went into the room and shut the door. After a few minutes, when I didn't hear the water running, I realized that he probably didn't know how to use the faucets. I myself had needed instruction from Tom Reese the first time I had used his shower.

I knocked on the door and asked Percival if he needed help. The brawny man opened the door part way and grimaced. "Yes, my lord, I'm sorry but I do. These devices are puzzling."

I showed him how to manipulate the faucets in the shower and how to use the shower gel and shampoo. Finally, I demonstrated how to flush the toilet, and then I went back into the bedroom while he cleaned himself up.

I started packing my clothing to take to the house, which occupied my time until Percival emerged, clean and still a bit damp.

"Let's get you back to the house. I'm sure Emily has your dinner ready by now. And by the way, she has begged clemency for you, Sir Knight."

"After what I did?"

"Yes. She is an extraordinary woman, and I expect you to guard her with your life when I ask you to do so. She is immortal, just as I am, but I have no wish for her to experience the pain and unpleasantness of injury or death, temporary as it may be."

"Of course, my lord."

Satisfied for now, I touched his arm with one hand, reached for my suitcase with the other, and transported us back to the house.

As we materialized in the living room, Percival staggered and said, "I have never been privy to such a feat of magic before, Lord Merlin, and it is most disturbing. I knew you were a sorcerer, of course, but it seems that you are much more powerful now than you were in Camelot."

"It's true, I am," I said, and left it at that. Let him wonder about my abilities. I did not trust this man.

I smelled food cooking and said quietly, "Emily, we're back, love."

She walked out of the kitchen and beckoned to my companion. "Percival, come on in and get something to eat," she said pleasantly, and then turned to me, "Merlin, can we go in the other room and talk for a few minutes?"

As the former knight sat down at the table and began to eat ravenously, she took my hand and led me into the bedroom, closing the door behind us.

She spoke to me silently. *Merlin, my love, what were you thinking to allow your emotions to have free rein like that? You could have killed the poor man!*

That is true, and he would have deserved it, Em, for threatening you.

Emily stood close to me, holding my hand and gazing up into my eyes. *This is one of those times that you scare me, magic man. In the fifth century, perhaps you could have ended his life without a second thought. But this is the twenty-first century, and there are extenuating circumstances. You had a shield in place to protect us, but even if it hadn't been there and he had cut me, he couldn't have killed me, correct? Or if he had, I would have come back to life like you did.*

I assured her that she was correct.

Then have some compassion, Merlin. Has discovering that you're really a god robbed you of your humanity?

I thought about this and knew she had a point. Although I couldn't access my god powers, the knowledge of my true self brought with it a feeling of detachment from human concerns. But I didn't think this was what was really happening here.

No, Emily, I still have my humanity; I have been acting like a primitive human male whose mate had been threatened. But you're right—I'm not being very compassionate, I'm sorry.

You know, Merlin, I would probably react the same way if someone threatened you, but I know that you can take care of yourself. And to a point, so can I. Remember, I was a law enforcement ranger for many years. I handled a number of dangerous situations quite competently. So I would hope that you would give me a little credit for being resourceful.

I felt properly chastened by this amazing woman who was my wife, who was not afraid to stand up to me. She was right, and I knew that I was fortunate to have her once again correcting my behavior. It was not Percival's fault that he had been transported to Moab without his permission, and I should be directing my ire towards whoever did this. I still felt very suspicious about this event, but it was time to set it aside for now.

You're right, Em, I do not give you enough credit. You're smart and you're tough—you're the perfect match for me. You love me, you're devoted to me, even idolize me, and yet you have the strength to put me in my place. You humble me, wife, and I adore you.

I reached out and caressed her cheek, and gazed into her eyes. With a satisfied grin, she thought, *That's better!* And she kissed me with enthusiasm. As usual, her unbridled sensuality instantly brought my body to full alert, which we would normally have addressed immediately. But we had a guest in the house and had to act with a certain amount of decorum. And he was probably wondering what we were doing, since our entire conversation had been conducted telepathically.

Emily walked ahead of me as we left the bedroom, which was fortunate as I had a rather unseemly bulge in my pants. As we entered the kitchen, Percival leaped to his feet and bowed, again pledging his loyalty, sincerity evident in his voice.

An hour later, as we finally went to bed, Emily thanked me for allowing Percival to stay in the apartment temporarily. I really didn't want him in our space, but I commanded him to stay in the bedroom until I came for him in the morning. Hopefully he would not disobey me and wander around the shop during the night.

"Gods, I'm tired, Emily," I mumbled as I fit myself to her back. Holding her, I cupped a hand around one breast.

"You know, if you're tired enough that you just want to go to sleep, this isn't the way to accomplish it, husband," she gasped, as I pulled her tightly against my groin. I responded to her statement with an unintelligible grunt, and found myself relaxing into unconsciousness, contrary to my original intentions. The warm and comfort of her body against mine felt so good, so right, that I...

CHAPTER 45
July 11

T HE NEXT THING I KNEW it was morning, and we were still cuddled up together. Emily's hair was tickling my nose and I reached up to brush it out of my face. I opened my eyes and glanced at the clock, suddenly remembering our "guest."

"Emily, love, we should get up. I forgot about Percival."

"Hmmm?"

I arose and walked into the bathroom. "Wake up, Em. I'll go and get Percival at the apartment if you would fix something for breakfast. I hope he hasn't decided to explore," I grumbled, as I finished urinating and flushed the toilet.

"Merlin, I feel sick..." Emily groaned as she elbowed me aside and vomited into the bowl.

I leaned down to hold her head as she heaved until there was nothing left in her stomach. I helped her up, flushed the toilet again, and then watched as she brushed her teeth and washed her face.

"How do you feel now, sweetheart?" I asked sympathetically. I had never been sick myself, but of course I had encountered—and treated—many forms of sickness as the Pendragons' Court Physician. "Why don't you sit on the bed for a moment and let me check you out?"

As I touched her forehead, looked into her eyes, and checked for swollen glands, I couldn't detect that any particular illness was present. And as she was now immortal it was unlikely that she was actually sick. I felt a stirring of excitement as I realized she was probably pregnant.

"Actually, I feel better now," she said. "And I know what you're thinking, Merlin. But I can't be pregnant since I'm taking birth control pills. Maybe it's just a twenty-four hour flu bug or something."

"I didn't know that bugs could make you sick, Em," I said, furrowing my brow as I teased her.

She gave me a half-hearted grin and said, "It means that it's caused by a virus, Merlin, not by bugs like ants, fleas or mosquitoes. Wait, you're teasing me aren't you?"

"I'm sorry, I shouldn't tease you like that, and I didn't mean to embarrass you, but I just couldn't resist. Emily, I may not have a diploma stating that I have completed a course of study to be a physician, but I do have quite a bit of knowledge and experience, particularly with diagnosing and treating common illnesses. Of course, I have the intuition that comes with having magic. Can we both learn to give each other credit when it's due?" I asked gently, embracing her and stroking her hair.

Emily held on to me tightly and sighed, "God, I love you. Yes, we can do that." She pulled away and said, "I'd better get dressed and start breakfast. While you're at the shop, please grab a potion for upset stomach or nausea. I'm feeling much better, but it couldn't hurt to have it on hand in case I need it later."

"I will do that, love," I agreed as I dressed in my usual shorts, T-shirt and sandals. I used my wife's hairbrush, put on my headband, and went into the kitchen to make coffee. Despite her insistence that she couldn't be pregnant, I knew that the will of the gods trumped mortal birth control measures. I smiled at the thought of a new baby in the near future, but decided not to say anything more at this time.

Once the coffee was ready, I teleported to the apartment. I needn't have been concerned about Percival—he was still asleep, sprawled out with his feet extending several inches past the end of the bed.

I cleared my throat and said, "Percival." He opened his eyes slowly, saw me standing there, and leaped out of bed to kneel in front of me, completely naked. I could hear his heart pounding in fear.

"You may get dressed, Sir Knight. I apologize for startling you," I said dryly. "Everyone else is used to me showing up out of thin air, and I did not think about how unsettling that must be. And that reminds me—you are not alone here in this time. Gawain and Lancelot are here as well."

"Lancelot? Gawain? I do not understand. Were they transported here also, from an earlier time? No, that cannot be. They both were killed early in the battle at Camlann..." Confused, Percival frowned as he hurriedly donned the garments I had given him the night before.

"They have been reborn in this time, at the command of the gods, to serve me," I explained. "Come, let's go downstairs for a moment, and then we can go back to the house for breakfast."

We hurried down the steep stairs, through the back room and into the front of the shop, and I chose a few potions for Emily. I then approached Percival, who eyed me suspiciously and flinched as I touched his arm.

"By the gods, just relax," I muttered impatiently.

Emily was putting breakfast on the table and didn't react when the two of us suddenly materialized in the kitchen.

She glanced up. "Oh, there you are. Breakfast is ready."

Percival stared at her and asked how she managed to be so calm at my abrupt comings and goings.

She shrugged and said, "I have my own magic and do things a little differently than my husband does, but we're linked to each other. I always know where he is, so he rarely can catch me unawares." Em smiled and kissed my cheek, murmuring, "Right, honey?"

"Right, my love," I said obediently. As she walked out of the room, my eyes followed her and I grinned happily.

Percival had watched us play our game, and said politely, "She is comely, my lord. Has it been long since you wed?"

I thought for a moment and was astonished to realize that it had been less than a week since we had been married in

Las Vegas. So much had occurred since we returned that it felt much longer.

"We were wed on July 6, but we have known each other for almost three months. I met her on the flight from England in April."

"Flight? England?" Percival pronounced the words carefully, but he obviously had no idea what they meant.

I touched his arm and sent mental images of the aircraft, and of the country called England that now ruled all of Britain.

The knight had jerked in surprise when I touched him, and then reacted in shock to the images in his mind. "A metal bird that flies from one land to another with hundreds of people sitting inside? By the goddess, I never could have imagined such a thing. And Camelot, our homeland...gone? Everyone living there, including my woman...dead for centuries..." He sagged as his predicament became real to him. He dropped into one of the kitchen chairs and closed his eyes, head in his hands.

"I'm so sorry, Percival," I said softly, feeling sympathy for his confusion and his sense of loss. I gave him a few minutes to grieve, understanding exactly how it felt to lose everything that was important to you.

"Percival, we had better eat our breakfasts or Emily will never cook for us again," I said, pouring coffee for both of us, and then seating myself at the head of the table.

Neither of us had an appetite, but we swallowed the food anyway, barely tasting it.

Noticing Em's phone on the counter, I reached for it and entered Ryan's phone number. "Hi, it's Merlin. There's someone here who would like to see you. And I thought we might as well have a brief meeting while you're here. Please pick up Gary if he's available and come over now if possible...Okay, thanks, I'll see you in a few minutes." I ended the call and put the phone down on the table in front of me. Then I noticed Percival staring at it as if it were about to bite him.

"I know how you feel," I said gently. "This century is truly advanced, and though I've seen many unique things over the past 1500 years, this time period has the most amazing technology."

"You were telling me the truth last night; you truly are the son of a god, and immortal," he whispered as he stared at me, all color draining from his face.

"Yes, it is true; my father is the Welsh god Llyr." I paused for a moment and then changed the subject. "Percival, Lancelot will be here shortly, hopefully bringing Gawain with him. You will not recognize Sir Lancelot, as his soul and his mind are now residing in a new body, but Gawain looks exactly as he did in Camelot. You were close friends with Gawain, were you not?"

"Yes, it should be a joyful reunion—I have missed him sorely since he died at Camlann," Percival said, different emotions flickering over his face as he struggled to comprehend the impossible.

We both had painful memories of that battle and sat silently until Emily came back into the room. She had, of course, sensed my mood, and she came right to me and slipped her arms around my shoulders, pressing her face against my hair. Her love and comfort flowed through me and I breathed a sigh of relief. "Thank you, sweet wife," I murmured, kissing her hand. She gave me another hug and walked out of the kitchen, heading back to the bedroom.

Just then, I heard Ryan knock at the front door. "Come in, Ryan," I said aloud as I sent the invitation telepathically as well. Gary was with him, and the two men came through the living room and into the kitchen, chatting about old times. As soon as they saw Percival, they both stopped in their tracks, stunned into silence.

"Percival?" Gary asked in disbelief.

"Yes, Gawain, I am here, oddly enough," Percival said

wryly. "And I presume this is Lancelot, although your visage has changed considerably, Sir Knight."

Ryan chuckled, "I am aware that I look nothing like my old self, but be assured that I am Lancelot. How came you here? You are not immortal like Merlin, and yet, like him, you still have your original body. How can that be?" Ryan turned to me in confusion.

"He was transported here from the past somehow." As I contemplated this puzzling occurrence, I noticed that Gawain and Percival had come together in a manly embrace, with much backslapping and grinning. "There is something happening here that makes no sense," I said slowly. "The gods may have planned this; they certainly could have managed to transport him through time. But Percival is no particular friend of mine—he still blames me for Arthur's death, as well as for yours and Gawain's. Sir Leon would have been a better choice.

"*I* might have been able to bring someone here from the past, but I know that I did not. Perhaps Nimue did this, but if so, it was not out of kindness; she would not have taken an action that would in the long run benefit *us*...gods, that's it. She has somehow enchanted Percival to sabotage our efforts against her!"

Ryan started to respond to me when there was a sudden disturbance in the bedroom, and I heard Emily shriek.

I immediately teleported to her side and saw, to my utter astonishment, Derek, standing next to the bed, holding the lamp that he had knocked off of the bedside table. Emily was next to him, clean laundry in her arms.

"How did you get here, Derek?" I suspected that I already knew the answer.

"I teleported from home," he said sheepishly, although there was a note of pride in his voice.

Emily was livid. "Damn it, Derek, you could have popped in here just as we were having sex!"

His face turned red and he stammered an apology.

Having heard the disturbance, the knights crowded into the hallway outside the bedroom door to see what was happening.

"Alright, the show is over, let's all go back to the living room," I exclaimed. As we entered the room, I pulled aside the newest addition to our team and said, "Percival, I would like to introduce you to Derek Colburn, my kin, who has been quite successful so far in learning to use the magical talents he inherited from me."

"I am honored to meet you, Derek, kin of Lord Merlin," said Percival as he bowed.

Then, I turned to my apprentice. "Derek, meet Sir Percival. He is another of Arthur's knights. In fact, he left Camelot only a few days ago."

"It's nice to meet you, too, Percival," Derek responded politely. Then he frowned as he stared at the tall knight, "I don't understand. How could he have just left Camelot?"

"He was transported through time and space without warning, and neither he nor I have figured out how it happened. Isn't that correct, Percival?" I said evenly.

"Yes, my lord." He bowed subserviently.

Derek looked at me and raised his eyebrows. *Why is he speakin' to you like a servant to his master?*

Because for now he is my servant. He attacked Emily and me the other night, and I had to show him the error of his ways. He and I are not friends. However, we will have to continue our truce, for our enmity cannot be obvious if we are to show a united front to our enemies.

I asked everyone to excuse us for a few minutes, and gestured to Derek to go outside with me. I shut the door behind me and said, "Now, we need to talk very seriously about your teleportation skills. Do you realize that you could have materialized inside a wall or a piece of furniture?"

"No, I didn't. Do you mean like what happened in that movie we watched?"

"Yes, exactly," I nodded.

Derek paled and said, "Shit, I never thought of that. This was my first attempt away from the house. Your energy is so strong and so much like mine that I can tune in to you—that's how I got here."

"But you were way too far off, Derek! I was in the kitchen and you ended up in the bedroom. Please don't attempt teleporting again until I have a chance to work with you," I said emphatically. "Now, we need to go back inside and have a short meeting, then go to work."

I discovered upon reentering the living room that Gary had invited Percival to stay with him, and I was very relieved. I was clinging stubbornly to my dislike of the knight and I knew it was wrong of me; I had never been so inflexible or unfriendly to any of the knights in the past. It felt like a festering wound, a splinter embedded deeply in my flesh, and I wondered if my intuition was trying to warn me of impending disaster.

I needed to meditate on this soon, but for now I shook off the sense of foreboding and began the meeting. I stressed the importance of gathering as many weapons as possible without alerting the authorities, and to start training the new people, or to continue training, in the case of our original group.

Since Percival had no idea what the coming battle entailed, I briefly described the circumstances, and how Nimue and her daughter have been tormenting me in particular, and the rest of the group by their association with me. More importantly, that she would do anything to keep Arthur from returning, so that she could dominate the entire human realm.

I emphasized the need to keep in touch by phone and email, and to arrange all personal affairs so as to be ready at a moment's notice. Percival, Emily and Alex were not employed, but everyone else was, and I knew it would be difficult to reconcile their jobs with the quest and the upcoming battle. However, if we failed, not only would employment be unavailable, but life as we now experienced it could cease to exist.

After I dismissed the three knights, I asked Derek to stay for a few minutes, whereupon he relaxed on the couch and put his feet up. I went looking for Emily and found her in our bedroom, lying down.

"Em, are you alright, love?" I asked gently. I again put my palm on her forehead and noted that her temperature was still normal. She looked up at me and yawned, belatedly covering her mouth.

"Sorry, magic man, I'm just really tired this morning—too many stressful days and late nights, I guess."

I sat down on the edge of the bed and took her hand in mine. "Then just rest today, love. If you need the potion for nausea it's on the kitchen counter. I have to go to the shop, but if you need me, just say my name and I'll hear you." I smiled at her and said, "And Emily, if you decide you want to feel more energetic, remember, you can connect to the energy inside of yourself at any time, and use it. You and I tend to forget that we are immortal, magical beings and we do not have to limit ourselves to human frailties."

Emily smiled back at me and said, "I do forget that sometimes. It's only been a few days for me, while you've had centuries to understand what you are and what you can do. I'll work on it, I promise. But in the meantime, if you'll get that potion for me, I'll take it now. I doubt I'm going to vomit again, but my stomach still feels unsettled."

I nodded and raised my hand to capture the small bottle as it floated into the bedroom. I had anticipated her request and called the bottle to me.

I uncorked the potion and handed it to her, whereupon she drank it down, grimacing at the taste.

"Thanks, honey. It tastes nasty, but if it works, that's what counts," Emily said.

"Okay, wife, Derek is waiting for me, so I'll see you later. I'll be here immediately if you need me." I smoothed her hair and kissed her mouth, tasting the herbal concoction I had given her.

I frowned. "That does taste rather unpleasant. I'd better add something to it or alter the spell—no wonder I don't sell much of it." I gave her a quick kiss on her forehead, got up and walked out of the bedroom.

Immediately I felt that something was wrong, as I was not sensing Derek's presence. I frowned, hoping he hadn't teleported again when I had forbidden him to do so. I entered the living room and as I suspected, he was no longer on the couch. *Derek, where are you?* I called out telepathically. I felt uneasy—it was not like him to disobey me. Could Nimue or Adrestia have taken him somehow without my knowledge? He was a sorcerer, but so new to the craft that it was possible he could be vulnerable if taken unawares.

I started to fear for Derek's safety. How could I have missed sensing the evil emanating from either woman? The answer was that I couldn't—that foul essence was unmistakable even from a distance, so it was unlikely they had come in unnoticed and abducted him. I quickly sent my senses out in all directions, as far as I could, seeking this man who meant so much to me. And I found him very quickly, at home, asleep. What the hell? I teleported myself to his side, and there he was, on his couch.

"Derek!" I shouted.

He jumped and sat up, flustered. "What?"

"Look around, Great-grandson," I demanded.

Derek realized that he was no longer at my house; he was home and obviously had no idea what had happened.

"How'd I get here?" Terrified, he leapt to his feet, staring at the familiar surroundings.

I stood still, my arms crossed, as my fear caused me to be more abrupt than I meant to be.

"You teleported in your sleep," I said sharply.

"My God, Merlin, I'm so sorry, I had no idea that I could do that," Derek said, trembling.

I took a deep breath to calm myself, and then stepped forward, pulling him into my embrace, holding him tightly against me. I felt like a father whose lost child had suddenly been returned to him. "Gods, Derek, I was sure that you had been taken from me!" I held him a moment longer and then let him go. "We can't wait to do this training, Derek, or next time could be disastrous," I said fervently. "Your powers are developing more rapidly than I could ever have imagined, but uncontrolled, they could be a danger not only to you, but also to those around you." I decided that I needed help and knew exactly whom to contact.

"Llyr, please come to me, Father. Your descendant has need of your assistance."

"You're callin' your father?" Derek swallowed nervously.

"Yes, my son, what is it?" Llyr's deep, disembodied voice suddenly resonated through the room, startling both of us.

"I humbly request your expertise regarding my great-grandson's powers," I said.

And then Llyr was standing before us, again in his shorts and polo shirt, and I bowed quickly, grinning at his attire.

Derek was more than a little flustered at the appearance of the tall god, and threw himself in full prostration before him.

Llyr looked at me with a twinkle in his eyes. "Are you *sure* he isn't your son, Merlin? He may not look like you but he is exactly like you in some ways. And you're right, he has come into his powers rather suddenly—especially the teleportation ability. He actually teleported in his sleep?" He chuckled and said, "Just like you did when you were a child."

"I did? I don't remember that," I said, surprised.

Llyr smiled at the memory, and looked at his descendant, still face down on the carpet. "Derek, you may get up now, my child. I accept your heartfelt offering."

Derek scrambled to his feet and looked up at the god, who towered over him by eight inches. "I...I'm happy to meet you, sir," Derek stammered. "Can you help me? I frightened Merlin pretty badly and I'd appreciate your help in learnin' how to use my powers. I've only known about them for a week or so. I feel kinda overwhelmed, especially with the unconscious teleportin' thing."

Llyr beckoned to us and we walked close to him. He put one arm around each of us and said, "I love you both. You are a credit not only to the human race but to the gods as well."

I was surprised and pleased that my father would say that, but Derek just glowed with pleasure at the compliment, and I felt his heightened emotions through our bond.

And suddenly, I realized that Llyr had imparted knowledge to both of us through that simple embrace. I now knew how to help Derek with any and all issues regarding his powers. What a wonderful gift from this god who was my father and at the same time, my fellow deity. How strange to remember that he and I had been together for millennia in spirit form.

Then I recognized the other gift of information that Llyr had given to me during that embrace, and my heart soared.

"Thank you so much, sir," Derek said earnestly to Llyr. "I will use this knowledge well and strive to make you and Merlin proud of me."

"We are already proud of you, Derek. Is that not so, Myrddin Emrys?"

"Yes, Father, that is so," I agreed wholeheartedly. And then Llyr was gone, back to the realm of the gods.

"Merlin, he called you Myrddin Emrys. I know that's

your Welsh name, but it's actually your god name, isn't it?" asked Derek, who was supposed to have forgotten my true nature, but like Emily, had seemingly been unaffected by Llyr's restrictions.

I grinned. "Yes, that is my god name, Derek, my son."

CHAPTER 46
July 11 Late Morning

D EREK LOOKED AT ME SUSPICIOUSLY. "Whoa, wait a minute. You just called me your *son*, Merlin, instead of your great-grandson. I know you feel fatherly towards me sometimes, but....What's goin' on?"

I couldn't hide my joy any longer. "Gods, Derek, no wonder your powers are so strong. I have remembered, with Llyr's help, that you really *are* my son!" I cried, as I threw my arms around him and laughed out loud.

"What? How? I don't understand..." He returned the hug because he loved me, but it was clear that he was deeply confused.

"When Llyr embraced us and gave us the information we needed to manage your powers, he also allowed me to regain my memory of your conception and birth. When I was still a young man, only twenty-two years old, I had sex once with a tavern wench. I thought I was in love with her and wanted to marry her. But Gaius convinced me that I should avoid sexual relations and never marry, to protect my powers. I never touched your mother again, but when she came to me months later, obviously with child, I continued to watch over her until you were born in 442. She named you Emrys after me. One evening, I was late coming to see you, and I discovered that her home was engulfed in flames." I had to pause and wipe the tears from my eyes as I experienced again the horror of that moment.

"I tried to douse the fire with magic, but it was already too late, and I was told that both you and your mother had perished in that conflagration. I must have collapsed from grief, because the next thing I knew I was back in the castle, and I had lost all memory of that time. Llyr had taken you away, and had erased my memories, so I didn't remember that you and she had ever existed. He brought you forward in time and left you in an orphanage, where your parents found and adopted you. He knew that we would meet in this century and come together as predestined." I stopped and took a breath, closing my eyes and centering myself. I regained my composure, and looked up to see Derek staring at me with his mouth open in astonishment.

He looked just like his mother, and I smiled.

"Merlin, I'm totally blown away. I ...I can't believe this is real. I was born in freakin' *Camelot*, in *442*? *You*...you're really my *father*? Llyr is my *grandfather*?" Derek was becoming hysterical and starting to hyperventilate. As I realized that he was going to pass out, I caught him as he collapsed, then carried him over to the couch.

I put him down gently, kissing his cheek, and remembered how much I had loved him when he was a baby. I then sat down on the floor next to the couch so that I could be there when he awoke.

I knew that Llyr had done what destiny had demanded, but I couldn't help regretting the years I missed—Derek's childhood and his transition to young adulthood. I pondered the fact that Llyr must have blocked his powers, so that they would not emerge until I showed him the previous week that he had magic. I thought about the vision Derek and I had experienced together. Llyr must have altered that also, or we would have known about our true relationship right away. And I wondered about his parents. Surely Llyr wouldn't have allowed just anyone to care for him—perhaps they had magic also and kept it hidden from Derek as he grew up.

And I knew that Derek would want to know about his birth mother, so I projected my memories into his unconscious mind for him to experience when he awoke.

Merlin, something monumental just happened between you and Derek, something wonderful—I can feel it! Emily's thought was so strong that it almost seemed that she was right there in the room, and I realized that in her excitement, she had actually spoken to me telepathically. I grinned and shook my head in amazement. My wife and my son had both made such progress in a short length of time.

Yes, wife, something wonderful has happened and as soon as Derek wakes up we'll be there with you to celebrate.

Wakes up? Why is he asleep?

We'll tell you all about it in a few minutes, my love.

Just then I felt a hand gripping my shoulder, and I turned around to see Derek looking into my eyes with so much love that I felt it to the depths of my soul.

"Merlin? Thank you for the memories of my birth mother. I love you...Dad," Derek said, his voice thick with emotion.

"You're welcome. I love you too, Son," I whispered, feeling the tears well up in my eyes. I took his hand in mine and squeezed it gently. "I know your parents raised you well, but I wish I could have been there for you as you were growing up."

Derek sat up and swung his legs off the couch. He looked at me with a crooked grin. "I wish that too. You know, I can relate to you bein' my father easier than I can grasp that I was born over 1500 years ago in *Camelot*." Then he remembered something else and his face lit up as he exclaimed, "Holy shit, I'm the son of a *god!*"

Suddenly he leaped up and yelled, "This is so fuckin' awesome!"

I laughed at his excitement and stood up. "Let's go tell Emily she's a stepmother..."

"Oh, crap, she's gonna *kill* me," he groaned.

We teleported to the house to give Emily the good news, materializing together in the living room, as she came hurrying out of the bedroom. She threw her arms around both of us and laughed, reveling in our joy and excitement.

"Now tell me what this wonderful news is," she demanded, glancing back and forth between us.

I nodded to Derek to go ahead and tell her.

Derek looked at me and grinned, then turned to her and said, "Emily, I don't know how to tell you this, but...Merlin is really my father, so that means you're my stepmother."

"What?" As the color left her face, her eyes rolled up in her head and she fainted. I caught her before she fell to the floor, and sat on the couch with her in my arms. I had a moment of déjà vu—I had held her exactly like this the day before we got married. I kissed her cheek and rested my head on hers, then glanced up with a smile. "It will be alright, Derek."

He looked at Emily with worry in his eyes and said, "I'm not sure *I'd* want a stepson my own age." He paused and then confessed something to me that I had suspected all along. "God, Merlin, I was *so* jealous of you when she introduced us at the Diner that night in April. I'd been hopin' she would finally see me as a potential lover, but she was waitin' for her knight in shining armor, and I didn't want to admit that I wasn't that guy. And then, there you were, exactly as she had described her dream lover to be. But instead of a knight, she ended up with a sorcerer." He laughed uncomfortably. "And you kept tryin' to share things about your relationship that I did *not* want to know!"

I grinned. "Yes, I remember."

Derek looked at the clock and said, "Well, I'm late for work, but what the hell, I'll just call in sick. It's already almost noon." He pulled his cellphone out of his pocket and called his supervisor, making up an excuse for his absence today.

I hoped that Derek wouldn't lose his job.

As he put his phone away, he said, "Nah, I won't lose my job. The government is pretty lenient about sick leave." He realized he had just responded to my thoughts, and winced, "Sorry! I guess I'd better watch that."

"It's alright. I need to be more careful about broadcasting my thoughts indiscriminately," I said, looking intently into his face for a moment. "I wondered why I felt such a fatherly affection for you. I was happy to know that we were related, and I have cared about you like family since we first met, but I was totally baffled that I felt *so* close to you, and protective of you. And I couldn't understand why you were so powerful in just a few days when our connection was so distant." I shook my head. "Now I know why. It makes perfect sense that my *son* would have inherited that level of power from me."

Emily finally stirred and opened her eyes. She looked puzzled for a moment before she remembered what happened. She struggled to sit up and I helped her off of my lap. She laughed weakly. "And I thought things couldn't *get* any more bizarre. How silly of me."

She looked appraisingly at Derek. "So you really are Merlin's *son*? You don't look like him, except maybe in the shape of your face. But I do remember you mentioning that the two of you seemed to be on exactly the same 'wavelength,' which didn't seem likely if you were so distantly related." She paused and looked back and forth between us for what seemed like an eternity, before she said, "I'm really happy for you both. You're absolutely beaming, and I don't blame you. Merlin, could you show me exactly what you experienced this afternoon?" I looked into her eyes and shared my experience with her. She began to cry as she saw the memories that Llyr had restored to me and felt my emotions as I relived that time when Derek was born.

"Derek was born in 442? My God..." Emily whispered, wiping her eyes as she stared at her friend. "You *do* look like your mother, but your intelligence, your loving heart, and your powers obviously came from Merlin. We really *are* a family now."

Emily and I got up off the couch and pulled Derek into a hug, which he returned enthusiastically.

"Merlin...uh...Dad, I think we should have some champagne, and I'm sure you can conjure a nice bottle for us, right? If *I* do it, it might not be drinkable," Derek chuckled.

"A brilliant idea, Son." I held out my hand and concentrated for a few moments. A chilled bottle of Krug Brut 1988 appeared, and I checked the label before handing it to Derek to open. We all headed for the kitchen, where Derek opened the bottle carefully and poured a healthy portion into each glass as Emily got them out of the cupboard.

I held up my glass and gazed at the two people I loved most in this world. "A toast, to the family I always wanted: To my wife, Emily—I love you to distraction, sweetheart; and to my son Derek Emrys—I am so proud and happy to be your father." The three of us touched glasses and drank deeply of the wine.

Emily giggled as the bubbles tickled her nose. She grabbed the bottle and filled our glasses again before raising hers high.

"A toast to the Reese family who loaned us their name, and to my two magic men, my husband and my best friend—excuse me, stepson—I will love you both forever..."

We tapped our glasses together and drank again.

Derek cleared his throat. "A toast to my dad, Merlin Ambrosius, the greatest sorcerer who has ever lived; also known as Myrddin Emrys, the god of magic and healin'. I'm honored to be in your presence, let alone to be your son."

I just watched, my heart full, as Emily and Derek drank to me, and then I began to smile; they were both getting a little drunk and silly.

Emily, who just that morning had been feeling nauseous, grinned and held up her glass to me, weaving slightly as she said: "An' I jus' want to thank my husban' for being so won'erful, an' for havin' the *biggest*..."

"Whoa, stop!" Derek put his hands up and shouted, looking shocked yet laughing at the same time.

"Wha'? I was jus' going to shay the biggest *heart*! What

did you thin' I was going to shay? Ohhh." She nodded wisely and looked directly at my crotch. "*I* know wha' you thought I was going to shay... Yeah, that too..."

I covered my face with my hand and shook my head. Gods, she was so funny, and at the moment, quite inebriated. I glanced at Derek, and although he was just as drunk, and laughing hysterically, his face was bright red. I realized that he even blushed like his mother. Cara was her name, I remembered suddenly, wondering how many other details Llyr, in his so-called wisdom, had helped me to forget.

By this time the two younger people had finished off the champagne and were both hanging onto the refrigerator door as they looked for something to eat, laughing uproariously at nothing in particular.

I steered them towards the kitchen table and sat them down while I took over lunch preparations. I listened while they chattered about their mutual friends and Derek's job. I truly hoped that Emily didn't regret ending her employment with the Park Service.

As I made sandwiches and heated soup, I used magic to cut a few corners in the preparation of our meal. Well, why not? We all had magical talents and needn't hide anything from each other ever again. And that train of thought led to another: Derek was probably immortal as well, but I'd have to check with Llyr before I discussed it with him. I would consider myself the luckiest being in any realm to have my family beside me throughout eternity. I prayed to the gods that we all survived this battle— being immortal didn't help if one's head was cut off.

I ladled the soup into bowls and put the sandwiches on a plate, then levitated the food to the table.

"Thanks, Dad," Derek said, obviously happy to acknowledge our relationship at every turn. His eyes followed me as I worked my simple magic with the plates and utensils.

Emily peered up at me and smiled crookedly, "God,

you're *so* sexy, maybe we should jus' skip lunch an', uh, you know..."

Derek choked on his food and coughed, grabbing his glass and chugging what was left in the bottom. "Jesus, Emily, how uncouth—I'm sittin' right here!"

"Alright, I think you both have had enough to drink. Please, let's just eat our meal and be grateful for each other," I suggested. "The battle is nigh."

At my reminder of the war looming over our heads, both of them calmed down and concentrated on eating. I had not intended to introduce a depressing topic of conversation, but rather to interject a little reality. I felt the relentless pressure of the coming conflict, and the fact that Derek's half-sister would be opposing us continued to disturb me greatly.

I started thinking about my two children and knew how ironic it was that all through the centuries when I had subconsciously yearned for a family, I already had one.

And I thought about Derek's adopted mother, and how she must feel, being separated from her son.

"Derek, as soon as you've finished eating, you need to call your mother and let her know how you're doing; perhaps even tell her you are aware you're adopted," I said suddenly.

Derek turned to me rather unsteadily. "Wha' brought thish, I mean this, on?"

"My intuition is telling me that it's time to contact her. What's her name?" I asked.

"Lisha, ah, Lisa Colburn," he answered, trying to shake off the effects of the alcohol. "Maybe I will call her. It's been awhile, and I know she gets lonely—she misses my dad, my adopted dad that is."

He pulled his phone out of his pocket and keyed in the numbers. I could hear the phone ringing and Heard her voice clearly in my mind when she answered.

"Hi Mom, how are you?" Derek asked carefully, managing not to slur his words, "It's good to hear your voice. I'm sorry I haven't called recently."

"I'm okay, Derek, I'm survivin'. How are you, honey?" Her voice was soft and gentle. I heard a slight accent in her voice, indicating she grew up in a different part of the country. That explained Derek's speech patterns. It was obvious that she was very pleased to hear from him.

He couldn't restrain his enthusiasm. "I'm doin' *so* great, Mom! I'm happy, and my life is *really* excitin' right now," he told her, glancing at me and grinning.

"You found him, didn't you?"

Derek looked puzzled. "What do you mean?"

"You found your biological father."

"How...how did you know?" he stammered.

I Heard her laugh as she said, "Oh, Derek, I'm so happy for you! And I presume you know about your magic, then? You must if you've found him."

"Mom, what are you talkin' about? How did you know about my magic?" Derek asked, profoundly shocked.

"I'm sorry we never told you, about being adopted I mean. We were instructed to let you live your own life, that when the time was right, your real father would make himself known to you, and would teach you about your powers. I'm *so* glad," she said with love in her voice.

"Yeah, my dad has been helpin' me to use my magic, but Mom, I don't understand. You mean that someone brought me to you when I was a baby? Wasn't I in an orphanage and you chose me?" Derek asked, confused.

"It didn't happen *quite* like that, Son. We were at an orphanage for, shall we say, gifted children, and were informed that you were a very special child, who would one day play an important role in savin' the world, and we had been chosen to take care of you. Oh, I guess I neglected to mention that your father was a wizard, and I am one also. It was difficult hidin' that from you all those years, but we must have succeeded. You never guessed, did you?" She sounded amused.

"No, I never guessed," Derek said weakly.

I motioned to Derek that I would like to talk to her, and he nodded. I took the phone and said, "Mrs. Colburn? Lisa? This is Derek's biological father speaking. I believe Derek is feeling a bit overwhelmed at the moment. I overheard your conversation with him, and I wanted to personally thank you for loving and caring for my son all those years."

"My goodness, you sound awfully young to be his father! But since you are the only one who could have released the spell blockin' his powers, you must be. We were never told your name, but you must be quite a powerful wizard," she exclaimed.

"Actually, I'm not a wizard, Lisa. My name is Merlin, the Sorcerer of Camelot. Your son—my son—is a sorcerer also, and a powerful one," I said.

She gasped. "Oh, my God. And who was the man that brought Derek to the orphanage?"

"It was the god Llyr, who is my father and Derek's grandfather," I explained.

"Derek is the son of Merlin and the grandson of a god? I can hardly comprehend that!"

"It's alright, Lisa, I know it's a lot to process. I am truly in your debt for what you did, and if you ever need anything, please let me know," I said gratefully, and handed the phone back to Derek.

"Mom, isn't this just the most incredible thing ever? And isn't it ironic that all my life I've loved stories about magic, and about King Arthur and Merlin? Mom, can you believe it? Merlin is my *father*! Of course, I loved Dad, and I hope you don't think...oh, well, good. I can't believe you and Dad had magic and I never knew..."

As Derek continued his conversation, I glanced at Emily, and saw that she was trying to stay awake. I walked over and gently pulled her out of her chair and into my arms, nuzzling her neck.

"We're going to have that interlude you suggested as soon as Derek leaves. I want you, wife," I whispered into her ear.

At that moment Derek concluded his call and cleared his throat.

"Looks like it's way past time for me to take off," he said, scowling, obviously uncomfortable with our display of affection.

I was surprised at his abrupt change in attitude; I wondered if his developing powers were causing mood swings.

"I'll be right there, sweetheart," I said as Emily headed for the bedroom with a smile. I then turned my attention to my son. "What's wrong, Derek?"

"Merlin, now that I know you're my father, it feels even weirder to watch you groping my best friend who is, oh, yeah, *my stepmother!*" Derek exclaimed sarcastically, his voice escalating.

I just stared at him, concerned and irritated. "Derek, I suggest that you lower your voice and have a little respect for me and for your friend, who is my *wife*, not some whore I picked up at a tavern. I might be wrong, but I think that you are still jealous that she married me and not you." I paused for a moment then continued, "In the last couple of hours you have found out that you were adopted, that your adoptive mother is a wizard, and that you are the son and grandson of gods. I do understand if you feel a little overwhelmed, but you are an adult, not a child, so you might as well adjust your thinking and behave appropriately." I was annoyed at my son's attitude, but I was trying to understand what was going through his mind.

"Does it make you feel strange to realize that I look young enough to be your brother?" I asked.

Derek answered cautiously, "Yeah, maybe that's part of it..."

"Well, despite my appearance, I assure you that I am more than old enough to be your father. And you, of all people, should know that. Let me show you what I would look like in my fifties, which is more or less the age I would be, minus all the centuries I was asleep."

I used the spell for altering my appearance and stood before Derek looking older: Hair streaked with gray, a few wrinkles on my face, my teeth slightly yellowed, and my body having lost its toned look of youth.

Derek's eyes widened as he saw the way I would look if I was a normal, middle-aged man in the twenty-first century.

"Or, perhaps it bothers you that your old, but young-looking, father enjoys sex so much?" I raised my eyebrows questioningly.

Derek's face flushed red as he nodded.

"Let me explain something to you, and I hope that you will comprehend how *I* feel. You know that I was born to a human mother, and I have a human body. But it is obvious to me, as it must be to you, that normal humans have a limited lifespan. Human bodies and minds age, as is only natural, and yet *I* have not aged a day in almost 1600 years, and my body still functions in the human way. It is the spirit inside this body, the immortal god, which keeps it from growing old and dying. The gods in spirit form cannot participate in the experience of physical love, sexuality, passion. So while I am in this body, I just want to experience those things; to share that love and passion with my wife. It had been *fifteen centuries* since I bedded a woman, Derek, and then miraculously, I met Emily and fell in love with her, and she with me. It was our destiny, Emily's and mine, to meet, to fall in love, and eventually to raise a family. I have been waiting for her all my life; can you even imagine the depth of the love I feel for her?" I had to stop for a moment to take a breath and blink back the moisture in my eyes.

Derek was quiet and contemplative as I continued,

328

THE HEART OF MAGIC

"Please don't begrudge my happiness with Emily. I never would have approached her or allowed her to become so enamored of me had I even the slightest doubt that it was right thing to do."

Derek looked embarrassed and uncomfortable. "Merlin, I'd be the most hardhearted person in this world to begrudge you, of all people, the happiness you have with Emily. I've been tryin' to cover up my feelings of jealousy, but they just keep comin' to the surface. I know that it's *my* problem if I'm embarrassed at somethin' you do in your own home. And it's definitely my problem if I can't remember to look past your external appearance to the amazing bein' that you are inside. After all those centuries of livin' without love, you deserve every bit of happiness you can get, Dad. I'm so sorry."

Derek looked into my eyes apologetically, then threw his arms around me and held me tightly, emanating a wave of love that filled my being with happiness. I hugged my son gratefully.

"Okay, *now* it's time for me to go home and let you spend some quality time with your wife. And I'm gonna do some soul-searchin' to try and figure out why I can't just let go of Em and find somebody else. You know, maybe I'll ask Maria out again as soon as this conflict is resolved." Derek took a deep breath, letting it out slowly. Then he squared his shoulders and said, "Also, it's time I took some responsibility for organizin' this battle. I'll meet with the knights and find out what the weapon situation is, first of all. Then I'll talk to the Gonzalez family, find out who else is comin' and what defensive spells they might know, and I'll go practice with them."

I nodded and said, "Alright, Derek, that's a good idea, because we *are* running out of time."

He slapped my shoulder companionably as he walked out of the kitchen and headed towards the front door. "See ya, Dad. And by the way, I'll let you break our news to the guys; they probably wouldn't believe me if I told them."

After Derek left, I felt out of sorts from our confrontation, so I just sat quietly in the living room breathing deeply and going into the light, until I felt calm and centered. Then, I went into the bedroom, to find Em asleep on the bed, naked. My breath caught as I marveled at the beautiful woman before me. Her scent was like the rose petals that had been scattered on the floor when Arthur married Guinevere. Emily rarely wore a fragrance, but I decided I liked this one—it was perfect for her. She must have showered while Derek and I were talking, and I decided to do the same. I quickly divested myself of my clothing and sandals, slipped quietly into the bathroom, and shut the door.

I turned the faucets on and got into the shower, letting the hot water saturate my hair and run down my thirty-two year-old body. I thought about what had happened just now with Derek, and I realized that I took so many things for granted: that I would live forever, that I would always *look* young even though I was very old, that I would keep my white teeth and my dark hair. I ran my hands over the muscles in my arms and legs and over my toned torso, and I even touched my genitals in wonderment. What an amazing, perfect male body I had been given. I *liked* having a young body. I smiled and reached for the shampoo, thinking about all the things I had experienced over the centuries, while I washed and rinsed my hair.

The steam got thicker in the room and I came out of my reverie long enough to notice that I had forgotten to turn on the exhaust fan.

And then I started to feel the signs of an impending vision. "No, not now!" I whispered urgently. There was no time to prepare before I stiffened and was immersed in a scene I had hoped never to see again—a battleground full of injury and death, blood, and carnage. I saw that the battle raged on the southern bank of the Colorado River, and that creatures of myth were flying out of The Portal, between the two cliff faces on either side of the river. The forces for good had exacted a heavy toll on the invaders, using a combination of weapons and magic, but seemingly endless hordes continued to pour out of the huge rift. The casualties mounted on both sides until I finally challenged Nimue to fight with me alone, one sorcerer against another...

And at that critical point my vision faded, leaving me shaken and exhausted. I leaned against the back of the shower and slid down until I was sitting in the tub, the water pounding on my head and shoulders.

CHAPTER 47
July 11 Afternoon

M ERLIN!" I heard Emily shout as the shower curtain was yanked aside and the deluge of water ceased.

I looked up slowly; even that slight movement a monumental effort. I finally focused on my beautiful bare wife standing above me, holding a large towel. I stood up carefully and she helped me step out onto the bath mat. I felt almost as weak as I had after I'd died and come back to life less than a week earlier.

"Magic man, what happened?" Emily asked, as she helped me to dry off.

I dreaded talking about it. "I …had a vision, a detailed vision, of the battle to come, but it ended before it was clear what the outcome would be. Gods, Emily, it was…horrible. People were severely injured, and there were a couple of deaths, although I could not tell who died. It's going to happen in a few days at most, Emily. It wasn't clear what will happen to the population of Moab…"

And I realized that I had not seen Percival's role in this catastrophe. Bollocks, I never finished telling Lancelot my suspicions about him. Immediately, I contacted Ryan telepathically, informing him of the location of the battle, and letting him know about the possible threat Percival represented. His thoughts when he replied were not very clear, but he did confirm that he had received my warning. I apologized to him for forcing myself into his mind; that I would not normally be so rude. He assured me that he understood, and that he and Gawain would watch Percival closely.

I breathed a sigh of relief and turned to Emily, needing to hold her. I kissed her as if it was the last kiss, and stroked her curvaceous body as if it was the last time I would be able to touch her.

She sighed and returned the kiss, touching my body with her soft hands. She slowly caressed every part of me as if she were memorizing each muscle, each limb, each angle. Maybe she was.

I threw the towel into the bathtub and pressed my hardness against her, letting her know how she affected me.

She backed away from me for a moment and gazed down at my erection. "My God, Merlin, I didn't think you could get any bigger, but I guess I was wrong!" And she ran her hands over the member in question, causing me to inhale sharply.

"Bedroom," I gasped and grabbed her, teleporting onto the bed.

Emily reached down and held the base of my erection with one hand while she lowered her head, capturing me in her mouth. I couldn't think straight, I could only feel the intense sensations she elicited. With her tongue and her lips she pleasured me almost beyond endurance, and I had to pull her up next to me to make sure she was ready. I reached between her legs and caressed her until she was panting with desire, and I sucked on her peaked nipples.

"Oh, Merlin, now, please," she whispered, as she opened her legs in invitation. I plunged deep into her body, only to retreat and thrust again, more slowly this time, drawing out the exquisite intensity. I worshiped her with my body, as was appropriate for a husband to do. I felt my consciousness merge with hers until we were like one being, and when we reached the peak, we experienced each other's passionate fulfillment.

Afterwards, we held each other close, unwilling to be separate. And while we were still basking in the joy of our union, I had a momentary glimpse of the future; a simple, sweet vision, of what our first child would be like. She had long dark brown hair and hazel eyes, her pert, freckled little nose so like her mother's, and high cheekbones and straight white teeth like mine. She had a sweet face, a mischievous smile and a habit of teleporting in her sleep. Derek's little sister. I opened my eyes and smiled at Emily, inviting her to share this with me. Her eyes widened in amazement and she whispered, "She's ours?"

"Yes, she's our daughter," I assured her, praying that nothing would prevent this miracle from coming to pass.

Later, after we had dressed and were sitting in the kitchen enjoying a cup of coffee, Emily asked carefully, "Merlin, what happened between you and Derek earlier, just after I left the room? I could sense that you were really annoyed by something he said."

I sighed. "Yes, he made a very sarcastic, disrespectful remark, and I took exception to it. The shift in his attitude really surprised me, so I tried to understand his perspective. Em, I think even after all this time, he still has deep feelings for you, more than friendship. He wanted to marry you, and therefore he is jealous of me. He normally hides it well, but because he loves me also, he feels very conflicted."

Emily frowned in confusion. "He wanted to *marry* me? Are you sure? He never said a word! I thought that he loved me like a sister; I had no idea that he felt like a spurned lover."

I hesitated, but I needed to know. "I hate to ask this, but did you and he ever have sex?"

Emily looked embarrassed and admitted, "Uh, yeah, twice, a long time ago, just after he and Chris split up. Even though the divorce was a mutual decision, he had a hard time at first and I wanted to comfort him. The second time, I...I knew I'd made a mistake, so we never did it again. I didn't realize..."

I sighed. "Oh, Em. Well that explains it, but it does not excuse the fact that he was so disrespectful. I strongly suggested that he learn to accept the situation and act like the adult that he is."

"And how did he react to your 'suggestion'?" she asked wryly.

"He was embarrassed by his behavior, and actually

seemed to pull himself together, so hopefully he won't do that again," I said.

I stood up and pushed my chair in to the table. "I can't believe it's already mid-afternoon. I really need to go to the shop and take care of some things. I dread what the next few days will bring, but there is no choice but to fight. I truly wish that I could just turn back time and change certain events so this situation never happens, but then there would be far-reaching consequences that I can't even imagine." I gazed out the window for a moment, lost in thought.

"I have a feeling that something is going to happen at the shop in a couple of hours, perhaps a meeting organized by Derek, so be ready. I'll come and get you." I leaned over and kissed her, at the same time inhaling her scent and feeling amorous all over again. I reached down and cupped one of her breasts.

Emily looked up at me and said, "Seriously? Merlin, *go*. You're the horniest man I've ever met; in fact, I think you're addicted to sex." Then she relented enough to say, "Anyway, there's always tonight."

"Besides the fact that you are the most desirable woman in the world and I love you, I think I'm making up for all those centuries without sex."

"And you're doing a good job of it, my love," Em said softly. "Now *go*."

"All right, I will leave now, and I'll see you soon." I kissed her again, then turned and walked out the front door.

CHAPTER 48
July 11 Late Afternoon

I HAD BEEN AT THE MOAB HERBALIST for several hours when I felt a powerful force coming along the sidewalk towards the shop. I had been expecting this. I strode to the door and opened it, and in marched all three knights, the Gonzalez family, and at least a dozen others I didn't know. Bringing up the rear was my son, with a determined look on his face.

As soon as Derek came through the door, I closed and locked it, turning the sign around to "Closed."

It was very crowded and noisy with so many people in a relatively small space. I glanced at Derek and asked him telepathically if everyone here, other than the knights, was magically inclined, and he nodded. *Did you tell anyone about our true relationship?* He shook his head and grinned. *Alright, I'll announce it as soon as I return with Emily.* Derek nodded once again and looked pleased. I teleported home, saw that she was waiting for me, and teleported back to the shop with her within a matter of seconds.

I knew I'd have a difficult time getting through the crowd, so I levitated myself up over their heads and onto the counter so that I could see everyone and they could see me. I noticed that the new people looked startled at my action; it probably appeared that I had flown. Well, they'd better get used to it.

"Thank you for coming," I told the crowd. "First, I have an announcement. Derek, please come up here." He had not had a lot of practice levitating but I was sure he could do it. He stared at me, nodded slightly and smoothly rose in the air, landing beside me perfectly. *Good job!* I praised him silently.

"Derek and I had originally shared a vision that we were distantly related, and yet our bond seemed much stronger than was warranted by a connection more than thirty generations past.

This morning he and I had the opportunity to be in the company of the god, Llyr, and it was revealed to me that Derek is actually....my son." The crowd started murmuring, and I heard a few claps, but mostly the people who didn't know me just seemed confused. After all, Derek and I looked more or less the same age. The knights looked shocked and yet pleased, each of them going down on one knee.

I paused a moment, then said, "And for those of you who do not know me, I am Merlin, the Sorcerer of Camelot, son of Llyr."

Pandemonium. Everyone began talking at once. The Gonzalez family, who already knew the truth, bowed deeply in obeisance. The new people had apparently not been informed of my true identity, and when they heard me announce my name, they all got down on their knees, awestruck.

I looked around at these people who were willing to fight and die for this cause, for me, and I allowed them the time to express their feelings. The god in me accepted their offerings with a regal nod, and the part of me that was Merlin felt humbled and a little embarrassed. I beckoned to Emily to join me. She made her way through the crowd and I brought her up next to me. "Ladies and gentlemen, this is my wife Emily."

And then something happened that I hadn't anticipated: both my son and my wife spontaneously kneeled before me, their foreheads on my feet, acknowledging their devotion to me. And the crowd roared its approval.

As I looked down on them and out into the group, I realized that this was my ultimate destiny, above and beyond my devotion to Arthur Pendragon. I was here in this realm to help, to save, mankind, when humanity was ready to acknowledge a god in human form.

I came out of the trance-like state I had slipped into and helped Derek and Emily to their feet. Emily grabbed my hand and squeezed it, and then she and Derek descended to the floor and waited with the rest. Everyone settled down and looked at me expectantly.

In the silence that ensued I began to speak in a resonant voice, "In the next few days the invasion begins, and the fate of the planet rests in our hands. I presume that Derek has informed you of the details?" I glanced around and saw everyone nodding. "Everyone needs to have their weapons of choice ready to go, including whatever defensive and offensive spells you know. If you have staffs or wands inscribed with protective runes, bring them. If you have special jewelry such as silver rings or pentacles, or various talismans that you use for focusing, bring them, use them. Be aware that the townspeople are, as far as I know, completely unaware of the existence of magic or the supernatural, so if any normal humans observe you employing magic, they will have to be enchanted to make them forget what they saw. I would be happy to help you with that spell if necessary. If I come up with a better course of action, I will let you know. Of course, I will take the lead out there, as I am the most powerful of us, and I am also the object of Nimue's vendetta." I hadn't even tried to be modest; it was the truth, after all, and no one disputed my statement.

"You may wonder how we will be able to keep in touch. If you have high quality two-way radios you're welcome to use them, but I plan on keeping track of everyone using telepathy. Are there any telepaths in this room, besides my wife and son?"

No hands were raised.

"Alright, that signifies to me that the rest of you are wizards of one level or another, rather than sorcerers." I noted that several people glanced at each other questioningly. "We need to trust one another and have each other's backs. I will not make light of this situation: This may be a battle to the death for some of you. At this point, if any of you feel that you cannot commit yourselves wholly to this cause, to me, then please feel free to leave now." I looked around and saw that each face was turned towards me, determination and commitment in every expression. No one accepted my offer to depart.

"Very well, let's do a quick training exercise. I am going to project a message into everyone's mind at once. Your job will be to allow me to enter, to be as receptive as possible. Start by closing your eyes and focusing on a point in your mind, letting go of any extraneous thoughts. If you have never experienced this before, if may feel strange; just let it happen."

I closed my eyes and prepared myself to project a single thought strongly enough that everyone in the room could receive it; that is, if they were open to it. I gathered my power and gauged the exact energy that I would need to accomplish the feat. I thought, *May the gods in all their wisdom be with us,* and I projected that thought to everyone. I heard a dozen responses, from gasps of fear, to "ahs" of satisfaction, to soft laughter, and realized that everyone in the room had heard at least part of my message. I glanced at my family and they of course were smiling and giving me "thumbs up." When I looked at Percival, he could barely meet my eyes, but it was obvious that he had heard me; he was sweating and looked nervous, frightened. My eyes narrowed and I suspected that he was hiding something...

Ryan looked pleased with himself—apparently he had heard me loud and clear. But Gary seemed confused, as if he had heard something but couldn't understand the message. *Gary, look at me,* I said to him alone. He immediately looked into my eyes and smiled tentatively; at least he had heard me say his name. I tried again: *Gawain, remember that you are fighting not only for this planet, but also to help bring King Arthur back.* And I saw a smile form on Gary's face and a look of satisfaction and determination replaced the confusion. Good.

"Is there anyone that needs extra help with this exercise?" I asked. No one answered so I presumed everyone else had heard me.

"Now, each of you in turn concentrate on me and form a

coherent message in your mind. You may not be able to actually project the thought to me, but I will hear you." And I listened for each person separately, learning their names and thought patterns until everyone had had the chance to communicate with me individually. It worked. I should be able to contact everyone.

As I gazed at the bravest people on the planet, I felt a pang of sorrow that many of them would not survive this battle.

"Thank you, all of you, for answering my call," I said sincerely, my arms raised as if to encompass the entire group. I didn't realize, until I heard gasps and murmurs of surprise from the crowd, that I had risen above the counter and had begun to glow with a brilliant pulsating white light—the light of the gods. I even heard someone compare me to Jesus. *Oh, no...*

As I descended to the counter and dampened the glow, I noticed that Emily and Derek both had concerned looks on their faces. I had been in a trance-state accessing my god powers and hadn't even realized it. I had just defied Llyr by displaying those powers to all the wizards in the room, who, despite having special powers themselves, were still human beings. *Bollocks.*

Derek teleported to the counter and took over for me as I made an effort to come back to full awareness. "All of you must remain on high alert from now on—Nimue could attack at any time. Merlin has had a vision that the battleground will be within the Matheson Wetlands Preserve, which is particularly dry this year. He expects that the area above the river and between the cliffs—the area we call 'The Portal'—will be the point at which the invadin' forces enter our realm. Apparently, it really is a portal from the Other World. Whatever you do, stay alert! Various dangerous beings, flying creatures of myth such as dragons, wyverns, griffons and gargoyles, will undoubtedly come through, and we must be prepared for anythin'. Whether you use physical weapons or magic, do not hold back—fight to *kill*. Because they will be tryin' to kill *you!* If any of these creatures get past us, no one will be safe; our world will be overrun with monstrous evil and thousands, maybe even millions, of people will die. Merlin has seen the future in a vision, and there is very little left of the world as we know it."

"Hey, Derek, most of us have no idea what those creatures look like; could you give us a quick description of each one?" Adam Gonzalez called out.

"Yeah, I can do that, but no matter what it's called or what it looks like, if it tries to kill ya, it's fair game. Dragons are kind of like great big lizards with wings, and they breathe fire. Wyverns have bodies like dragons but their tails are like snakes, and they also breathe fire. A griffon has the body of a lion and the head and wings of an eagle, so watch out for the beak and the talons. Gargoyles are roughly the shape of a man but have wings and look pretty hideous. I'm not an expert—there are dozens of mythological flyin' beasts and we could see them all. But I sincerely hope not. So the bottom line is, kill first, ask questions later.

"The call to battle, when it comes, will most likely be telepathic, but we'll utilize cell phones if necessary. There's a sign-up sheet at the end of this counter—please write your name and contact information, weapons you'll be usin', and any unusual magical talents that you may have. If you need a weapon and don't have one, please stay after this meetin' and we'll see what we can do to get one for you. If you'll need transportation, please indicate that on the sheet.

"We're done for now. Go home, or to wherever you're stayin', eat well and get plenty of sleep tonight. If you haven't already done so, get your affairs in order. Thanks."

As people came up and wrote their information on the sheet, then started filing out the door, Derek turned to me and put his hand on my arm.

"Dad, what's goin' on? I thought Llyr had blocked you from accessin' your god powers?"

I couldn't answer him. I blinked and realized that I had

CARYL SAY

been out of my body again, and in that time I had seen my future. I looked into Derek's eyes and said quietly, "I think I'm going to die…again."

CHAPTER 49
July 11 Evening

W HAT? WHY DO YOU SAY THAT?" Derek asked, panic obvious in his voice. *Emily, get over here—something's
wrong!*

I could hear Derek's silent cry in my mind and Emily's
reply as she hurried over to me. *I felt something strange happen
to him...Merlin? Oh, God...*

I'm right here and I'm fine; there is no need to shout, I
thought calmly. I may have to die to accomplish what I needed
to do, which was to kill Nimue. If the death of my body truly
was my destiny, there wasn't anything I could do about it, but it
seemed odd that I had not been aware of this before. I was sure
now that Llyr had been keeping things from me. And it was ironic that I had just been admiring my body when it appeared that I
was about to lose it. I *should* be able to come back to life as I had
done before, so I needed to trust the gods. But if I couldn't come
back from this death, I prayed that my wife and son would be
able to understand and accept it. I knew that would be very hard
for them. I would live on, in spirit form with the gods, but knowing that would not comfort them since I would not be with them
physically.

I was immersed in a state of tranquility and detachment
that seemed natural for the god in me, but was not a natural state
for the rest of me. I deliberately pushed the detachment aside and
returned to being Merlin.

I immediately felt more aware of my surroundings and
was able to smile at the two worried faces in front of me.

"Everything will be alright, you two—don't worry." I
looked around the empty shop. "It appears that everyone has
gone, so we can lock up, set the wards, and go home."

I touched them and teleported all three of us to the door.

I opened it so we could step through, then closed and locked it. "Derek, will you do the honors? You used to hear me say the spell even before you knew you had magic, so you should remember it."

"You knew I could hear you? Weren't you afraid I'd figure out who you were?"

"It had crossed my mind. But you didn't, did you? Go ahead," I encouraged him.

Derek closed his eyes for a moment. *"Contego,"* he whispered.

I felt the powerful energy of protection surge outward until it covered the entire building. "Very good," I said, pleased that he was learning to harness his power and to focus it into appropriate channels.

Emily turned to look at Derek and said, "By the way, you were awesome in there. You took charge and were extremely well organized. I'm really proud of you..." she gave him a big hug and kissed his cheek, and then continued, "...Stepson." And she grinned at him innocently.

"Seriously, you're goin' to play the stepson card? Jesus, Emily, we're the same age!" Derek started to get upset, then he saw me staring at him, one eyebrow raised, and decided he'd better just accept it. He took a few cleansing breaths, gritted his teeth, and said, pleasantly, "Why, thank you, dear Stepmother."

"That's better," I murmured.

As there were tourists still strolling along the sidewalk on this warm summer night, we couldn't just disappear in front of them, so we walked home as we did most of the time.

When we arrived back at the house, the three of us went inside and Emily reached into the refrigerator for three bottles of cold beer. The silence was deafening, and I could sense the fear that they were trying to hide from me. Finally, I knew I couldn't put this off any longer.

"I owe both of you an explanation for what I said just

before we left the shop. But first I need to tell you what happened to me," I said hesitantly, not expecting them to understand, because I certainly didn't. "Somehow, I have become strong enough to break through Llyr's restrictions on the use of my god powers."

"Merlin, I don't understand, if you have access to your god powers, how can you possibly die?" Derek asked.

"If I was utilizing those powers at the time, no, I couldn't die no matter what was done to me. But to prevail over Nimue I may have to do something different, so that I wouldn't have my god powers to fall back on. In one of my trance moments, I realized that I now have access to a new power; the ability to shapeshift. Shapeshifting might be the only way to gain the advantage over my enemy, but I must beware while in a form other than my human body—I would not be immortal and could be killed, permanently.

"I...I saw a future in which I *did* change shape, and *did* kill Nimue, but in doing so....I died." As my voice tapered off, I could hear Emily crying as if her heart was breaking.

"No, Merlin, please, don't die, I can't bear it," she sobbed. "What about our family, the children we were going to have? What about that sweet little girl we saw in your vision? Derek's little sister?"

Derek stared at Emily, "My God, I'm going to have a baby sister?"

I closed my eyes and sighed; what could I say? "Yes, Derek, our first child will be a daughter, your half-sister, and I promise that I will utilize my god powers to overcome death to be here for her; for all of you."

I was just turning to Emily when time stopped. I looked up into the face of my "father." Llyr was standing directly in front of me, as angry as I had ever seen him.

"Merlin, you arrogant *fool,* you've done it again, and revealed your god powers to a roomful of wizards—mortals, humans. And you've made a promise to your family that will be virtually *impossible* to keep. Are you *trying* to upset the balance in the entire universe again? I agreed millennia ago to support your scheme to become human, but you were supposed to follow the rules, and instead you have deliberately broken *all* of them. I cannot continue with this farce any longer, and—"

As Llyr berated me, the being that I truly was, ancient long before there was life on Earth, finally interrupted and said coldly, "Am I not Myrddin Emrys, the god of magic and healing? Do you not remember that I am older and stronger than you? How can you hope to control me? How *dare* you criticize me?"

Llyr stood silently staring at me for a moment, shaking his head in frustration, and then he said carefully, "Merlin, the combination of a human ego and knowledge of your god powers is a dangerous one, and you are obviously unable to control yourself. Long ago you warned me that this might happen, and you instructed me in what I would have to do. My son, my oldest friend, although I love you dearly, this stops now. I *am* sorry."

There was a blinding flash of light and I lost consciousness.

CHAPTER 50
July 11 Night

EMILY, DEREK, AND I WERE SITTING in the kitchen drinking beer, discussing the success of the meeting we just had at the shop. Smiling, I reached for Emily's hand and held it gently in my own. Then my smile faltered as I realized her face was streaked with tears, her eyes red and swollen from crying. "By the gods, what is wrong, my love?" I asked softly, my brow wrinkled in concern.

"I don't know." She looked puzzled as she wiped the tears away.

I glanced at Derek and he had a strange look on his face, as if he had been upset but now couldn't remember what was wrong.

Something had occurred, I realized; time had been rewound and circumstances had been changed. And there was only one being I knew that would have been able to accomplish it: Llyr.

"You two sit tight; I need to pay a visit to my father," I said grimly, and proceeded to close my eyes and go into the light, seeking the realm of the gods.

Oh, Merlin, what are you doing here? Llyr sighed.

Father, something strange has happened; you changed something I did, didn't you?

Yes, Merlin, I did. There were actions that needed to be erased and words that needed to be rewritten. One day you will understand, and hopefully, you will forgive me, old friend. I truly cannot tell you any more at this time. When God decides that you are ready, you will remember everything, Llyr said compassionately. He showered me with his love, and sent my consciousness back to my body.

347

I inhaled sharply and opened my eyes. My wife and my son were sitting in their chairs, staring at me as I came back to myself. I had been gone mere seconds.

"What happened, Merlin?" Derek asked.

I brushed my hair back from my face in frustration; my headband was gone. "I wish I knew. Llyr changed something that happened in the last couple of hours, but he wouldn't tell me what it was. And he said something strange. 'One day you will understand, and hopefully, you will forgive me, old friend.' I'm his son, why would he call me 'old friend?' I have a really bad feeling about this."

Emily frowned. "I feel as if I should know what it all means, but I can't remember."

"It's what he changed, what he erased from our memories, somethin' that was so earthshakin' that he couldn't let us remember it," Derek exclaimed.

I sighed. "Well, there's nothing for it but to trust that the gods know best and will be watching over us. The three of us are a family and *that* we do remember, thankfully," I said as I reached out to my wife and my son and held their hands. I sent my love and appreciation to them and felt them return it.

"Everything will be alright; the gods will protect us," I said softly. "Now, let's get some sleep. Derek, do you want to stay here tonight?"

"No, thanks, Dad, I'm just gonna to pop home. Wish I could remember where I left my truck," he muttered as he disappeared.

Emily smiled crookedly as she watched her oldest friend disappear from our kitchen. She turned to look at me. "Sometimes I can't believe this is real. I'm married to a sorcerer and my best friend just happens to be his son, so he's a sorcerer too. And I'm part Elf and am now immortal. I know that we have a battle looming, and something serious just happened that we can't remember, but I feel like this is all completely amazing."

I watched her facial expressions as she spoke. My life had become so much more satisfying and precious since this woman had entered it. Just knowing her made me a better man. I prayed to the gods with all my heart and soul that we would be able to continue our lives together.

Emily talked about various subjects, but all I really wanted to do was watch her mannerisms; the way she tucked her hair behind her ears, and...her ears! The tops of her ears had become slightly pointed. I grinned and tugged her to her feet, pulling her into the bathroom.

"Merlin, what the hell?"

"Look at your ears, Em," I said softly, as I turned her to face the mirror. She looked at her reflection and gasped. She pulled the hair completely away from both her ears and confirmed what I had seen: She was transforming into a true Elf.

"Oh my God," she said faintly.

"I think it's cute," I said, and put my arms around her, kissing each delicate ear with its pointier shape.

She leaned back against me and felt the evidence of my desire. "You're insatiable, magic man, what am I going to do with you?"

"Well, I have some ideas, and they all start with removing our clothing."

"Okay, I get it," she whispered as she turned around and kissed me deeply. And we ended up in the bedroom, once again joining our bodies, our hearts, and our minds in passion. Sleep claimed us quickly afterwards.

It was dark, and I was standing on a hill, gazing down on a scene lit by torches; a scene of horror, the stench of blood and death filling my nostrils. Knights in old Roman-style armor were hacking their way through the Saxon hordes, falling beneath the relentless advance of mounted warriors. Screams reached my ears as I searched with all my senses for the one man I was sworn to protect with my life. I raised my arms and focused my magic through the staff, throwing lightning bolts into the ranks of the enemy, but they just kept multiplying. Finally, I spotted a regal form, leading a group of men further into the fray.

As I prepared to join Arthur on the battlefield, I noticed that his enemies had surrounded him, and although I threw bolts of powerful energy over and over against the threat, they kept advancing until they had overcome and mortally wounded Camelot's king. I was helpless to reach him in time, and all I could do was watch him fall...

"No, Arthur, nooo..." I screamed in anguish.

"Merlin, love, wake up!" Emily shook me as I cried out, and I heard her voice as if from a great distance. I was still in the throes of the worst nightmare I had experienced in more than a thousand years.

I awoke as if crawling out of a deep pit, sobbing, having relived again the most ghastly experience of my life.

Emily pulled me into her embrace, stroking my hair and gently kissing my cheek, sending her magic into my being, healing the still-open wounds of my memory.

I gradually calmed down, taking long deep breaths, letting go of the pain that lingered.

"Oh, my love, it's okay, it's okay," Emily crooned, rocking me like a child.

I opened my streaming eyes and recalled once again that the battle at Camlann had been over for many centuries. I felt comforted, held in my wife's arms, and I rested my head against her breasts.

"It's the knowledge of the coming battle that has brought these memories to the forefront," I whispered, as if speaking quietly would keep them from erupting full-blown in my mind again.

"I know," Emily said, rubbing my back, continuing to soothe me. "But remember the vision that you showed us recently, of Arthur waiting until the time is right for you to help him come back. Merlin, you need to stop torturing yourself. The battle at Camlann happened so long ago; it is over and done with. Camelot is gone, my love, but the idea is still alive. The legends and stories about you and Arthur and the Knights of the Round Table have persisted all these centuries because people *want* to believe in justice, gallantry, and magic. And this battle will be fought against the one who has always been the antithesis of that, one who would see this world bend to the yoke of evil and oppression. *You* are the hero, Merlin, *you* are the only one who can save this world so that Arthur has a place to come *back* to."

I lifted my head and stared at Emily as she made the most impassioned speech I had heard since Guinevere spoke to Arthur before he left for Camlann.

"You're right," I said, resolutely. "I'll do this for Arthur and for the world. After all, it is part of what I came here to do."

We got up for a few minutes, used the bathroom and got drinks of water. As I rinsed the tears from my face, I heard Derek's voice in my mind, faint but clear as he asked if I was alright. I told him I was, related what had happened, and promised that I would talk to him in the morning. Finally, Emily grabbed my hand and said quietly, "Come on, let's go back to bed."

We settled down again and attempted to sleep. Although Emily was finally able to rest, her breath soft and slow as I held her against me, I lay wide awake for the rest of the night, staring into the dark.

CHAPTER 51
July 12

THE DAWN BROKE AND ANOTHER beautiful summer day in Moab began; the residents and tourists totally unaware of what would soon transpire. For hours I had been contemplating what I would have to do. At our meeting the previous day, I had taught the wizards how to enchant someone who had seen them using magic against the supernatural invasion, but now I decided to do something different. I would place an enchantment over the entire town and its outskirts, which would prevent people from seeing anything outside of their normal mundane purview. Even people passing through the area would fall under the influence of this ambitious enchantment. It was a bold move, but I knew I was powerful enough to accomplish it. I would take care of it this day, even though the invasion most likely would not happen until the following one.

I slipped quietly out of bed, allowing Emily to sleep a little longer. I pulled on clean clothes and my usual sandals, quickly brushed my hair and affixed my headband, and went out to the kitchen to start the coffee. As it brewed, I stepped outside and sat on the porch, much as I had done my first morning in Moab. I heard a faint sound and looked around the yard for its source. A small, furry body bounded up the steps and proceeded to rub against my legs, purring loudly.

I smiled as I stroked the cat's head and back. I whispered, "I'm glad to see you, my friend."

And I am glad to see you, my lord. The cat spoke to me in my mind. *I know of your upcoming battle, Merlin, and I wanted to assure you that all of us would be there to assist you.*

All? What do you mean? I asked.

All of us who have the ability to shift will help you, the cat replied.

You are shapeshifters? You can become larger, more fearsome creatures?

Oh, yes, my lord; just imagine fangs and claws on a creature as tall as this dwelling. I felt a surge of ferocity from this small animal.

Your assistance would be much appreciated—thank you. I was stunned by the selflessness of this being.

"Merlin? Where are you, honey?" Emily called from inside the house.

"I'm here, love, come and meet a friend of mine," I responded, hoping the cat would allow it.

Would you stay and let my wife see you? I said to the little feline as I got to my feet.

As you wish, my lord.

Emily, in a summer robe, pushed the screen door and stopped short as she saw the little black animal staring up at her.

"Well, hello, who are you?" She asked, squatting down to pet the cat.

My name is of no consequence. I serve Merlin, my lady.

Emily looked startled for a moment, then grinned. "Yes, I imagine you do, little one," she said softly, glancing up at me with shining eyes. "As do I."

I smiled at my wife. "Let's get some coffee, shall we?" I helped her up, and then looked for the cat, but it had already left the yard. I was amazed that these shapeshifting creatures would support me in this important stand against evil. In truth, I could use all the help I could get.

"That's the cat you mentioned when we were at the City Diner, the night we met Gawain, isn't it?" Emily asked, as she poured our coffee and joined me at the kitchen table.

"Yes, and it was quite presumptuous of me to think that such a being would want to be our pet," I said, grinning as I took a sip from my cup. My amusement faded as I recalled that soon I would have to face my daughter Adrestia on the battlefield. I sighed and closed my eyes for a moment, profoundly saddened that she would be opposing me, following her mother's plan to exact vengeance upon me for something that had ceased to matter centuries ago.

"Merlin?" Emily said softly. "I know you're worried and upset, but for a little while, let's just enjoy being together, okay?"

I looked into her eyes and knew how far away I had been for a few minutes. "You're right, let's enjoy each other's company while we can," I said solemnly, reaching for her hand and gently squeezing it.

Eventually I left for the shop, troubled, yet anxious to get to work. I spent the better part of an hour crafting the spell and honing the energy that would cause any non-magical individuals in and around Moab to forget whatever magic or supernatural creatures they would encounter in the next twenty-four hours. This in turn would allow the practitioners of magic to concentrate more completely during the battle. I would do my utmost to protect the mortals from harm, but I had no way to keep everyone safe, unless…hmmm.

I had an idea that could work. I went back to the original spell and altered it. The element that I had needed to add to protect the entire population was going to require an immense amount of not only energy, but focus, and there was only one person that I knew and trusted to assist me with this. I contacted him telepathically and he immediately materialized in the shop's back room.

"I didn't want to reveal myself to any of your customers," Derek explained quietly.

"Thank you, Son, that was very thoughtful of you," I replied with a smile. His skills had improved markedly since we had seen Llyr, despite the fact that the two of us together had not had the opportunity to implement his suggestions. It was apparent that Derek had worked on them by himself.

We discussed my plan exhaustively for the next hour. The spell I would invoke from the Rim was a variation of my forgetting spell combined with a special protection spell. Once I accomplished this task, I would visit the site of the future battle and set special wards around the perimeter of the preserve, using an enchantment similar to the one I had used to blanket the Delicate Arch area. I wanted to keep the mortal citizens of Moab away from the area as much as possible, and with a slight twist perhaps I could discourage the enemy forces from moving out of the vicinity of the preserve.

Derek was able to assist me with the power needed to prepare the spell, but I was hesitant to involve him in the actual working of the magic as it could be well past his ability. When I mentioned this, he immediately responded as I guessed he might. "Dad, I can do it, you know I can. Please let me help you!"

I looked at him, considered the exponential growth in his abilities recently, and decided to give him the chance to prove himself. "Alright—here is what I want you to do..."

Later, when I was ready, I teleported to the Rim, and stood on the very edge of the cliff overlooking Moab. I had been so preoccupied that I hadn't considered the possibility that hikers might have witnessed my sudden appearance. I looked behind me, preparing myself to use a forgetting spell if necessary. *Bollocks!* There were two young women halted, frozen in mid-step, staring at me wide-eyed from a mere ten feet away. I could easily hear their thoughts, full of fear, amazement, excitement and...recognition? I was so surprised that I stared back at them, hearing in their minds, *OMG, it's Merlin...*

Quickly, while the three of us still had eye contact, I retrieved an illusive memory from one of them as I waved my right hand in a wide sweep in front of their faces and intoned the spell, *"Alieno Mihi."* Only when the girls had forgotten about me and walked away did I allow myself to examine the memory I had seen. A clear picture of myself in The Moab Herbalist emerged, and I realized that I had seen these two in my shop during one of my reading sessions. They had been sitting on pillows on the floor staring up at me, a touch of hero worship evident on their faces. Good gods, how had they guessed my real name, and how had I not sensed it sooner? Did others know? Frustrated, I knew I would have to set this conundrum aside for now and focus on the task ahead.

Dad, what's going on? Are you okay? I heard Derek ask.

I'm fine; give me a few minutes to prepare myself. I closed my eyes and first of all sent an entreaty, a prayer, to the gods to guide me. Then, I reached deep inside myself and called upon the magic that existed in every part of me, mind, soul and body, and upon the vast power residing in the surrounding rocks, air and sky. I also drew upon the power in the river and added it to the rest of the seething, pulsating energy harnessed within me. I could feel myself growing and expanding to accommodate this massive amount of magic waiting, at my fingertips, to be bent to my will.

I readied the spell in my mind, and then sent a telepathic message to Derek, who waited on the cliff on the opposite side of the valley. His job was to act as a shield of sorts, a deflector, to channel the energy containing the spell along the line of the eastern rim in both directions. He had been gathering energy himself as he waited for me to give him the signal; this would be a true test of his abilities as a sorcerer. Inexperienced though he was, I had faith in my son's innate strength, abilities and determination. Not to mention the love and loyalty he felt for me.

I reached for the power surging through me, and lifted my arms high and wide, my rune-marked staff held horizontally. I adjusted my stance for better stability and threw my head back, hair streaming in the breeze passing over the edge of the Rim.

"*Oblitus invasore! Oblitus creaturae! Oblitus vidisti! Custodire mortalis!*" As I shouted these words, I thrust the spell through the staff, the runes creating an immense force which hurled the spell across the valley. I could see the wave of energy moving as if alive, and expanding as it crossed to the far side, sparks of light emanating from it as the wave traveled towards Derek on the eastern rim.

Derek, get ready, Son!

I'm ready, Dad...

And in my mind, I saw Derek spread his arms, and I heard him telepathically as he invoked his own spell to deflect the magical energy along the predetermined path. As easily as any seasoned practitioner of magic, my son accomplished his task. I could see the energy being deflected to each side of him, smoothly covering the area as planned. I sent my senses out to confirm that the spell-laden energy had covered the area completely, and discovered that we had been successful. I knew that the spell would last for several days.

"Excellent," I murmured. *Derek, we have done well. Meet me at the entrance to the preserve.*

We both teleported to the designated location and found that the parking lot was full of tourists, who saw us wink into existence, then promptly forgot about us as the spell took effect. We glanced at each other rather smugly as we began the task of setting up an enchantment around the perimeter of the Preserve. We experienced a deep sense of satisfaction creating magic together, father and son, despite the fact that the reason we were doing it was not a happy one. As we worked, we witnessed the departure of the visitors until the last one had finally gone.

It was now well past five o'clock and we decided to go back to my house for a beer. I had not talked to Emily for several hours and was anxious to check on her. Normally, we felt each other's presence continually through our bond but with the intense effort Derek and I had been making all afternoon, I had not been as attentive as usual.

We teleported into the living room and I immediately called out, "Emily?" The only sound I heard was a thin, high-

357

pitched wail coming from the bedroom and it chilled me to the bone. I was by her side in an instant and folded her into my arms. "What is wrong, my love?"

Emily was pale and distraught, not seeing me, experiencing something I could not see, and she did not respond. She was apparently having some kind of vision that terrified her. I attempted to reach inside her, to See what she was seeing, but I failed to do so. I was frantic to bring her out of the trance in which she was ensnared. I tried various spells and to reach her through our heart connection, but to no avail.

Derek tried to bring her back using the methods of mortals; shaking her, shouting her name, passing smelling salts under her nostrils. Nothing helped.

"Llyr, I know I've called upon you many times lately, and have been the source of much vexation for you, but I beg you to help Emily, for I cannot," I cried out, beseeching my father for his assistance.

"Merlin, what is wrong now? Oh, I see," Llyr immediately saw Emily's state and took her from me, holding her as he exuded a warm soft light that encompassed the two of them. Emily gradually relaxed and breathed normally, blinking her eyes as she returned to consciousness and realized who held her.

She looked up at my father and smiled weakly, whispering, "Thank you, Llyr."

My father released her and she quickly bowed before him, touching her forehead to his feet.

"You are most welcome, my daughter-in-law. Now rise and go to your husband as he is quite distraught," Llyr said calmly, glancing at me knowingly.

"Emily, love, what happened?" I reached for her and held her tight against me, returning my father's look gratefully.

"Merlin, I...it was horrible!" She burst into tears. "I was finishing the housework when I felt this darkness come over me, and I was totally cut off from you. I tried everything to reach you, but it was like being encased in ice. I tried to access my powers but I couldn't find them."

"I'm here now, Emily," I said quietly, gently rubbing her back. I exchanged another look with Llyr; it had to have been Nimue.

"Thank you, Father, for your kind assistance," I said gratefully, releasing Emily for a moment to bow before him subserviently; something I had not done lately. Then he was gone, and I arose from my position on the floor and embraced Em again.

Derek had stood immobile all this time, seemingly an onlooker in this most recent family crisis. Now he came forward and gripped my arm, his face ashen as he gasped, "Merlin, I just had a vision, or a premonition; I think they're comin' through The Portal in less than three hours."

CHAPTER 52

July 12 Evening

I BLANCHED AS I STARED INTO Derek's eyes and Saw images of the vision he'd experienced. The evil was indeed close to breaking through. An intense pressure was building in the Other World at The Portal, the rift a weak spot between worlds.

Heart pounding, I started contacting the knights and the Gonzalez family and had them in turn contact as many of our warriors as possible. By telepathy and cell phone, we sent out the call to arms.

I was thankful that Derek had experienced such a timely premonition. I was very proud of him and amazed at his most recent accomplishment—I had never expected my son to have that particular gift. But at the same time I felt a trace of unease that *I* had had no warning at all about the imminence of the invasion. I suspected that Llyr's recent actions were affecting my powers. There was no time to dwell on it, however, nor was it wise to leave room for fear; it would do no good, and could certainly do a great deal of harm. Nimue would take advantage of any lapse in judgment on my part.

I turned to Emily, who was standing at my side with a worried look on her face. "It is time to prepare; we must leave for the preserve and be ready when the rift in The Portal opens. No matter what happens, Em, remember that I love you with all my heart."

Emily held on to my arms, looked directly into my eyes and said urgently, "Merlin, we have to believe that we will survive this! Otherwise, why should you have had such clear visions of our future family and of the gods protecting us?"

I lifted her hands up to my face and kissed her palms. "There are many possible futures, love, and the choices we make from moment to moment determine which paths lead to each one. Gods willing, the actions we take and the choices we make this night will lead us to the future we long for."

The three of us clung to each other for a moment, and then we hurried to get our things together.

It was almost eight o'clock when Em and I drove into the parking lot at the Matheson Preserve in my old black Chevy pickup truck. There were quite a few people standing around talking solemnly. When they saw the truck, they straightened up and started towards us. I got out and immediately went around to the back for my sorcerer's staff and my pack. Emily shut the truck door behind her with a determined bang. Derek, who had gone home for his own supplies, pulled his truck up beside ours and leaped out.

"Everyone, we have very little time, so gather around me quickly," I said loudly, glancing around for the knights; Sir Percival in particular. They were all there, staring at me expectantly. Adam and his family were present, as well as the other wizards making a stand with us tonight.

"The battle begins here—Derek and I have both seen it. I apologize for the short notice, but here we all are, ready to fight for a future free of supernatural evil. We will prevail here because we *must!* Be aware that I have cast a spell upon this entire area to protect the population and to ensure that they forget the magic they will undoubtedly see. It will not affect anyone here who wields that magic. I felt that this would be far more effective than handling each case individually, and would enable all of us to concentrate on the task at hand."

I went on to brief them as best I could, considering the fact that we did not know how many beings would come through the rift in The Portal nor how long it would take for us to win this conflict. As I was speaking, I noticed many animals, mostly cats and dogs, approaching the group and I knew that my little feline friend had brought reinforcements. I pointed out these animals to my group of warriors and explained that they were shapeshifters who had pledged to assist us. I made sure that everyone understood what they would look like once they had changed forms so that they would not be considered part of the invading army. I wanted no harm to come to them.

I began to place people strategically throughout the grounds according to skill and type of weapon being used. I noted that the knights were armed not only with swords, but with crossbows as well; supplied by Ryan Jones, I presumed.

Ryan—Lancelot—have you been able to determine anything regarding Percival's intentions? I asked my old friend silently, as he and the others spread out across the field in preparation for the attack.

No, I am afraid not, my lord. I'm sorry, but I can't help but suspect a deep-seated enchantment that will be triggered when we least expect it. You and your family are the most likely targets, but as you and Emily, and perhaps Derek, are immortal, what could Percival do to you?

My thoughts exactly, and I wondered if keeping him close by would be best or if such an action could prove disastrous. *Thank you, Lancelot, I appreciate your diligence and your loyalty.*

Ryan did a little half bow in my direction. *You are most welcome, Lord Merlin, and I...*

Suddenly the air exploded with flying, writhing shapes, bursting from the rift above us and immediately fanning out in all directions. Shouts and screams erupted from the scattered warriors as Derek and Ryan directed the others in reacting to the onslaught. I heard Derek screaming, "If in doubt, chop their heads off!" Firearms discharged, at first haphazardly, and then with increasing accuracy as my warriors fought the invading army. I witnessed the shapeshifters become the size of pickup trucks and larger, and align themselves with the wizards, who nodded to them and continued to use any means at their disposal to fight the enemy.

And I heard in my mind, *I love you, Merlin*, and almost overlapping that came, *I love you, Dad*, and I felt bursts of love from both my wife and my son. I returned the sentiments along with all the love in my heart.

I leaped into the air, levitating to a point opposite the center of the huge opening, and sending out massive bolts of energy from my staff—I intended to cut down as many of the opposing forces as possible. I noticed that many creatures had already been hit, whether by magic, by bullets ripping into their nearly impenetrable hides or by arrows sent flying from the knights' bows, and the wounded or dying beasts were slamming into the field below me. It was a miracle that no one had been crushed so far. Varied creatures continued to pour out of the rift, but I knew that I would have to magically control or destroy the falling bodies or all of my warriors would be killed before they'd really begun to fight.

With my left hand I sent a broad arc of killing force towards the enemy, and with my right hand I directed a focused beam from my staff to obliterate the bodies. And I managed to stay in the air as I accomplished these monumental tasks. Many of these monsters, being magical constructs created from the substance of the Other World, would have eventually dissolved, but I couldn't take the chance in the meantime that they would cause harm or be an obstruction to my fighting force.

I listened to everyone's minds to keep abreast of developments on the ground. Since it was still early, everyone's energy was high. But none of the wizards had ever utilized their magic to maim or kill and it was obvious that they were having a difficult time adjusting. I communicated with them often to help them to remain focused.

There had already been a few minor injuries but nothing life-threatening so far. We had been fighting for less than an hour, although it seemed much longer.

I could feel myself surpassing my own preconceived ideas about my magical capabilities, as I added more and more tasks. I was like a beacon in the air, sending out dozens of beams of light, energy and magic wherever they were needed. Despite Llyr's claim that he could not participate nor take sides in this battle, it appeared that he was supporting me in a subtle manner anyway, by enhancing my powers yet again.

Time passed and there seemed to be no end to the progression of beings coming through the rift in The Portal. Surprisingly, we seemed to be holding our own, and the few creatures that got by my warriors and by the shapeshifters were repelled back into the center of the fray by the special inclusion in my perimeter spell.

I kept expecting Adrestia to show up without warning and attack me directly, but I never saw her, nor did I feel her presence. Had I been less occupied I think I would have pursued her, if for no other reason than the fact that she was my daughter.

And then I heard cries of agony from below, and knew that several of the out-of-town wizards were down, blood pumping from deep wounds as well as from numerous shallow cuts. I knew that Emily was rushing in with first aid supplies, and I heard Derek yelling directions to Gary just before he let loose with a largely uncontrolled stream of magical energy. I heard a shriek of fury and pain from his target and realized that Derek was battling a beast that could prove to be well beyond his ability to destroy. Many centuries ago, at the beginning of Arthur's reign, I had bested a griffon that had been sent to wreak havoc upon the kingdom. It had been one of my first experiences with Lancelot; in fact he and I had worked together to bring the creature down.

*Derek, I'm coming to help you, Son...*I projected forcefully, needing him to know that he was not alone.

Dad, hurry, I'm...

I felt a jolt of agonizing pain that was not mine and I ex-

364

perienced fear such as I had never known. "Derek!" I screamed out loud.

I teleported from mid-air to the location where Derek's pain was most intense, and as I materialized I automatically created a barrier between the creature and the downed warriors.

I faced this beast that seemed to have been conjured from a nightmare, and I roared my fury, growing to almost twice my normal size as I directed a blast of magical energy so intense that it literally burned the creature to ash in seconds.

Afterwards, still larger and stronger than normal, I picked up my son and two of the wizards to get them out of harm's way at least temporarily. I spotted Percival, who had witnessed the destruction I had caused, and realized that he was frozen in terror, having seen me carrying out a feat of magic that I had warned him about only a few days ago.

I sent him a message telepathically: *Take heed, Sir Percival.*

*Yes, my lord...*I heard him respond weakly.

I set the young men down some distance from the fighting at the edge of the preserve and discovered that all had sustained major injuries. *Oh, gods, Derek!* I was terrified that I would lose him. He had not shown any particular abilities in healing himself, and so far I had no real evidence that he was immortal, so I knew that I was his only chance of survival. But the other men were just as badly injured as Derek if not worse, and I suspected that I would have to accomplish a major feat of healing. I could sense Emily frantically running towards me, but I could not wait to do this; Derek and the others could die in the meantime. I would not allow that to happen.

I went deep inside myself to that familiar place that felt like home, and I connected to the brilliant white light there. I then placed one hand on Derek and directed the other hand towards the other injured men, and I pulled forth that light and enveloped them in its healing energy. I sensed the extent of each injury and healed them all simultaneously. I had no concept of time while I performed what Emily later called "my miracle." I was told that it was no more than a few seconds until everyone's wounds were healed and the men all stirred and sat up.

I was still inside myself, almost unaware of what was transpiring before me when I heard, as if from a great distance, Emily and Derek both calling my name.

Finally, I focused my attention outwardly and saw my family staring at me in awe, holding on to my still-glowing hands. In fact, I realized that it wasn't just my hands—my entire body was glowing. Derek was whole and completely healed, repeating *Dad*, over and over again in his mind.

And now I remembered what I had done to cause Llyr to turn back time, twice, and I remembered exactly who—and what—I was. My true nature was too strong to stay in the background any longer, but now I knew that I had control over it, and I had to keep this knowledge to myself for the time being. There had been no visit from a furious Llyr, so apparently God had sanctioned the remembrance and use of my god powers to heal others.

As the god of magic and healing I could probably stop this entire scenario from playing out by merely halting time and sealing the rift; destroying with a glance all the creatures still living that had already come through. But I was wiser now, and I realized that this was the destiny of all of us gathered here, and I could not interfere any more than I already had.

And most difficult of all, I had to allow several other people to be injured and others to die because it was their fate. Being a god came with decisions and responsibilities that would weigh heavily on me, I knew, but there was no other choice.

"Merlin, *Dad*, are you okay?" Derek was asking me for the fourth time, and I could feel Emily's fear and love, mixed with pride and awe at my accomplishment.

I smiled at both of them, confident that I could now experience being a god and being Merlin at the same time, but at least for now some slight prevarication was necessary.

"Yes, I'm okay. I'm glad you and the others are alright Derek; apparently Llyr loaned me some extra power so that I could heal you. Emily, love, come here and let me hold you. I know this has been traumatic, but you've acted bravely and I am really proud of you."

Emily came into my arms. "Merlin, my powers are working, kind of. I found that I can release short bursts of energy but it's not very reliable, so mostly I've been administering first aid."

"I know. You're doing great, sweetness," I murmured as I rested my head on hers for just a moment.

"Now, we must get back to the battle, and pray that we have not allowed any creatures to escape the perimeter of this preserve. And I *will* contact Nimue and somehow end this debacle; this has gone far enough."

CHAPTER 53
July 12 Nightfall

UNFORTUNATELY, IN THE TIME that we had been absent, there had been casualties, one of them Adam's older brother, Alex Gonzalez. I had not gotten to know him as I had Adam, but I wanted to weep at the terrible waste of a promising young life. Yet at the same time I knew in the depths of my soul that this was his fate. I would have to try and console his parents later, but winning this battle would go far to making his death meaningful.

The knights, as accomplished as they were at combat on the ground against non-magical forces, were obviously exhausted and could not hope to continue much longer this night without food and rest, although I knew that they would fight to the death if I asked it of them. They were as devoted to me during this battle as they had been centuries ago fighting for Arthur Pendragon.

Ryan informed me that Sir Percival had been throwing himself into the fight almost maniacally, apparently trying to impress me, or possibly to try and overcome a compulsion spell placed upon him by Nimue. Derek and the wizards I had saved had returned to the fighting, destroying many more of the creatures coming through the rift. It was getting close to dark and I became concerned that the vampires and trolls that I had seen in my vision of the future would soon be entering this realm.

I returned to my position aloft, swiftly dispatching as many bodies as I possibly could, all the while wondering why there had been no sign of either sorceress.

I heard Emily's weapon discharge and knew that she had decided to take a more active part in the fighting. I felt not only her fear and frustration, but also the growing anger in her regarding my nemesis. I agreed with her, and proceeded to increase my efforts.

Some time later it appeared that we had prevailed to some extent, but our warriors had suffered many injuries and there had been two more deaths.

I knew that I could not continue fighting much longer; my heart was sore with the horror of it all. Many had fallen tonight that need not have perished, and my anger towards Nimue had reached a point that it could cause the eruption of my god powers. That would truly end my stay here forever—Llyr would make sure that I returned to the realm of the gods with him and he would wipe clean every trace of Merlin from this century. I remembered now that I had made him promise to carry out that dire action if I was unable, or unwilling, to comply with God's directive.

And wouldn't that just fit perfectly into Nimue's plans?

I was still in the air, my levitation skills having become so natural that I almost didn't notice the effort to keep myself elevated. I gathered my energy and sent a powerful message telepathically that I knew would reach through The Portal and into the Other World, demanding that Nimue cease the flow of deadly creatures through the rift and face me herself, fight me alone, one sorcerer to another, letting the outcome depend upon that individual battle. I hoped that she would accept my challenge, but there was no guarantee of it.

As I waited for Nimue's reply, I sent my senses out to the warriors below. I felt their exhaustion and their pain—there was not one person left who was uninjured—yet I also felt their unflagging commitment and determination to prevail against overwhelming odds. I was proud of everyone, even Percival, and I promised myself that, if possible, when this was over, I would try to send him back home to Camelot.

There was a lull in the onslaught of beasts, and I heard the voice from my dreams, from my distant past; a voice oozing such hatred that it made my skin crawl.

"Well, Merlin, giving up so soon? Just when I thought I

would be able to destroy every one of your so-called warriors. But, then again, it has always been *your* pain and suffering that I truly desired above all else. You miserable bastard, I will see you pay for your actions. And by now I'm sure you're aware that I have irrevocably turned our daughter against you."

"Nimue, why would you pursue me like this, and cause such untold suffering to justify your own actions? Instead of letting go of the hurt I unintentionally caused you so long ago and living a normal life, you have held onto this anger and pain for over 1500 years, magnifying it far out of proportion to the original issue. And to force an innocent child to grow up conditioned to hatred and vengeance—even *naming* her for the goddess of revenge—is inexcusable. I will fight you and you alone, one sorcerer against another, to the death if necessary, but you will close the rift in The Portal now, before any more creatures can come through. And furthermore, you will allow my warriors to leave this place unmolested, and you will never come to this realm again. Is that understood?"

"And who are you to dictate to me what will and will not be done, spawn of the Devil," she sneered, obviously unaware of my true identity.

"I am your executioner, your destiny, and your doom, Nimue," I replied with deadly intent.

"Oh, to the contrary, Merlin; I am *yours*. I accept your challenge."

And immediately the rift closed. The remaining creatures were summarily dispatched by the least wounded members of my army, and the shapeshifters who had survived the fighting began to resume their original forms and depart the bloody battlefield.

I could hear everyone's thoughts as they expressed their grief and their horror over their losses. Emily and Derek had already sensed my emotions and had guessed that I had been communicating with Nimue, but no one else had actually heard the vituperative exchange between us.

It was no longer necessary for me to remain suspended in mid-air, so I slowly descended to the ground, wondering how and when Nimue would attack. I didn't have to wait long for my answer.

"Merlin, I am here, you coward—face me!" Nimue hissed, appearing suddenly in front of me. It was the first time I had seen her in many centuries, but she had not changed: The clear skin, intense blue eyes and lustrous brown hair accenting the classically beautiful face were the same. But the cold, calculating evil that emanated from her betrayed to all what she truly must be—the daughter of a demon god. She raised her arms to unleash a massive amount of magical energy in my direction.

Quickly, I created a shield to divert the magic back towards her, but she disappeared just as the powerful burst of energy would have hit her. Instead, it roared across the field and hit the side of the cliff above Kane Creek Boulevard, causing an avalanche of rock to fall onto the pavement.

She reappeared above me and sent such a powerful bolt of energy at me that I tumbled backwards for several hundred yards. I ended up on my back with the wind knocked out of me, feeling as if every bone in my body was broken. I healed myself with white light and levitated straight up as I sensed she was preparing a bolt of lightning to finish me off.

I was seething with anger and wanted to annihilate her once and for all, but as she was also an immortal being, I wouldn't be able to do more than incapacitate her temporarily. My only consolation was that she did not have the enhanced self-healing skills that I possessed, and therefore would take longer to come back to normal when injured.

We traded major blows back and forth, each of us inflicting more and more damage on the other, but every time we were able to heal ourselves and continue.

I knew that Emily and Derek and the knights, although

injured, were watching us fight from a place of relative safety, and showed no intention of leaving. I could hear Emily's soft weeping and could feel my son's suffering on my behalf.

Finally, I realized that I had no other choice: I had to shapeshift and draw Nimue away from the preserve. The perimeter spell had weakened and was almost gone, so there would be no impediment to traveling through it.

I leaped into the air and shifted form—to a small bird with a blue-gray back appropriately called a merlin, a tenacious falcon used for hunting.

Below me I felt Nimue follow suit, but she chose the form of a larger bird, a raven, in many cultures revered as a god. In this form she had more bulk, but much less maneuverability than I had. I hoped that this choice of hers would end up being the flaw in her plans that could help me destroy her.

I heard cries of distress from below as my family realized that the future they had dreaded was coming to pass. Apparently, once again, both Emily and Derek had regained the memories Llyr had sought to erase.

As I traveled up and away from the preserve, Nimue gaining on me with her larger more powerful wings, I spared a thought for myself: Finally, I was flying! It was a wondrous experience, even though I knew it could not last. I could hear Nimue approaching behind me, and I knew that the end was near. I had so many regrets, but there was no other choice to end this.

Nimue, in her avian form, drew alongside me and thrust her beak viciously into my body, causing a painful wound that I could not heal properly. I had known that shifting into another form would change everything, but it was the only way to destroy her. With difficulty I flew up above her more cumbersome body and attacked her with my beak over and over, buffeting her with my wings. I then reached out with my talons and ripped into her eyes, causing irreparable damage.

I heard her furious screams of agony in my mind as I

thrust my beak into her body over and over again. *It is time to die, Nimue, you insufferable bitch.* I still had my talons deeply imbedded in her eyes and in her neck, and I continued to cling as she fought to dislodge me. We had started to spiral down towards the ground and she fought frantically to get loose from my hold and regain the altitude we had lost. But it was too late. As the two of us plummeted faster and faster and I knew I would soon die, I reached out to Emily and Derek and sent them a last message. *I'm so sorry that it must end this way. I will try to come back to you, but it may not be possible. Please forgive me if I don't see you again. I will love you both forever...*

And I heard frantic, terrified screams from not only my family, but from everyone waiting below as they saw two birds falling to earth.

I was aware of the moment when Nimue hit the ground under me, then an unimaginable pain tore through me and there was only darkness.

CHAPTER 54
In the Light

I KNEW I WAS IN THE REALM of the gods, and there was nothing but light and harmony. All the human trappings were gone. They were unnecessary, as no human consciousness was present to see them. I was with Llyr and the other gods in my true form—pure spirit. It was wonderful to be home, but I wanted to be back on Earth in my body, Merlin's body, with my family.

I was curious what had occurred after I perished. I was not even sure how long I had been with the gods.

Just seconds, Myrddin Emrys. Welcome back, bro! Llyr sounded happy.

Seriously? "Bro?" You spend too much time listening to your "grandson," Llyr, I responded.

It is over now, just let it be. You had a fine time playing at being human, or partially human, and I enjoyed the experience of fathering you, but now it is time to get back to the god business, Llyr's disembodied voice replied.

I did not respond as I was busy trying to sift through the layers of the human realm to find the Matheson Preserve in Moab, Utah.

You're out of practice, "Son." Here, let me do it. Llyr pulled up the right time and place for me.

If I'd had eyes, I would have cried. Emily and Derek were reaching to gently move my obviously dead human body off of an equally deceased Nimue so that Percival could decapitate her, making absolutely certain that she would never return. He had to swing the sword more than once, as his injuries prevented him from making a clean cut. Gawain and Lancelot, in pain from their own severe wounds, were also very upset but more inured to the consequences of war. I had tried to prepare them all for the possibility that my immortality might not extend to an alternate form. But it seemed that none of them had wanted to believe me as they hovered around the body I used to inhabit.

Oh, how I wished I could be there with them, to reassure them that I still existed—just not in the same form. I knew that I could send my voice to them but was not sure it would be the most prudent thing to do.

I followed the scene below as everyone escorted my corpse back to The Moab Herbalist and laid it on the counter, straightening my shattered limbs and broken neck. I saw my widow carefully wash the face and comb the hair of the body she had loved, all the while sobbing brokenheartedly. Devastated, my son was still calling for me in his heart and mind. I could yet feel a remnant of the amazing bonds I had shared with both of them, connections that transcended the physical plane into this one.

I was now pure spirit and supposedly had no emotions, but I truly could not stand it any longer. I closed the connection to the human realm and tried to forget my family, my friends, my quest to bring back the Once and Future King... all was lost and my sixteen-centuries-long adventure was over. But there was something that was bothering me, something that I knew...wait!

*Llyr, I need to go back! I **will** go back, with your help*, I exclaimed into the ether.

Oh, no, must I? Llyr pretended to sigh in frustration.

Yes, you must. Do you not wish to be my father again? And pretend to be the god of magic and healing on occasion? I wheedled.

Well, now that you mention it...

CHAPTER 55
After Midnight

I SLOWLY BECAME AWARE that I was back in my body, in excruciating pain. I had brought the healing light back with me from the realm of the gods and began to heal my internal injuries and broken bones and to renew my already atrophying organs. I had apparently been dead for more than two hours. I was able to hear everyone's thoughts and feel everyone's emotions, and I became aware that Derek had been attempting his own ineffective healing magic on my empty shell of a body. Emily had called upon her Elven magic, and Lancelot, Gawain, and Percival, all three in need of medical attention, had been at my side praying to any and all gods and goddesses for me to be restored to them. All efforts had proven unsuccessful and they had given up, saying their final goodbyes by touching my body and pouring out all the love in their hearts.

I couldn't let them go on thinking I was still dead, but I was so newly "reborn" that my voice was at first only a slight mental nudge, *Emily,* then a weak whisper "Emily..." I hoped that she heard me, and I tried to move my fingers.

"Everyone be quiet, I thought I heard something!" Emily exclaimed.

"Don't torture yourself, Em. He's gone," Derek said sadly.

"No," Ryan cried. "I heard it, too."

I kept manipulating the light inside of my body until my fingers finally curled slightly.

"Oh, my God, I just saw his fingers move," Emily said in a hushed voice.

I got my lungs working again and inhaled slightly through a haze of pain. And then, I was finally able to open my eyes and whisper softly: "Is Nimue...?"

Emily started to weep again, but this time with joy, and as she held me she said, "She's dead, my love. *Most definitely* dead—Percival cut her head off."

"Thank the gods..." I said softly, resting for a moment. "Derek and Emily, stand on one side of me, please, and the three knights come forward and stand on my other side."

And I manifested a healing white light around all of us that was so brilliant that everyone had to cover their eyes. When I knew we were completely healed, I allowed the light to fade away. Emily's and Derek's wounds had been minor and had quickly disappeared. The three gallant knights, all of whom had been severely injured, were now whole and healed in a manner of seconds. They immediately got down on their knees and bowed in gratitude and obeisance.

I realized that I was naked under the thin sheet that covered me—they apparently had been laying me out for burial. With Emily's help, I wrapped the sheet around me and sat up on the counter. I took a deep breath—I was alive and well once more, although extremely weak. Someone threw a blanket around me, noticing that I was shivering with cold and fatigue.

Derek had been staring at me, speechless, until I looked into his eyes and said weakly, "Don't I get a hug?"

"Merlin, *Dad*, oh, my God, you're alive," Derek gasped, and threw his arms around me, holding me so tight I almost couldn't breathe.

"Easy, Son, I'm back now, it's alright." Derek released me, albeit reluctantly, with an affectionate pat on the back, and moved back so that Emily could step into my arms.

Emily could hardly speak she was so ecstatic. "Merlin, you came back to me! I was so afraid that this was truly the end. You died in your altered state and we assumed you were gone forever." She was giddy with relief and her smile widened as she gave me a look filled with love and renewed hope for the future.

I stroked her tangled hair and kissed her precious lips as

I explained, "I was with the gods, sweetheart, and I saw you grieving for me. I couldn't stand knowing how much pain you were all in, so I instructed Llyr to send me back, uh, I mean I *begged* him to send my spirit back to my body. And there is another reason that I came back here to be with you, Em. You are carrying my child."

EPILOGUE

SIX MONTHS AFTER THE BATTLE, after the death of Nimue and my own death and subsequent resurrection, Emily was so heavily pregnant that she was more than ready to deliver our baby. She was only about six and a half months along, having become pregnant on our wedding night it seemed, and she was very close to giving birth. Apparently a child of immortal parents did not require the usual nine months of development. Em and I had already anticipated that the birth would have to occur at home, away from mortals. Our child was unique, a miracle, her mother part human and part Fae, her father a god in human form, and we preferred not to take the chance that mortal eyes would witness something magical. Of course, I could always make the hospital staff forget what they had seen, so perhaps it would be more accurate to say that I just wanted to keep this experience private.

We had moved into a larger dwelling a few months earlier, right across the street from Derek, so having the birth at home was no hardship—there was plenty of space, it was comfortable and we were afforded complete privacy. But I missed the little place we had lived in when I came to Moab, where Emily had first told me that she loved me.

Ryan, Gary and Percival constantly dropped by the house, anxious to be doting uncles. Llyr finally admitted that *he* had brought Percival to Moab, not Nimue, so I had persecuted the poor man for no good reason. I had offered to send Percival back to Camelot and remove his memories of this time, but he decided he wanted to stay in the twenty-first century and assist with the quest. I had not had any contact with Arthur since the previous summer, but then again, time passed at a different rate in Avalon. I was absolutely certain that I would hear from him when the time was right.

Derek started dating, having finally let go of his unhealthy attachment to Emily, but he found it difficult to appear "normal" when he wasn't. He was my son in every way, an accomplished sorcerer; I couldn't believe that I had ever thought he was a distant relation. And Llyr finally confirmed his immortality, which could obviously be a problem in a relationship with a mortal woman. Derek confided in me that the intense sensation he experienced when he worked magic was better than sex, so perhaps he wouldn't pursue finding a life partner. It was certainly his decision to make.

One cold clear night in January, Emily was feeling restless, so I teleported us out to Arches National Park, and we stood in the dark near the rock formations gazing up at the heavens. We held each other and kissed passionately, keeping each other warm. It was lovely and romantic and we both thoroughly enjoyed the short outing.

"Oh!" Emily gasped as a contraction took her breath away, "Merlin, I think we'd better go back…"

Instantly I took us home and we prepared for our daughter's imminent birth. She arrived in a rather unexpected way, by teleporting out of her mother's womb and directly into my arms.

As I held my daughter and looked into her eyes for the first time, I said softly, "Welcome, Lumina…"

ABOUT THE AUTHOR

Caryl Say is a writer based in Moab, Utah. A new voice in fantasy fiction, she looks forward to continuing Merlin's saga in her second book—*God of Magic, Child of Light*—coming in early 2015. You may contact her at carylsay.author@gmail.com.

Made in the USA
Middletown, DE
29 September 2023

39457204R00216